Faeries Gone
Wild

Faeries Gone Wild

MARYJANICE DAVIDSON

LOIS GREIMAN

MICHELE HAUF

LEANDRA LOGAN

St. Martin's Paperbacks

This is a work of fiction. All of the characters, organizations, and events portrayed in this novel are either products of the author's imagination or are used fictitiously.

FAERIES GONE WILD

"Tall, Dark, and Not So Faery" copyright © 2009 by MaryJanice Davidson.
"Pixie Lust" copyright © 2009 by Lois Greiman.
"Dust Me, Baby, One More Time" copyright © 2009 by Michele Hauf.
"A Little Bit Faery" copyright © 2009 by Mary J. Schultz.

All rights reserved.

For information address St. Martin's Press, 175 Fifth Avenue, New York, NY 10010.

ISBN: 0-312-94568-X
EAN: 978-0-312-94568-8

Printed in the United States of America

St. Martin's Paperbacks edition / June 2009

St. Martin's Paperbacks are published by St. Martin's Press, 175 Fifth Avenue, New York, NY 10010.

10 9 8 7 6 5 4 3 2 1

Contents

Tall, Dark, and Not So Faery

BY MARYJANICE DAVIDSON

Every time a child says "I don't believe in fairies," there is a little fairy somewhere that falls down dead.

—James M. Barrie, *Peter Pan*

Only a human would be that arrogant.

—the Violent Fairy

If I have seen further it is by standing on the shoulders of giants.

—Isaac Newton

Now that one I can get behind.

—the Violent Fairy

Only when you love someone else as much as you love yourself will the curse lift.

—Archmage Karonen, to his cheating girlfriend, April 1949

Acknowledgments

Thanks, as always, to the family, the friends, the Yahoos, the editor, the agent. . . . If I wasn't so hungover, I could probably remember some of their names. . . .

Author's Note

This novella takes place a year or so after the events in *The Magicka*, which can be found in the anthology *No Rest for the Witches*.

Also, fairies really are quite anal, and they do feel better if they can count things. They are the OCD sufferers of the paranormal world.

Also, Cannon Falls is a real town in Minnesota, the farm Ireland and the gang live on is a real farm, and over a quarter of a century ago the Violent Fairy used to hang out there.

Prologue

Once, a long time ago, there lived a giantess who forgot she was one. So she met and married a former Gophers basketball player and they had a son who was five feet tall by the time he was six. And then the giantess got distracted, as members of their species will, and wandered away.

The boy never saw his seven-foot, nine-inch mother again.

But he grew and grew and grew.

Chapter

1

Cannon Falls, Minnesota
Pop.: 6,661
7:28 P.M. CST
Tuesday, during the *Law & Order* marathon on TNT

She came out of the woods like an arrow, a six-foot, four-inch arrow with the huge diaphanous wings of a dragonfly and the split ends of a beach bum, and she didn't float, or flitter.

None of her kind did.

She moved smoothly, like a machine, her toes always exactly 1.3 inches off of the grass and, as she neared the house, the gravel.

She was holding a clipboard and a pen, and her eyes were the color of ice. Her hair was the color of tree bark, and hung halfway down her back in a riot of rich brown waves.

She moved up the driveway, eyeing with some trepidation the gray Escape that now appeared much closer than she had first assumed. In fact, it was rolling toward her, the gravel crunching beneath the wheels.

No one was driving, which, although she wasn't entirely

surprised, still made her uneasy. She'd heard rumors, of
course, which was part of the reason she was here, but
surely *all* the rumors couldn't be—

"Nice wings. You look like an escapee from a children's
ice-skating show." The small SUV came to a stop six inches
from her toes. "This is private property, you big dumb
dragonfly, so why don't you hit the bricks?"

She was intimidated enough by a fairy's natural un-
easiness around machinery; being spoken to by a vehicle
was even more unsettling. "I—I'm here on official business."

The car stereo chortled static. "Official dragonfly business?"

She had no idea if the machine was joking or not. The
voice was feminine, with a raspy edge. In her nervousness,
her feet settled to the gravel. She tiptoed around the SUV
but didn't have the nerve to turn her back on the vehicle
and continue up the drive. "Official fairy business. I'm a
counter."

"Kitchen or bathroom?"

She pondered that for a moment, puzzled, then answered,
"Household. I count things."

"Why?"

She blinked and hugged the clipboard to her chest. "Because. Because that is our nature. We count."

" 'We' being uptight accountants with wings . . . ?"

"Fairies."

"Huh." The engine thrummed thoughtfully and the
headlights popped on, then dimmed. Almost as if—ha-
ha!—the machine was deep in thought. "Must be the brat.
Must be."

She was edging around the hood and now she was walking backward, still far too rattled to fly. "Yes, well, I have
to count."

"It's just as well," the vehicle called after her as she

began an undignified scramble up the steps. "It's been really dull around here! Hey! Get back here. Where d'you think you're going? We're having a conversation, aren't we? Hellooooo?"

Chapter

2

She congratulated herself on her composure during the frightening interlude with the vehicle. Sure, she

hadn't run away at all, no indeed, not at all,

had been intimidated but acquitted herself well, she thought.

She squared her broad shoulders and knocked firmly on the door. Why, the king wouldn't have sent her if he hadn't believed she could do the work! All of her kind counted, but many couldn't function under stress. But *she* had done very well. Yesyes! And surely now the worst was—

A vampire answered the door. Still rattled from her driveway encounter, she dropped the clipboard. And, moving with the spooky grace common to his kind, he had bent, snatched it out of the air before it could clatter to the tile, and handed it back to her before she'd had a chance to realize she'd even let it go.

"Good evening, young lady." He was tall—for a man who had once been human, anyway, probably about six four—and cadaverously thin.

"Good evening, sir."

His hair was the color of peat; his eyes were black. She couldn't tell where his pupils ended and the irises began;

looking into those eyes was like looking into a well where children had drowned. "Isn't it a little late to be selling Girl Scout cookies, my dear?"

She had no idea what that meant, so she plunged ahead. "Good sir, I am here from the king of the—"

His head snapped around and he lost all interest in her as he shrieked, "Ireland Shea, I *hear* you rustling around in my closet! Stop borrowing my shirts and do the damned laundry!"

From somewhere inside the house she heard sinister laughter, and then a door slammed.

"You get out of my room right now, you sloppily dressed wretch!"

Abruptly the door slammed in her face and she could hear the vampire dashing down the hallway.

She puffed her bangs out of her eyes, waited a minute, and knocked again.

Chapter

3

She had to pound the door for some time to be heard over the vampire's yowls and someone else's shrill giggles, but eventually the knob turned and she was once again face-to-face with—

with—

"Hello," the werewolf said. "Sorry, it's a little chaotic around here right now. My friend just had a baby and my other friend has been stealing my *other* friend's shirts. Are you taking a survey?"

"Yes," she said, grateful someone in the house was— what was the human phrase? Over the ball? "In fact, the king himself has sent me to your fine home in order to—"

"Say, are those *wings*?"

She fought the urge to preen. But then, she had glorious wings. She couldn't resist fluttering them as she replied, "Yes, they are. Thank you kindly."

He was examining her critically, eyes wide with interest. "But they're so light, and you're so—uh—not light. How do they work?"

She smiled; she couldn't help it. "Haven't you heard that bumblebees can't fly? Some human proved it, with numbers and such. It's impossible. But they fly."

She made her wings flutter again so that they were a lovely blur, and cautioned herself to be wary of vanity. Really, it was so kind of the tiny werewolf to notice.

Again, she reminded herself not to judge other species by the standards of her own. He wasn't that tiny, she supposed—about five nine. He had very pretty hair, too—shoulder length and white blond. And his eyes were really quite lovely, sort of a bright, shiny blue. He was in excellent shape (although, to be fair, she'd never seen a flabby werewolf), with sleek muscles and strong hands.

"Are you a friend of Lent's?"

"In a manner of speaking, yes, I—"

"Well, does he know you're here?"

"No, I—"

"Well, jeez! Wait right there. I'll go get him." And the werewolf galloped down the hallway, leaving her standing on the porch.

Chapter

4

She wondered if it was appropriate to enter the house without an invitation. The door *was* hanging open, but she wasn't sure that counted as an actual invitation. She took a step forward, hesitated, then took a step back.

From behind her, she heard a blaring honk, followed by, "Are you gonna hang around on the porch all frickin' night? Why don't you get back here so we can finish our talk?" She fervently hoped the machine couldn't navigate the trees and sidewalk.

She heard footsteps, but they were far too light to belong to the Violent Fairy. And when the woman rounded the corner and stood in the doorway, she nearly gasped with shock.

It was a dryad! Oh, the king would be amazed—none of her kind (well, except for the Violent Fairy, obviously) had seen one in decades. The dryad was willow-slender and her hip-length dark hair moved even when there wasn't a breeze. The dryad's legs and arms were stick-thin (not literally) and her eyes were as dark as her hair; she was wearing a clingy knee-length dress several shades lighter than her tanned skin.

She was holding an infant, an infant with the same-colored dark wavy hair and eyes, but with creamy skin. A chubby infant dressed only in a diaper, sound asleep, the small pink mouth slightly open. He or she smelled strongly of milk.

The infant had wings.

So it was true! She fought the urge to scribble notes on her clipboard. A dryad/fairy hybrid! The implications were staggering. First, who knew anyone other than a dryad could successfully mate with a dryad? Second, would the child be a true mixture of both worlds, or would he or she favor the mother? Third—

"I greet," the dryad said.

"Yes, hello. What a charming infant. I congratulate you and bring congratulations from my king. May I come—"

"Greet, greet, greet."

"Yes. Uh . . . I greet you back?"

The corners of the dryad's mouth turned up. She had no idea if the creature was actually smiling, or aping human behavior. "Greet," she said again, and gave the baby a gentle squeeze. The baby peeped, then resumed snoring.

"I greet your infant as well." She tentatively smiled back at the dryad. "It's very nice to meet you and your baby," she said, calmly and carefully. "My name is—"

"Lent."

"No, Lent is the name of one of my kinsmen, and your—mate? Husband?"

"You. Lent."

She was amazed that a creature that was mostly tree could speak at all. . . . Nothing she had read (and her people, if nothing else, adored writing things down) indicated dryads could. Perhaps Lent was teaching her?

"Yes," she replied, thinking it was odd that although the dryad was fairly monosyllabic, there was never any doubt about what she meant. "Lent and I are of the same species. In fact, our king sent me here to—"

"I leave," the dryad said, and wandered back down the hall, propping the baby up on her shoulder and patting it.

She fought the urge to stamp her foot.

Chapter

5

She had decided to creep a step or two into the house when a horrified shriek nearly split her eardrums.

"For the love of Mike! You people are costing me a fortune! Who left the damned door open? In *April*! Do you think I'm trying to heat all of Goodhue County?"

She heard someone stomping down the hall and edged back from the doorway. Then a tall (again: for her species) redhead with eyes the color of rich loam was standing in the doorway, staring at her.

"Ah, hello," she began, more than a little rattled by the events of the past ten minutes. "I—"

"Look, no offense," the human interrupted, "but we don't want any. Normally I like to at least listen to the pitch before saying no, but I don't want to waste your time."

"I—"

"It's nothing personal, but my friend just had a baby, nobody's sleeping very well, the full moon is only a couple of days away, I'm all out of clean shirts, and I—I—" The redhead's pale complexion took on a distinct greenish hue and she lurched past her, bent at the waist, and was noisily sick in the lilac bushes.

Awkward. Some humans wanted total privacy when

they were ill; others sought company under the very same circumstance. She had no idea which type of human this one was. "Shall I fetch someone?" she asked as the woman retched and groaned.

"Nooooo." The redhead straightened and wiped her mouth with the back of her hand. "Morning sickness, my ass!" She gestured so wildly at the darkened yard she nearly fell into the lilacs. "Does that look like morning to you, or does it look like eight o'clock at night?"

It was possible the human was deranged, so she answered politely, and hunched her shoulders so she wouldn't appear so large. "It's quite dark now."

"I knoooooow!"

"Perhaps, if you're ill, you should have some privacy? Maybe I could go inside and—"

The redhead snorted. "Why would I want privacy now? I've barfed in four cities, every room of *this* damned place, the gym at the elementary school (we went to the sixth-grade production of *Life's a Bitch, Charlie Brown*), the supermarket, the post office, my doctor's office, the Target in Hastings, the Target in Northfield, the St. Olaf campus, Walgreens, the bakery, the car—*man,* did I hear about that from Judith—"

"Judith?"

"—the bed-and-breakfast my husband and I went to, the *other* bed-and-breakfast my husband and I went to, Applebee's, the truck stop, Bachman's, Hallmark, the Mall of America, the Burnsville mall—"

"How long have you been with child?" she asked, appalled. She didn't think humans gestated for several years, but it certainly *sounded* like—

"—an eternity, honey—Burger King, Perkins, Scofield's drugstore, my *other* doctor's office, the—"

Suddenly a tall man—her height!—with a perfectly unlined face and snow-white hair was framed in the doorway.

The old-man hair was a startling contrast to his youthful face.

"Ireland! What the hell are you doing wandering around out here without a coat? It's only fifty degrees!"

The redhead made a sound. It sounded awfully like a snort. "I'm not 'wandering around'; I'm—"

"Ankle deep in mud," the strange-looking human interrupted. He reached out a long-fingered hand and the redhead clasped it without hesitation. "Now come inside," he coaxed, the frown disappearing like magic—the only kind humans could do, she often thought—and his voice going from scolding to tender just as quickly. "Your tea's all ready."

"I've drunk so much tea my insides are sloshing," the woman protested, but without much heat, and he led her inside and shut the door.

She stared at the door. The human male was so besotted with the redhead he hadn't even seen her. And that, she knew, was rare. She was no raving beauty, but she *was* a six-foot, four-inch fairy with wings almost as long as her body.

She wondered if she dared knock again.

What in the world had His Majesty gotten her into?

Chapter

6

She stood, shifting her considerable weight from foot to foot, for almost five minutes. It got colder, which she should have expected for the climate and the time of the year, and she needed to find shelter soon.

Finally, she hurried back down the sidewalk and called, "Excuse me? Madame Vehicle?"

"Oh, I like *that,*" the SUV replied at once, the lights flicking on and spearing her like a bug on a card. She heard gravel crunch as the SUV rolled toward her. "I like that a lot. Madame Vehicle, haw!"

"I am relieved," she said, speaking nothing but the truth, "I have not offended you."

"Except the name's Judith, okay? And why the hell are you lurking out here like a moth that doesn't know which light to kiss? You realize you've been banging on that door for over half an hour?"

"I—I can't seem to get in." She gestured helplessly toward the house. "I've been trying, and . . . and I was wondering if you might . . . if you might tell me—"

"Spit it out, O winged freak, lest I squasheth thee 'neath my tires like a bug."

"Well, I have some concerns, but I also have a task, a task I must complete, and—and—"

"You're a fairy, right?"

"Yes, Madame Ve—yes, Judith."

The engine made an interesting grinding noise, and after a moment she realized . . . it was laughing.

"So talking to me must make you want to pretty much pee your pants. 'Cuz if memory serves, your kind isn't too fond of machinery, iron, that sort of thing. Right?"

"Yes."

"Well!" The car sounded as if it—she—suddenly cheered up. "Good for you. Face your fears and run 'em over, that's what I always say. What do you want to know?"

"Are the people in the house—"

"Those nitwits? Don't get me started."

"Are they dangerous?"

"No more than I am." Another grinding sound as the car laughed again. It was a much less pleasant sound this time. "Of course, I'm pretty damned dangerous."

She backed up a step, thinking, *I am far too rattled to even attempt flight. If she wants to kill me, I imagine there is little to be done.*

Oddly, that thought made her calm down. If there was nothing to be done, she might as well try to get *work* done, at least until one or more of these strange creatures killed her. She had her orders, and they came straight from His Majesty.

She itched to count.

"Thank you for answering my question. May I ask you something else?"

"Shoot."

"Are you a car who has been bewitched to think it is a woman? Or are you a woman who has been bewitched into a car?"

"The latter, honey, and take my advice: Don't cheat on an archmage unless you make damn sure you won't get caught. Or unless he's dead. But they get madder when you cheat on them after they're dead," she added thoughtfully. "Nothing worse than having a dead archmage on your ass."

She made a note on her clipboard, then underlined *ensorceled man-made vehicle: Judith.* Then she marked it: one.

"Counting," she said, calming down further, as counting *always* calmed her kind. "Counting one Judith." And then, "Good night."

"Yeah, g'night, *freak*!" the car called after her as she once again trudged toward the door she could simply not get past.

Chapter

7

She was raising her fist to knock when the door was yanked open and her countryman Lent, who had pleased himself by selecting the name the Violent Fairy, stood in the doorway.

Well. *Filled* the doorway, of course, as she would have expected. He was a splendid, typical specimen of *Hominus spritus*: wide shoulders, enormous wings, wheat-colored hair, and violet eyes. He was so large he made her feel small.

He blinked at her. "You."

"Yes, Lent, it's me."

He blinked again. "Sent by the king."

She noticed it wasn't a question, and wasn't surprised: even for their kind, Lent could be blunt. "Yes, Lent."

His generous mouth quirked into a smile. "To count."

Relieved, she again said, "Yes, Lent."

"To count my infant."

"To count all of you. May I come in?"

His wings fluttered as he thought. She wanted to fidget and wouldn't let herself. The Violent Fairy had gone rogue over five decades ago. He didn't—this was so astonishing she could never say it; she could barely *think* it—he didn't count.

He did as he pleased. No one could order him, and certainly no one could make him do anything, even if he hadn't been so large. His willful streak was well known to the kingdom, and she had the impression he could have been smaller than her and no one could make him do anything.

Also, he was brother to the king.

Older brother.

So no one ever knew what odd thought he might take into his head, and because of that, she knew there was a good chance he would refuse her entry into the house. She had come here anticipating that . . . even if she couldn't have anticipated his odd roommates. Yes, the Violent Fairy might indeed send her away . . . refuse (gasp!) to be counted. What she would do if that happened, she did not know.

But she had to try. She had been told to try.

After a long moment, which she knew really had been less than two seconds, he stepped aside, his diaphanous wings fluttering in the spring breeze. He shrugged his massive shoulders at her. "Come in and count, then."

"Thank you, Lent."

Relieved, she followed him in.

Chapter

8

Coffee Ray parked the tow truck next to the ditch, shut the truck off, opened the door, and stepped down onto the gravel.

"Having trouble?" he asked, and the twentysomething woman in the red business suit wobbled toward him on high heels, her car half in and half out of the ditch.

"Oh, thank God! It feels like I've been out here in the middle of nowhere for hours!" He heard a click as she snapped her cell phone shut. "Fucking deer, they all ought to be in a damned zoo somewhere so people don't go off the damned road trying to—*Christ*!"

Coffee sighed inwardly. She'd gotten close enough to see how big he was. And she hadn't liked it.

Nobody really liked it

(not even Dad, especially Dad, because you remind him you remind him you remind him of her),

but he couldn't blame her. A woman, driving alone, her car off the road in the middle of nowhere (but really just on County Road 8, only six miles from the high school), when a strange man in a tow truck shows up. . . .

A certain type of customer, he knew, was always uneasy around mechanics, tow truck drivers . . . like that. Not only did he work with his hands and speak the secret language of engine blocks and oil changes, but he was a strange man on a dark country road who was over seven feet tall.

She was backing up, and he bet she didn't even know it. "We'll get you back on the road in just a sec, ma'am," he sighed. "Then you can head on back to . . ."

"Say—Say—Saint Paul," she managed.

"Right." He could see in the dark the way she could see in the daytime—not that he was going to tell her—and realized at once that the car didn't need a tow at all.

Just a yank.

He moved quickly—faster than most would believe a man his size could move—and seized the front bumper. Then he dragged the car up and out of the ditch.

"There y'are," he said, smiling and trying not to pant. She was cowering away from him and he doubted she realized it. He had hoped she would relax when she saw how quickly he solved her problem, but it was having the opposite effect. "You can head on home now."

"Yes, I—I will. Th-thank you. Here, I—" She was groping for her purse, frantically digging into it, and turned her ankle because she was backing away from him in the gravel. She went down with a muffled cry in an ungainly business-suited heap, embarrassed as well as frightened.

He bent over her, picked her up out of the dust, and brushed her off much like a mother brushed off a wayward toddler. She was staring up at him, amazed. "There y'are," he said again. "That's all right. On the house. You run on home."

"I—I—thank you. Thank you." She hurried to her car, got in, and he heard the dull thud as she engaged all the locks.

It started up on the first try, and she roared past him, kicking up a spume of dust.

And then Coffee Ray was alone. Again.

Chapter

9

"So you're like a paranormal census taker?" the redhead—Ireland—asked. "With wings?"

"Yes, indeed," she replied.

"And you're here to count us?"

"Yes."

"But why? Who cares that we're here? And who in God's name wants us to be counted?"

The Violent Fairy scowled. "My stupid brother."

She gasped at the heresy, then fixed him with a look. "Do not speak so of the king, Lent. Not even you."

"Who else, if not me? He was an idiot when he was still pissing his shirts, and he's an idiot now."

"Then perhaps you should have kept the crown for yourself!" she snapped, then clapped her hand over her mouth and blushed for shame. To speak of such things among those not of her kind! But then, Lent had always had that effect on her. Blunt (even for a fairy), abrupt, rude, with a bubbling contempt for the royal family that went back more decades than she could imagine.

"I said he was stupid. I didn't say he couldn't run the government. He was born a bureaucrat."

She shook her head, alarmed. . . . They must not speak

of these things among others! And the king was more than a—a—what was the phrase? Paper pusher?

Although technically, her entire race was a race of paper pushers. . . . Perhaps that was why Lent had left. He never could abide the real purpose of the Fey.

"Hey, relax," the werewolf told her, smiling easily. "We won't tell. This house has more secrets than dust bunnies."

"Perish the thought," the vampire muttered. "That reminds me, we're out of Clorox wipes."

"Excuse me," the human male said—the pregnant one's mate, she had already guessed. "But who are you, exactly? We haven't really been introduced. I'm Micah, and this is my wife, Ireland."

The redhead nodded, then went back to gobbling crackers.

"This is Ezra . . ."

The vampire nodded.

". . . and Owen . . ."

The werewolf tipped her a casual salute.

". . . and this is Willow; she's Lent's mate. . . ."

"Greet," the dryad said. The baby was nowhere to be seen; she assumed it was sleeping.

"We heard you'd taken a mate. Of course," she added sweetly, "it was only a rumor, since you haven't been interested in keeping us posted. Any of us."

Lent yawned and she bit off a retort, namely: *How dare you choose a mate without the king's permission?* Infuriating, irritating male!

"And I'm betting you met Judith."

"Oh, yes."

"And of course you know the Violent Fairy. He—"

"No no no." Lent shook his head. "I told you, gotta change it."

"Change it?" She was startled. Fairies had two names, always: the one they were given at birth and the one they chose for themselves after twenty summers. With his purple eyes, Lent had chosen a riff on "Violet Fairy," and it had certainly suited him.

It was as unheard of to change a name as it was to—to—well, to go live in a strange house with an assortment of creatures and never, never see your homeland again. And never—ahhh, even the thought burned like the fire of a thousand suns—count again. "You can't change it; why would you change it?" Unspoken: *What in the worlds is wrong with youuuuuuu?*

The vampire—Ezra—sighed. "We were at a comic-book store in Burnsville, looking at some graphic novels, and it turned out that there's a comic-book character with the same name."

"So?" she asked, trying to keep the scorn out of her tone. "The doings among these people have nothing to do with us, or the name you chose."

"Perhaps more relevant," Ezra continued dryly, "are the copyright laws in this country, and in fact, names cannot be copyrighted."

"Really?" Ireland asked, lightly spraying the vampire with cracker crumbs. "I didn't know that."

Ezra sighed and wiped his cheek. "Neither can titles," the vampire added. "I used to be a lawyer. A long, long time ago."

"So I could write a book and call it *Gone with the Wind*, and nobody could sue?"

"Correct. Although your publisher would likely try to talk you out of it because really, is the planet large enough for *two Gone with the Winds*? I think not. Just as there is only room for one Vivien Leigh. Or Tobey Maguire."

"And I could write a story about—I dunno—bugs? And name one of the bugs Rhett Butler?"

"Correct. But whyever would you?"

"I'm not having the same name as some stupid human

comic-book character," Lent grumped. "So quit calling me the Violent Fairy."

"But Lent! You gave yourself that name over sixty years ago! It was perfect because of your *real* name, and your eyes."

"That's true," the Violent Fairy admitted. "It was perfect."

"Barf, barf, barf," Owen said cheerfully.

She ignored the taunt. "You had it first. He should change *his*."

"No. It's tainted; it's ruined. I don't want it anymore."

"You're insufferably stubborn," she snapped. "As always."

"So?"

"You named *yourself* the Violent Fairy?" Owen asked, then let loose with a cheery, soul-lightening laugh.

"We give ourselves our second name," Lent replied testily.

"Lent! That is the private business of the fairy kingdom and you know it well."

He shrugged and she ground her teeth. She had managed to forget, over the years, just how annoying the man could be. "Besides, it's ridiculous to change your name just because someone else in the world has it."

Lent sighed. "Tell the stupid humans your name, little sister."

"Little sister?" Micah, Owen, and Ireland gasped together.

"Oh. You didn't tell them? Odd. You seemed to have blurted out everything else. I am a princess of the fairy realm, third in line to the throne after my dear younger brothers." She paused, and hoped she had a pleasant expression on her face, though she felt as though she were chomping on limes. "Lent is my oldest brother."

Now the group was staring at her brother. "*Prince*

Lent?" Owen finally said, sounding as if he were laughing and choking at the same time.

Her brother shrugged sullenly. "You didn't tell them your name, little sister."

"Oh. Well." She glanced at the floor, then at the others. "It's, ah, Scarlett." She had been born the year the book had been published and, for the scribblings of a human, it was not a bad tale of love, loss, and revenge.

"Just a minute," Ezra said, and cleared his throat. "You're telling us that Lent is a prince, you're a princess here to—what was it?—count us? A fairy princess who's a Margaret Mitchell fan and accountant wannabe?"

"Yes, yes, and yes."

"But he's your older brother. . . . Why isn't he the king?"

"Because he abdicated to, apparently, come *here.*"

"Weird," was Ireland's comment, and Scarlett couldn't have agreed more.

Chapter

10

Judith prowled the driveway—well, as much as a small SUV could prowl. In reality, she drove up and down, then across eight or nine feet, then up and down again. Across. Down. Over. Across. Down. *Argh.*

After what seemed a very very *very* long time, her most special friend

(after Ireland but you don't think about Ireland the way the way the way you think about him isn't that right?)

came bopping down the sidewalk to talk to her.

Finally.

"Hiya, Judith," he called cheerfully, and she perked up right away because he was always happy, always cheerful, always cute and funny, and

(oh stop it haven't you bought yourself enough trouble for one lifetime you stupid silly bitch?)

she was glad to see him. It was true. She was. She always was.

"About time," she grumped, because he must never, ever know how she felt. The last time she told someone how she felt, she'd ended up in a goddamned Ford SUV hybrid.

"Sorry, sweetie, I came down as soon as I woke up."

He yawned and stretched, arching up on his toes like a ballet dancer, and she watched the biceps and thigh muscles bulge, and tried not to pant. Which she managed to cover by stalling, then furiously starting herself again.

"Ack, *ack!*" she coughed, revving her engine. She made herself simmer down. "Come quicker next time. I've been waiting forever."

He yawned again. "Why didn't you beep for me?"

She had no answer for that—at least, none she was willing to share. Judith knew Morse code and had taught it to her fr—, her bu—, her ch—, her lackeys—yes, that's what they were, and she had taught it to them. So when she needed to talk to a specific denizen of Hell House, she just had to beep their name in code over, and over, and over.

Ireland, I need an oil change.

Ezra, Beyoncé is getting married again.

Owen, I'm bored; come cheer me up.

Only the Violent Fairy dared ignore her summons.

If she were in one of those silly romantic stories, her character would think something sappy like, *I couldn't have said when my feelings had changed from mere friendship into something deeper . . . more meaningful . . . more crappy and insipid and oh, this is such bullshit!* Because she knew exactly when her feelings had changed.

Halloween, two years ago. Ireland hadn't yet met Micah, so she, Owen, and Ezra used to go clubbing now and again. They'd been coming back from the Mall of America, soused to the gills (one advantage of having a friend who was a car: there was always a designated driver). They'd been burbling about what zany costume they'd wear or some such crap, and then Owen had shut up and, after a few seconds, deliberately changed the subject. Almost as though he'd realized that for her, every damn day was Halloween.

Yup, every day was Halloween; for her November 1 would never come. She'd be stuck in her costume forever.

Or until she broke the curse, which amounted to the same damned thing.

Owen had even talked to her about it. That very night, in fact. And when she saw he was serious, that he really cared about her answer, he was—jeez—what was the word? Concerned? Was that it?

Yeah. When she saw it wasn't a trick, or a joke, or something to talk about until a more interesting topic came along . . .

She told him.

"Sure, Ezra's a vampire, but he doesn't have to drink blood every minute he's awake. He's got time to go to the movies, to read one of those stupid celebritoid rags he's always yakking about. He's got time to be a regular guy. And you—you're a wolf, at night, for . . . what? Two, three nights a month, tops? The rest of the time, you're Owen; you're a guy who goes to the gym or bakes brownies or runs choir practice."

Owen had politely pointed out that he didn't do any of those things, which was so beside the point Judith ignored him.

"And Ireland, shit, her parents left her all this money, she doesn't even have to *work*. And even if she wasn't rich, she wouldn't have to worry about hiding her true nature part of the time. And Lent, he can fool people so they don't even know he's a fairy. But me, I'm a car all day and all night. Every day. And every night. I can never get away from it. I can never take a break and have a muffin and a cup of coffee. This—this metal shell is my costume, and I can't ever take it off." *And I deserve it,* she'd thought but hadn't said. *All this and more.*

After that, he'd come out and talked to her for hours every day. Sometimes at night, too. Even when he was in wolf form, he'd come out after gobbling down a couple of rabbits and just lie down in the gravel beside her. More than once he'd woken up naked in the driveway (and boy, did Ireland bitch about that!).

Unlike the others, he didn't see her as a mode of transportation first and Judith second. To him, she was always Judith.

But she would never tell him how she adored him for that, how she spent part of every single day wondering when he would come out and talk to her.

"So what's going on up there?" she demanded, forcing herself back to the here and now. "What's that winged freak want, anyway? What took you so long?"

"Sorry, sorry, calm down." He eyed her tires, making sure she wasn't going to "accidentally" run over his toes.

"You bums didn't come out to tell me about that weirdo with the wings . . . and here it is, the next damned afternoon! Kee-rist!"

Owen yawned. "Yeah, well, some of us were up pretty late last night. Don't blare your horn like that; it's like a lightning bolt through my brain."

"What brain?"

"I've got enough on my mind what with tonight being the full moon."

"Say, that's right. D'you think she'll come around again?"

Last month Owen had run across the scent of a female werewolf. He had no idea if she was in town for him or if it was just a coincidence. Judith knew he had left the Pack under murky circumstances, but didn't pry.

Owen shrugged. "If she does, she does."

"You should run her off. This is your territory. Haven't you peed on all the trees by now?"

Before he could reply, here was Ireland, that redheaded

dolt, hopping down the steps like she was on meth or something. Ah, and there was the ubiquitous box of Ritz crackers. Good. *Anything to keep the wench from barfing on my upholstery.*

"Hi, Judith."

"You can cram your 'hi.'"

Ireland laughed at her, one of the few beings on the planet who could get away with it. Actually, the *only* beings who could get away with it all lived on this farm for weirdos.

"Always a pleasure, Judith. I can't imagine why someone disliked you enough to slam your soul into an SUV."

"You know how long I've been waiting out here?"

"No," Ireland said, and Judith laughed in spite of herself, which sounded a bit like gears grinding. Sometimes she couldn't resist Ireland Shea, even when—especially when—she was barfing all over the rear bumper.

My God, I'm getting so soft in my old age. "So what's going on?"

Ireland climbed up on Judith's hood and sat cross-legged, munching. "Check this: the big gal with the wings? The Violent Fairy's sister! And the V.F. is a prince!"

Judith snorted. "That lumbering hulk?"

"Yup."

She gave it a minute to gel, and it made sense. She'd met her share of princes of the blood, and on one level or another, they were essentially the same man. "That would explain his innate, oddly jarring sense of superiority."

"And here comes the best part: he was supposed to be the king of the fairies, only he abdicated to, I dunno, wander the world, and that's how he eventually settled down here."

"Jeez," Judith said, impressed. Who would have thought the big hulk had it in him? She knew too well how difficult it could be to turn your back on family, never mind the trappings of royalty. Shit, it was one of the reasons she was a damned Escape hybrid.

"So this gal, his sister Scarlett, is here to—"

"Whoa, whoa. *Scarlett*?"

"I know, I know. Anyway, she's here to take a census."

"Yeah, she counted me last night."

Ireland shook her head. "I gotta say, real fairies are as far from the Tinkerbell mythology as they can get. Instead of being teeny and delicate, they're—"

"Huge hulking things with big feet and wide shoulders, not to mention afflicted with some weird kind of OCD."

"Yeah, and instead of sprinkling fairy dust on things and flitting around all delicate and stuff—"

"They're accountants who write down numbers and freak out if they can't count shit."

"Yeah."

"Weird," they said in unison.

"So what happens once she counts everything?"

"She'll move on, I guess."

"Huh."

"I know that tone," Ireland said suspiciously. "What are you up to?"

"*Moi*? As usual, Ireland, you're way off."

"Sure. That's why I live in a house stuffed with paranormal creatures."

"Oh, yeah, blame us, Ms. All-powerful Magicka."

Ireland grimaced and Judith chortled inwardly. This whole Magicka thing had come up last year, when Micah showed up out of the blue (funny how often that happened around here) and told Ireland she was her generation's Magicka, charged with the protection of supernatural creatures.

Apparently she, Owen, Micah, et al., hadn't come here

of their own free will at all. . . . They were drawn to the Magicka, a sort of supernatural guardian. Micah was her Tutor, charged with teaching her all a Magicka's responsibilities.

Yawn.

Besides, Judith was the mistress of her own damned destiny. She was on Shea Farm on *her* terms, not because she was—it was laughable—drawn to Ireland because she was some sort of supernatural guardian of all things weird.

"Don't start with that Magicka crap," Ireland grumbled.

"Oh, boo-hoo. You think you've got problems? Anybody ensorcelled *you* into any machinery lately?"

"No," Ireland admitted, finishing the box. She upended the box and sprinkled the last crumbs into her mouth. Yes indeed, it was a miracle she'd been single when Micah had happened along. "Other than puking every half hour, I've got it made."

"You think Lent's sister is going to hang around?"

"Doubt it. She has to get back to the king and give her report."

Judith didn't care for that one damned bit. This was *her* family, dammit, and she didn't approve of bewinged *spies* flitting around—not that the big gal exactly flitted—writing stuff down and then reporting everything to some king she'd never heard of.

Screw that.

So . . . how to keep her here, at least for a little while?

"I need an oil change," she said abruptly.

"What? You just had one last—"

"Are you gonna take me to Coffee Ray's, or do I have to park on your foot again?"

"All right, all right. Let me get something to eat and then we'll go into town."

"Take your time," Judith said cheerfully. She didn't want to get to the shop until just before closing, anyway.

Then we'll see, she thought, starting her engine and popping into drive. *Yes, we will.*

Chapter

11

Coffee Ray was talking to his boss, a very nice woman named Sue Dalton (who, for the owner of a garage, had the cleanest hands he'd ever seen . . . and beautiful nails!), who was trying her best to follow his comments.

"—because then I figured it was probably the carburetor, and it turned out I was right! Only we didn't have one in stock for—for—that reminds me, we need to run another inventory because the last one was way back in February and—and—my dad sent me a valentine; how weird was that? Did I tell you that? I haven't even seen him since I moved north. That reminds me, I still have some boxes in storage from my move—the moving guys were really nice, I—"

"Coffee Ray!" Sue shouted, snapping her fingers in front of his face. "How many times do I have to tell you? Say it with me: Rit. Uh. Lin. Ritalin! Possibly intravenously."

"I hate needles and I don't take pills. And speaking of pills—"

"Coffee Ray, I've got to go. Do you mind waiting around for Ireland Shea? Her hybrid needs an oil change."

He perked up. "Sure, be glad to."

"You don't have to actually do it till tomorrow—"

"That's okay. I'll stay late."

"If you do, I'll be glad to cough up time and a half."

"That's okay; I don't mind. Besides, I got time and a half yesterday when I helped that gal from Saint Paul out of the ditch. And speaking of the state capital—"

"Coffee Ray, I love you, but I've had enough of trying to follow your tangents for one day. I'll catch you tomorrow, all right?"

"Sure, boss."

"Nice teardown on Mr. Wolper's Mercury."

"Thanks. It was pretty easy once I—say, that reminds me, I—"

"Night, Coffee Ray."

"Night, boss."

He watched her go, a petite blonde comfortably padded in all the right places. She ran the best shop in town, and didn't seem to mind that he was almost three feet taller.

He began to pace, hoping Ireland would drop off Judith very soon.

He had a secret, a wonderful secret.

Ireland Shea's SUV talked to him.

Chapter

12

Ireland hopped out of Judith and waved at Coffee Ray, who came toward her wiping his hands on a ball of paper towels.

"Hello, Coffee Ray." As far as she knew, nobody ever called him just Coffee. "I need another oil change . . . my husband's outside in his car, so is it okay if I leave Judith overnight?"

"Sure," Coffee Ray said, smiling. Ireland was struck, as she always was, both by the man's size (over seven feet tall, easily the tallest man she'd ever seen . . . and she had thought Lent was huge!) and his good looks.

Coffee Ray had eyes the color of his first name, shoulder-length jet-black hair with a thick shock of bangs that constantly fell into his eyes, and the long, slender fingers of a surgeon. He was wearing denim shorts—Ireland couldn't imagine how much trouble he had getting jeans that actually fit—and a flannel work shirt. He was famous in town for both his height and the fact that he wore shorts all year round, even during snowstorms. He was, Ireland had long ago guessed, impervious to cold.

"I'll come pick her up sometime tomorrow, is that all right?"

"Sure. How are you feeling?"

Ireland grimaced. "Don't ask. Are you going to finish that candy bar?"

He handed her the other half of his Twix. "Knock yourself out."

"Bye, Coffee Ray."

"Bye, Ireland."

He watched her head out, climb into the passenger side of her husband's Volkswagen, and wave. He liked Ireland a lot. . . . She was one of the few women in town who weren't afraid of him. She either honestly didn't notice his great size or didn't care. Word around town was, being raised by a crazy mother (literally crazy; schizophrenic, he thought) had made her impervious to weirdness in others.

"She's gone," he said, seemingly to the air.

"About damned time," Judith grumped, and he grinned.

Chapter

13

"You don't really need an oil change," Coffee Ray told her, as if she didn't know.

"Duh, Coffee Ray. I just wanted to get off the farm for a bit." A lie, but he wouldn't figure that out till later. "Too much weird shit going on out there. Don't get me started."

"Oh, I'd never dare."

"Wipe that smirk off your face before I spit oil all over you next time you're messing around under there. You remember the rules, right?"

"I haven't told anybody you talk to me. Why would I? They'd lock me up somewhere."

"That'd be a good trick, since you could probably knock down just about any door they tried to shut on you," she muttered, and Coffee Ray threw back his head and laughed, a booming sound that filled the garage. "Be sure to add 'fee fie foe fum' to that."

He stopped laughing at once. "Quit it, Judith."

She quit it, because she didn't want to scare him, or make him mad. But she knew his secret, as he knew hers. And had kept it to herself, as she had promised.

That didn't mean she couldn't *use* the information, however.

"So, check it, Ireland's got *another* houseguest."

"That woman collects more strays than the Humane Society," he agreed, settling his long frame on a custom-made cart and scooting beneath Judith. "Hmm, looking good under here."

"Stop peeking, perv. You know damned well there's nothing wrong with me. I keep myself in perfect—Ack! Quit, that tickles."

"So how's everybody out on Shea Farm? Did Willow have the baby yet?"

"Two days ago."

"Boy or girl?"

"Boy. Which is interesting, because he might be in line for the fairy throne."

"Willow must have had the baby at the house. She could hardly go to a hospital. . . ."

"Yeah, but she was in labor for, what was it, a whole half an hour? She was all 'infant arrives' and pop! There was the baby, yowling like a cat on fire. I got the whole scoop from Owen."

"Speaking of Shea Farm and their odd inhabitants, I was out in your neck of the woods last night."

"Yeah?"

"Yeah, this out-of-towner swerved to miss a deer and ended up in the ditch."

"Moron."

"Quit it," he said absently. "So, I gave her car a yank and off she went."

"Without so much as a fucking thank-you, I bet."

He shrugged.

"Coffee Ray, you're the dumbest nice guy I've ever met."

"Why, thank you, Judith. You're the angriest SUV *I've* ever met."

"I keep telling you, I'm not an SUV, I'm just stuck in

one. Why do you keep doing favors for these ungrateful idiots?"

"Because it's my job?"

"I bet you didn't even charge her, you gigantic soft dumb ass."

"It took a whole two minutes of my night," he said mildly.

"Yeah, and she probably broke her leg getting the hell away from you."

"No, but she did turn her ankle." He scooted out from beneath Judith. "You can't really blame them, Judith. I look like a scary guy."

"And I look like an Escape hybrid, except I'm not. I'm just stuck in one. You don't see me getting walked on, right, dumb shit?"

He laughed. "Who'd ever dare?"

"Hey, get in here. There's something I want you to take a look at."

"What's the matter?" he asked, circling the car and opening the driver-side door. "You have a bulb burned out or something?"

"Something," Judith agreed as he climbed in. She locked all the doors.

"Uh. Judith?"

She put herself into reverse, relieved Coffee Ray hadn't shut the main garage door, and scooted out of the garage.

"Judith?"

"Hold on tight," she chortled, and left a few feet of rubber in Coffee Ray's parking lot.

Chapter

14

Scarlett peered at the infant, which was the smallest baby she had ever seen. That made sense, given that his mother wasn't a fairy, but it was startling all the same.

"Counting," Scarlett said, making a note on her clipboard. "Counting one infant, hybrid; father: fairy; mother: dryad."

"That, ah, seems to relax you, I've noticed." The vampire had been leaning in the doorway, watching her with cool curiosity, his arms folded across his chest.

"It is our purpose," she said simply. "It is why we are here. How do *you* feel when you don't drink blood for a day or so?"

"Wretched," he admitted.

"How did you come to live with Ireland?"

"Some things"—He smirked, wandering away—"will never be told. Count *that*. Now, where did I put the *TV Guide* . . . ?"

She scowled but didn't go after him. Her curiosity would have to remain unsatisfied; she was here to count, not take down life (and death) stories.

But it was awfully queer.

She had, in the course of her life (and how did humans

stand their puny eighty-year life spans? They were like candles in a hurricane that way) seen all these creatures. Separately. As far as she knew, vampires and werewolves didn't even believe in each other, much less become roommates. And Lent was a notorious loner; she would have been able to understand him living alone in the woods somewhere, but having all these roommates? In a house built by humans, for humans? It was so *odd*.

She could hear a strange sound coming from outside, and realized after a moment that the vehicle, Judith, was honking. Blaring, really, absolutely leaning on the horn.

An attack? Someone trying to hurt Prince Lent? Or the new prince?

Despite her size, she could move when she wanted to, and she very much wanted to. She was the first one out the door.

Chapter

15

The others were right behind her as she rushed down the steps and ran to the driveway. The SUV was parked sloppily, two of its (her?) tires on the grass, two on the gravel.

There was a man inside.

"Oh my God," Ireland moaned behind her, then retched.

"Judith, what have you done?" the vampire asked, horrified.

The man waved at them, looking more than a little bemused.

"You kidnapped your mechanic?" Owen asked, and Scarlett had the odd impression he was trying not to laugh.

"Oh my God," Micah, Ireland's husband, groaned. When Ezra flinched, he absently apologized. "Judith, what have you done?"

"What?" Judith snapped, sounding annoyed. "What's the big deal?"

"Oh, sure, it's just a *federal freaking crime,*" Ireland snapped. "And how are we going to *explain* you to poor Coffee Ray?"

Scarlett could see the man's lips moving. He didn't seem angry, or even aggrieved.

"Heh," her brother snickered. "Stupid crazy Judith."

"Shut up, you winged freak," the SUV told him coldly. And, startled, Scarlett realized that her (and her brother's) wings were out in the open, plain as day. It was too late to throw a cloak over the human's mind.

Fairies couldn't hide their size (and why would they?), but after years of moving among the humans, counting, they had gotten quite good at cloaking the feeble, tiny human brain. It wasn't terribly difficult; it just took sustained concentration. They simply fooled the humans into thinking they didn't have wings. And given how monstrously self-centered most humans were, it wasn't hard at all.

Too late now.

The man behind the wheel was politely tapping on the glass. Judith rolled the window down about two inches.

"Nice night for a drive, I guess," he said cheerfully.

"Judith, what the hell is *wrong* with you?" Micah thundered.

"Off my case, Casper. You guys can show up out of the blue whenever you want and move in, but I can't have a friend over?"

"That does sound unfair," the man in the car agreed.

"Have a friend over?" Ireland managed, sounding as if she was choking. "Is that what you call a federal kidnapping charge?"

"I won't tell," Judith said smugly, "if you won't tell."

"I won't tell," the man said.

"Do you think I should count him?" Scarlett whispered to her brother.

"If it makes you feel better," he replied, amused.

There was a *chunk* as Judith's locks disengaged. The man opened the door and climbed out. He stood up. And up. And up.

Scarlett gaped up at him, completely amazed (a common occurrence, she was beginning to think, on Shea Farm).

He was easily the tallest male she had ever seen. His shoulders would fill a doorway and perhaps more; she suspected he could only enter a room if he turned sideways. He had hair the color of good soil, long in the back, and his eyes—his eyes! They were the exact color of wet grass. She'd never seen such green eyes before. Most of her people had lavender or blue eyes; humans, she knew, tended toward brown and blue and hazel.

He towered over her.

She felt positively petite.

"Hi," he said, staring down (!) at her. "I'm Coffee Ray."

"Scarlett," she said. He held out a hand. She looked at it. Her brother poked her rudely between the shoulder blades and she suddenly remembered the human custom. She held out her own hand and it was engulfed by a rough palm and long, slender fingers. She remembered another custom: "It's nice to meet you."

"Thank you," he replied in a deep, comforting voice. "Can I have my hand back, Scarlett?"

"Hmmmm?"

Another poke nearly sent her sprawling into the man. She released his hand and turned to glare at her brother, who was smirking in an infuriating way.

"It's okay, you guys. I'm not, you know, going to blow your cover. I already knew Judith could talk."

"You did?" the werewolf and vampire chorused.

"Sure. We've been friends for a couple of years."

"Judith . . . made . . . a friend?" the vampire asked.

"Y'know, Judith," Coffee Ray said, leaning against the vehicle, "if you wanted to take me for a ride, you could've just asked."

"Asking is for chumps," the vehicle replied. "So are you guys going to stand out here staring at my friend, or are you going to remember your damned manners and invite him in?"

"She's lecturing *moi* on manners?" Ezra asked.

"The irony's so thick, I'm going to start gagging," Micah said sourly.

"Ooooh," Ireland groaned. "Don't say 'gagging.'" Then she turned and darted up the stairs.

"Well." Micah tilted his head back to look Coffee Ray in the eye. "Want to come in? Have a cup of coffee, maybe?"

"No coffee for me," the man replied, falling into step beside Micah. "Stunts my growth."

Scarlett stared after him for a moment, then raced back to the house to find her clipboard.

Chapter

16

"So Judith's been talking to you for *years*?" Ireland was saying as Scarlett hurried into the dining room, where the others were sitting and standing all over the room. "And you never said a word?"

"She said she'd park on my face if I blabbed," Coffee Ray said. Everyone knew he wasn't joking. "And speaking of parking, you should see the rubber she left all over the lot when she stole me. And speaking of stealing, did you read in the paper about the art room getting broken into last week? I didn't—"

"But why did she bring you here?" Micah asked.

Coffee Ray shrugged.

"Are you supposed to do something?"

"Uh-uh. Least, I don't think so; she's all tuned up and she sure doesn't need an oil change. Speaking of oil changes, I had a truck in last week that hadn't had the oil changed in fourteen months! Who does that to their truck? I just about cried on the spot. I—"

"Uh, Coffee Ray, if we could please stay on track?" Ezra asked pleasantly. "Why do you think Judith brought you here?"

"Dunno."

Ezra leaned close and caught the large man's gaze. "Think *hard*, Coffee Ray. I'm sure you can recall, if you put your mind to it."

"Say, uh, Ezra, is it? You're kind of in my personal space. And speaking of personal space, I met a Close Talker in the shop the other day, talk about offputting! He was so—"

Micah was staring at Ezra. "Are you telling me what I think you're about to tell me?"

"I can't seem to, what's the phrase? Work my mojo on him."

Scarlett knew that vampires could "catch" humans with their gaze and make them do . . . well . . . anything. It was part of the reason fairies just couldn't take humans seriously as a species. Too small. Too dumb. Too self-centered. And too, too easy to fool.

But Ezra couldn't catch Coffee Ray. And that was quite curious, wasn't it?

Coffee Ray put large hands on Ezra's shoulders and gently pushed him into a chair. The vampire, astonished, allowed himself to be maneuvered. "There," Coffee Ray said comfortingly. "Now you're out of my space, and seated in a nice dining room chair. And speaking of dining rooms, did you guys hear what happened to Mrs. Dunman's dining room set? Her kid was smoking pot and got all confused and spilled his bong water all over—hey, nice wingspan, Scarlett. Can those things actually lift you off the ground? Are you related to Lent? Lent's the best-kept secret in town, mostly because he stays on the farm and never—"

"What are you?" Scarlett asked.

"A Leo. Well, technically I'm a Virgo, but I was due during the Leo stretch, and I had my chart done at the state fair five years ago and— Say! Have you guys tried those deep-fried Snickers bars they have? They have everything on a stick at the fair. And speaking of sticks, did—"

"What *are* you?"

"Uh—an organ donor?"

Scarlett was clutching her clipboard so hard, her knuckles were dead white. "What *are* you?" she demanded. "Are you an elf, a sprite, a wizard, a leprechaun? Are you a pixie, a brownie, a witch, a mutant human, a lycanthrope, a dryad, a naiad? Are you a merman, a banshee, an elf—"

"How could he be an elf?" Ezra asked.

"Or a sprite? Or a pixie?" Owen asked. "I mean, look at him!"

Scarlett ignored them. "A gnome, a hochigan, a jinn, a naga, a nymph—?"

"A *nymph*?" Micah asked, trying not to laugh.

"A sylph, a troll, a skinwalker? A buru, a kobold, a silkie, a glaistig?"

"She'll feel better," Owen said, "if she can categorize you and then count you. It's best to go along."

Coffee Ray sounded equal parts annoyed and amused. "Count me?"

"I know how it sounds, dude. Please just humor her," Owen begged. "You do not want to see an aggravated fairy. Not when they run that size," he added thoughtfully, nervously eyeballing the agitated winged brunette.

"Speaking of running, did you guys hear the track team is going to State? I didn't think they—"

"Do you want a hint?" her brother asked, bored.

"You stay out of this!" she snapped. "You couldn't count something if it flopped over on its back and died at your feet."

"Speaking of feet, my boss has the tiniest feet you've ever seen; you can't even imagine it; they're like goat feet—"

That's it. And it was staring me in the face the entire time. The tiny attention span should have tipped me off sooner. She couldn't imagine why it hadn't occurred to her earlier; her only excuse was that she had never before met a non-fairy bigger than she was.

That and Coffee Ray's kind had, they had all supposed, died out over a century ago.

She advanced on Coffee Ray, who raised dark eyebrows but held his ground. She squinted up at him and asked, "Was one of your parents a giant?"

Silence fell over the group with an almost audible thump. And after an uncomfortably long pause, Coffee Ray said, "My mother. But she left when I was little. Uh, so to speak."

"Of course she did," Lent said. "She was a giantess."

"Huh?" Ireland asked.

"Giants are known for several things," her husband replied. "Among them great height, great strength, an ability to resist enchantment of pretty much any kind, and—this is why they can't be enchanted—a murderously short attention span."

"Ah-ha!" Owen said. "Is that why Coffee Ray's always going off on these weird tangents? Because he's part giant?"

"Duh," Lent said with annoying smugness. He glanced at his sister. "You must be losing your touch, little sister."

"You hush right now, prince or no prince," she snapped. But he was right, of course. It was one of the more annoying things about him.

Abruptly Coffee Ray left the dining room, and a few seconds later they all heard the front door slam.

"Was it something we said?" Owen wondered.

Without knowing why, Scarlett ran after Coffee Ray.

Chapter

17

"Judith."

"What?"

"Take me home."

"What, *now*? You were only in there for ten minutes."

He fought the urge to kick her tire, knowing his foot would probably go through the rubber. He wasn't sure Judith could feel pain—she never complained during oil changes—and didn't want to find out. "Now, Judith."

"Don't be such a damn crybaby. Give 'em a chance. They'll grow on you, kinda like mold. You're too weird and sad to be by yourself all the time."

"Judith, I'd like you to mind your own business and *take me home*. Now!"

"Wait! Please wait, Coffee Ray!"

He turned, surprised, and saw the tall brunette with the beautiful wings and pretty eyes come galloping down the steps toward him.

She skidded to a halt, stumbling in the gravel, and he grabbed her elbow and steadied her. "I haven't counted you," she panted. "You can't leave yet."

"You'd be surprised," he muttered. He was desperately embarrassed. Out of all the people in that room, the pretty woman with wings was the last one he'd want to know the truth about his mother. Naturally, she had been the one to guess.

"Please don't leave. I just—in all my years of counting, I have never seen a human/giant hybrid before. You're—you're quite fascinating."

"Yeah, me and the dog-faced boy," he said glumly.

"Boo fucking hoo," the SUV snarled. "You think you're the only freak on the planet? Shit, you're not even the only freak in this driveway. So suck it up, crybaby."

"You hush," Scarlett said. "I've already counted you."

"You know what you can do with that clipboard, you winged freak?" Judith began. "You can take it and jam it sideways straight up your—"

Scarlett grabbed Coffee Ray's hand and, to his astonishment, started pulling. "Come on," she said. "Let's walk."

Stunned, he let her lead him out of the driveway.

Chapter

18

Scarlett had to keep sneaking glances up at Coffee Ray. It wasn't just that he was taller than she was . . . though that was distracting enough. He had a presence, a kind of comforting calm about him that, though she'd known him for a short time, she instinctively responded to.

"Thank you for coming away with me."

He snorted. "I sure wasn't gonna hang around in there for much longer. Counting fairies and talking SUVs . . . why do I have the feeling I'm in a hospital room somewhere, deep in a coma?"

She didn't know what a coma was, but it didn't sound pleasant. "You are unique," she said, hoping to cheer him. "In all the world, I've never known of a giant/human hybrid before."

"Great."

Puzzled, she stared at him in the deepening gloom. It was almost as if—but that made no sense at all—yet what other explanation could there be?

"You are . . . shamed? By your parents?"

He said nothing, but his strides lengthened. She had to hurry to keep pace with him. "But why, Coffee Ray?"

"Why? *Why?* Seriously, you're asking me why?"

"I believe that is exactly what I asked."

"My God, you're a literal one, aren't you?" He turned to face her and she could hardly make out his expression in the shadows. That made her oddly glad, because his tone was frightening enough. "What's to be ashamed of? Hmmm? Let's see, my mom had so little interest in me that she took off when I was five. And my dad never forgave me for it."

"*Forgave* you?" A thousand thoughts crowded her brain and jammed her mouth. She actually gagged on the words for a moment before blurting, "Coffee Ray, don't you even know how extraordinary you are?"

"Extraordinary," he said flatly.

"Giants have murderously minuscule attention spans, you strange, strange man! That's why they don't marry, they merely mate and move on. Haven't you ever wondered why your mother's people aren't the dominant species on this planet?"

"Uh—"

"Giants are stronger, faster, more durable and resistant. But they can't focus on more than one thing for very long at all. *Homo sapiens* can. Giants are very poor caretakers. . . . I find the fact that your mother stayed until you were five to be extraordinary."

"You—you do?"

"It's unprecedented. She stayed for you, Coffee Ray. She resisted her nature as long as she could, and you had her for five years. Do you have any idea how long five years is to a giant?"

"No," he admitted.

"A very long time, Coffee Ray."

"I like the way you say my name."

"You—what?"

"Everybody else puts the emphasis on 'Coffee.' You put it on 'Ray.' "

"All right."

"That's pretty interesting, that stuff about giants. I didn't know any of that stuff."

"How could you? We have different jobs. I count, and you—er—you do whatever it is you do."

"Know what I'd like to do right now?"

"No." But she was hoping.

"This," he said, and bent down, and put his arms around her, and kissed her for a lovely long time. So long a time, in fact, that she forgot to count the seconds.

Chapter

19

The sun had gone down. Judith was waiting patiently in the driveway, watching. And eventually, the moon came up.

The full moon.

A silvery howl split the air, and she knew Owen had gone through his Change. He had assured her many times that it didn't hurt, but she had seen it and had her doubts. It would be like Owen to protect her from unpleasant truths. The big dumb ass.

She heard him slip through the wild raspberry bushes on the north side of the property and then there he was, trotting down the driveway. He was the size of a golden retriever with the coloring of an albino: pure white fur, enormous blue eyes she could see gleaming even in the near dark, wide white tail waving a greeting.

He grinned at her, showing many long teeth, and she said, "Piss on my tires and die a painful death, Owen."

He barked and whipped around, chasing his tail for a few joy-filled seconds. Then he froze, stiffened, and trotted to the end of the driveway and crossed the road.

Another howl shattered the cool dark—one coming from the field across the road. Judith was so startled she nearly stalled.

It's that lone female he was telling me about! Is she here for nooky? Or a fight? Judith wasn't sure which prospect was more upsetting.

She crept to the end of the driveway, navigating by her fog lights. She could hear muffled barks and growls, saw the tangle of fur and limbs that meant a fight, and realized at once that Owen was in trouble.

She slammed herself into drive, roared out of the driveway, and arrowed straight across the road into the field. Her headlights picked out the female, a wolf about Owen's size with black fur and about a thousand teeth.

Oh you fucker you should have left my family alone I'm going to park on your face *I'm going to run over your head you piece of shit you bitch you cowardly puke you get away from him right now right now right the hell now you get away!*

She was bearing down on the black female, blaring her horn and hoping the cavalry was on the way, when suddenly there was a blur of white fur and Owen—Owen was standing in front of the female, Owen was *right in her way,* and she frantically tried to put on the brakes but had built up too much momentum, and as the black female jumped out of the way Judith plowed right into Owen.

At the last second she managed to wrench her wheel to the left, so instead of hitting him head-on she clipped his left side. It was hard enough to knock him back several feet but not

(please God it wasn't hard enough please please)

hard enough to kill him.

Owen was perfectly still, a mound of white fur sprayed with dirt from the field. The female had backed up in alarm and was whining, circling Owen's form and sniffing him. Judith blatted her horn and the female took off like she'd been scalded. Great. They were probably doing the werewolf equivalent of a handshake, and in response Judith had run over her friend.

"Owen? Owen? Oh my God, why did you do that? Oh, Owen, please be okay, please please be okay, I'm so sorry, I thought you were in trouble, oh God, please help him, I'll do anything," she babbled, not quite sure who she was talking to . . . or even sure if anyone was listening. "Listen, if you make him be okay you can take me, you can do anything to me, but please please let Owen not be hurt; please be okay, Owen; I'm so sorry; please be okay, please!"

Abruptly the wolf rolled over and was on his feet. He shook himself briskly and dirt flew.

He grinned at her, tongue lolling.

"You *prick*! You've got a lot of nerve not being seriously injured, Owen! How could you do that to me? You scared me to death, dumb shit! And who jumps in front of a charging SUV to save a stranger?" Her wheels chewed up dirt as she lunged at him; Owen avoided her easily and ducked behind old man Willow. "Oh, sure, *now* you're Mr. Nimblepants! Why didn't you do that before? I'm never forgiving you for this, you furry psycho!"

He barked once, sharply, and she roared around in a half circle and drove out of the field, cursing him at every foot. She was so angry, she was exhausted. She was so angry, it was hard to think. She was so angry, once she was back in the driveway she fell asleep . . . fell asleep for the first time in over half a century.

Chapter

20

Coffee Ray was rolling around in the ditch with Scarlett, kissing every inch of her he could reach, touching her, running his fingers through her hair. And she was an enthusiastic partner, returning his kisses, his embrace, with raw passion that was making it hard for him to breathe. Or to think.

"It's a ditch," he managed.

"What?" she said after she had shredded his shirt.

"We're in a ditch."

"Yes."

"It's a ditch."

"Yes," she replied, somewhat impatiently.

"I don't want our first time to be in a ditch."

Her head jerked up. "Our *first* time?"

"Well. Yeah. You know my disgusting shameful secret and you didn't head for the hills. Think I'm letting you go now?"

"You must," she replied seriously. She blinked her big pretty eyes at him. "I must make my report to the king."

"So. I'm coming with."

"You are?" She mulled that over, seeming to taste the words. "You are. But why?"

"Don't you believe in love at first sight?"

"I have never counted it before," she replied seriously.

"So if you haven't counted it, it doesn't exist?"

"No! Oh, no. There are many things in the world I have not counted. I—I only meant that I had no experience in that. In love at first sight." She paused, then forced it out: "In love."

"Well," he said, pressing his lips to the hollow of her throat, "it wasn't love at *first* sight. I fell when you told me about giants. So it was more like love at second or third sight."

"I'd like very much to introduce you to the king. And my other brother."

"So you're allowed to show up in the fairy kingdom or whatever with strangers?"

"By the time we get there, you will no longer be a stranger," she said slyly, and he laughed.

"Seriously, Scarlett . . ." His shorts went flying. "A ditch? We've got to come up with a better story for our grandchildren."

"I would like it very much if you would not talk the entire time we are naked."

"But it's a ditch," he whined, then gasped and clutched at her as she flexed her wings, as they whirred and blurred . . .

. . . and then they were soaring straight up into the star-studded night.

Chapter

21

"Whoa," he managed some time later.

Scarlett giggled.

"I—uh—wha? Whoa. *Whoa.*"

"Are you well?"

"Barely. You've spoiled me—forever! Flying sex is way better than masturbating alone to Internet porn."

"What?"

"Never mind. Also, you're the most incredible lay in the history of getting laid."

The events of the past few minutes whirred through his brain: her lips, her mouth. Her long, strong legs wrapped around his waist. Her inner heat, her silky limbs . . . and all the while he thrust and groaned, they were flying through the dark, and once an owl kept pace with them, hooing questions they both ignored. Scarlett hadn't even counted the bird.

"And gorgeous," he said, wrenching himself back to the present. "And big-time smart—and I know about big. I'd feel sorry for you being stuck with me if I wasn't hip deep in afterglow."

"'Stuck' with you? Not at all. It will be a good match.

Your life span is much longer than if both of your parents had been human."

"Fairies have longer life spans than humans?" he asked sleepily.

"Nearly every species on this planet has a longer life span than humans," she almost-but-not-quite-sneered. Then, "Oh. I apologize. I didn't mean to insult your honored father."

"Honored father," he snorted. "Shyeah. Change of subject, please."

She obliged. "And you are not tiny, as you would have been if both your parents had been human, which also suits me very well."

"Tiny?" he asked, delighted. "Who are you calling tiny?"

"I assume that is a reference to your penis, which we both agree is not tiny. And, thankfully, because your father was human you won't get fatally distracted and walk off a cliff."

"Is that an occupational hazard for giants?"

She shuddered. "Extremely so. So, as I said, this will be a good match."

He stared at her. They were floating just a couple of feet above the woods that covered the southern part of Ireland's property. It was so dark, and they were so far out in the country, the only lights were from the stars overhead. "Is that how fairies get hitched? They make—I dunno—the logical choice? Does love never enter into it?"

"Love comes after," she assured him.

"After what?"

"I will love you, as you will love me, because our union is so logical."

"Well, I'm not going to be the only one in this relationship who's in love. So hurry up and fall in love with me already."

"I shall make a point of it," she said gravely . . . then ruined it by giggling.

"Gee. That's so romantic I may— Yeek!" he yelped as she pinched him in a sensitive place.

"And now," she whispered, drawing him close—her hair smelled like secret flowers. "Now, you will love me again."

So he did. Very thoroughly.

Epilogue

Ireland Shea, Magicka guardian of her generation, groaned, flopped over on her stomach, and cracked open a bleary eye. She glared at the clock and wondered what had woken her up . . . at 6:15 in the morning!

More honking from the driveway. Her husband groaned and sat up. "What fresh hell is this?" he asked, shamelessly cribbing from Shakespeare. At least, she was pretty sure it was Shakespeare.

Ireland, who had gone to bed in sweatpants and a T-shirt, didn't have to dress. She waited impatiently as Micah shrugged into yesterday's slacks; then they hurried toward the god-awful noise.

Ezra wasn't there, of course—the sun had been up for five minutes. But everyone else was—even the fairy Scarlett and Coffee Ray! He must have spent the night.

Ireland saw Coffee Ray and Scarlett were holding hands, and smiled.

The Violent Fairy ("Stop calling me that; it's tainted") was also outside, arms folded across his massive chest. Willow stood in front of him, hugging their baby to her chest.

Owen was transfixed, and Ireland had to poke him three times before he looked at her. "What's going on?"

Owen pointed wordlessly, and Ireland looked. There was Judith, parked in her usual—

Wait.

There was a woman standing beside the SUV. Hanging on to the mirror, actually. Naked, and bewildered. Her short blond curls were a mess, her feet were black with dirt, and even from where she was standing, Ireland could see how blue her eyes were. She looked like a Dresden doll.

"Hello," Ireland called. She was long used to strangers showing up on her property—and they were naked an alarming amount of the time. "Are you hurt? It's okay. We won't hurt you."

"I know that, you nitwit," the blonde snapped in a weirdly cherubic voice. Though the words were acidic, her voice was high and sweet. The woman was a Barbie doll come to life.

"Okay. That seemed uncalled for," Ireland admitted. "Are you—"

"It's Judith!" Owen cried, and ran to the nude blonde, and scooped her up, and swung her around in two big circles before he set her back on the gravel.

"You knew me!" Judith said, and hugged him back, and even from where she was, Ireland could see the tears falling like rain down Owen's back.

"Of course I knew you, you awful bitch. I've always known you."

And Ireland realized with a staggering shock that the SUV the blonde was leaning on was just that. An SUV. And that Judith, after decades of imprisonment, was home.

Pixie Lust

BY LOIS GREIMAN

To Tara Rose, the most magical person I know.

Chapter

1

"These feet," said Avalina, and, bending, stroked the broken stems beneath her, restoring them to full health. "They are as large as moons. I cannot seem to bend them to my will."

The slow-flowering sedum that covered rock and root granted forgiveness, though it did little to hide its grumpiness. But that was the way of ground cover, wasn't it? Rather grasping, and generally irritable.

Avalina glanced about. Dusk was falling soft and dreamy from the sleepy places of the earth. Fragile, silvery mist lifted gently, filtering over fig and fern. It was the first night of her first visit to the Mortal Realm. Smiling a little, she lovingly folded the knobby root of a willow herb in a length of weevil silk, then tucked it into the little hemp bag that crisscrossed her torso and hung at her hip.

She was strangely garbed, dressed in garments humans would not find unusual. Or so she hoped, but the species was notoriously fickle, prone to change fashions as easily as their moral code. Each century brought new styles, new speech, new foolishness, while Faery remained the same for time immemorial. There was, after all, little reason to change perfection. Still, Ava could not bear the thought of losing Mortal's lovely species to mankind's capricious foolishness. Thus she had come.

She had been given little enough time to study Mortal ways, however. Her plans had been rushed, for the portal between their worlds would not long remain open for her kind.

Gazing through the soft, descending darkness at the quiet glen, Avalina adjusted the garment that chafed her skin and restricted her breathing. It was called a corset, or so she believed, and it was horrid uncomfortable. As was the itchy dress that covered her from throat to ankle in hot, restrictive folds. Foolish folk, these mortals. Did they know nothing of petal fabrics and corn silk gowns?

Still, it was unkind of her to mock them. They were a young race by Fey standards. Raw, uneducated. Dangerous by many accounts. Foolhardy by all. Perhaps they did not deserve the mesmerizing flora with which they had been blessed, yet here it was, springing forth like rushing water, so lush and green with fragrant newness that she longed to caress each leaf, to drink in every newborn scent. For a moment she felt compelled to twirl gleefully, to feel the oddly heavy air rush through her hair, push against her unfamiliar clothing, but she stifled the idea and chided herself; this was no childish game she played, no frolicsome sport, and she no mischievous bogle. Neither was she some impish pixie, prone to bouts of ridiculous thievery or juvenile pranks.

Oh, aye, tales of yore suggested that all the wee folk had once been one and the same . . . all wild pranksters who lived for naught but strong drink and merrymaking. For decadence and foolishness and frolicking with mortal men. 'Twas said, in fact, that they had, long ago, *all* been irresistible to humankind. But only in olden tales most forgot did a Fey find a mate who would become her *rant-*

inn, the one soul who was willing to give up the very essence of himself for her. Then and only then would they be bound for eternity and travel, forever joyful, between the realms.

But Avalina believed no such tales. For as long as she could recall, no mortal had come to the land of the Ancients, though more than a few sex-drunk pixies had tried to smuggle in their besotted lovers.

Ava shook her head at such idiocy, for she was not so foolhardy. Nay, she was stalwart and steady. She had a task to fulfill and she would see to it, no matter the circumstances.

Placing a protective hand on her pouch, she glanced about the glen in which she stood. She would do that for which she had come and leave posthaste, though this was indeed a magical spot. *Airil,* they would call it in the early tongue. Surely even the barbaric human would recognize the beauty possessed here, with the mercurial mists just rising from the fragrant bog and the deep-throated frogs only now tuning up for their nocturnal songs.

Mortal was indeed an intriguing place, a land filled with flower and thistle, with grasses and herbs that bloomed and twined and sprouted. But it was the ferns that fascinated her most. She was, after all, a Fern Fey. A Learned One in her own right, descended from the wise folk of Gelda. Not frivolous like the flower faeries with whom she had arrived.

Avalina scowled a little at the memory. Silly creatures all, they had come to Mortal on the pretense of studying godetia, but she knew far better; they had no wish to learn of the fragile blossoms that grew in profusion in certain Mortal regions. Instead, they planned a week of debauchery with any male foolhardy enough to linger with them, which, by all accounts, were many.

Queen Barilla should have known better than to allow

them to come. Though indeed, Avalina was lucky to have the excuse to accompany them. The portal opened only once a century, and 'twas the flower folk who had convinced the queen's Chosen to permit them to come. The flower folk with their beguiling eyes and winsome features. The flower folk who had giggled at the sight of her heavy garments. They had dressed in their usual gossamer gowns. But theirs was a mission of decadence, while Avalina had come for entirely different reasons.

Indeed, hers was a rescue mission of sorts, for she had come to retrieve the illusive Pinquil Fern, which was said to have been seen here hundreds of long years before. It was for that mission that she had abandoned her own frolicking gardens to hear every tale told of the revered fern— the Pinquil with its feathery foliage and reedy roots, with its musky fragrance and potent medicinal properties. Perhaps those properties did not pertain to humankind. Perhaps that was why the mortals, with their self-centered natures and enormous appetites, felt no great need to save it. She did not know, though she had spent some time studying their ways so that she might blend in. Might appear as one of them to avoid interruptions by some passing buffoon.

But perhaps "buffoon" was no longer a word oft used. She scowled into the rising mist, musing. A lazy shaft of sunlight shimmered through the gauzy leaves, gilding thorn and berry alike, but she was lost in thought.

What of "buffoonery"? she wondered. Was that a term yet used? The study of history had confused her no small bit, for the stories oft differed with the teller. Faeries had no need of written records, of course, for the Fey did not easily forget, and each tale grew in lushness and depth when passed from mother to daughter, from queen to princess.

But all agreed that for time beyond memory humankind was bent on atrocities. The very earth upon which she stood told the tale, chanting of battles the species had waged amongst themselves, but now the foolish Mortal seemed determined to declare war on the ferns as well.

Ava scowled at the thought. Off to her right, near the gnarled feet of a reticent maple, a frond nodded in the last, slanted rays of the vanquished sun. She caught her breath. Could it be? Might she have found the Pinquil already? she wondered, and rushed over. But it was only a timid leatherleaf. She touched its unfurling stem and it bobbed gracefully, but beneath her pinching slippers the flora complained. She shuffled apologetically aside, restoring broken herbage with a touch.

"How long will you be with us, Mistress?" asked a reedy sprig of lamb's-quarter.

It was not easy to decipher its dialect, for it had taken on a Mortal twang, but Avalina had not spent long hours in study for naught. "Six days yet," she said.

There were "oohs" in response. "And all in mortal body?" asked a bending sapling.

"Nay indeed," Avalina said. "I would spend every moment in my own form if ever I could, but it requires a great deal of energy here in Mortal. Still . . ." She glanced about again. The fireflies were just winking to life, lighting the bog with mercurial magic.

No mortals had passed this way for some hours. She had seen a leather-faced fellow wandering down a meandering path while it was yet fully light, but he had seemed intent on his own mission, stopping now and again to gaze at some particular plant or scribble something on his parchment.

Most probably at this late hour the mortals were well settled in, having gorged themselves on the flesh of their fellow species and content to lounge about until well past morning light. "I think it safe to make the change now," she said. "Full darkness is nearly upon us; thus I must say farewell until the morrow."

"Good night, Mistress," sighed the maple.

"Good night," chirped the sapling.

"Until the dawn."

"May you sleep with the dew," added a woody bur.

"My thanks," she said, and, closing her eyes, let her mind slip away to her homeland. The memory 'twas all that was needed to transform her. Feelings swamped her, immersed her. It was warm in the land of the Ancients, gently sultry, washed in color and light and fragrances so rich and fresh, it all but made one giddy. She filled her lungs with her thoughts and felt the change take her, felt the magic touch her and fill her and form her.

The flora gasped and oohed as the Mortal Realm rose and grew around her. She felt the rush of possibilities, the bloom of everlasting hope. With a sigh of relief, she smiled and opened her eyes. Upon her back, glowing wings fluttered past her shoulders. With naught but a thought, she lifted from the ground. A score of voices raised their good-byes as she zipped above the sleepy grasses. Then, light as a breeze, she glided through the glen in search of the smiling poppy she had spoken with some hours before.

Dammit! He was late again.

William Timber stood silent in the darkening woods. It was a pretty spot. That much he could admit. His mother would have been giddy at the sight of it. Would have probably given it some foolish name just as that idiot Braumberg had. Would have coohed over each pointy leaf, each scurrying bunny.

But William's mother was dead. Had been for more than twenty years, in fact. A heroin overdose, the police had said.

And they'd been right, of course. Old hippies often died that way. Old hippies whose lovers had abandoned them to the harsh realities of the world *usually* died that way. Leaving terrified little boys trying to feign bravery and fend for themselves.

"Elder Mann?" The first officer on the scene had tried to smile when he'd addressed William. The boy was frail, short, too small for his age, but smart. Certainly smart enough to know that he should not be dressed in mismatched socks and pink pajamas. But his mother had not believed in color-coding the genders . . . as she called it. "That your name?"

The boy had managed a nod and wiped his nose with the back of his frayed sleeve.

"You don't look real old." The cop's hair had been as gray as platinum.

William had fisted his hands, throat tight, eyes dry. There was no time for tears. Never would be again. He had known that with a terrible certainty. "It doesn't pertain to age," he said, words perfectly enunciated, and the old man had scowled.

The boy had legally changed his name not twelve months later. Had left the foolishness behind to become William Timber instead. William because it was rich with traditional practicality. Timber because it spoke of strength. He had been William Timber ever since. William Timber, self-made millionaire. Well . . . millionaire if you counted all assets, which he did. Counted and recounted, and configured and contrived.

He would not die in some musty, run-down apartment above a Vietnamese restaurant that reeked of burnt sauces and aloeswood incense. He would make a name for himself. In fact, he had done just that.

Snorting silently at his own wit, or lack thereof, he moved on.

Emily was one of the few who seemed to appreciate his dubious sense of humor. Or maybe it was his capital gains that she found heartening. He wasn't, after all, foolish enough to believe that a woman such as his fiancée would have taken notice of him if her iron-fisted father hadn't declared him to be an up-and-comer.

It was no secret that Emily Meier wanted to up-and-come. And William, never one for undue passion or wayward idealism, had wanted rather desperately to make inroads with Meier Conglomerated. It was a match made in financial heaven.

Still . . . He glanced around the sleepy woods. Purple wildflowers bloomed in riotous profusion. Lupine, if he remembered correctly, standing tall and proud on their spiky stalks. Fireflies flitted amongst the greenery near the bog. His mother had said they were sparkles of moondust come to life. She had a weakness for fireflies. In fact, she had many weaknesses, but for one shining moment all he could remember was her smile. It shone in his mind, the personification of love, of adoration.

Half-forgotten memories stole in, shadowed by sadness, illumined with laughter. But William plowed them aside, focusing on his mantra: another day another million. And this place had tremendous monetary potential. Within an hour's drive of Seattle and ringed by old-growth trees, it was the perfect spot for an upper-income community. A year from now there would be row upon row of two-story houses and brick patios. He would keep the best of the mature trees, of course. But the rest would be razed, plowed under, sodded over, paved, made ready for SUVs, overworked septic systems, and humming air conditioners.

Tonight, however, he had promised to dine with Emily, and she wasn't one to be kept waiting.

A tired trail wended through the woods, barely visible

now in the waning light. It had almost certainly been made by Braumberg. Damned, dehydrated tree hugger. He was probably higher than a rocket ship by now. High and still plotting how best to save the glen from succumbing to progress. But it didn't matter. Meier Conglomerated had money and it had clout. Those who couldn't be ignored could be bullied. Those who couldn't be bullied could be bought. Even hippy-dippy environmentalists had their price. They had to pay their dealers, after all.

Off to William's right, a poppy nodded heavily. It was tightly closed against the oncoming night. Tiny many-fingered leaves cradled its sleepy head. The blossom inside would be white with the faintest hint of lemon hues.

Emily preferred white to every other color. White on white on white. What did that say of her?

Bending with a mental shrug, William tore off the blossom and turned toward home.

Chapter

2

Avalina awoke with a start and struggled to her knees. The alba poppy that housed her was trembling with violent urgency. What was amiss? Had a windstorm sprung up unexpectedly? Had some beast attacked her bower?

Pressing her palms flat against the smooth-veined interior of the blossom, she drew in the flower's fragrant emotions and immediately knew the truth. Alba was in the throes of death.

Lurching to her feet, Avalina glanced frantically about. Had the blossom been torn off by the wind? Severed from its stem by a flailing branch? Ripped—

But no. The sound of heavy footfalls below her stopped Avalina's breath in her throat, for suddenly she knew the truth. Alba had been intentionally decapitated.

Panicked now, Avalina pushed against the closed petals with all her trembling strength, but it was of little use; the flower had already passed away, never again to smile at the morning sun, to sip nectar from the giving earth, to open at her command.

The footfalls stopped abruptly, tossing Ava from her feet. She struck the already-wilting pistil and bounced back up, breath held, waiting. A noise clanged, sharp and metallic, but there was no time to dwell on the sounds, for suddenly she was dipped violently downward, tumbling against a stamen before rolling to her feet. It was dark and silent for an elongated second, and then something roared.

She covered her ears, trying to shut out the agony, but a thought struck her suddenly: perhaps her captor knew nothing of her presence. Such behavior seemed likely from the ham-fisted humans of whom she'd been told. But regardless whether her abduction was intentional or not, she might not live long enough to escape. Already she could feel her powers weakening, for instead of taking strength from the blossom that cradled her, she was being drained. Drained by her separation from the earth, from life itself, the life that was the Fey's very identity. Stretching out her arms, she pushed against the petals once again, but it was no use. They had closed to the world, preparing to give their life to the soil. There was nothing Ava could do just now. Thus she sat, huddling against the stem, desperately absorbing what little energy remained.

She would wait, bide her time, and hope to retain strength enough to escape when the opportunity presented itself.

"Emily." William had pulled his Pontiac into the driveway seconds before, only to find his fiancée waiting by her car. Her sleek body was encased in a white satin sheath, her hips pressed against her Porsche's gleaming ivory fender. *Luscious hips*, or so Dean Abbot had declared them. Lifting the flower from the passenger seat, William stepped out of the car and slammed the door. "What are you doing here?"

She pushed away from her vehicle, eyeing him from beneath dark lashes, glossy pink-frosted lips curled up. Dean called it her sexy-as-hell expression, but it always looked a little predatory to William. As if she may have skipped one too many meals and was considering devouring him whole. "Don't tell me you've forgotten our date again."

"Okay." Jostling his overstuffed briefcase, he headed for the door.

"You forgot," she said.

"I didn't," he countered, and, turning on his stoop, handed her the flower. It seemed silly suddenly. Silly and sophomoric. Though he'd never been either. "I picked this for you."

"Oh." She drew back dramatically, pressing her fingertips to her breasts. A discreet amount of cleavage showed between her French-manicured nails. "It's lovely," she said.

But it wasn't. It was dead, wilted, and droopy in her carefully moisturized hand.

"Maybe if you put it in water it'll open," he said. Feeling foolish, he slipped his key into the lock. "It's a California poppy."

"Really."

He pushed open the door and motioned her inside. She gave him a glance from the corners of her eyes. Also sexy, according to Dean. But Dean found most things suspiciously erotic . . . frying pans and cobwebs included. Dean obviously needed the help of a licensed psychotherapist, but he was one hell of an architect.

"And how do you know that?" she asked.

"What?" William glanced at her, refusing to be irritated by her presence. She would soon be his wife, after all, and was, therefore, liable to be nearby now and again.

"That it's a California poppy."

"Oh," he said, and followed her into the foyer. "Common knowledge."

"*I* didn't know it." She was twirling the flower between her fingers.

"Maybe you're not common enough," he said, and took the poppy from her hand. The kitchen was just down the hall. A half bath was situated to the right, a small office adjacent.

He didn't own a vase, so he retrieved a glass, filled it with water, and dropped the stem inside. The single bloom floundered, drowning. Plucking it out, he hooked the lower petals over the rim and stared at it as a host of rambling memories rushed in: Flowers woven into a head of glossy curls. Laughter. Butterflies streaming like sunlight through an open window.

His mother had called herself Poppy; her real name had been Louise. He hadn't realized that until the day of her funeral. But he was certain that had nothing to do with his reason for picking the flower. He didn't admire her, after all. Hardly that. In fact, he was damned lucky he hadn't followed in her footsteps. The flower-child gene seemed to be a particularly virulent one.

"A renowned single-minded developer who knows the names of wildflowers . . . very intriguing," Emily said.

Making some sort of noncommittal noise, he drew himself back to the present.

"A man of mystery." She smiled . . . devastatingly, according to the ever ludicrous Dean, then changed the subject. "You know, if you'd give me a key, I could have waited inside," she said. She was leaning against the kitchen's rough doorjamb. Next week when he had a few hours to work with his hands, he would take it out, widen the entrance. It would open up the entire house. Increase its value dramatically. If the damned real estate market would rebound, he would make a decent profit.

"I could have made you dinner," she continued.

He glanced at her in surprise. As far as he knew, Emily Meier had never cooked so much as an idea in her entire life.

"If I hadn't just gotten a manicure," she said, and laughed. Dean said she laughed like a virgin goddess. "And speaking of cooking . . ." She sauntered toward him, hips swaying, but not too much. Emily Meier would never be mistaken for provocative, at least not by anyone but Dean. "I'm famished. Why don't you get dressed and take me to Mixtura?"

Getting dressed meant Armani and Kenneth Cole. A visit to the yacht club called for a carefully pressed polo shirt, linen pants, and leather loafers . . . the casual look. Just now, however, William was rather in the mood for a beer and a bag of Doritos. On the other hand, he was always in the mood to marry money.

Which meant, of course, that it was entirely possible that he was an ass, he thought as he headed for the bathroom. Or maybe Emily knew exactly what he was in the mood for and had an appetite for the same. Maybe he should ask her, he mused. But he wouldn't, which probably proved beyond a shadow of a doubt that he *was* an ass.

"I'll be back in a minute," he said, and stepped into the bathroom. It was messy. He closed the door behind him, simultaneously realizing he still held the glass that housed the pathetic flower. Setting it on the faux marble, he leaned against the vanity and examined himself in the mirror.

He looked about the same as he had on the previous day, weathered, with a slightly crooked nose and a five o'clock shadow cast daily just before noon. He was tall, dark haired . . . and probably an ass. But he wasn't getting any younger. According to the far too verbose Dean, Emily was a great catch what with her rockin' body and sizable inheritance. She was also probably great in bed. Supposedly, the cool ones often were. William couldn't attest to the fact. Presumably Dean was also just hypothesizing. Perhaps it should bother him that he wasn't sure and had never cared enough to ask.

Turning on the shower, William peeled off his clothes and left the garments heaped on the floor.

The water pressure was pathetic in this aging section of Seattle, but the heat felt good against his back. Poppy had said that water was the essence of life. That—

The sound of shattering glass tore apart his musings.

"Emily?" he called.

A crash answered him.

Slamming off the water, he tore the curtain aside, glanced toward the door, then dropped his gaze to the floor.

A woman lay sprawled on his yellowed linoleum, legs spread, hair scattered, absolutely naked.

"What the hell!" he rasped, but she was already lurching to her feet, backing unsteadily toward the door, eyes as wide as the horizon, wild hair spread about her in a golden tangle. "How—"

"William?" Emily called from the far side of the door, but he failed to notice.

The girl's breasts seemed to be sparkling. Breasts didn't usually do that, did they? His throat felt suddenly dry, his heart overtaxed. "Who the hell are you?" he croaked.

"William, honey." Emily knocked again. "Are you all right?"

No, he wasn't all right; he was, suddenly and unmistakably, horribly aroused. The girl had a face like an angel, a body like a wet dream. Snatching a towel from a plastic peg, he hooked it around his waist, ineffectively hiding his erection as he stepped from the shower.

"Who are you?" he asked again.

"William!" Emily's voice had become strident. "I'm coming in," she said, and snapped the door open.

The girl stared, buttocks pressed against his vanity, tousled hair flowing like molten gold over glittering breasts to curl protectively about her sweetly curved hips.

"Who the hell is that?" Emily rasped.

Somewhere in the dim part of William's mind not demanded by his southward rush of blood, he realized he'd never heard her swear before. Then again, he'd never had a naked, sparkling angel backed against his vanity, either. And all he could do was stare.

"William!"

Dammit. Was he still staring?

"Who the fuck are you?" Emily demanded, and took a threatening step forward. The girl skittered sideways, inadvertently brushing William's arm.

Emotions and feelings and instincts bumped savagely to life in Will's overheated system. They swirled and congealed, galvanizing his desire, bracing his protective instincts, and effectively sending any lingering brain waves skittering off to attend his nether parts like water down a flume.

"I am . . ." The girl darted her evergreen gaze to his like a forest creature on the run. "I am his," she whispered.

Chapter

3

"Mine?" the man rumbled.

"*His*?" the woman shrieked.

Her voice was a barded barrage against Ava's shattered senses. Her head felt swollen, her limbs weak. Where was she? *Who* was she? She glanced down. And shouldn't she be wearing clothes?

"William, get her out of here!" the woman demanded.

Avalina snapped her gaze fretfully to the other's face, but as she did so the world seemed to shift around her. The floor buckled up like a swelling wave and suddenly she was falling, slipping into darkness.

"Hey! Hold on," he said, and caught her against him at a slanted angle. Feelings as primitive as hope shimmied through her, firing up emotions, igniting unadmitted instincts. She raised a hand shakily to his chest. It felt solid and hard and strangely alluring. She focused on it with an effort. His skin was warm, his hair coarse and dark, sparking her imagination, tinkling her fingers. She blinked as feelings washed through her in lavender waves. The woman had called him William, but it seemed wrong somehow, too dull, too rigid. "Hair," she said, though she didn't truly know why. It simply seemed a strange place to be hirsute. She let her gaze slip lower. His hair narrowed to a silky trail that traveled the length of his tight-muscled abdomen and disappeared beneath the bumpy, white cloth that encircled his waist. She reached for it, curious.

"William!" snapped the woman.

Ava yanked her fingers back.

"Just . . ." William lifted his free hand, palm out. His other arm cradled Avalina's back, holding her tight against him. His skin felt supple and lovely against hers. "Just give me a minute. I think she's sick."

"Sick!" The woman's face was screwed up like a snarling goblin's, her voice an abomination to Ava's ears. "I don't care if she's dying. She's naked!"

"Well, yes." He had a lovely voice. Low, beautiful, resonating from the core of him. His gaze held hers. "Yes, she is that." From beneath the towel, part of him moved, nudging her hip. She turned toward him without thought, lips parted, ready. Though, if the truth be told, she had no idea what she was ready for.

"William!" the woman gasped. "Do you have a hard— What the hell is going on here?"

He was tall, towering over Ava, but somehow his lips were only inches from hers. They moved. She rose on her toes, eager to taste their sound, to feel their emotion.

"William!"

He jerked his gaze away, straightening abruptly. "I . . . I'm not sure. I . . ."

"You're not sure!"

"I think she needs help."

"She needs a quick kick in the ass," Emily rasped, and grabbed Ava's arm.

The grip was hard and cold. Avalina tried to pull away, but her head was reeling. And then she was falling again, tumbling end over end into darkness.

Still, she felt him lift her, felt herself being carried through the door and away. Something yielded against her back. She fluttered her eyes open, and he was there, singularly alluring, strangely irresistible. She lifted one hand toward him, and for a moment it seemed he approached but suddenly he jerked away, moved out of reach, cleared his throat.

"Just . . . just rest for a minute," he said, and disappeared from sight. She tried to follow his departure, but the world was so hazy. Confusing and cold and frightening. Her eyes fell closed.

The woman hissed something, but they were already moving out of earshot and the darkness was so alluring, so quiet, so seductive.

"Let go of my arm," Emily ordered, which was strange, because William hadn't actually realized he'd been gripping her arm. He dropped it now, rubbed his hands together, and tried to clear his head. It remained patently unclear.

Emily took a step back. Her eyes were narrow, her perfectly frosted lips pursed in hard lines. "Well?"

He cleared his throat again and glanced guiltily toward the bedroom door, which was also strange because he didn't do guilt. It was one of those unnecessary emotions he'd purged from his life nearly a decade before. He didn't clear his throat, he didn't feel guilt, and he didn't become so aroused he was in danger of spontaneous combustion. Hell, there was a whole damn list of things he didn't do . . . until now. "Well what?" he asked.

"What is she doing here?" Emily could, it seemed, speak with her teeth tightly clenched. Interesting.

"I'm not entirely sure," he admitted. Generally, he did not make vastly ridiculous understatements, either.

"What do you mean, you're not sure? Who is she?"

He glanced toward the bedroom again, wanting, with rather desperate longing, to step through the door, to see her there, to watch her sleep. "She didn't say."

"Didn't say?" Emily's perfectly arched brows rose above narrowed, crafty eyes. The careful diction was back in place. The serene, seductive expression was not. "Tell me, William, do slutty teenagers often show up naked in your bathroom?"

He nodded, though he had no idea what he was nodding about. His head seemed to have taken on a life of its own. As had other parts. "It's uncommon." He glanced toward the bedroom again. The urge to watch her sleep was growing. He itched to sit by her side. To feel his fingers envelop hers. To see her awaken. And . . . well . . . to do more.

"Get rid of her."

"What?" he asked, and dragged his gaze back to the woman who might, if he remembered correctly, be his fiancée.

"I want her gone. Now! Do you understand me?"

"But . . ." He studiously kept himself from staring at her door like an abandoned bloodhound. "I think she might be ill."

"Ill! Yes, she very probably is, William. Diseased! The little whore! Get her out of here."

"Whore?" The word seemed oddly incongruous when put in conjunction with the angel in his bed. The angel was sparkly. Whores didn't sparkle. He was sure of it, though, in actuality, he knew very little about whores . . . or angels, come to that. He was a hell of a contractor, though. Had devoted nearly two decades of his life to it, but suddenly he didn't much care.

"William!"

He pulled his gaze back toward Emily with some difficulty. "Yes?"

She gave him a thin-lipped smile. "Perhaps in the past you've enjoyed flaunting your . . . trashy foreigners. But in the future you'll be both judicial and discreet."

"Trashy—"

"I want her gone," Emily hissed. "Do you hear me?"

Was she saying she didn't care if he had affairs? Was that normal? Shouldn't she care? "I'm not sure I do."

"I'm leaving now," she said, frosty tone level, eyes deadly hard. "You'll get rid of her. You'll not see her again. And we'll not speak of this again."

He had a bad feeling he might be stupidly staring again.

"Or else," she added.

"Or else . . . ?"

"I'm gone! Along with Daddy's money, Meier Conglomerated, and your future. Do you understand?"

She wasn't speaking some kind of cryptic code. He was sure of it, and yet it was oddly difficult to focus on her words, or *her* . . . or anything that wasn't the angel with the sparkly breasts.

"Don't disappoint me, William," she hissed, and, storming through the house, slammed the door in her wake.

He stared at the reverberating portal, but that didn't seem to be particularly productive, so he turned and stared at the bedroom door for a while. That, too, seemed less than fruitful; he let his legs carry him to it. The knob felt strangely surreal beneath his fingers. It turned in his hand. He pushed the door open and realized suddenly that he was holding his breath.

But she was still there, lying perfectly still upon his blessedly lucky sheets.

He crossed the floor silently and stared down at her. Her eyes were closed, but it didn't matter. He could remember them exactly. They were purple. Not blue, not aquamarine. But a purple so deep and pure it stole your

breath and froze your senses. The lids that covered them
were a rusty hue, and the lashes . . .

He marveled at them, finding that he wanted to touch
them, to run his fingertips along the downy fringe and
watch them lift. They were gold. Not blond, but gold, as if
each strand were made of the finest gilded mesh. He
shook his head. It was foolishness, of course. They were
obviously fake. And surely she was wearing tinted lenses.
He hadn't immersed himself so deeply in his career that
he had failed to hear of such things.

But her face. He actually reached out to touch it. Just
stopping himself inches from her cheek. It was astounding. Miraculous. Although, if asked, he couldn't have said
why exactly. It was, after all, just a face. Nevertheless
there was something spectacular about it. Something bold
and shy all at once. Something almost comical yet strik-
ingly intelligent. Broad at her apple-bright cheeks, it narrowed to a pointy, clefted chin. Her lips were a tiny curved
Cupid's bow, whimsically lifted into a half smile even as
she slept. And her hair . . .

He let his gaze follow the curling, twining length of it.
It tumbled over her shoulders, trilled over her breasts, and
fell . . .

Well, he couldn't really look past her breasts, for they
were mesmerizing. Perhaps he had imagined the sparkle,
but perhaps not, for it seemed almost that when he shifted
his gaze the slightest degree, the tone of her skin changed
almost imperceptibly from a golden hue to a soft, inde-
scribable shade of . . . lavender?

He shook his head and pushed his gaze downward
over the flat plane of her belly to— But he stopped
abruptly, blinking. Where was her navel? he wondered,
but in that moment she shifted, drawing his gaze down to
where her legs joined, only to find that the long golden

sweep of her hair had curled past her hip to effectively cover her private parts.

Nevertheless, he felt himself buck with desire and moved closer, almost reaching for her. But he stopped, crunching his fingers into fists and remaining very still. His lips felt dry and his throat strangely tight, but he did not touch her.

No. That would be asinine. And he was never asinine. He was disciplined. Controlled. He had his life organized, planned down to the minute. Down to the dollar. No extravagant expenditures, no ridiculous risks, just solid, careful investments and hard work.

But still his gaze slipped along the length of her legs, up one slightly raised thigh to her right knee. Sweat trickled down his back, though he was sure, absolutely *certain*, that her knee could not possibly be irresistible. It was just a knee, after all. Much like her other knee, which . . . He skipped his attention to the peaked cap in the center of her left leg and found it to be just as fascinating as the first.

Still, he managed to force his gaze away, down the long, slim muscles of her calf to where one foot lay gently atop another. They were graceful and delicate and sweetly pointed, with each little toe capped by a shell-like nail in mother-of-pearl hues.

He had no particular fondness for feet. No fetishes. No odd fantasies. And yet, to his vague amazement, he found himself seated on the bed, reaching for one long, dainty foot.

And then she awoke.

He knew the moment she came to. Felt it in his questionable soul. He glanced breathlessly at her face and watched her eyes flutter open. The deep purple captivated him, held him. She sat up slowly. Corn silk hair slipped over her nipples, half-hiding, half-teasing. Her knees bent, opening her core to him, but he was still held in her eyes, in her thoughts.

She wanted him. He knew it long before she touched him, felt it in her gaze, smelled it in the very air.

She rose to her knees. Her hair moved like a living thing, as though she were floating in the sea, as though it was tossed by an invisible wind, but her eyes never shifted. They remained fixed on him, slanted like a cat's, wide and deep, filled with a thousand sorrows, a million joys. And suddenly he wanted to laugh and cry and shout all at once, but she was reaching for him, her fingers smooth and slim and magical.

He watched her move closer, her nails gleaming in shades of silver and periwinkle, her digits curving up slightly at the ends like an avid pianist's.

Her fingertips touched his cheek, and even though he had braced himself for contact, he felt the first spasm of orgasm strike him like a tidal wave.

Chapter

4

"Holy shit!" he rasped, and lurched to his feet, spilling her sideways. She tumbled onto the bed, eyes wide, endless legs sprawling. But he didn't care. Hardly cared at all.

Good God, was she hurt?

And was he panting? Panting like a hound? "What . . ." His voice sounded like a croak. "What the hell just happened?"

She blinked at him, lashes gold against amethyst eyes. "Is aught amiss?" she whispered.

"Aught? Amiss?" He stared at her, boggled, trying to get his bearings, but his damned bearings were gone. His dick, however, was pointing due north. It throbbed, taut and erect, and just on the socially acceptable side of full ejaculation. He wanted to grab her and kiss her and make love to her with a desperation so deep he was about to implode, but he held back, gritting his teeth, fisting his hands. "Amiss?"

She blinked again, gathered her sensuous legs under her, and settled back on her buttocks, watching him. Her hair shifted again, though he could have sworn her magical body remained still.

"Who are you?" he asked. Or maybe he panted. It was

entirely, disgustingly possible he was still panting. Which would have been disconcerting if he were coherent enough to think about it.

She shook her head.

He drew a careful breath, reminding himself not to fall on her like a mail room boy at lunch break. "Where did you come from?"

A scowl marred her brow, but she was now only more beautiful. It made him want to kiss her and sing to her and . . .

Sing to her? Good God! What was wrong with him? Was he concussed? Was he delirious? Was he nuts?

"Are you French?" he asked. Dean said Frenchwomen always breakfasted in the nude. That's what made them so horny. *Note to self*, William thought hazily: *Fire Dean*.

She shook her head, but the movement was uncertain.

"Italian?"

She only blinked this time.

"Do you speak English? I mean . . . you speak English. Right?" He'd heard her speak English. Good God, he'd heard her say that she was his. Something pounded in his chest at the memory. He hoped it was his heart.

"Listen. . . ." He opened his mouth, searching for something to call her, but he had nothing. "Do you have a name?"

She chewed her lower lip. He found he wanted to do the same. Chew her lip, lick her neck, stroke her slim, pointy feet. Her feet? What the hell!

"All right. Okay," he said, and pulled his gaze from her toes to turn and pace the length of the room. It was the hardest damn thing he'd ever done in his life, because it wasn't okay. He was nuts. So nuts, in fact, that by the time he turned back he felt desperate to see her again, to look at her, to make certain she was well and safe and . . .

A trickle of blood ran over the slim muscle of her calf

and smudged the sheet below her. At the sight of it, his breath stopped in his throat. His heart bumped to stillness.

"You're bleeding." His voice was throaty, helpless.

Her frown increased.

"Blood," he said, and stepped toward her. She reached for him with unconscious grace, but he reeled himself back moments before it was too late. Before he crossed the point of no return and fell like a brick into ecstasy. What the hell was going on? Was she a witch? Was that it? Had she cast a spell on him? Had she—

Oh, for God's sake, there was no such thing as witches!

"Blood," he said, and pointed, careful now to go no closer, to stay at arm's length, but his hands were already shaking. He closed his eyes and tried again. "On the bed."

She glanced down. Her lips moved into a little moue of dissatisfaction and she shifted, smearing blood across his sheets.

"You're hurt."

She blinked.

"Let me see. Stand up," he ordered, and she did so finally, stepping with forest-creature grace onto his squashed carpet. Good Lord, her feet were pretty. And her legs and her . . .

He was feeling faint by the time he got to her kneecaps, but he braced himself on the wall to his left and remained erect . . . in so many ways. "Turn around."

She blinked. Why did she keep blinking? Didn't she know it made him want to do less than acceptable things with her?

"Around," he repeated, and made a motion with his hand. She pirouetted slowly, revealing her back, her waist, her . . .

"Holy crap," he said, and stumbled back to sit on the chair near the door.

She turned her head, gazing down. Her hair, fine as silk, brushed past her shoulders to tickle her buttocks like gilded fingers. Her buttocks that were soft and golden brown and split by an irresistible crease that housed the hot core of . . .

"I be injured," she said.

He slammed his ridiculous thoughts to a halt and focused. Somehow he'd failed to notice the blood that smeared across her buttocks. Her buttocks that were as luscious as . . .

Oh, dear God!

"What happened?" he asked.

But she only shook her head.

"How bad is it? Does it hurt? Do you need a doctor?"

She was scowling again and turned toward him. And holy crap, her breasts *were* sparkling, but he tore his gaze away.

"Doctor. Doctor!" he said, and felt like roaming around in a circle like a rabid animal but managed to remain where he was. "That's what we need." It was a great idea. A brainstorm. He'd deliver her to the hospital, let them deal with her. He looked away, knowing his limits, then jerked to his feet, intent on rushing her out into the world as fast as possible. Storming across the distance, he grabbed her arm.

But suddenly, inexplicably, she was kissing him. Their lips met with a clash. Desire roared through him like a volcano. He pressed her backward, heading toward the bed, toward orgasm, toward ecstasy.

But sense came back with a start. He broke off the kiss and jerked away, breathing hard, longing desperately. "What the hell," he whispered.

Her lips were still parted, her breasts rising gently with each breath. "Is aught amiss?"

"Yes, ought is amiss," he rasped. "Lots of oughts are

amiss. I . . ." He ran his gaze down her shimmering body and managed not to swoon. "Listen. . . ." He stumbled backward, gripped the back of the chair with all his might, and held on tight. "I don't know what's going on here, but . . ."

"You are *rantinn*."

He cocked his head, for her voice, always breathy and ethereal, seemed now to shimmer somehow as if imbued with an unearthly quality that made him shiver with desire. "What?"

"You are *rantinn*. Yes?"

"Does that mean what I think it means?"

She didn't reply. But of course it meant what he thought it meant. Who in their right mind would talk about anything else at a time like this?

"No," he said. "No. No *rantinn*. I'm taking you to the doctor. They can find out—"

What? What would they find out? That Meier's soon-to-be son-in-law had been keeping a ridiculously beautiful and incomparably naked woman in his house? A woman who spoke only limited English. A woman who was . . . very possibly . . . an illegal alien. A woman who was injured.

"Listen . . . honey. . . ." Honey? He didn't call anyone honey. Not his dog, if he had one, which he didn't. Not his co-workers and certainly not Emily. Emily was Emily and sometimes Ms. Meier. "I want to make l—" He stopped himself before the dastardly honesty spilled out. "I want to *help* you."

She nodded and stepped forward, arm outstretched.

"But not . . ." He tightened his grip on the chair and squeezed his eyes closed. "Not like that. I . . . I'm . . ." What was the word? "Engaged. To be . . ." Dammit! "Married!" The word came to him on a breath of relief.

She scowled.

"And you're so . . ." He gritted his teeth and motioned hopelessly toward her lissome body. "Fantastically . . ." Dear God! "Hurt," he finished.

Enlightenment seemed to dawn on her heavenly features. She turned again, showing him her backside. He felt his knees buckle and his erection buck, but he braced himself.

"You tend," she said, and glanced down at herself.

"Tend . . . ," he breathed. "Tend. You want me to see to your wound. Oh, yes. Well . . ." Shit, he was gibbering like an inebriated monkey. "Do you know what happened?"

She shook her head erratically.

"There was a crash and . . ." He glanced toward the bathroom. "The glass. I think you may have . . ." Prying his fingers from the chair, he managed to force himself into the hallway and beyond. And sure enough, the glass he'd left on the vanity had been shattered. And the flower . . . The flower had burst into a dozen pieces that were scattered over the floor like wayward confetti.

"Yes. See," he said, and turned, but she was already there, entering the bathroom. Small as she was, she seemed to fill the space like a light show, and suddenly he couldn't breathe, couldn't think. He tried to back away, but there was nowhere to go. His back pressed against the wall, and then she was touching him, her hands petal-soft against his chest.

Disoriented and randy as hell, he rasped something nonsensical, some gibberish about control and discipline and life plans. There may have been something about capital gains, too. But then she kissed him. Her hands were like velvet against his skin, her lips were like magic against his, and suddenly everything seemed clear. He had to make love to her. Here, in the bathroom, then in the bedroom, then the kitchen, possibly the sink or . . .

Dammit!

"Honey!" He grabbed her hands, pulled them down, swallowed hard. "I can't. I'm sorry. My life . . . It's . . . structured. I'm sorry." He glanced down. She was sparkling again. He closed his eyes and shivered. "I'm maybe the sorriest creature that ever lived. But I can't."

A tendril of her hair had somehow become curled around his wrist and seemed to be caressing his forearm. But that was crazy.

"I'll just . . ." He took a breath, fortifying himself. "I'll just put some . . . something on your . . ." God help him. "Your fantastic . . . Your *cut* and then . . . Then we'll find you some clothes so you're not . . . naked." What was he talking about? What the hell was wrong with him? She should always be naked. Naked and wet and . . .

He had to get a grip. "Then I'll take you home."

"Home?" She scowled.

He nodded. "Yes. Home. Where . . . Where is that exactly?"

She shook her head, scowling. "Morning glories."

"What?"

"Heather?"

"I don't—"

"I see them. . . ." She nodded, touched her fingertips to her breast. He managed to resist passing out by sheer willpower alone. "Here."

"You see flowers. In your . . . your . . ." He couldn't stop staring. Her nipples were as pink as apple blossoms, her breasts as round as passion fruit. He yanked his gaze away. "In there?"

"Yes. Flowers and . . ." She thought hard. "Green."

"Plants."

She nodded. "They grow . . . profusion."

"Do you live in a rain forest? South America? New Zealand?" He searched desperately. "The Congo?"

She blinked.

"Do you speak Spanish? "Hablas español?"

She was shaking her head again.

"French? Italian? German?" It was amazing how few languages he could think of. Or maybe it was amazing he could think at all with her breasts doing that sparkly thing. "You must have hit your head," he said. "On the vanity. When you fell." From where? Holy nuts, this was crazy. "I should get you to a doctor."

She was still scowling. How could it be so adorable?

"Concussions can be serious. They could keep you overnight. Do tests."

He wouldn't have thought her eyes could get any wider. Any more expressive. But he would have been wrong.

She shook her head. "I wish to stay."

"Listen, you can't—"

"Here." Somehow her hair had blown around his back and curled about his waist. It felt as soft and surreal as a dream lover's kiss.

He shook his head, but her eyes were glistening.

"I beg you," she said, and suddenly he was nodding though he didn't know why. He had no intention of keeping her in his house. He *couldn't* keep her in his house. His fiancée would leave him. His fiancée, whose name was . . . *Dammit!* He sharpened his thought. She had a father. A fitness fanatic. He was a wealthy man, and vindictive. And someone had mentioned a pair of thugs he kept on retainer.

Ahh there, motivation to think with his head instead of his . . . whatever. But he couldn't throw the girl out on the street. And taking her to the hospital seemed cruel. But maybe she *was* concussed. He stared into her eyes, checking the size of her pupils. But she didn't seem to have any. Was that a good sign?

"We need a name for you," he said. "What—"

"Flora."

He raised his brows. "What?"

"Fern. Green plants that . . ." She made an undulating motion with her hand. It made him feel faint. "Fern be lovely."

"Not as lovely as you," he murmured.

Her lips twitched. It was only the slightest of smiles and yet the expression made him feel like yodeling. He refrained . . . from everything. Cleared his throat.

"Okay, listen . . . Fern. You don't look like a Fern, but . . . I need to get that . . ." He glanced downward, not actually daring to look past her elbow. "I need to get that cleaned up."

She nodded.

"So I'll just . . ." He jerked his head toward the kitchen and wondered if it would be possible to let her go. "I'll get some things."

Another nod.

He pried his hands open and backed away. She remained where she was, not following, not disappearing like a fevered dream. He made it through the door, managed to turn and head for the kitchen.

With a few feet of space between them, his head was clearer, working again. He didn't know how she had gotten there. The front door had been locked when he'd arrived, but maybe she had come in after. In fact, maybe . . .

Dean!

The name exploded like a cherry bomb in his head. Of course! Dean had planted her there. Dean, who thought he was funny. Dean, who thought it would be amusing to put some poor foreign girl in his bathroom and see what happened. Or maybe he wanted to break up him and Emily. Either way . . .

The phone felt solid in his hand.

"Yeah?" Dean sounded distracted. Voices yammered randomly in the background.

"What's the penalty for prostituting a minor, Abbot?" Will growled.

The line went momentarily silent, then, "Hang on a sec. I think I have that information for you, sir," Dean said, then covered the receiver and murmured to someone else, "Just a moment please. Very important call. I'm going to have to take this in the conference room."

His chair squeaked. Footfalls sounded, but William didn't wait. Anger coursed through him like boiling lye. "You sorry bastard. Where did you find her?"

"Certainly. Just a minute.

"Hey, Baxter, how's it going?" Dean asked. Then a door closed and he spoke more clearly. "Okay." The footfalls stopped. He was breathing hard. "Start at the beginning."

"What the hell were you thinking about?" Will's voice sounded like a snarl to his own ears. Rage spurred through him.

"Probably sex, but—"

"She can't be over eighteen."

"Eighteen. Holy f— Okay . . . so there's a girl," Dean said, struggling to remain calm. "Is she naked?"

"How'd you get her in here? What'd you do with her clothes?"

Abrupt silence, then, "I'm coming over."

The anger flared into rage. "You show your ugly face in my door, I'll put it through a wall."

"Timber?" Dean said. "Hey, buddy, is that you?" Perhaps he was surprised by the passion. He wouldn't be the only one. William was nothing if not pragmatic. He was known for it.

"Bastard!" William snarled, and hung up.

His hands were still a little shaky when he opened what some might laughingly call his medicine cabinet. It contained a half a tin of Band-Aids and two Q-tips. Shit.

He took down the tin and the Q-tips, then rummaged around in a couple of drawers, but they were unhelpful. Finally, he reached into the liquor cabinet . . . much better stocked . . . and pulled out a bottle of vodka.

She met him in the hallway.

"Oh." He didn't know why he was surprised to see her, but he was. He had a sneaking suspicion that if he saw her every day until the end of eternity he would still be surprised. And hopelessly thrilled. "Here. I found . . ." Nothing. He lifted the vodka. "Disinfectant."

She glanced at it, then found his eyes again.

"Why don't we go in there?" He nodded toward the bathroom. "The light's better. I'll sit down and . . ." He tried to catch his breath, but it was slippery. "I'll do what I can."

Which, in his current condition, wasn't a whole hell of a lot, unless it involved his dick, in which case he felt like freakin' Superman.

He followed her into the bathroom. Her hair swayed like willow branches in a subtle wind, offering intoxicating glimpses of her back, her shoulders, her buttocks.

He took a chug of vodka and wiped his mouth with the back of his hand. Turning, she watched him, and he shimmied around her, careful not to touch. Setting his limited supplies on the vanity, he found a clean washcloth in the second drawer down and ran it under the tap.

She watched, scowled, then stepped forward, dipped her fingers in the stream, and smiled. "Life," she said.

"What?"

She scowled, thinking, then, "Water. Life."

"Yeah." Poppy had called water life. "Turn around." What the hell was going on? Maybe it hadn't been Dean who had set this up after all. Maybe it was someone else. A competitor. Someone who wanted to distract him. Which was very effective, he thought, and watched the girl turn, watched her hair caress her hips, watched her legs move.

Shutting off the water, he dropped the toilet lid and sat down, face-to-face with her . . . everything.

Shit! Reaching over, he grabbed the vodka bottle by the neck and took another hard swig.

She glanced over her shoulder. Her hair swayed, brushing his bare knees. He felt a little light-headed.

"Life?" she asked, motioning toward the bottle.

"This? No. Strength," he said, and, setting the vodka aside, braced himself for the impossible.

Chapter

5

It was hell and heaven and purgatory all wrapped up like a damned pig in a blanket.

But somehow William had managed to finish the job, had cleaned and bandaged her wounds. They weren't serious. Just . . . *Holy crap!*

He paced the kitchen, carrying the vodka with him. It was almost midnight. She'd been asleep for over an hour. Asleep, in his pajama shirt. He'd thought it would be safer that way. But it wasn't. Oh, no, it wasn't. She'd looked like a miracle, like a gift wrapped for Christmas, with her corn silk hair flowing about her like living gold. He'd put her in his bed. What else could he do? She was injured, after all, and disoriented. And maybe concussed.

Maybe he should check on her. He stopped his pacing and stared, tense and leaning toward his bedroom as if there were a hard wind at his back. Weren't concussion patients supposed to be awakened? He took an involuntary step in that direction, but just then the doorbell rang, bringing him up short.

His footsteps were almost silent across linoleum and carpet. He was still barefoot. Barefoot and crazy.

"Who is it?"

"Hey, buddy," Dean said from the far side. "Let me in. There are mosquitoes the size of helos out here."

Will debated letting the bugs have him, but curiosity or anger or a half-dozen emotions he couldn't identify made him jerk open the door. "What the hell are you doing here?"

"Me? I was just in the neighborhood." Dean skimmed the house. He was still in his dress pants, wrinkled shirt almost tucked in, blond hair tousled. Dean rarely went through a day without looking as if he'd been hit by something that would register fairly impressively on a Richter scale. "Hey, you okay?"

"Sure. I'm great." William ran his fingers through his hair and tried to remember to breathe. "Why wouldn't I be?"

"Uh-huh." Eyes skimmed again. "Say, you said you had some company earlier?"

William turned back toward the living room, then sat down on the couch and propped one foot over the opposite knee. It was hotter than hell, but he'd dressed in jeans and a long-sleeve button-down shirt. It seemed safer that way. The more clothes the better. He'd give his left testicle for a nice suit of armor. Well, maybe not a testicle. An arm perhaps. "Did you pay for the concussion, too?" he asked. "Or was that just lucky happenchance?"

Dean sat down on a nearby recliner and nodded to the bottle still clasped in Will's fist. "You sharing that vodka or you planning on killing it yourself?"

Will considered swinging it at the other's head but finally passed it over. Dean took a swig. "Maybe you should start at the beginning, huh, buddy?"

What was with the damned patronizing tone? As if he were a yammering idiot. "Maybe *you* should."

Dean stared at him a moment, then nodded and took

another swig. "Okay. I got a call about eight fourteen. I was busy with potential clients, but I answered on the fourth ring. The call was from a Mr. William Timber, who seemed a bit distraught. He spoke of an eighteen-year-old who was naked. . . ." He paused, canted his head a little. "Did I get that right? . . . Was she naked?"

The room fell into breathless silence. "Are you saying you had nothing to do with this?"

Dean threw up both hands. The vodka splashed noisily. "With what? What the hell's going on?"

William watched him. If the bastard was acting, he should be on the stage. "A girl showed up in my bathroom tonight."

Dean's brows shot into his hairline. "Your bathroom?"

"Yeah."

"Was she naked in your bathroom?"

Will jerked to his feet. "Get the hell out of here."

"No. Wait. Wait a minute." He held up a soothing hand. "I'm just trying to get the lay of the land."

"Uh-huh," Will snarled.

"No, really. I'm intrigued. Where did this girl come from? How'd she get in?"

Will paced, gait jerky. "I don't know and I don't know."

"Did you ask?"

He stopped his pacing to glare. "Of course I asked."

"And she . . ." Dean shrugged, waiting for the other to fill in the blanks.

"She doesn't speak much English."

"You're kidding!" He said it as if he'd won the lottery. "A foreign chick?"

"Keep your voice down."

"Them foreign girls are—," Dean began, then stopped, mouth open, mind closed tight. "You telling me she's still here?"

Will glowered, wishing like hell he'd popped the bastard in the nose as soon as he'd opened the door. But maybe it wasn't too late.

"Is she here?" Dean asked again, quiet now, stabbing a finger at the floor as if she might be buried in the basement. "In this house? Right now?"

William narrowed his eyes and refrained from doing something he might regret if incarcerated for aggravated assault. "You swear to God you had nothing to do with this?"

Dean raised his right pinky finger. "I swear it on Britney Spears' underwear."

"Then where do you think she came from?"

He shook his head with vague uncertainty. "Heaven?"

"I considered that."

"Really?"

Yes. "Don't be stupid."

"No," Dean said, and leaned closer. "Think about it. You're about to get married. I mean, not that that's a bad thing. Emily's hot and everything. But marriage! Whew! Maybe God thought, Hey, you-know-who needs a little fun before he—"

"I should have taken her to the hospital," William said, and paced. "But she looks so young and . . . and she doesn't have any ID."

"No." Dean made a face and shook his head. "No ID. 'Cuz she doesn't have any clothes, right?"

What would happen if Will hit the idiot in the head with a chair like they did in the movies?

"Just out of curiosity . . . is she naked right now? In your bedroom? Is she naked?" Dean asked.

"Leave her alone." The words sounded a little gritty, a little dangerous.

Dean's brows now resided in his hairline. "Sure. Sure I will. I'm just trying to help. And I thought . . ." He shrugged again. "Maybe if I took a look I might recognize her. You know. From a strip club or—"

Anger sizzled through Will like summer lightning. "You think she's a damned stripper?"

"No! No. Of course not. But . . . maybe I've seen her . . . somewhere."

"She's not from around here."

"How do you know?"

"Her voice. It's . . ." He tried to think of something that wouldn't sound idiotic. But there was nothing. "It's like music."

"A naked chick with an accent?" Dean sounded dreamy, and maybe pre-orgasmic.

Will leveled a glare. "I think it's time for you to leave."

Dean opened his mouth but then just took another swig of vodka and nodded. "Yeah, I suppose you're right. I should leave you alone. You got things to work out." He turned toward the door, shook his head. "Emily's going to have a shit fit."

Try as he might, William couldn't seem to recall his fiancée's face. He was pretty sure she had one. "She already has."

Dean stopped dead in his tracks, turned back, croaked a laugh. "You told her?"

"She was here."

"You're shittin' me"

"I wish I were."

"She was *here* here?"

Will slammed his gaze to the bedroom, but the door remained closed. "Keep your damned voice down."

"And you still kept the girl in your house?"

William winced.

"Ballsy! Dumber than hell. But ballsy." Dean chuckled, then jiggled a little. "Hey, can I use your can quick? Got half a quart of vodka on top of a gallon of coffee. Bladder's about to erupt," he added, but William had already turned toward the bedroom. She was in there. So close.

"Buddy?"

"Yeah, sure. Just be quiet."

Dean slapped the bottle into the other's hand and hurried toward the bathroom.

Outside, something scraped against the house. What was it? Or *who*? Nerves taut, William paced through the living room and stepped outside, but a cursory glance showed nothing. Shutting the door behind him, he pattered onto the sidewalk and looked around. All seemed quiet. Only the ethereal girl in his bed was strange.

Going back inside, he shut the door and stared at nothing in particular. He'd have to sleep on the couch. There were no other options, of course. He had some spare sheets in the bedroom, but when he glanced in that direction, he saw that the door was open.

"Fern?" he said, but there was no answer. Reality hit him like a jackhammer. *Abbot!* He stormed into the bedroom, heart pounding. And there was Dean, standing beside the mattress, staring through the dimness at the girl.

William was about to curse, to call names, to toss the other out on his ass, but the angel in the bed was all-consuming. Her silk-soft hair wisped in undulating waves around her body. Her lips were slightly parted as she slept and her lashes, lowered in repose, seemed somehow to be whispering to him.

"Holy hell," Dean said, and vaguely William remembered he wasn't alone with the girl.

She was lying on her side with one supple endless leg slightly bent. Her borrowed pajama top had worked up, showing the sweet curves where her thighs met her buttocks. Desire stormed through Will like a spring blizzard, but with it came something else. Something achingly akin to jealousy.

Reaching out, he snatched the crumpled blanket from the foot of the bed and whipped it over her golden legs. Then, grabbing Dean by the shirtfront, William dragged him into the hallway and pulled the door shut behind him.

"Holy hell," Dean muttered again, and turned his head robotically toward the bedroom.

"Go home," Will rasped, and nudged him toward the front door, hand still fisted in his shirt.

Dean stumbled a little but went nowhere. "Good God! She's . . . She's . . ." He shook his head. "What is she?"

"Get the hell out of here."

"An angel?"

"Keep your voice down."

"A mermaid?"

"Shut the hell up."

"A nymph?" Dean said, and then, for reasons Will would never quite understand, he drew his fist back and struck his best friend square in the nose.

Chapter

6

Avalina awoke with the dawn. Stretching, she drew in a breath, tasted the air on her tongue, and scowled. Things smelled strange. And felt strange. Coarse and . . . She glanced down and frowned at the blue-striped garment that covered her torso. Something was wrong, she thought, and then memories rushed in. Memories of a whisker-shadowed face, a tall form, hard and solid. A male. The thought came to her easily. He had held her against his body. Had felt warm and potent against her palms. She squirmed a little at the hot flow of feelings, then stopped, for her actions seemed odd, out of character. But what was her character? Surely 'twas to enjoy a male's touch. To take pleasure and give the same.

Searching her memory, she found scant information. Just a few scattered remnants of scents and sounds. Of colors and feelings. Greens and reds in a tumble of fragrances. The distant sigh of a morning lark's call.

Where was she? *Who* was she?

Rising from the bed, she crossed the room. The flooring felt scratchy beneath her bare toes as she stepped into the hall. One glance told her she was yet in the strange abode in which she had found herself the previous night. The abode with the lovely male with the lovely voice and the lovely . . .

She stopped, for he was there, sprawled across the settee, his right foot draped diagonally over the edge, his left leg bent beneath him. One arm dangled over a cushion while the other was stretched above his head. He lay on his back, but his eyes were closed and his chest was almost entirely naked. And strangely, unmistakably beautiful. She smiled and took a step toward him.

William moaned and shifted, warmed by his improbable dark velvet dreams. The angel princess was kissing him, lips like plum wine, hands like music, touching his face with delicate fingers, caressing his chest with tender strokes. He tried to reach for her, but his left arm felt strangely drowsy. He jerked at it. Feelings tingled irritably from his fingers to his shoulder, but he remained as he was. Waking grudgingly, he grimaced as he tried to change positions.

That's when memories stormed through him in wild waves. Memories of an angelic face and devilish body. Memories of an idiotic attempt to keep himself from the most luscious—

"Who did this?"

He opened his eyes with a snap and she was there, sitting inches away, lips slightly parted, tousled hair caressing his chest. He jerked, only to find that his left hand was tied to the couch.

"Hi." He cleared his clogged throat and sat up uncomfortably, feeling foolish and startled, and hopelessly hard as he tried to wrestle his shirt back over her chest. "Hello," he said.

She remained as she was, scowling a little, then reaching

out, touched his tied hand. Tilting his head back, he steeled himself against the feelings that crashed through him like thunder.

Her fingers trailed from his fingers to the rope as she shifted her worried gaze to his. "Why?" she asked.

"Oh . . ." He tried to breathe and forced a laugh. It sounded like the bray of an inebriated ass. "That. I just . . . I like to sleep that way." *What the hell,* he thought, and made another vain attempt at sanity. "Sometimes I . . ." Trying to shift upright without touching her, he reached over to untie the cord with his right hand, but it had pulled tight during the night. "Sometimes I sleepwalk."

She was still scowling at his foolishness. Maybe *he* was the one who was concussed. Or maybe it had been a stroke of genius to truss himself up like a Thanksgiving goose. At least he hadn't ravaged her during the night despite her unearthly appeal, her petal-soft skin, her flirtatious hair, her—

"I walk in my sleep," he explained, desperately fiddling with the rope. "And I didn't want to . . ." He glanced at her face and abruptly lost his train of thought, his breath, his bearings. Good God, she was beautiful, as fresh as the sunrise, as . . .

She laid her hand on his chest.

He actually gasped as he jerked his head back. But he was capable of little else, for he was frozen, mesmerized, breathless. Her hand felt like a whispered prayer against his skin, and then she was leaning in, lips parted.

Jailbait! The word burst inside his cranium like a squashed melon, and suddenly he was scrambling backward, arm still caught on the leg of the couch as he stumbled over the back of it.

She rose to her feet, devastatingly bewildered.

"Clothes!" he rasped. "You need clothes. I shouldn't be lying around all day when you don't have any . . ." He made the mistake of lowering his gaze to the edge of his pajama top. The damned lucky edge. The edge that ended just below her crotch. "Holy crap," he ended poorly, bent nearly double over his secured arm and working wildly at the knot. For a moment he entertained a rabid, fleeting thought of chewing off his arm, but she came around the corner of the couch, forcing him to move to the end of his leash. He held his breath as she bent, but she only touched her fingers to the bond. It fell away. He straightened and tried to run, but it was no use, for she had already taken his hand in hers and was smoothing it with her fingertips.

Hope flowed through him. Hope and happiness melded irrationally with hot need.

"Are you well?" she asked.

It took him a moment to find his voice, longer still to quell the demands from below. "Yes. Well. Quite well."

"Your hand, it does not hurt?" she asked, and kissed his knuckles with mind-numbing tenderness.

He jerked spasmodically, then found his senses with a jolt.

"No!" he croaked, and yanked his hand away. Feelings of bereft confusion gasped through him, but he held himself steady. "I'm fine! Good. Fine."

She stepped toward him. He stepped back, swallowing. "Have you . . . Have you remembered anything? Your name? How you got here?"

A smile tugged at the corners of her mouth. "I remember *you*," she said, and reached out.

But he was still backing away. "Good. Excellent. But listen . . . Fern, I have a lot of work to do today. Another day, another million." He laughed croakily. "So you're going to have to . . ." What? What was she going to have to do? Haunt his thoughts until he was so horny he was nothing but a greasy spot on the carpet? "You're going to have to . . . leave."

The world went silent.

She blinked. Her eyes looked unearthly bright. Was she going to cry? Dear God, what if she cried!

"I mean . . ." *Shit. Shit, shit, shit, shit, shit.* If she cried, he'd crumble, spewing apologies and promises like a TV evangelist caught flagrant delicto. "Not immediately. I'll get you some clothes and . . ." He glanced at her legs again. They didn't end. Ever. And her feet . . . "*More* clothes. Anyway . . . we'd better get going. Here." He rushed toward the bedroom, found his pajama bottoms with soaring, painful relief, and tossed them at her. "Put those on. I know they won't fit 'cuz you're so . . ." There were no words to describe her. No thoughts even. Just colors and sensations and dreams. "So . . . Holy crap! But . . . I know . . ." Bending, he untied the distal end of his tether and held it out to her, mind tumbling, words at an end. "Here," he said finally, tone defeated and hushed. "You can use this for a belt."

But Wal-Mart seemed to be the only store open at 7:00 A.M. that offered clothing. Stupid retailers. What did they expect a man to do when he found a naked angel princess with plum-wine lips and musical fingers sprawled on his bathroom floor?

An angel princess who looked adorable even in his ridiculously large pajamas and mismatched tube socks. He'd been unable to find shoes that would fit, and barefoot was out of the earth-shattering question. So she padded across the parking lot beside him, wide-eyed and half-smiling, motioning now and then to a car or a tree or a sign, and stopping dead in her tracks as a jogger trotted by with a terrier on a red nylon leash.

Her eyes were as bright as candlelit amethyst. "What?" she asked, pointing.

It took him a moment to make sense of her question, for once again he was struck dumb by her gilded beauty, pulled under by her incomparable allure. But he had to get over it, accept it, move on. It was what he did. Another day . . . and all that crap. "Terrier," he said. "Airedale, I think."

She nodded. Her cheeks were dimpled, her eyes bright with intelligent interest. "Airedale," she repeated.

"Good. Very good." Maybe her memory was returning. Maybe soon they'd be discussing politics, the price of salami, and why, oh God why, he couldn't look at her without thinking of swimming naked beneath moon-drenched waterfalls. And where the hell did he get the word "moon-drenched" anyway?

She was still gazing after the jogging pair. "Never," she said, and shook her head in wonder.

"You've never seen an Airedale?" They were almost to the gaping maw of the mega-store. A trio of men had stopped dead in their tracks near the cart corral to watch her walk by. "Well . . ." He glared over his shoulder at them. Bastards. Hadn't they ever see an angel princess with plum-wine lips and musical hands before? "They're fairly rare, I think."

She trilled her fingers up the rough cornerstone of the building and seemed not to notice that two more men and a gangly teenager had stopped to stare. The kid's pimply jaw dropped like a bad investment and stayed there. Maybe it was because of the pajamas. Will glanced at her. Maybe not. His own forehead felt damp, his joints uncertain, but he soldiered on.

The glass doors slid open before them. Fern twitched and held back, but he urged her inside.

"What?" she asked, half-turning in awe.

"Automated door," he said. "They're activated by a sensor that's—"

"Door?" she said, and turned back toward it, but he curled a hand carefully around her arm and tugged her past the suddenly speechless greeter. He was as old as dirt and absolutely bald except for two hairs that grew from the exact center of his head, but he turned nevertheless and tottered after them.

"*Automated* door," Will said, and scowled at the small parade of men who seemed to be trailing behind.

"Door," she repeated.

The rest of the trip was equally surreal. As they roamed through the women's department, she touched most garments and smelled several. When she touched the tip of her inquisitive tongue to the sleeve of a cotton jacket, he almost passed out. But he didn't dare, for her fan club seemed to be expanding. There was not, he noticed with growling irritation, a woman in the entire transfixed troupe. In fact, there seemed to be an angry mob of females gathering near Housewares.

"Choose anything you like," he said, still eyeing the men and nodding toward a pair of boxy trousers. "Anything that will . . . ," he began, but she was already weaving her way through the racks, only to stop in the swimwear department. He scurried after, a human barrier between her and the restive pack of jackals.

His heart did a little trick beat as she touched a glittery bikini, but then her eyes lit and she lifted a long garment to her face, grazing it along one satin cheek.

"Comely," she said.

"Comely? Oh, pretty. Yes." And it was. Made of sheerest emerald gauze, it boasted a tiny frill at the plunging neckline and a flirty ruffle at the hem. The thought of it sliding off her sun-gold shoulders made his knees shudder like wind chimes.

"Mine?" she asked.

He swallowed hard and tried not to imagine her wearing it. Or not wearing it. "Ummm, well . . . ," he said, "I believe that particular garment was meant to be worn over swimwear. I don't think you can—"

"Swim." She dimpled shyly and suddenly the image of her floating on her back filled his head like lightning. She was skimming through velvet blue water, with the emerald gown translucent against her glorious skin and her hair flowing around her like molten gold, hiding and revealing, teasing and caressing.

His brain felt hot. "Well . . . ," he said. "Okay."

Still smiling, she flipped open the top button of his oversized shirt. One sparkling nipple shone like a harvest moon above the flannel. He gasped like a B-movie starlet, then grabbed her hands. Steeling himself against the lightning bolt of skin against skin, he ignored the glower of the man mob and stilled her movements. "Not here, though, honey. Not here. Just a minute."

By the time they had exited the store, he was as hard as a Roman candle, but he had managed to buy her three garments. The emerald gown plus a pair of khaki pants and a sweatshirt baggy enough to hide a Honda. They were, very probably, the ugliest clothes ever made.

"Well . . ." He started his car, glanced at his watch, failed to register the time, and tried not to think about her nipples or her legs or her kneecaps. "Listen." He turned onto Maplewood Street. "I had better get to work, so . . ."

Her stomach rumbled. She put a hand on it. He wanted rather desperately to do the same. To skim his fingers beneath his blessedly lucky pajamas, to feel her heart beat against his palm, to . . .

He closed his eyes for a second and remembered his mother. She would gladly have abandoned everything for love. In fact, she had. Had turned away from her parents, who had insisted that she give him up. Had nurtured him and laughed with him and taught him the meaning . . .

But what the hell was he talking about? He wasn't in love. He probably wasn't even in like. He was just in some sort of dazed lust.

Reaching into his back pocket, he pulled out his billfold. "Here. I'll give you a few dollars and you can get yourself some breakfast." He tugged out a pair of tens and handed them to her, but she only blinked. He drew them back. "Listen, Fern, I'd love to have breakfast with you, but I have a job . . . and a fiancée and . . ."

Her stomach rumbled again.

Thirty seconds later he had parked the car. A little bakery stood across from McClenna Park. Flower baskets hung dismally above round, rickety tables that cluttered the sidewalk.

The screen door squeaked as they stepped inside. Fern eyed the glass cases like a mischievous child, peering wide-eyed and adorable at the goodies while a few tendrils of lively gilt hair pressed to the display case as if admiring the apple fritters.

His mouth felt a little dry as he watched her, but he steeled himself. It was more difficult with some parts than with others. "Whatever you like," he said. He'd buy her a couple sweet rolls and drop her off at the police station. Fini. End of story.

She pointed to a selection.

"The turnover?"

She nodded and shrugged simultaneously.

He gave her order to the employee behind the counter, but Fern gasped and pointed again.

"We'll have a caramel roll, too," he told the employee. She was female. He was pretty sure because her mouth was pulled down like an angry boxer's as she stared at Fern. Thus far men had proven incapable of looking less than euphoric in her presence.

By the time they stepped out of the shop, Will had spent thirty-two dollars and twenty-seven cents, but she was smiling, making the world seem strangely, indescribably right.

But just then a Mercedes cruised past, zapping his mind back to reality. What was he thinking? He had plans, goals, strategies.

"I have to get to work," he said, forcing out the words. They felt hard and gritty against his teeth.

She was standing a few feet away, stroking the petals of a stunted, drooping blossom. And when she turned toward him, he saw that her eyes were as bright as meteors.

"What's wrong?" he asked. If she cried he'd topple like a prefabricated two-bedroom.

"*Pesolaania*," she said.

He stared, mesmerized by the musical stroke of her voice. "I thought they were petunias."

She looked thoughtful, immersed in the moment, then touched the next blossom. "*Reybannya*."

"Latin? Do you speak Latin?"

She shook her head, but the motion was vague.

"You know the names of the flowers, but you don't know your *own* name?"

She touched the other three baskets of blooms, then gave him a smile filled with hope and reached for the bag of goodies. He could do nothing but pull out a chair for her.

"Have a seat," he offered.

She did so. He set down a carton of milk, then glanced down the street toward his office. He wasn't absolutely positive, but he suspected there was some sort of activity he sometimes engaged in this time of day.

But her eyes were shiny, her dimples devastating, and he was weak.

"Eat," he said.

She looked up at him. Her hair had twined around the twisted metal back of the chair.

"Go ahead," he said, and, taking the opposite seat, reached into the bag to remove a fritter.

She followed suit, pulling out a turnover, and touched it delicately with the tip of her candy apple tongue. After that, there was nothing he could do but stare, transfixed, mesmerized. For she made every bite seem irresistible, every scent delectable. By the time she had finished, five rolls had been consumed. He was fairly certain he'd eaten none of them.

Across the street in McClenna Park, a piebald animal of uncertain heritage chased a Frisbee.

"Airedale," she gasped, and, grabbing his hand, lurched to her feet, leaving the thirty-seven-dollar bag behind.

Will paused for a second, glancing behind to grab the remainder of their breakfast, only to find that it was lost beneath a trailing profusion of petunias.

He staggered back a pace. "Holy crap! What happened?"

She blinked, uncertain.

"The flowers!" he said, motioning wildly. "What happened?"

"Oh. Better now," she said, and smiled.

Chapter

7

"Better?" Will stared at her. His brain felt swollen. Minutes before, the flowers had looked anemic and weather-worn. Now they were . . . taking over the table . . . possibly the universe. "Better? What—"

"Airedale," she said again, and tugged him across the street.

He tried to stop her, but she was unreasonably strong. Then again, she was fueled by a half a ton of sugar. So they stood in the park, watching a teenager toss the disc, watching the animal bound after. Will tried to focus on the weirdness of the exploding flowers behind him, but her hand felt like morning in his palm, and her laughter, when the spotted animal caught the toy, was somehow magical, a musical, silvery song of joy.

"Airedale . . . astounding," she crooned.

"Well . . ." He pulled himself from her eyes with a Herculean effort. "I don't think it's actually an Airedale."

She scowled up at him. He refrained from kissing her. But it hurt to do so.

"It's just a . . ." He shrugged and didn't tug her into his arms even though it seemed the sensible thing to do. "Dog."

"Dog?" Her eyes were shining like polished river stones, and a wayward finger of hair had blown up to caress his cheek. He didn't fall to his knees and proclaim his everlasting adoration.

"Surely you've seen dogs before," he said, and forced a chuckle, because it seemed more law-abiding than laying her down on the grass beneath their feet and kissing every inch of her mind-numbing body.

She shook her head, apple-cheeked and ridiculous in her borrowed pajamas, which he had somehow failed to make her change out of.

He scowled. "But dogs are everywhere. Where—" he began, but in that moment she kissed him.

His breath stopped. His heart raced, and suddenly there was no one, nothing. Only her with her jewel-bright eyes, her sweet-nectar laugh, and resistance was not only futile; it was downright stupid.

He moved closer, giving in, giving up. But suddenly she shrieked, jerked out of his arms, and darted behind him. It took his stuttering mind a moment to realize the kiss had ended, a moment longer to realize the dog had leapt into the air only inches from them. It stood now, Frisbee in its mouth, watching them inquisitively, head cocked, one ear bent, crazy, off-colored eyes curious.

"Fern . . ." Will turned toward the girl, but she was clutching his biceps in a tight-fingered grasp. "It's just a dog."

She peeked past his arm.

"A pet. It won't hurt you," he promised, but her eyes were unbelieving.

William glanced at the teenager who was loping toward them in a disjointed manner. In a moment he ordered the dog to sit. It dropped to its haunches, tongue lolling, Frisbee atop its spotted paws.

Still, it took a few minutes to convince Fern to ease out

into the open, longer still for her to dare to touch the animal. And when it lapped its tongue across her fingers, she giggled with ringing happiness.

Five minutes later, when they'd left the poor besotted boy peering after them, forgetful of his dog, Will sat in his car and stared across the armrest at her. The windows were open. The air felt balmy against his skin. She had pressed a palm flat against the gray fabric of the passenger seat.

"Soft," she said, and tilted her head at him. "Alive?"

"Fern." He looked into her face, feeling breathless and hopeful and strangely melancholy. "I have to take you to the hospital. To get help."

She scowled. "Something is amiss?"

He would have laughed if he'd had enough saliva left for the job. "Honey," he said, and headed east, trying to remember his mission, "you don't remember dogs."

She glanced toward the retreating animal and smiled. "Alive," she said.

"Lots of things are," he countered, but she scowled, staring out the window.

"Many are not."

He followed her gaze, slanting his attention up at the bulky gray buildings that blocked out the sky.

"Where is the green?" she asked.

"Green?"

He turned onto Lakeside, heading north, but when he glanced back at her, his breath knotted in his throat; her eyes were dark with a sorrow so deep it ground at the very heart of him.

But that was ridiculous. He shook his head, looked forward again, and tried to be sane, tried to think, and realized, quite suddenly, that he was a fool. "Tell me the truth," he said, voice quiet against the humming traffic.

He could feel her attention turn toward him but dared not look at her.

"You had me going," he admitted, and slowed to follow the line of vehicles just creeping through a green light. "You're a hell of an actress, but who are you really?"

"I . . . ," she began, but suddenly she pointed excitedly to their right. The glistening width of Lake Washington sparkled like diamonds beyond Baker Beach.

"I know. Life," Will said, and, feeling the dark burn of cynicism, followed the accelerating line of cars, but a scratch of noise distracted him. He snapped his gaze to the side just in time to see the girl scramble out the window and onto the street.

"Fern!" he gasped, but she was already on her feet. The pickup in the right lane honked its horn and screeched to a halt. She skittered around its bumper and disappeared. "Fern!" he yelled again, but a dozen horns were blaring now. He slammed on the accelerator, careened into the first left turn, and jerked into the nearest parking space he could find.

In a minute he was streaking down the sidewalk, lurching past trucks with ear-shattering horns and galloping toward the beach. By the time he found her he felt queasy. His hands shook and his voice was raspy.

"Fern."

She glanced up at the sound of his voice, her expression far away. Her feet were bare, he noticed, her mother-of-pearl toes drinking in the lapping waves.

"Why does she call you William?" she asked.

"Fern . . ." His joints felt stiff with residual terror. "You could have been killed."

She canted her head. A silky wisp of hair brushed with tantalizing softness against his wrist.

"You do not feel like a William."

He stared at her for a moment, trying to remember who he was, who he had been, who he should be. But it was too immense. Too convoluted. "I just . . . You scared the—"

"Not here," she said, and touched her palm to her own chest. "Here you feel caring."

The world dropped away. There was only her. Her in her sparkling glory. "Who are you?"

"Here life is all."

"Where are you from?"

She scowled, looking inward, searching. "Somewhere you would like, I believe."

"I like it here," he said.

She shook her hand once, then slipped her hand into his, and suddenly his old life seemed strangely distant. Yet the world was remarkably clear. They walked along the beach while she pointed out shells and seabirds and trailing pieces of herbage that washed up on the sand. And every tiny bit of life seemed immeasurably fascinating.

"Emily . . . ," she began finally, and he glanced down at her. He had no idea what time it was. The sun was spent, no more than a golden memory, but he failed to care. His cell phone had rung several times, but eventually it had ceased. It was entirely possible that he had left it on the park bench where he had abandoned his shoes. "She does not cause you to smile."

He didn't argue. There was little point.

"I wish for your smile," she said. Pulling him to a halt, she stretched up on her toes, and cupped her palm against his cheek.

Light streamed into his soul. Her fingers felt like sunwarmed satin against his skin. She pulled her hand away, and suddenly her shirt was gone.

He growled something inarticulate. It may have been a protest against public nudity, though he doubted if even he was that foolish, for she was a dream. Her hair blew about her in adoring waves, caressing her shoulders, her breasts, her sharp-curved waist.

Her skin seemed to glow like moonlight, and when she

kissed him his mind soared, conjuring up a thousand erotic thoughts until he was mad with longing, but he tore away.

"I can't! Really. I just . . ." He was breathing hard. Possibly having a heart attack. He glanced along the shore. "People will—"

"No people," she said, and he realized she was right. The long stretch of beach was irrationally empty but for a leftover castle and a sandpiper stalking the silver-capped waves.

He turned back toward her and was immediately caught in her eyes, in her thoughts, in her boundless allure. "How old are you?" he whispered.

"I am old," she said, and touched his face. His erection jumped with desire.

"*How* old?" he asked, and forced a chuckle. He sounded certifiable. "Sixteen? Seventeen?" Good God, he should be in prison.

"Far older than you," she said, and skimmed her hand down his chest. He'd left his suit coat in the car, and somehow his shirt had fallen open.

"Right. Of course." He shuddered at the hot rush of potent feelings. "You can remember that you're aged, but you can't remember—"

But in that instant she touched his erection.

His head jerked back. Reality ceased to be.

"I feel it," she said, and, dropping to her knees, stretched out on the sand. "I am old like the oak."

The oversized pajama bottoms had disappeared and she was entirely naked. Moonlight gleamed on her skin, casting her in gold, the dip of her belly, the swell of her hips. Her hair framed her face, flowed over her moon-shadowed breasts. Desire shone hot and avid in her deep purple eyes.

And suddenly he was beside her, on his knees, so close he could feel her thoughts. "I'd like to believe," he breathed.

"You *do* believe. Come. It is time," she whispered, and suddenly, miraculously, he was as naked as she. Her hair wove about his back, tugging him closer. One sensuous leg draped over his, so they were hip-to-hip, heart-to-heart, and suddenly there were no choices.

He rolled onto his back, bearing her with him. The sand felt sugar-soft against his skin. He kissed her, slow and reverent, feeling the deep beat of her heart against his. She whispered something he failed to understand, but he shuddered at the hot feelings her words evoked. Her hands were velvet joy against his chest, against his belly. She arched into him like a frolicking dolphin, and when she slipped around him he closed his eyes. The world went still for an endless heartbeat, and then she stroked him, moving against him like a dream. Her body was limned by moonlight, her belly shadowed, the long, smooth length of her thighs like polished gold beneath his hands. Feelings swelled euphorically inside him, hope and need and yearning so great it felt like he would burst. She squeezed around him, gripping him harder, riding him toward the sky. Her hair wafted behind her in an unseen breeze, lapping him boldly. He sucked in a breath, and she smiled, riding faster, breath coming hard now, lips slightly parted. He tensed, pulsed, thrust until the moon tilted and exploded in the sky. The world went momentarily black. He dropped through the sand. She gasped a moan and fell with him, soft and sated against his chest.

It took a lifetime for him to come to his senses, longer still to realize she was asleep, nestled beside him like a long-legged kitten in the sand. Rising unsteadily, he slipped into his pants, then wrapped her in his shirt and lifted her into his arms. She seemed almost weightless, almost unreal, and as he trod across the sand toward the parking lot, he realized they had never left Baker Beach.

Chapter

8

Will carried her to his house and laid her gently on his bed. She slept like a toddler, like an angel. He watched her, scrubbed his face with his hand, then wandered into the kitchen.

What had he done? A lot of things. Possibly a lot of felonious things. A lot of felonious things he longed to do again. He fisted his hand and paced a circle around the table. She was probably a minor. Probably a foreigner. Probably some dignitary's cherished daughter who had fallen off a boat or . . .

Holy shit! He had had sex on a public beach. What the hell was wrong with him? He had to call it off. Get rid of her. Tell her immediately. He stormed into his bedroom to do just that, and stopped, staring, speechless, breathless.

"*Rantinn*," she breathed, and suddenly he was in her arms. They made love. Slowly this time, savoring every minute, filling, yearning, aching until they fell together into the satiny folds of sleep.

He awoke to broad daylight and she was there, watching him, amethyst eyes lit like a flame.

He reached up, touched her face, felt the jolt of desire

diffused by something strangely akin to love. "Who are you?" he whispered.

Her lips twitched merrily. Dimples winked past her kitten-soft waves of hair. "Who are *you*?"

She managed, somehow, to make every phrase sound exciting, stimulating, as unexpected as Christmas in June. He sat up. She was naked. The world was as it should be.

"My mother named me Elder," he said, and was surprised by his own words.

She put a hand to his chest and gazed into his eyes. "'Tis a good name."

"No." He shook his head and crushed her fingers in his hand, though if she had said the world was octagonal, it would have been difficult to disagree. "It was a foolish name. She was a foolish woman, worried more about a hundred inconsequential things than about her own son."

She studied him, eyes aglow with thoughts so clear he could almost see them. "Hence you took the name of William, for it is not foolish."

"It was strong with tradition, with practicality. And I was . . ." He lost his breath searching her eyes, remembering a hundred things he should have done differently. "I was weak."

"As was she," Fern murmured, watching his eyes. "But that does not mean that she loved the less."

And watching her, he believed. "What of you?" he murmured. "Do you love me?"

"This I think you know," she whispered, and he made love to her again. Once on the bed, once in the closet, and once on the counter between a jar of blue-ribbon huckleberry jam and two chipped glasses, because he could. Because she was irresistible.

Later, they sat cross-legged on the floor, where he fed her peanut butter from a spoon.

"Move in with me," he said.

"I believe . . ." She gazed into the distance for a moment, eyes serious, mouth strawberry red from kissing. "I think my home, it is in the woods."

"The woods! Fern! You're a genius," he said, and, grabbing the emerald gown, pulled it over her head. Perhaps he knew she should have worn something more substantial, but that would seem wrong, and in a minute they were in his car.

It was evening by the time they reached the woods that surrounded Sunshadow Glen. She looked like a small slice of heaven in the fading golden light. He had been here dozens of times, but it seemed different now. So different when seen with an angel in your arms. For that was where she was. He carried her through the grasping underbrush, unable to let her go. She was weightless and warm against his chest, face glowing in the waning light.

Below them, the river flowed midnight blue. Beneath its sheer banks, a chorus of amphibians tuned up. An owl called mournfully from a nearby conifer.

Slipping her hand behind his head, Fern kissed him, making him instantly dizzy with hope and desire.

"We'll build our house here," he murmured.

"Swim," she said, and pointed to the water.

"In there? Oh, no." He shook his head, loving her. "It's not safe."

Her brow furrowed, her eyes saddened. "Unsafe?"

"Chemicals, runoffs." He shrugged, strangely guilty.

"Life is good," she said, and, dropping to her feet, slipped from his arms.

"Wait," he said, but in that moment her fingers parted from his. A second later she dove.

There was nothing but a flash of green and gold, and then she was gone, slicing through the water like a clean blade.

"Fern!" he yelled, and frantically searched the surface,

but she was nowhere to be seen. He swore, then, ripping off his pants, dove after her. He hit the water like a box of rocks, then scrambled to the surface, screaming her name, but she was already there, inches away, bobbing effortlessly in the water and smiling.

"Life," she said.

"Holy shit, woman!" He was gasping, breathless with relief and worn terror. "You scared the hell out of me."

"Not bad."

"What?" His heart rate slowed to a gallop. "What's not bad?"

She motioned toward the world at large. "Life. Green." She shrugged, and her gilded tresses, ever playful, twined around his back. "You."

The touch of her hair was shockingly erotic. Soft and pliant, like a living thing that pulled him closer, drew him in, and suddenly they were inches apart, breathing the same air. Thinking the same lurid thoughts.

He touched her face, because he could not resist. "Where do you belong?" he breathed.

Their gazes met and melded.

"With you," she whispered, and the world simply ceased to be.

He awoke slowly. They were lying on a narrow spit of sand. She was pressed against his back, her hair a warm, soft blanket across his side, though one wayward lock had curled around his hardening desire. He rolled onto his back.

The sight of her struck him like a blow. Her body was almost covered with the long sweep of her locks, but here and there he could see the glowing ecstasy of her skin.

Her eyes opened slowly, like a sleepy cat's. "Good morningtide," she said, and stretched, unembarrassed, unashamed, every sinuous muscle taut, every sweeping hollow tempting.

He was immediately aching. Her eyes turned mischievous. Her hair tightened around him.

"Not again," he breathed. "You'll kill me."

But he was wrong. He didn't die, though it felt for a moment as if he had, as if he had succumbed to her charms and been lifted to heaven, as if he were floating into another realm where there was no such thing as mortgages and investments and other meaningless things. He pulled her closer, feeling the euphoria of her skin against his. Nothing mattered, nothing except the sweet feel of her against him, but suddenly voices sounded from the shore.

He darted his gaze to the bank, shielding her from their sight, but there was no need. Whoever was traveling through the woods passed on unaware that beauty itself lay nearly at their feet.

Still, Will waited several minutes until he was sure they were alone, then, tugging her along the slender trail of beach, found their clothes and pulled on his pants. She slipped into her gown and he did his best to resist touching her, lest he find he could never stop.

"Stay," she implored.

But he shook his head and struggled into his shirt as he crested the escarpment. Foliage grew in a lush, undulating line along the edge of the sharp declivity. "I can't stay, honey. I have to talk to Emily. Tell her what I've done." Her hair blew across his knuckles, caressing gently. "Tell her the wedding's off. That I . . ." He laughed. It sounded giddy, idiotic. "I don't even know who you are."

She smiled as she stepped into the grasping weeds. "I am yours," she said, and reached for him.

But he caught her wrist. "Oh, no. No, you don't." He

was grinning like a buffoon. *"Buffoon," where the hell did that word come from?* "Not this time. You can't distract me again. I brought you here . . ." He glanced about, gathering his wits. "To show you where I want to build our home." She touched his face. Passion burned through him, but he turned away, holding her hand, tugging her through the scrub. Plants reached up, snagging on their clothes, but he plowed through.

"Home?" She sounded disoriented. But so was he. Disoriented, shocked, dizzy with happiness.

He turned back, breath held, searching her face. Ferns brushed their legs, but he didn't notice.

"Will you marry me?" he asked.

She glanced down at the unfurling fronds and scowled.

He looked into her face, trying to read her thoughts. "I'll help you remember who you are. But it doesn't matter."

"Fern," she said.

He laughed. "I don't think your name is Fern. You look like a—"

"Avalina." She jerked her gaze to his, eyes as bright as flares.

"Avalina." He nodded and laughed, then dropped to one knee. "Avalina, will you marry me? I'll build you a mansion. Right here in this woods. We'll tear out the underbrush," he said, and knocked the ferns aside with one hand.

She reared back as if struck. "Tear out—"

"It's all scheduled for development. There'll be a road through here. And a row of houses. We'll keep a few of the trees."

"A few." She looked pale, shocked, devastated.

"We'll have the biggest house of all. With a pool and a fenced yard. You can have a dog. An Airedale if you like."

She was shaking her head, backing away.

He rose to his feet. "What's wrong?"

"You cannot. I—" She glanced about, stopped, frozen, eyes wide with horror. "Pinquil Fern."

"What?"

"I am entrusted to find it. To save it. To take it back to . . ." She fisted her hands, put them against her mouth.

"What are you talking about?"

"You must not tarnish this land," she breathed.

"Tarnish? What the hell's going on?"

"It is sacred." She grasped his wrist. "Do you not see? Look about."

But he didn't. He was looking at her, seeing her in a different light. Seeing her for the first time. "Who are you?"

She straightened, dropped her hand. "I am Avalina, friend of the wild things."

Silence filled the woods. Reality shifted, settled, cemented. "You're one of those damned tree huggers." His voice was a whisper of disbelief.

"I have come to save the fern."

"Save the fern!" He grabbed her arm. Rage spurred through him. "You lied to me."

"I did not—"

"Prostituted yourself for some worthless weed."

"It is not worthless. It is precious. It is invaluable. Do you not see? Do you not realize what you are about to lose?"

"Lose? Are you threatening me? Is that what this is all about? Blackmail?" He felt breathless, aching. "You're underage. Is that it? You think that'll ruin me?" He leaned in, gritted his teeth.

She cowered away. There was fear in her eyes, but he didn't care.

"I do not wish to ruin you. I . . ."

"Nothing ruins me," he snarled. "Nothing has; nothing will."

"You're hurting me."

"What'll it take?" he rasped.

She was pulling away, her hair wrapped tight about his wrist. "I do not understand—"

"What'll it take to keep you from going to the press?"

"Press?"

"To keep from telling what happened here?"

"I have no intention of telling—"

He grabbed her arms, shook her. "Don't lie to me."

She drew herself slowly to her full height, as regal as royalty, as solemn as a stone. "The fair folk do not lie."

He stared at her, breath coming hard. "Who are you?"

Her eyes held him for a small eternity, then, "I am but a memory," she said.

"What the hell does that mean?"

"Farewell, Elder," she said, and suddenly she began to glow with a sparkling light.

He stumbled back. A noise brushed him, a rustle of wind, and she was gone.

There was nothing in her place, nothing but an emerald dragonfly fluttering on a ribbon of wind.

Tears streamed down Avalina's face. The touch of the fern had returned her memory with a scorching jolt. She remembered everything, her character, her purpose, her home, and so she had been able to transform, to leave him.

She swiped the tears away with the back of her hand. She knew better than to trust mortals. Never had she compromised herself. Always she had felt naught but disdain for the foolish flower faeries with their preening, decadent ways, but when she had lost herself, she had become everything legend claimed her to be.

She was back now, however. She was back and she would not forget the betrayal. She would find the Pinquil, would take it back to Faery, would put this shame far behind her.

Or maybe . . . Maybe she should go to those he feared. Maybe she should tell what he had done. Find him trouble. Maybe then the land would be safe from him. Would be free.

Just as she was safe. As she was—

Something swung from the sky. Instinctively, she darted to the right, but in that instant pain struck her shoulder. She fell, spinning downward, spiraling into a mounded bed of leaves.

"Jay!" a voice boomed. Footsteps thundered against the earth. "What are you doing? You gotta be careful."

"But Max." The childish voice was close, reverberating in Avalina's ears. "I found something."

"There are lots of amazing things in Sunshadow, Jay." An immense shadow blocked the sun. Ava cowered backward. "Berries. Ferns. They don't know what they're about to lose. That's why we have to convince them to protect—"

The voice stopped. The shadow leaned closer.

"Balls!" Max puffed.

"Isn't it funny looking?"

"Grab the juice bottle."

The smaller form scrambled away.

"Empty it. Hurry now."

The sound of running water filled Avalina's head.

"Don't be scared. Don't be scared, little one," crooned the towering form. But Avalina *was* scared. Terrified. She crunched backward, but the huge hand descended, bearing the net around her. She fought with all her might, scratched and bit and scrambled, but the net tightened around her, suffocating her. "Hold up the jar, Jay. Hold it up!" he shrieked.

Suddenly she was lifted into the air, and just as suddenly

she was falling. She tried to gather her wits, to fly, to escape, but her senses were reeling. She hit the hard bottom with a jolt.

"Get the cover!" hissed the man, and then the sky thundered down, shaking the surface on which she lay. "Grab the bag," the voice echoed like a drum, and suddenly she was thrust into darkness, as black and deep and hopeless as a hobgoblin's hole.

Chapter

9

William drove straight downtown. He parked in the ramp he had used for the past fifteen years and walked the two blocks to the office. The two blocks during which his mind was usually filled with ideas and plans and schemes. But today there was nothing. Nothing but a wide, blank whiteboard without a single message.

"Andrea," he said, passing the reception desk. She opened her eyes wide and half rose to her feet as he passed by.

She blinked. "Good morning, sir," she said.

His office was silent. Colorless, still. He closed the door behind him. *Another day, another million,* he thought, and wondered what it meant. He sat down behind the desk.

Minutes passed like scattered dust motes. Fragments of conversations murmured politely in the hall, but he didn't try to decipher them, not until there were no options and the voices were crowding in on him.

". . . how nice to see you."

"Thank you." A familiar voice. Feminine. "Oh, what a lovely scarf. Is Mr. Timber in?"

"Yes, but I don't think—"

"That's nice. I'll only be a moment," said a voice, and then the door opened.

A woman stepped inside. Her name was Emily. He was pretty sure of that much. Her face was absolutely without expression. He wondered dully if he had ever found her attractive.

"Where the hell have you been?" Her voice was abrasive, her eyes flat.

"Listen, I'm pretty busy right now," he said, and, glancing down at a smattering of documents, forgot to read the words.

Striding toward the desk, she slammed her palms atop the polished mahogany. "You were with that little whore, weren't you?"

His mind felt sodden, saturated. "I don't think I know any whores."

"You were fucking that hippy whore, weren't you? Well, Daddy's not going to stand for it." Her voice was a deep, feral growl. "You can forget the deals. Forget—"

The door opened. Dean Abbot stepped inside, snapped his startled gaze to William's, and stared.

"Hey," Dean said.

"How are . . . things coming along?" Will asked, though, for the life of him, he couldn't think what those things might be.

"Things . . . well . . . umm . . . need a little work yet.

"Hey, Emily, how are you doing?" Dean asked.

She didn't answer but turned away.

"What have you been doing?" Will asked. It sounded like something he might have said in another life.

"It's been a little hectic," Dean said. "Listen, Emily, maybe Will and I could have a few minutes alone."

Will could feel her glare, but it bounced off him, deflecting into nothingness. "That's a good idea," she hissed.

"If you want to keep your pathetic little jobs, you'll talk some sense into him."

"Right. Thanks for your input," Dean said, and ushered her to the door with a hand at the small of her close-cinched waist.

In a minute he had returned. "Hey, buddy." Did his voice sound as if he were talking to a trauma victim? "What's up?"

William scowled and tried to remember who he was, who he might have been. Outside the broad expanse of his triple-paned windows, clouds were bubbling, gray, and bumpy. He wondered if it would rain. How the drops would feel on his skin. Where dragonflies went to sleep. "What do you mean?" he asked.

"Well . . ." Dean paused. "I'm no fashion critic or anything, but I think your shirt's on inside out."

Will scowled down at himself, mildly surprised.

"Is that . . . is that algae on your shoulder?"

"What if it is?" Will asked, and rose restlessly to his feet. Turning around the corner of his desk, he struck his toe on the thing's solid leg, and hobbled painfully onward.

"That a new look for you, buddy?"

"What?"

Going to the window, Dean glanced outside, looked both ways, then pulled the shades, and turned back toward the center of the room. "Correct me if I'm wrong, but don't you usually wear shoes to the office?"

William blinked, focused, and realized with sudden confusion that he was barefoot. It was then that his thoughts erupted with a thousand tumultuous memories. An ever-clear smile, bright mercurial laughter, an angel's touch, so soft and tender it rattled everything he'd ever known, ever believed. He stumbled backward, holding his head, and Dean grabbed his arm, directing him toward a chair.

"Sit down. Take it easy. Breathe deep."

William tried to do all three, but the images kept flying at him, untamed and breathtaking. There was a girl, so achingly beautiful it actually made his heart hurt. He put a hand to his chest.

"How the hell much did you drink?" Dean asked loudly, and, glancing toward the door, plopped into a nearby wheeled chair.

They'd made love in the water like sea otters, her hair dancing around them, binding them.

Dean pulled his gaze back to Will and scooted his chair up close. "It was the girl, wasn't it?" Dean whispered.

"Her eyes are purple."

"Well, it's hard to tell when you're higher than Christ on—"

"Her hair was like fingers," Will murmured.

Dean glanced toward the door again. "What's that?"

"Her hair . . ." He reached out, her image so real in his mind, he could almost touch her. "It could hold things."

"Things like—"

"My hand, my arm." He remembered the feel of it against his skin, as soft and heaven-bright as rain. He touched his own skin, feeling the rasp of his fingers against his wrist.

"Listen, buddy, let's get you home before old man Meier—"

"I don't think she's human," William said, and glanced up abruptly.

Dean jerked back, laughed nervously. "Listen, you're starting to sound just a little crazy," he said.

But Will grabbed his hand. "She appeared in my bathroom. Just appeared."

"She probably just slipped in."

"How?"

"I don't know. Maybe the guys at Imperial wanted to mess with your head and—"

"The flower!" His voice sounded dark and gritty to his own ears. He jerked to his feet. Dean lurched to his, staggering back. "She was in the flower. When I brought it to the house, she was inside."

"Yeah, that's probably it. Inside the flower." He was nodding emphatically. "Listen, buddy, I think you should go home before somebody calls the—"

"She can get really small." The world tumbled into silence. "The size of a paper clip. That's how she disappeared."

"Listen, buddy, we need to either sober you up or find you a shrink."

"No." Retrieving his suit coat from the back of his chair, he pulled it onto one arm, letting the rest dangle. "I need to find *her*," he said, and left the office.

Chapter

10

"Lucy! Finally!"

Max's voice wrenched Avalina from her somersaulting dreams. Her little world was stale and narrow, but the jar had been removed from the bag and set on some elevated surface. She rose to her knees, peering through the glass.

"What's wrong?" The woman who rushed into the room was small by mortal standards. Her hair was a dark, burnished brown, pushed back behind one ear. Her brow was furrowed, her voice scratchy. "Did something happen to Jay?"

"No. No. Everything's fine." Max shook his head, dreadlocks jostling.

"Then what's going on?" Fatigue had filtered into her tone. "Jeez, Max, you scared me half to death. Couldn't this—"

"Listen, Luce." His voice was as jittery as his hands had been. "We've found the answer to our prayers."

There was a pause, long and fragile. "What are you talking about?"

"Sunshadow Glen. We found a way to save it."

"Max. . . ." Her voice trailed off and she bent out of view, then reappeared, a patchy roan rabbit tucked under one arm. It tilted up its twitching nose and Lucy scowled, scratching distractedly beneath its jaw. Its left ear was ragged and curling at the end. One oversized hind foot jerked spasmodically with the rhythm of the woman's ministrations. "I really appreciate you taking care of Jay. Teaching him about nature and conservation and . . ." Her eyes were dark and troubled, her brow furrowed beneath a wayward fringe of shiny bangs. "You're a good man, Max, the best, but people don't care about ferns and katydids. You did everything you could, but it's time to face facts." She set her jaw, pursed dry, unpolished lips. "The glen's going to be developed. Maybe if we're lucky they'll save the little acreage by the bog."

"But there are things there," he said, and fisted veined, brownberry hands. His face was as weathered as a revered oak. "Magical things."

Lucy's expression broke for a moment, but she pulled the shroud of practicality around her. "The plants are precious. We're losing them faster than we can discover their potential. I know that, but I can't worry about it all the time. I'm tired, Max, and Jay needs new jeans. Stability. I can't waste all my time on Sunshadow."

"It's not a waste. Not—"

"I barely make enough to cover the rent."

"Then crash with me." He was animated suddenly, ancient eyes alight in his wind-weathered face. "You wouldn't have to pay day care no more. That place is just a kiddy prison anyhow. Jay and I'd have a great time. He can help me sketch the plants we—"

"I can't live with you, Max. You know that. It's bad enough I let Jay stay once a week. I can't allow him to become any more attached than he already is. He loves you like a . . ." Her voice trailed off. "When you leave, I'd— Anyway, listen." Her tone was brusque, businesslike. "I just came because I thought there was trouble. But

I've got to get some sleep. I promised to be in at seven and the bus—"

"It's a faerie," Max said, and Avalina closed her eyes in misery. It was bad enough that she had been captured, but it was unthinkable that she'd allowed her true identity to be revealed. And all because of William Timber. She hated him. *Hated* him, she told herself, and yet the shivery memory of his hands on her skin made her eyes well with tears. What was wrong with her? She was Fern Fey, proud, educated.

"What did you say?" The woman's voice sounded wispy, translucent.

"Jay and me, we caught a faerie."

The room fell numbly into silence. "Max," she said finally, "you promised."

"I'm not using, Luce. Swear to God. Here, come look," he said, and, turning, flipped a switch. Light burst alive. Desperate, Ava dropped back into a ball, squeezing her eyes closed, sheltering herself with her wings. The jar trembled as he lifted it from the table.

"Look," he said again, voice suddenly hushed.

The jar quivered, then steadied.

"Max, it's a bug."

"A bug! No." He tapped the glass. Noise echoed in Avalina's head, but she remained where she was, curled tight, unmoving. "Luce, I swear to you . . ." His voice dropped to a whisper. "She's a faerie. She's just sleeping."

"Max—"

"Perfect little legs. Little hands. Eyes like violets in—"

"This is crazy. I—"

"Crazy lucky!" His voice was breathy, awed. "Don't you see? People don't give a shit about plants. I know that now. They wouldn't care if they brought Christ himself back to life, but a faerie . . ."

"Max, listen to me. I want you to get help. I can't let Jay—"

"No! Look," he said, and tilted the jar closer to his chest. Avalina slid along the bottom of the glass, but she was ready, tensed, prepared. Noise grated through her very being as he unscrewed the cover. A draft of air curled in, and then she leapt, springing upward, wings unfurled, soaring toward freedom.

But the lid slammed down, barely missing her fingers. She hovered against the glass, gasping, terrified.

"Look! Look at her!" Max rasped, and Avalina zipped down to the bottom to hide beneath her wings once again. "Did you see her?"

There was a heartbeat of silence.

"What was that?" Lucy sounded shaken, fragile.

"It's a faerie." Max laughed, giddy. "She's a faerie."

"No. Max. It . . . It can't be."

"Then it's something else. Something we've never heard of before. Either way, Sunshadow wins. *Everyone* wins, even if they don't know it yet."

Elder sat in front of his pc, eyes gritty, hands shaky. He'd searched the woods for two days. Had called her name, had begged forgiveness, but she hadn't answered. So now he searched the Internet, dredging up any shred of information he could find.

Pinquil Fern, she'd said. She'd come to save the Pinquil Fern, but he could find no information about such a plant.

Behind him, the television droned. The noise grated on nerves already worn raw, but he dared not shut it off. Just in case. In case there was a report of someone finding a magical girl with purple eyes.

He'd contacted every hospital in the Pacific Northwest.

He had also called the police, but telling them he was missing a woman with purple eyes and grasping hair had gained him little credibility. So now he sat alone, memories burning holes in his mind.

Where was she? Was she safe? Was she angry? Did she hate him as he deserved to be hated? He was an idiot. Had been for years. Maybe his entire life. But no. He remembered back to his childhood, when he had believed in good, in right.

The phone rang. He glanced at the number displayed on the screen. Emily again. He'd answered the first time she'd called. Had answered and apologized. Said the wedding was off. Said he wasn't good enough for her. She'd cursed him until he'd hung up, then called back a half-dozen times. He hadn't responded. Not even when her father had pounded on his door, telling him he had lost the account and could very well be taken to court. Lawyers would become involved. But none of it mattered.

Avalina was out there somewhere. She wasn't human. He knew that, but somehow such an insignificant detail failed to matter. She was light and hope and—

". . . the glen slated to be developed."

Will jerked toward the television, skittering across the floor to turn up the volume and stare at the screen from inches away.

David Jackson, local news anchor, was standing, well dressed and perfectly groomed, in front of a stretching swath of nature. "Greenworld hasn't said what species they have found in the woods fondly referred to as Sunshadow Glen, the woods that so many have hoped to preserve, but the small yet tenacious environmental group does assert that it is a specimen so rare that there will no longer be any question of disrupting this untouched setting."

William's heart was pounding like a racehorse.

"Franklin Meier of Meier Conglomerated disagrees," said another talking head.

Meier's face appeared on-screen, confident, handsome, solidly reassuring. "Of course we will proceed with all due caution if an endangered species has truly been found, but so far we have no reason to believe that is the case. These environmental groups, while well-meaning, are not always credible sources."

"In retaliation, Max Braumberg, president of Greenworld, stated that Meier Conglomerated has one of the worst environmental records in recent history."

Braumberg's craggy, sun-hardened face appeared. It was surrounded by dreadlocks, creased by years, and showcased by a pair of half-crazy silver-shot eyes. "We're not going to allow Meier or any other greedy corporation to ruin what's left of one of Washington's few remaining pristine areas."

The anchor's face reappeared. "And in national news," he said, but Will was already back at his pc, slamming Max Braumberg into his system. He'd never met the man in person, but by 2:00 A.M. Will had found out all he could about the environmentalist/artist. Will paced the length of his living room, chafing to be off, to speak to Braumberg in person. Did he have her? Had he found Avalina? Or was this just another hopeless ploy like the medicinal plant he claimed to have found in the glen some months before? The plant that had turned out to be nothing more than a seldom-seen weed.

A few hours of sleepless tossing later, Will parked his car on Tay Street and hurried up the cracked walkway to Elmhurst Apartments. They were constructed of dirty bricks and dirtier stucco. He rang the bell for 418 and waited a lifetime for a response.

"Yeah." The voice that answered sounded grainy, tired.

"Max Braumberg?"

"Yeah."

"My name is Elder Mann. Can I speak to you for a minute?"

"That depends on what you want, man," he said, then chuckled rustily at his own wit.

Will fought for sanity. "I'd like to discuss the future of Sunshadow Glen."

There was a moment's hesitation before the buzzer rang.

Will took the stairs three at a time. By the time he reached the fourth floor, Max was already standing in his open doorway, baseball bat in hand, tattered-eared rabbit at his feet.

"What do you want?" he asked.

Will slowed his pace, tried to do the same with his heart. "Can I come in? Just for a few minutes?"

Braumberg narrowed his eyes, jerked up his chin. "You with Meier?"

"Who? No."

" 'Cuz I can't be bought. Meier knows that."

"I'm not trying to buy you," Will said. "I'm just a concerned citizen. Like you."

"Yeah?"

"It's terrible what they plan to do to the glen," he said, and suddenly he meant it. Felt it like an open wound in his soul.

"You a member of Greenworld?"

Will's mind raced. "No."

"Tomorrow's Branches?"

Where was she? Was she in his apartment right now? Was she safe? Was she afraid? "Since '06," he said.

"There's no such organization," Max growled, and, tightening his grip, pulled back the bat.

"Wait a minute. Wait. I'm sorry. Listen. I saw you on TV last night."

"Yeah?"

"And I think . . . I think I can help you."

"Help me how?"

His mind was racing. "I'm an entomologist. If you'll let me see your specimen, I can verify whether it's truly rare or—"

"An entomologist?"

"Yes."

"What makes you think I got an insect? The news clip didn't say."

Shit. "I assumed. It's unlikely to be a mammal."

"What about amphibians?"

Frustration burned him. "What?"

"We've lost more than a hundred kinds of frogs just in the last thirty years."

Will felt dizzy, sick. "Frogs?"

"Entomologist, my ass!" Braumberg snorted and shooed the rabbit back inside with his foot.

"Listen, I'm sorry. You're right," Will began, but Max was already closing the door. "I failed her," he rasped.

Braumberg peered out, crazy eyes narrowed. "I don't know what you're talking about."

Will's knees felt weak, his mind mushy with hope and love and a million emotions he'd never tried to catalog. That had seemed unimportant until this moment. "Her name's Avalina."

Braumberg looked wary, disturbed. "You're dippy, man. Get yourself—"

"I had forgotten about love."

There was a moment's hesitation, then: "You'd better get out of here before I call the cops."

"How it grabs your heart. How it makes you alive."

"I'm sorry," Braumberg said, and stepped back.

"She has purple eyes!" Will rasped.

"Balls," Max whispered.

"You have her, don't you?" He felt weak with hope, aged with longing. "Is she okay? Is she—"

"Timber!" a voice boomed. Will turned. Franklin Meier was storming down the hall toward him. "You bloody bastard!"

"You're with him?" Max hissed.

"No, I swear—," Will began, but the door had already closed. And suddenly he was swung around. He tried to turn back to plead with Braumberg, but Meier swung a fist, plowing him against the wall.

"So you're behind this damned hoax!" he snarled.

Will straightened, wiping blood from his mouth with the back of his hand, mind slowing, thoughts tumbling. "Yes," he said. "I'm behind it, but it's not a hoax. I've found a never-before-seen species."

"Yeah?" Meier's eyes were crafty. "What are you doing here then?"

"Braumberg had the connections to Greenworld. Immediate press."

"So Braumberg has the . . . thing?"

Will forced a gritty laugh. "Sure. I trust him with a billion-dollar discovery."

"You're lying. I don't believe you've become a damned tree hugger."

Will dabbed at the blood with the back of his wrist. "So the rumors are true; you're *not* as dumb as you look."

Meier narrowed his eyes, drew back a couple of inches, nodded. "You plan to make a profit off this."

Will smiled. Blood smear across his teeth.

"Then what's your price?"

"More than you can afford, Meier. Once Max there spreads the word, every do-gooder on the planet will be screaming, 'Preserve and conserve,' and I'll be a damned hero. An environmental genius. I've got people working up sketches for interactive nature displays round the clock. The government will seize the glen, and you'll be a laughingstock."

Meier swung again and Will let him. The blow caught Will across the jaw, knocked him back against the wall, but it was almost refreshing. Certainly deserved.

Chapter

11

Will waited in the darkness. He had left his car a few blocks back and crouched behind a leaning arborvitae. It was cold and damp, the air heavy with impending rain, but it didn't matter. Braumberg would be moving Avalina. He was sure of it. Maybe his own lies to Meier had bought the gangly tree hugger a little time, but even Braumberg wouldn't be idiotic enough to believe Meier and his goons would stay gone forever.

Which meant . . .

Something creaked in the night. William strained his eyes, watching the outline of the apartment building's back door, but it remained closed. Braumberg wouldn't risk the front door. Will was certain of that. At least he had been. He rubbed his eyes. Midnight had come and gone hours before, but he wasn't tired. Guilt and fear and raging hope kept him awake, alert, but the tinny sound of metal against metal scraped his consciousness, and suddenly he knew! The fire escape! Max had exited by another route.

Racing around the building, Will was just fast enough to see a bike disappearing into the gloom.

The Pontiac seemed ungodly loud as it gunned away

from the curb, but within minutes it was clear that Max was gone. Will dropped his head against the steering wheel. Defeat crushed him, but in his mind an angel princess laughed as she touched a drooping petal and danced down a winding path. The river sighed. The maples whispered, and . . .

He snapped his head upright. If Max wanted to save the glen, he needed the public to believe he had found her there. What better way than to film her in that habitat?

In an instant, Will was roaring through red lights and careening onto I-5. A bumpy exit brought him to an abused blacktop just south of the glen, but he dared drive no farther and risk being heard.

Rattling down a ditch into a blueberry field, he killed the engine and stepped out of the car. Furtive night sounds fluttered around him, and in a moment he was running, scrambling through the tenacious foliage toward the woods. Beneath the towering branches, his breathing sounded hoarse and heavy, but he kept climbing until he came to an opening in the trees. Below him, Sunshadow lay quiet and dark. No moon illuminated the little valley tonight. Nothing disturbed its waiting tranquility. All was dark. He scanned the hollowed area until his eyes burned. Hope dwindled and sputtered, leaving a bitter taste, a terrible agony.

And then, just to the east! A flicker of light! So faint it seemed an illusion, but Elder was already gone, scrambling downhill, toward hope, toward redemption.

"Braumberg!" a voice hissed from the darkness.

Max's heart was beating like a hammer against his ribs. He was hunkered down in the shadow of a towering alder, breath held, hands unsteady. The faerie was hidden beneath a mound of old leaves three hundred strides due south at the base of a rare widespread maple. She was still in her jar, tucked into an earth-toned drawstring bag. Emerald, he called her, because of the color of her wings. He hoped to God she was all right. He'd given her a tiny piece of organic fruit every day, but she hadn't eaten. Neither had she spoken, though he was certain she could. So certain, in fact, that he had talked to her for endless hours. Apologies, explanations, stories. He'd told her of his failed attempts to protect the glen, of the burning addictions that kept him sleepless and jittery, of Lucy and Jay, the only reasons he could think of to fight those addictions day after day. But the tiny creature had made no response. Sometimes she had watched him with morning-bright eyes. But in the past few days she rarely moved. Once the world knew, though, once they believed, Sunshadow Glen would be safe and she could go free.

"Who's there?" he asked, and rose unsteadily to his feet only yards from the newcomer.

"Christ!" rasped the other, and started. "You scared the shit out of me."

Max tried to see through the darkness, but the moon had abandoned him. "You Jackson? From television?"

"Of course I'm Jackson. Who else would come all this way on a damned bike in the middle of— Hey!" He shielded his eyes from the beam of light Max shone in his face. "Christ, are you nuts?"

He didn't answer. It was a definite possibility. "You come alone?"

Jackson snorted. "Nobody took me up on my offer to exercise this time of night."

Max turned off the torch and shifted from foot to foot. He was tired and he was scared. Meier was no one to fool with and Max was no hero, but he'd told Jay he'd find a way to save the glen. He'd given his word. Sometimes that was all a man had. "You think this is a joke?" he asked.

His voice sounded wheezy in the still darkness, not at all like he'd hoped.

The other was silent for a moment, then: "You tell me what it is, Braumberg," His tone had lost a little of its TV pomposity. "Why'd I have to come all the way out here in the middle of the night?"

"'Cuz folks gotta see the magic of the real thing. Where I found her, where she lived. Then maybe they'll understand," Max breathed.

"*Her?*" Jackson asked. Maybe he was trying to sound jaded and worldly, but there was an airlessness to his tone.

"Swear you came alone," Max demanded, jumpy and afraid and so hopeful it made his heart quiver in his chest. "Swear it."

"I came alone."

"Swear you'll tell this story just like it happened. You'll take the pictures and tell the story."

"Why do you think I came here?"

"Swear to God," he ordered.

"Okay, I swear it."

Max fisted his hands to stop the quiver, then nodded. "Wait here."

A splinter of lightning crackled in the ebony sky.

"Where you going?" Jackson asked. His tone sounded spooked, and Max smiled. *Urbanite.* He didn't know the glory of a moonless night, didn't understand the awe and grandeur of *life,* but maybe he would. Maybe this would help. Maybe, for the first time in his life, Max Braumberg would make a difference.

Once he turned on his flashlight, he found the bag easily. It was right where he had left it. Rapidly switching off the torch, he extracted the jar and stared through the glass at Emerald. She was up, standing erect, her palms flat against the glass. She knew she was home. He was sure of it. "I'm sorry," he said. "I'd like to let you go. You know I would. But I can't. The glen. It's where I met my Luce. Where—"

"Turn around, nut job," a voice hissed from the darkness.

Max froze, breath held, and then he turned. A shape stepped out from behind a tree. Lightning split the sky. It illuminated the world for just an instant, but Max had seen enough movies to recognize the metallic gleam of gunmetal.

"What do you want?" he asked, and found he was too frightened to move, nearly too frightened to speak.

"Hand it over."

"What?" He eased the jar behind him, hands already slick with panic. "What are you talking about?"

The shadow took a step toward him. "Meier said you were an idiot. Give me the damn thing."

"I swear I—," he began. His garbled mind was trying to figure a way out of this, some clever means of extracting himself and saving the day, but blinding fear numbed his brain. Panic filled him like a toxin, and suddenly he bolted, lurching through the foliage brush like a drunken deer.

Behind him, the goon cursed, but in a second he was thundering after.

"Run, Braumberg!" shouted a voice.

Max slammed his gaze to the left. A figure was racing toward them from the trees. Lightning flared, illuminating Timber's face for an instant.

Hope screamed through Max. He surged forward on a burst of adrenaline. From behind came an *oof* of pain as bodies tumbled to the ground. But he didn't quit running. Emerald was safe. The jar was still in his hand. He cradled it against his body as he careened through brambles and berries, but suddenly there was a rush of footsteps. Something struck him from the side, bowling him over. He crashed to his hip, holding the jar aloft, praying and cursing.

"Fucking tree huggers," growled his attacker, and, lurching to his feet, kicked Max in the ribs. Pain exploded like fireworks. He doubled up, holding the fairy close for protection. "Give it here," ordered the other.

Max's ribs were broken. He was sure of it, felt it in the nauseous pit of his stomach. "I don't know what you're talking about." His voice was guttural, unrecognizable.

"Hand it over," growled the thug, and kicked again.

Darkness slammed toward Max, but he squeezed it back, holding on.

From the left, he could hear heavy footsteps running toward them. Hope soared for a moment, but the voice from the darkness swamped it.

"You get him, Hank?"

"Yeah. Fucking asshole," wheezed the thug, and aimed another kick at Max. The blow caught him in the thigh.

"Let's finish this up. I lost my damn gun, and that other prick might wake up any minute."

Max held the jar as steady as he could and forced himself into a half-sitting position. His ribs burned like fire and his stomach roiled.

"The press," he gasped. "The press is here."

"What?" Hank's tone was a frightening meld of panic and anger. "You said this would be an easy job, Beef."

"That musta been the bastard I already took out."

"There better not be any goddamned press."

There was a rustle in the brush, then: "Put your gun down."

Max jerked his attention to the right, heart barely daring to beat. Timber was back. He was almost invisible in the darkness, but his voice was steady.

"Who the fuck are you?"

"I found your gun," Timber said.

"What the hell . . . ," Hank hissed.

"Shut your mouth," warned Beef.

Max glanced from one to the other, breath held, mind tumbling.

"Put down your weapon or I'll shoot you where you stand," Timber said.

"Okay. Okay," Hank said, but suddenly he jerked his hand up. Fire spat from his fingertips.

Timber staggered and fell, his face momentarily lit from a flash of lightning. Max scrambled to his feet, but he was yanked back down and slammed onto his stomach.

"We wasn't supposed to kill anyone!" rasped the man on Max's back.

"Just get the damned jar."

Max's captor was breathing like a Labrador, breath hot and hard against his neck.

"Hand it over or you'll be as dead as he is," Hank said.

"Please," Max pleaded, and raised his hands as best he could. Inside the jar, the fairy stood, arms stretched wide, violet eyes catching his.

The world slowed to a grind.

Courage. Courage now or never, Max thought, and, reaching over, twisted off the lid.

"Godspeed," he whispered.

There was a buzz of wings and a flash of light, and suddenly she whisked out of the jar, glowing like a candle in the air.

"Get it!" Beef ordered, and jolting off Max's back, made a swipe at her.

She zipped to the right.

Hank lunged toward her, pawing with a ham-sized palm.

"Go!" Max yelled, but she hummed in the air, glowing, hovering, just out of reach.

The thugs lurched toward her. She dipped and swirled, and suddenly they were chasing her, scrambling through the tangled foliage, the noise of their retreat diminishing steadily.

Max cradled his ribs, rose to his knees.

Behind him, there came a rusty rasp. He turned, remembering Timber. Scrambling to his feet, he staggered over and dropped back down.

Even in the darkness, he could see the dark stain seeping into the other's shirt. But his eyes were open, his teeth clenched.

"Shit, man. . . ." Max's hands were shaking. "Are you—"

"Is she safe?" Timber gritted.

"You've been shot. I gotta get you to—"

But the other reached up, grasped his collar, pulled him close. "Avalina!" His voice was raspy. "Is she safe?"

"I hope so, but I don't know. She—"

"Then go find her." Timber pushed at Max's chest. The movement was weak.

"Listen, I think you're hurt pretty bad. I—"

But suddenly a light winked in the air nearby. Max gasped. Timber dragged his gaze sideways. There was the hum of tiny wings, a faint popping, and like a scene from a third-rate fantasy, a woman appeared, squatting beside them, golden-haired, naked, so beautiful it hurt his soul.

"Ava," Timber rasped.

"Elder." She touched his face. She glowed gently, lighting the area with a golden flush. "You are wounded?"

"No." He gritted his teeth. "I'm fine. You have to get out of here. Go back to . . ." He paused, battling for breath. "Go back to where you came from."

She was silent for a second, then spoke again, voice like a song in the quiet meadow. "I find now that I have no wish to leave you."

"Go." His tone was grating, desperate. "Before they come back."

"They are busy with fireflies," she said.

"Fireflies . . ." His voice was weakening.

"By the swamp. Near the illbane," Max rasped.

"Pinquil Fern," she corrected, but didn't glance up.

"You found it," Timber murmured, and, chuckling, raised his hand to her face.

"It is precious," she said, and lifted her right hand. A small, humble sprig was clasped between her magical fingers. "The healer of faeries."

"Clever girl," he said. "Clever pixie."

"I am Fern Fey," she said, and one corner of his mouth quirked up in a smile.

"I would stay with you," she said, and for a moment his eyes lit with an illuminating hope. But a spasm shook him.

"No. I'm marrying Emily. You know that. Go! Before it's too late. Before—," he began, but his words staggered to a halt. His hand fell from her face.

"Elder. Elder! What is amiss?"

Max inched closer. "He's been shot."

"Shot?" She turned toward Max and for a moment he was speechless, struck dumb by the enormity of her presence.

Timber's breath rattled in his throat.

"I think he's dying," Max rasped. "I think—," he began, but just then a shot sounded, pinging into the dirt two yards from where they huddled in the grass.

Max jerked around. Shadows raced toward them.

"Emerald," he gasped, "you gotta go."

"Please," Timber moaned, voice feverish, hands rustling ineffectively. "Please go."

"Our time," she said, voice soft in the darkness. "It was special."

The ghost of a smile lifted the dying man's lips. "The best of my life. I would give anything . . ." He paused to breathe. "*Everything* to be with you."

Another shot ricocheted off a nearby tree.

Max covered his head, but the girl only leaned down, staring into her lover's eyes. Their gazes met and locked.

"*Rantinn*," she murmured. "The mate of my soul."

"Yes," he said.

She smiled, and then, reaching out slowly, she cupped his face with her hands and closed her eyes.

There was a moment of utter stillness, as if the world held its breath, and then, like a wayward whisper of thought, they were gone.

Max dropped back onto his rump, stunned, gasping. A moment later two lights flickered in the sky.

Hank and Beef stumbled to a halt beside him, wheezing, winded.

"Where the hell did they go?"

Max could only shake his head.

They turned on him, shoulders bunched.

"Tell me where—"

But suddenly a beam of light bobbled over the glen. Voices shouted from the distance.

The thugs cursed in unison, delayed one uncertain second, then fled, plowing through the lousewort.

Max watched them go. Listened to the shouts of the pursuing police. Watched the flashlight beams dance and twist toward him and away.

"You okay?" David Jackson's voice was breathy as he rose from his hiding spot behind a fallen conifer.

Max turned toward him in a daze. "How long have you been there?"

"Long enough," said the other, and, raising his camera, snapped off a shot.

The flash lit the meadow, and Max gaped. "I thought that was lightning."

"Lucky for me, so did they," said Jackson, and while Max laughed, two tiny lights blinked and disappeared.

Epilogue

It was a strange ceremony. The bride was barefoot and laughing. The best man was a six-year-old who couldn't stop grinning, and the ring bearer was a scraggly bunny with a tattered ear and a collar of daisies that it would nibble at indiscriminately.

Evening stole gently over Sunshadow Glen. A white-breasted horned lark sang as it soared overhead. Hopeful chorus frogs chirped for their mates.

It had been more than a year since the faerie photographs had been published in the *Seattle Times*. Shortly thereafter the story had exploded across a startled planet. For the first few months, the world was abuzz with the news. Police had been called in to quarantine the glen, but folks still snuck in to comb the woods for faeries. Finally, though, it was the damp Pacific cold that drove them back, that made them lethargic, that caused them to return to the comfort of their homes.

But not everyone forgot. Not the publisher from Intelligence Press who offered a sizable fortune for the story. Enough of a fortune, in fact, to allow Max to buy Sunshadow Glen from Meier, who needed cash for litigation. Jackson's photographs had not been stellar, but they were good enough to identify Hank and Beef. Good enough to get them indicted. Good enough to make them turn with mind-boggling speed on their boss.

"We did it," Max said, and smiled into Lucy's laughing eyes. Tiny wooly daisies circled her head, looking like a delicate halo against her dark, short-cropped hair.

"*You* did it," she corrected.

Fireflies blinked to life, echoing their joy, and in the branches of a red cedar far above, Elder kissed Avalina with a passion that would never dim.

Dust Me, Baby, One More Time

BY MICHELE HAUF

Chapter

1

Reverie, MR (Mortal Realm)

Sidney Tooth snuggled her head between the Spider-Man flannel sheet and the heavy weight of a goosedown pillow. Wriggling, she squirmed her body into the tight squeeze until only her ankles felt the humid breeze of a summertime snore.

Shuffling about with her hands, she mined for the prize—a lateral incisor. A tooth. And, pray, a brushed one, at that.

This was the last stop for the night. She couldn't wait to get home and watch TiVo'd *Sex and the City*. Sidney wasn't into fashion or girlfriend chats. But the sex? She didn't have a lot of options here in the Mortal Realm, so for now, Mr. Big was it. Too bad he belonged to Carrie.

Who did a faery have to do to get her own sheet-twisting orgasm?

Sidney knew the answer to that one, but she wasn't willing to sacrifice her night job in the MR for sex. She had just bought a house here in Reverie, beyond the willow park. She was an official member of the community—so long as she continued to toe the line.

Beneath her a flat-faced flannel superhero gave her the glad eye.

"Sorry, Spidey, not here for a swing on your web. I'm working. Besides, I prefer men who don't wear tights."

A crinkle in the dark depths alerted her. Her fingers slid over something smooth yet untoothlike. A piece of notebook paper? The frayed ends, ripped from around a spiral binder, tickled her nose.

"No tooth?" Sidney muttered between the smothering flannel. "This can't be good."

She clutched a corner of the paper and began to shimmy backward.

Jimmy Hanson had shown up as a TLFR on Sidney's ScryeTracker™ this evening. Hanson was an eight-year-old mortal male. A known drooler, occasional snorer. Sidney had retrieved two TLFRs from the boy previously. A TLFR was a Tooth Left For Retrieval.

Sidney had been born and raised a tooth faery, a fine and noble occupation. It was a family profession. Take the tooth and leave the cash. There were days she couldn't recall the names of some of her twenty siblings, but she never forgot a tooth.

The notepaper sprang free from beneath Jimmy's pillow. Sidney, clutching the end of it, sailed feet over head in a mid-air somersault. Her crinolined skirts ballooned. She flapped her wings to gain control and halt a dangerous trajectory.

Coming up straight to hover below the NASCAR ceiling fan, she shot a glance to the bed—snores and drool. The kid remained oblivious.

Wasn't as if he could see her anyway. When she was small—*not* her normal size—glamour naturally cloaked her from mortal eyes and made her appear but a shimmering light, much like a glow bug. The only living things that could see her were others of her kind.

There *were* certain mortal children who could *See* faeries. Sidney flew a wide path around them after an encounter last year, which had seen her fleeing for her life from a huge insect net. A kill jar reeking of deadly chemicals had glinted wickedly, wielded by a grimy kid hand.

Tucking the crinkled paper under an arm, Sidney buzzed out of Jimmy's bedroom and headed down a dark hallway toward a dim light.

In the kitchen, Sidney landed on the glossy black stovetop with a skid. Losing balance, she slid, wobbled, and finally crashed into the backboard control panel, cheek smashed to the digital *Bake* button.

"Another anal housewife," she sputtered. "Can't be satisfied with a clean surface, no, it's got to be slick as a river stone and flash back her perfectly coifed reflection."

Standing and casting a glance over her shoulder, Sidney ensured her awkward landing had gone unseen. If there were brownies lurking in the corners, they'd snicker gruffly and tell the entire realm of Faery, gossipmongers that they were.

Satisfied she was alone, Sidney read the note: *Dear toothe fairy. You doo not egzist. My mom says soo.*

The note fluttered to the black-and-gray-speckled stove surface. Standing there, utter shock prickling the back of her neck, Sidney couldn't find her voice. Her wings shivered. Her heart squeezed and missed a beat.

"What the—? Why would anyone—?"

It was a given that eventually children grew out of Belief. It was a necessity to her job. Else Sidney would be collecting wisdom teeth and dental crowns from the geriatric set. And she didn't even want to consider how much adults would expect to get paid for their teeth. Kids were cheap.

But this note.

She dropped her gaze across the words, scrawled in purple crayon. "I don't exist?"

Curling her fingers into a fist, Sidney stomped the stovetop. She tore the paper and then kicked the shreds to the floor.

"I do exist!"

Her bottom lip quivered. Erratic thoughts flooded her better senses.

"This better be the only one. If everyone starts thinking like Jimmy's mom, I'll be out of a job. I like my job. I *need* my job."

Without her job, she'd have to move back to Faery. Her entire career had been focused on following the rules and ensuring a permanent position here in the MR.

There was nothing for Sidney in Faery, except to take up pixie-pestering or something mundane and stupid like mushroom farming. In Faery she had been less than someone, lost amongst a sea of Tooth siblings, and always the last one to be considered when hand-me-downs were passed on or seconds at meals were passed around.

She liked the Mortal Realm. She liked television and TiVo, and 800-thread-count sheets, and hot showers with high-tech showerheads that put the rain to shame.

And the food. Cheetos and gooey Hawaiian pizza. And oh, did she love strawberries. Faery didn't have strawberries. She had no idea why not, but it was true. If she must claim an addiction, it was to the sweet red fruit bejeweled with crunchy minuscule seeds.

Here in the MR Sidney Tooth had a purpose. She held down two jobs and supported herself, just like the mortal career women she admired. And she was proud of that, if a little tired from working so much.

She had already sacrificed so much, including sheet twisting. But if she had to work twenty-four hours straight to remain in the MR, she would do so.

"I'm not giving up my strawberries. I refuse."

Even more, she knew the satisfaction of being needed was something she'd never find back in Faery.

"This is just . . . one kid. One mom. One pestiferous non-believer!"

Sweeping her wings to flight, Sidney sullenly fluttered through the kitchen.

She wondered what the non-believing mother had done with the tooth. Sidney got paid per tooth, though Faery currency was only good in Faery. Here in the Mortal Realm she had a mortgage to pay, which necessitated the day job at the Reverie library.

Flying a wide arc past the stainless-steel refrigerator, Sidney noticed the white flyer secured to the fridge door with a plastic Spider-Man magnet. She fluttered closer.

She read the print beneath a picture of a cartoon faery: *Ban the Tooth Fairy.* A big red *X* had been stamped across the faery's body. Sidney clutched a hand to her chest. *Reverie High School, Tuesday night. 7:00 P.M. Please attend to discuss a citywide ban on the Tooth Fairy. Refreshments will be served. Bring a treat to share.*

"'Ban the . . .'" The sickening thud of her racing heart made Sidney swallow back a wail. A gasping stutter followed. "Th-they want t-to run me out of Reverie?"

Below, a huge white cat pounced at the bottom of the fridge, dislodging a grocery shopping list and a magnet advertising Prozac. Cats could see faeries.

Sidney summoned the urge to kick feline butt. Catastrophe threatened her well-being. When facing dire consequences it never hurt to slap around a few cats.

Right. And that would prove what?

That to the cat nation she was the most dangerous faery around. Or maybe that she had to get her frustrations out by kicking fluff-balls? Or was it that she was sexually frustrated? Did lack of orgasm cause anger issues?

Her forehead slapped the flyer and she hung there, wings barely flapping. "Wait one mini mortal second. What am I doing? This has nothing to do with my sex life. That's another issue entirely."

A non-issue, actually. If she didn't have sex, how could it be issue-worthy?

Quirking a brow and stiffening her wings, Sidney mined the fortitude that had seen her through many a tough pickle (as well, many scrapes with housecats). "They can't ban me. I won't let them!"

Determination focusing her path, Sidney zoomed through the dark hallway toward Jimmy's room. The speed of flight moved her as if a beam of light. Anger fisted her fingers. She was upset. She was a little worried, actually.

And she wasn't looking where she was going.

Sidney slammed into a hard object that happened to be flying in the air at the same level as she. Stunned to a stop, she briefly hung in the air. Dust spumed about her— and not her own.

She got a look at the faery who'd just dusted her. Tall, blond, and sun-bronzed sexy. Then she dropped, wings snapping up like a malfunctioning propeller, and hit the floor snoring.

Chapter

2

The faery dropped like a rock. Dart Sand zoomed to the floor. His toes sank into the low-pile tan carpeting.

As usual, he'd dusted without trying.

"I've got to stop doing that."

What did a faery expect when she collided into another faery going mach speed? This one needed warning lights!

He leaned over the sleeping flight hazard and got an earful. She snored louder than Cooper Henderson, Reverie's resident carpenter.

Dart looked over the splay of limbs, wings, and polka dots. "Must be a tooth faery."

That was the only other faery who would be in a mortal's house at night. Besides brownies. Those sturdy-bodied clean freaks were a vicious lot. Dart still sported a scar on his ankle from the time he hadn't flown from the path of a troop of determined house brownies.

He hooked his hands akimbo and leaned in for closer inspection.

An indeterminate shade of brown hair scattered about the tooth faery's head in a non-style. Dart hadn't seen the color on any of his kind. Ever.

His own hair was golden. It could stun the eye for leagues away, and he always wore it the same color, even when wearing glamour.

One wing was folded behind her back, the other crooked out over her shoulder. The usual sheen a faery's wings gave off wasn't evident. Dart's wings were bright as chrome but twenty times more dazzling.

"She looks more mortal than faery," he mused over the fallen faery.

Dart had never discriminated against looks when dating. He liked females, young, old, tall, short, plain, or sexy. And . . . vacuous. He preferred them a little stupid or, rather, accepting. Man, did he need them to be accepting.

"Definitely thinks she's mortal," he decided of the faery. "Must spend a lot of time here in the MR."

Because he felt sure the red and white polka-dot skirt would give any faery a laughing fit. And what was with those sensible white shoes? Big silver buckles glinted and captured Dart's reflection. *Hmm . . .* He checked his hair. As he adjusted his glamour, the gold locks sprang into perfection.

As for his own mortal glamour, he preferred stylish suede pants and a stonewashed T-shirt. Organic, of course. A tight shirt stretched across his abs and pecs made all the faeries swoon. Yeah, even the males, but that didn't bother Dart. He was comfortable with his sexuality, and it was the females he preferred, all the way.

Faeries were all about pleasure and gratification, especially the personal kind. Too bad he couldn't seem to keep them beyond the first date.

Thing is, Dart wanted to get serious. He was ready to settle, to have a wife to come home to each morning after a long night of dusting. And a little one to train in the family profession of sandman. He'd call the boy Fleche, and he would be the first of a large brood.

The dream of family tormented, because the truth always smacked Dart back to reality.

"It's because you like the fluttery flower faeries. Easy on the eyes and fast to bed. You'll never find a woman with the patience to get to know the real Dart Sand. Patience?" He chuffed out a breath. "Look who's talking."

And then there were the rules of the Night Worker's Guild. Made it difficult to have a relationship in the MR beyond a stolen quickie. So patience wasn't even the issue.

Huffing out a sigh, Dart knelt over the snoring faery and stroked the hair from her face. Despite the awkward clothing and mortal-blah hair, her face was beautiful. Round and delicate, and the color of moonbeams. Her lips parted to emit a raucous snore—but they were red, plump lips, deserving of a kiss.

Dart leaned in, yet before getting lip-to-lip he noticed she smelled like strawberries. A mortal delicacy. Just like her? He had to find out. So he kissed her.

And it hurt.

Head swinging back and to the left, Dart yowled as the force of the punch knocked him off balance. He caught himself yet landed in a sprawl across the entrance to Jimmy's bedroom. "What in Turkish toadstools are you doing, woman?"

"Me?" She fluttered up to float before him, wings beating the air and fisted hands to her polka-dot hips. "You had your lips on mine."

"That *is* how a kiss generally works."

"A kiss? Do you always steal your pleasures from unconscious women? What did you do to me?" She swiped a hand over her eyes. A few particles of sand dust fell away. "Uggh! You're a sandman. You dusted me to sleep!"

"Sorry. Sometimes I can't control it."

Dart stood and brushed himself off. That was the first time he'd been punched for a kiss. "Nice polka dots."

She smacked an elbow into her palm, fist balled, serving him a nasty mortal gesture.

"Chill, tooth faery. Who put up your hackles? I'm just trying to make conversation."

Slapping her arms across her chest—a nicely abundant chest, Dart noticed—she tipped up her nose. "I don't see how my choice of attire should be a topic for rude remarks."

"I said the polka dots were nice."

"Facetiously."

Yeah, well. This wasn't going as it should. Time to rewind and start the conversation over.

"I'm Dart. Dart Sand."

He offered a hand to shake but guessed correctly it wouldn't be reciprocated. Smoothing the untouched palm down his abs, Dart stretched back his shoulders and puffed up his chest. "So, I've never run into you on rounds before. You do all of Reverie?"

"I *live* here. And I've never heard of you, either. Do you live in the MR?"

"Sort of."

"Care to expound?"

"Nope." What was there to say? That his libido always got him in trouble and reassigned before he could begin to consider settling in a town?

"I don't need your kind of trouble, Sand," she snapped.

"Tr-trouble? Who put the bee in your bonnet? And for that matter, where is your bonnet? Shouldn't mortal wannabes at least play the part?"

"Mortal?" Her left eyelid quivered. A stern thrust of spine drew her up stiffly, a fist slapped aside her hip.

Okay, so the mortal *comment might have been too much. Take it down a notch, Dart.*

"Dart Sand, eh?"

She gave him the once-over and, Dart noticed, lingered his muscles. Females never could look away.

He turned up his palm, which twisted his forearm and bulged the biceps tighter. "That's my name. What's yours, pretty lady?"

"You," she said pointedly, "are fraternizing with a fellow Night Worker, I'll have you know."

"Hey now, this doesn't need to get ugly."

Night Workers were not allowed to fraternize in the MR. That was a big no-no in the guild rule book. Three strikes and you're busted, back on a fast retrieval to Faery. Dart had tallied up a fair share of strikes, but the Sidhe Special Force goons hadn't caught him. Lately.

"And anyway, you're fraternizing, too, Miss Tooth."

"Not for long." She spun and gave him a flitter of her lackluster wings.

Again that strawberry scent touched Dart and he inhaled, drawing her into his being. By all that was green, she smelled great. Lickable.

"That's Sidney Tooth," she said over a shoulder.

"Can't wait to run into you again, Sidney!" he called.

She returned yet another rude gesture and was gone in a flit, buzzing through Jimmy's room toward the open window.

Dart couldn't help but smile. "Cranky faery."

And then he smiled even wider. "Pretty, though. Not so much cranky as a spitfire. Different from any of the faeries I've dated."

"Date" being his euphemism for "slept with."

The tooth faery wasn't his particular kind of woman.

She didn't seem at all accepting, and far removed from the stupid scale, to boot.

"I think you need another kiss, Sidney Tooth. No one turns down Dart Sand's kisses. And I'm not about to break that record."

Chapter

3

Exhausted after a night of unpleasant surprises, Sidney stomped into her bedroom. When not on night rounds, she assumed normal appearance, which was as close to mortal size, coloring, and shape as she could be. She lived in a mortal house—though redesigned by a Faery construction crew; it was iron-free and very spare with electronic devices. Sidney existed in this realm right alongside mortals. It took a lot of energy to be small, but her job was worth it.

Daylight appeared on the horizon, brighter than a cartoon sun on a cereal box. Her shift at the library started in half an hour.

The sandman's infuriating comment really twisted her wings the wrong way.

"I happen to like polka dots."

She smoothed her palms over the wide skirt poufed even wider thanks to the crinoline beneath. This outfit was her official tooth faery costume. Should a kid ever *See* her, this was exactly the image Sidney wished to portray: not overt, but homespun, very kid-friendly. It's what her mother wore, and Sidney had fond memories of catching a few moments of her mother's time when she was younger.

She shed the skirt and crinoline with a mental command and they dropped to the floor, followed by the white ruffled shirt.

"Mortal?" she muttered the sandman's other insult. Her left eyelid quivered. "Mortal?"

That one hurt. Just because she preferred the MR didn't mean she wanted to *be* mortal. A faery could hardly hold a mortal job without glamour to mask her wings.

"Where's that mirror?"

Shuffling a path through clothing strewn about the bedroom, Sidney mined her way to the corner of the room. Dragging away shirt after skirt after scarf after shawl finally revealed a floor-length mirror.

Standing there before the mirror in big-girl panties and a sensible bra gave Sidney a startle. Had it really been so long since she'd looked at herself in a mirror?

She tugged out the elastic waistband of the panties and then released it with a *snap.* Just because everyone else was wearing dental-floss underwear didn't mean she had to. It was a mortal fad. Faery women didn't subscribe to the foolish fashion. Did they?

But stones, this pair really did ride high. None of the women on *Sex and the City* would be caught dead in the style. The elasticized cotton completely covered her hips. Sidney had hips. She even had a waistline. But the last time she'd dressed to show off her waistline, mortal women had worn hip-huggers and tie-dyed blouses.

And what about this pitiful bra?

A faery could only summon wardrobe glamour after viewing the actual clothing in a magazine, catalog, or store or even on a person. Then it became a part of the faery's collection. Once worn, it could be removed by shucking the glamour. Or the faery could physically take off the clothing—as mortals did—and place it in a closet, for future use. Which Sidney preferred. It was easier when she could see everything she owned, as opposed to mentally tallying through her collection.

Turning to examine the side view of her body, she smoothed her hands down her ribs and over her hips. Glamour put a mortal costume to a faery, but it didn't change them physically (save to hide their wings and non-mortal hair colors). If mortals really looked, they might see the extra joint in a faery's thumb or the pointed tip of an ear.

"How dare he call me mortal."

And yet the costume screamed mortal.

A costume she felt comfortable wearing. The glamour protected her.

Crunching a fist about a wodge of drab brown hair, she blew out a sigh. "I do look mortal."

And what in toadstools are these clothes protecting you from?

"I've stopped caring," she decided.

As the middle child out of twenty-one siblings, she was accustomed to being overlooked. That's why she'd headed for the MR first opportunity and hadn't looked back.

Yet, over the decades, she had focused exclusively on following the rules. On holding a day job so she could buy a house.

Most Night Workers traveled from the Mortal Realm to Faery daily. Rare were those faeries who lived in the MR. Sidney enjoyed staying in one spot. No constant traveling from realm to realm for her. She had established Reverie as a base for over three mortal decades.

Faery had a tendency to reassign Night Workers yearly. Didn't want anyone getting too comfy and settling in. Unless they'd proven they were reliable and didn't rock the boat. As Sidney had done.

And yet, sometime over the years, Sidney had overlooked herself.

She had fulfilled a dream, establishing residence in the MR. And then she'd stopped dreaming.

"I don't need dreams. I'm happy. Mostly."

What dreams could top what she'd already accomplished? New car? Nah, faeries didn't do mortal vehicles; too much iron. Riches? She made enough at the library to support herself, and if she ever required home repairs, her tooth salary covered that. Fame? Get real. Love?

Hmm . . . Well, love was a good one but, unfortunately, unattainable here in the MR. There just weren't that many faery men to consider. And should she find a candidate? That no-fraternization rule loomed.

"He *was* a handsome sandman," she whispered.

A handsome sandman who'd packed a wallop of a kiss.

She'd woken herself up with her own snoring outside Jimmy's bedroom. And she'd looked right into a set of gorgeous smiling eyes. And pursed lips. He'd moved in for the kiss. And she had reacted.

Course, now that she thought on it, she had reacted a little slowly. No sense not accepting a freebie kiss when offered. Because the last time Sidney had had a kiss— toadstools, some hot sex—had been too long ago. Oh, she wasn't celibate. She had lovers. They came. They left. But she knew better than to begin a relationship. That would see her retrieved back to Faery in no time and branded a rule breaker. Not a mar she wanted on her sterling record.

Didn't matter. Of the few lovers she had known, none satisfied her. None understood her needs.

"I don't even understand my needs." Sidney sighed. "I'm set in my ways. I don't know *how* to let a man take care of me. But some sheet twisting would be"—another sigh—"splendid."

The Brigade of Mothers Against Ridiculous Beliefs met in room 101 at Reverie High School, which was also the middle school and the town bomb shelter. The school mascot was a possum, which looked very ratlike on all the school insignias and ultimately led to rival schools calling Reverie teams the Reverie Rodents.

Despite the moniker handicap, they were 10–0 so far in the season curling tournaments. Every year at least one senior went on to join the Olympic curling team.

While she waited for the meeting to be called to order, Sidney studied the glass trophy case. Apparently curling involved heavy disks of stone and brooms.

"That must be one clean playing field," she said.

Team pictures featured gawky, pimply teens sporting brooms and broad smiles. "That's Timmy Nelson and Ryan Olson and, hey, Brian Anderson. Nice canines on that kid."

Sidney knew the inner workings of the mouths in all of Reverie. She knew who was a good brusher and who could stand to use mouthwash. She could follow a child's growth from the loss of their first central incisor to the last yanked pre-molar. And she often checked in on those she suspected would need braces. (She had an ongoing wager with the tooth faery from the neighboring town. Each placed bets on the kids they suspected would need braces. She'd only lost once in thirty mortal years.)

"Ladies! Find a seat."

Uncomfortable standing amongst the gathered women, Sidney realized her contact with mortals was mostly with teenagers who hung at the library and children who poured off buses for field trips. Despite living in the MR for decades, she hadn't established close relationships with neighbors or any of the ladies in the community. So much time was spent simply working to survive.

Her future in the MR was at stake. She needed to be here.

Inhaling a breath of fortitude, Sidney shuffled into a

chair, which was attached to a desk with a contorted steel bar. She'd known better than to wear her costume amongst mortals, but she wondered now about the choice of plaid pants and ruffled shirt.

A few curious stares captured her attention. Linen suits and horn-rimmed glasses and smooth coifed hairstyles everywhere. All manicured and salon-prepared.

"What?" Sidney asked the pink cashmere number who boldly gave her the evil eye.

A rap on the chalkboard lured all eyes to the front of the room.

The blonde who directed the meeting must be a size 2 for the anorexic bones the fabric hung on. She pushed up thick black plastic-rimmed glasses and pursed her thin red lips.

"We all know what we're here for, ladies, so there's no reason to beat around the bush. I believe our banishing the Easter Bunny last year has proven very successful. Our children can now focus on the true meaning of Easter and we mothers aren't stuck dying eggs and hiding the damn things only to discover a rotting one a week later in the dog's bed."

The room agreed with nodding heads and a couple "you know its!"

So that's what happened to the Easter Bunny.

Sidney's fingers curled about the edge of the desk. What kind of power did these materialistic mortal primps wield? To take away the joy of the Easter Bunny because they didn't want the hassle of dying eggs?

"No more cheap stuffed bunnies, either," one of the mothers intoned. "I am so grateful."

"Not to mention that awful Easter chocolate. I've lost six pounds since the banishment."

"I hear you."

"All right, ladies," the head non-believer said, "so we are agreed the Tooth Fairy is another painfully tedious ritual none of our children should be subjected to. To actually believe there exists a tiny being who takes away their teeth and leaves behind money? How will our children ever learn to make their own money and grow up to be respectable Reverie citizens?"

Who put the meanie mojo on this chick?

"But the Tooth Fairy does—"

Head non-believer glared at the woman who had spoken up from the front row, stopping her declaration with a choke and a shrug. "Don't tell me you believe, Stella?" she defied with an intonation of evil incarnate.

"Er . . ." Stella glanced to her cohorts, who all looked down at the desktops.

It was obvious to Sidney the chick in front held some sort of mastery over them all. Sidney cleared her throat and shuffled on the chair.

The leader cast a keen eye her way. Her gaze oozed over Sidney like slug slime. The leader compressed her thin lips and pushed the humorless glasses up the bridge of her nose. "This doesn't work, people, unless we're all on board. Remember, Stella, you wanted the groundhog abolished last year because six more weeks of winter prolongs your SAD."

Stella nodded and bowed her head submissively.

"So, is it unanimous?" the leader gleefully chirped. "As of this day we banish the Tooth Fairy, and no further mention shall be made of it to the children. They will not receive cash payment for lost teeth, and instead we'll toss the nasty tooth out with the trash, as it should be."

Horrors!

"Ahem," Sidney tried. Loudly.

The entire room turned to look at her. She heard mutters:

"Who is that?" "I've seen her before. She works at the library peddling romances and how-to manuals," and, "Looks like someone's dotty aunt."

That last comment made Sidney's eyelid twitch. A dotty aunt?

Did dotty aunts kick feline butt? Could a dotty aunt work every night, 7:00 P.M. to 7:00 A.M., then put in another six to eight hours *peddling romances* without vacation? Why, she could teach the entire room a thing or two about the wonders of Belief, not to mention manners.

"Did you have a question?" the leader called. "You there, in the back with the . . . plaid? What was your name?"

Feeling as if the entire room stared icy shards into her forehead, Sidney shrugged down a little in the chair.

And then she straightened. *What's up, Sidney? You don't shrink from a challenge. Ever.* She wasn't about to let these primped bits of silk and cosmetic shellac abolish her livelihood.

"I'm, er . . ." She didn't have any kids. And the town was so small they would know if she made one up. "Right. I'm someone's, er . . . aunt."

Oh, the humility.

"I just think it's wrong," Sidney said. "Kids have so much to deal with nowadays. Homework and peer pressure and angry teachers and, er . . . divorcing parents."

Sidney angled the evil eye on leader chick, who appropriately stiffened.

"What's wrong with a little Belief? The tooth faery isn't hurting anyone." But she could so go toe-to-Manolo with Anorexia Divorsosa. "And besides, who made you queen of the town?"

"I beg your pardon?" If those lips stretched any tighter, they'd snap. "You do know the Tooth Fairy isn't real?"

"I, er . . ."

Pestiferous non-believers. Sidney felt sure a few of

them believed, but they were so cowed by the leader they didn't dare speak up. Hadn't the woman ever experienced the joy of shoving a lost tooth under her pillow, only to find a shiny coin there in the morning? "I know she's, er . . ." This was going to hurt. "The Tooth Faery isn't . . . real." *Ouch.* "Per se."

"You're an aunt," the woman sitting to Sidney's right said. "You don't get a vote. It's parents only, right?"

"Oh, I agree," was muttered from somewhere at the front of the classroom, and others mumbled their solidarity.

"So it's settled then," the leader called, avoiding eye contact with Sidney. "The Tooth Fairy does not exist! Meeting adjourned!"

Sidney opened her mouth to protest, but the room cleared out faster than a gang of candy dealers at a dental convention. She heard a few more mutters: "Do you see what she's wearing?" "Someone needs to send Auntie back to school so she can get a real job."

The hallway erupted in giggles.

Sidney caught her chin in hand. Sulking upon the desk, the room silent save for the thumps of her aching heart, she sighed loudly.

"I have a real job. *Had* a job until you creeps decided to take it away."

She toyed with the hem of her shirt. "So that's it? Good-bye, tooth faery?"

She tugged out her ScryeTracker™ from the waistband and switched it on. It registered all pickups for the evening. Usually a good dozen per night kept her busy.

The violet LED blinked to ready. The screen remained blank. Not a single TLFR.

Sidney laid her arms over the desk and put her head down. "I'm doomed."

Chapter

4

On her way home from the school, Sidney plodded through the park across the street from the Reverie library. With her glamour intact, all mortals would see her as their kind. It took a lot out of her to wear a full glamour. But it was a greater effort to drop what had become a comfortable costume.

But if her best efforts at glamour produced whispers about being a dotty aunt . . .

"I'm no one's aunt."

She stomped a yellow dandelion and marched through the emerald grass. Children never played in the park.

"Because their mothers banned fun," she grumbled.

"Hey, Sidney."

Pausing, Sidney noticed the portly man seated on a park bench, a box of Krispy Kremes coddled on his lap. Desiccated wings hung from his back. Ah. It was only Steve. The Faery.

"Hey, Steve the Faery." She stomped over and stood before him, hands to her hips. The scent of sugar and grease-laden dough clung to him like an aggressive after-shave. Steve didn't have to have a doughnut anywhere near him and he still smelled like them. It was all he ate. "How's life treating you?"

"Miserable."

"Of course."

Steve was Disenchanted.

Disenchantment to a faery was like cancer to a mortal. It drained the faery of *all* his or her glamour. No longer could he disguise himself from mortals. His wings would be clearly seen. Yet those wings would slowly deteriorate, until they hung lifeless at his back.

There was no returning to Faery, either.

It was heart-wrenching to look at a Disenchanted faery. And a cruel warning to Sidney never to forget her yearly vaccination—concerning which, the vaccination clinic was being held tomorrow.

Sidney had never asked Steve how he'd become Disenchanted. She respected his obvious misery.

"Let me ask you something, Steve the Faery."

He insisted on the moniker because Reverie citizens thought of Steve as the crazy old fat *mortal* guy who wore dimestore faery wings and fed pigeons doughnuts. Little did they know the wings were real and that Steve was forever trapped in a realm not his own. That would give any faery a dozen-doughnut-a-day habit.

"Ask me anything you like, Sidney."

"All right."

She swung her hips, twisting at the waist. While Steve the Faery was a friend, she'd never confided in him before. There were very few male faeries in the MR, which made it easier to follow the rules. If a girl wanted to scratch the itch, she could go back to Faery. Not that Steve lended to any scratch-worthy feelings.

And the last time she'd had a girlfriend was when Suzy Sprite had run away from Faery. Suzy had gotten involved with a band of spriggans, dark denizens of the Realm (sexy bad boys to a young sprite). It hadn't ended well.

Sidney burst out, "You like plaid?"

To judge his confused expression, he didn't immediately understand, but soon his pale gray eyes took in Sidney's dress. "Not really. It makes you look . . . erm . . ."

Sidney leaned in. "Fat?"

"I didn't say that."

"But you were thinking it."

"No, it makes you look mortal, is all." Steve the Faery cringed. He recovered by flipping open the top of the Krispy Kreme box. "Want a doughnut?"

"Mortal?" Fisting a hand in her palm, Sidney pounded it before the flinching faery. "Mortal, you say? Why, of all the—"

"You should really try the glazed chocolate ones. They're excellent. Don't ask me questions like that, Sidney. I know nothing about women and plaid. It would have been easier if you'd asked me if it made your butt look big."

"Oh, yeah?" She swerved a glance behind and over her shoulder. "Does it?"

Steve the Faery shrugged. "Not really."

Just so.

But mortal, eh? Why did every faery man think she looked mortal? No wonder she wasn't twisting the sheets lately. Rare was the faery who desired a mortal in his or her bed.

There was one true test to determine her decline. This would hurt.

"Would you . . . er . . . date me, Steve the Faery?"

The doughnut box went flying. Steve plunged to his knees before Sidney. His pitiful wings shivered. "Oh, yes, Sidney. You mean it? I clean up real nice. I'd bring flowers, and treat you to a real meal. Not just doughnuts. Promise. Can we do it tonight?"

Desperate expectation glittered in the Disenchanted faery's eyes.

Sidney's heart dropped to her gut with a splash. "Oh, crap!"

Sidney clocked in for a short morning shift at the library as a favor to a co-worker. Lisa was clocking out. The stylish young woman slung a black leather DKNY bag over a shoulder and shrugged when Sidney asked if there was anything that needed to be done.

"Is there ever anything?" Lisa was twenty-two and never let a shift pass without complaining of her bad luck to work at the *library,* where gorgeous single men never tread.

It was true. Single men did enter these hallowed walls, but they were usually bald, pudgy, or hidden behind Unabomber sunglasses.

"What's this pile?" Sidney picked up a children's picture book. The title made her cringe.

"Oh, Wayne had me pull all books about tooth fairies. Seems his wife has a thing against them. Weird chick. But then, all the old ladies in Reverie are just so . . ."

"Uptight?"

"You know it."

Sidney clutched the book to her chest. "They're really serious."

Lisa snapped her gum and drew her gaze down Sidney's figure. "Whatever. So that's an interesting ensemble, Sidney. Are you shopping the Goodwill again? I told you, you'll never catch a man until you snaz up your wardrobe. Please, go online. Shop Macy's, girlfriend. You'll thank me for it. Bye!"

Lisa sashayed out, leaving a cloud of choking cologne in her wake.

"At least I won't kill them with my smell." Sidney waved her hands to dispel the lingering odor.

A glance to the stack of children's books made her heart fall in her chest.

The afternoon dragged like a cinder block chained about a feline's neck. No one came in. Not even a wide-eyed kid searching for a little Belief.

Sidney stuffed the Tooth Fairy books in a box destined for the basement. To her right she caught her reflection in the floor-length mirror Wayne kept in the office.

Lisa was right. The purple paisley ruffled outfit was . . . "Too froufrou."

Her reflection in the mirror agreed with a pitiful shake of frizzy hair.

"Maybe I am out of touch with fashion. But that shouldn't make me look mortal."

The dilemma was that she had to look mortal to work her day job and walk about the community. Sidney could live with that. But to have learned how unattractive she'd become to her own kind?

This afternoon the vaccination clinic made a stop in Reverie. All Realm workers were required to be vaccinated against Disenchantment and iron sickness.

"Maybe I should change before I go. Put on something . . . sexy."

Sexy?

It wasn't as if she had to impress the giggling flower faeries who showed up in droves for the clinic. They were all vapid bits of petal and fluttering lashes. Sidney could never hope to compete with any of them. And why would she want to? Flowers were so common. Teeth were where it was at.

There would be myriad other faeries attending as well. House brownies, pixies, sprites, and faery godmothers. Perhaps a faery princess or two.

And a sandman.

"Dart Sand," she said, kind of whispery and soft.

Sidney stroked her lips.

That kiss . . . had not been so special. Or so her reflection tried to convince her with a firm nod. Could be his MO—crash into them, dust them sleepy, then lean in for a stolen kiss when they were groggy? A guy like that had to have a dozen girls on the hook.

He wasn't worth the effort.

"And have *you* made an effort lately, Sidney?"

No, she hadn't. Because she had been so focused on following the rules. As a result, she had a great house and respect from the Realm. But no sex life to speak of.

"Just because *relationships* are not allowed doesn't mean I can't have a quickie, right?"

And Sand was quickie-worthy.

"What are you thinking? He's . . . out of your league. He thinks you're too mortal!"

The only other viable option sat on a park bench.

Sidney blew out a huff. "He won't be there. And if he is, I'll probably show at a different time than he. I'll never see him again. And I don't care if I do."

That's what her mouth said, but her reflection blinked hopefully.

Chapter

5

The line at the vaccination clinic curled around the roller rink twice. The old rink had been purchased by the Realm decades earlier and served as the official meeting place for Faery events. The Realm owned old, nondescript structures like this across the mortal nation.

As faeries entered the building, they shed their glamours. This was one opportunity to relax and be with their ilk. Brownies stomped about, short and stout. Pixies flittered above everyone's heads, giggling and dusting indiscriminately. Sprites, tall and slender and a brilliant shade of fuchsia, danced in flowing silks.

Sidney kept up half her mortal glamour; it was too comfortable to completely release. But her wings swayed with the breeze that curled inside each time the auditorium doors opened and closed.

Flashing her credentials, displayed on her Scrye-Tracker™, to the receptionist, Sidney was then directed to the queue.

Disenchantment usually set in within a week to those faeries not vaccinated. And the vaccine was only available to the flower faeries and Night Workers, which made it difficult for other faeries to travel to the MR. The exclusive selection process kept the secret of Faery as it should be—a secret.

And woe to those who forgot their vaccinations. Steve the Faery being the example.

She was halfway through the line when she spied Dart Sand. A difficult figure to overlook. She'd bet if he were one of dozens of siblings, no one would ever occasionally forget to feed him.

Free of glamour, the sandman oozed a brilliance that reminded Sidney of moonlight on a humid midsummer night. His huge muscled shoulders must shine the world bright. And that hair. Golden deliciousness. Dart's wings beamed like chrome but were liquid and probably warm to the touch. That faery must literally glow in the dark. Which, now that she thought on it, must come in handy during his rounds.

He absently smoothed a hand across his abdomen. The motion pressed his shirt to the rigid washboard beneath. What it must be like to see him completely naked, glowing and proud.

Every part of Sidney softened and went melty. Her jaw fell slack, and she sighed.

The sound of her sigh stirred her from the silly reverie. "What?"

Caught drooling over the cookie jar.

Had anyone witnessed her delirious idiocy? Sidney cringed and hid behind the broad shoulders of a house brownie anxious to get her shot and march back to work.

And then Sidney grew a spine. "Just because he looks like the moon doesn't make him special."

Yet, try as she might, she couldn't keep her attention on the line. Her eyes strayed toward the sandman, surrounded by silly giglets whose wings fluttered nervously, and some suggestively.

"Blatant fan girls," she muttered.

Faeries were not inhibited like mortals. They expressed their desires as freely as other emotions. Yet Sidney felt compelled to roll her eyes as one of the flower faeries *accidentally* slipped a dress sleeve to expose a breast.

"You call that a breast?" she murmured tightly. "I've seen bigger ladybugs."

The sandman flexed an arm, displaying a muscle Sidney felt sure wasn't required to dust people to sleep at night. She preferred her men slender and aerodynamic, thank you very much. Yet when Dart turned his fist outward, the pectorals beneath his thin shirt bulged.

Much like Sidney's heart bulged. And then her face flushed, as if she'd just flown through a sauna. "Perhaps I've overlooked the value of brawn."

"What was that?" The house brownie shuffled her sack of cleaning tools flung over one broad shoulder and eyed Sidney. "Oh, you're staring, too?"

"Huh? At what? Staring? Nope."

"Oh, I saw you." The brownie cocked her head, though how, when she didn't seem to possess a visible neck, proved quite the feat. "Everyone stares at Dart Sand. Even a few of the men. Wouldn't you love to lick those abs?"

Startled by the heathen suggestion, Sidney took a step to the right, away from the neckless brownie. Their sort were territorial and fiercely punctual. One never messed with a brownie.

Licking abs? Hmm . . .

"He's nothing special," Sidney offered dismissively. "Arrogant, if you ask me."

And not a bad kisser, if she recalled correctly. Which she did. But that was neither here nor there.

A kiss didn't mean anything. It had probably been an accident. He'd been leaning over her. She had sat up from her induced sleep too quickly. *Smack!*

The flush warming Sidney's face moved down and

across her chest. It tingled and woke up parts of her she'd thought gone dormant. (No, not even Mr. Big could get a rise out of her lately.) The sensation kept moving lower, there, to swirl about her big-girl panties. Felt good.

"Your wings are turning," the brownie noted.

Sidney folded down her wings and slid her arms back to try to hide the tips with the excess fabric of her skirt. A futile effort. When faeries became aroused, their wings turned violet or some dark lush color like emerald or azure or crimson.

The brownie smirked knowingly. "Been a while, eh?"

"A while since—?" Sidney clapped her mouth shut. "Not at all. I am a perfectly satisfied faery. Life is sweet, couldn't get better. I don't even worry about my job. The teeth will never stop falling out. Who could ask for anything more?"

"I could." The brownie sighed, blowing a hank of mud-dull hair from her eagle-beak nose. "I'm a long-timer, just like you. Been in Reverie seven years."

"You have your own home?"

"I rent, but it gives me a feeling of—"

"Satisfaction?"

"Annoyance. I've been considering transferring back to Faery. Too frustrating here with the no-fraternization rule. A girl's gotta have sex once in a while."

"We *can* have sex, just not relationships. I have sex."

"Sure you do, honey." She nodded across the room. "Oh, you can look, but if you'd heard the rumors about Sand, you wouldn't be staring so fiercely."

"Rumors?"

"I hear . . ." The brownie leaned in, and Sidney, much against her desire to remain disinterested, cocked an ear to listen. ". . . that he has a problem with"—she glanced to the left and right (again, a feat for lack of neck) checking for listeners, then spat out—"premature dusting."

"Premature—?"

"You know it. All the flower faeries whisper about him. Seems he takes them home. Beds them. But he can't hold his dust. The dude gets excited and—poof! Not exactly Casanova, after all."

"You don't say."

A glance to Dart's brilliant glow spied him whispering in the ear of a violet-winged flutter-twit. A premature duster?

Yet, even with the rumors, none could resist his allure. The sandman charmed the color into the flower faeries' wings.

"Worth a few good fantasies." The brownie nudged Sidney with a thick elbow. "If you know what I mean."

"Sure. Fantasies." Even a fantasy of the gregarious sandman had to prove better than the action she'd been seeing lately: a TV character named Big and a flannel Spider-Man. "Pitiful, Sidney. Just—"

"Next!"

With a shove from the brownie, Sidney stumbled up to receive her vaccination. It hurt, and the base of her neck would be sore for days, but it would allow her to work in the Mortal Realm for another year.

Rubbing the back of her neck, Sidney strode through the old rink. Another year in the MR. Another year of mortgage payments—which utterly thrilled her, no matter the sacrifice. Sidney Tooth was an independent woman who could take care of herself.

Very well, so the independent part scratched her the wrong way once in a while. She had the house. But it was so big, and . . . lacking another presence.

Said presence being a man. She wouldn't mind a man. A faery man. But how to do the relationship thing when it wasn't allowed?

Hell, she had to *know* a faery man before she could

start thinking about relationships. When had she stopped noticing men? And wanting— "Sex."

"Excuse me."

Walking without paying attention to direction, Sidney stumbled back a few paces after colliding with a solid force. Only this time the solid force didn't dust her.

"Sex?" the sandman wondered gleefully.

A flower faery in a pink gossamer toga winked at Dart as he walked by her. Sweet. He hadn't seen her around before. Must be a new recruit. The Reverie Horticulture Club boasted a decade of State Fair grand prize wins. Faery was constantly dispatching new flower faeries to keep that record strong.

Just as Dart was going to introduce himself, a concoction of purple paisley—mumbling about sex—bumped into him.

"Sex?"

"Oh, I'm—" Wide green eyes stared up at Dart. Just as quickly, the green orbs shifted to the side, then right back at him.

Entranced, utterly. They could never look without falling madly in lust. He was used to the look.

But when the lustful swoon slipped away and fists formed at her sides, Dart lost his charm-them-into-bed smile. "Sidney?"

"You have a problem with navigating, buddy? I can't seem to get within a foot of you without a crash." She thrust her nose a little too high. "Dust any tooth faeries lately?"

"Only the pretty ones."

"Oh." Her fierce expression dropped, as did her paisley shoulders. "I see."

"I meant you, Sidney."

She didn't realize she was pretty? Maybe it was hard to

see beyond all that crazy fabric, and the frizzy hair that migrated to her eyes as quickly as it was swiped away. Why didn't she drop her glamour completely?

No matter. Dart was glad he'd run into her. "So you were talking about sex?"

She rubbed the back of her neck. "No, I actually said, um . . . pecs. Yeah, that's it. Pecs."

Uh-huh. Liar.

But still. Dart flexed a muscled arm. "You like?"

She rolled those gorgeous eyes. "I think it was Max, actually. That's it; I was thinking about my friend Max."

Really bad liar.

He detected the scent of sugar on her. Sugar and strawberries. Like a meadow of fresh sun-plumped fruit enticing him to dive in for the feast.

A finger snapped rudely before his face. "Do you always look at women like that? Like you're going to eat them? It's rather discomfiting, I'll have you know."

"Uh, sorry." Dart swiped a palm over his face and let out a sigh. Yeah, this one was different. The usual tactics weren't going to work, as they did with the flower faeries. Bye-bye, patented sex smile.

"Now you look lost," she said. And then she giggled, and it tinkled like bluebells splashed with raindrops.

Feeling her laughter spread over him was like inhaling desire into his pores. Mm, she sounded scrumptious. And he wanted another taste.

"Oh!" She slapped a hand over her mouth. It was as if she'd caught herself doing something naughty.

"I like your laugh," he said. "You should do it more often. But not around other faeries."

"Why not?"

"Because I don't want too much competition. I wonder if you wouldn't mind a walk in the park?"

"Me?" She looked around, but no one stood even remotely close. "Uh, I don't know."

"Max waiting for you?"

"Who's Max? Oh! Oh, him, no. I have another shift at the library. Then my night is full. Rounds, you know."

"Too bad. The park is awesome this time of year. The bees have pollinated the honeysuckle and the smell of pollen in the air is heady."

She looked down her nose at him. "You trying to get me drunk, Sandman?"

He shrugged. "I'll try anything once."

Chapter

6

Having turned down the sandman's invitation didn't make Sidney feel smart or superior. She had been thinking long-term, about maintaining her spotless record. But a simple walk in the park wouldn't lead to sex and then a relationship, and then the complete and utter loss of all that mattered to her.

Would it?

"Whew. You are so uptight sometimes," she muttered as she scanned the card catalog for a biography of Sir Arthur Conan Doyle. "Why *not* go with him?"

She knew the answer to that one. Because Dart Sand was a threat, deep down, on some inner level that established Sidney Tooth as a staunch and independent woman. She wasn't about to let anyone mess with her mojo.

"Like you have a mojo. You *need* a mojo, Sidney. You certainly need something."

Sighing, she plunked down on the stool behind the checkout desk and stared out the front doors that looked over the park. Steve the Faery's favorite bench was empty. He must be doing rounds at the Krispy Kreme. At least the sweet treats kept him happy. But they probably disguised a deep inner pain. The pain of losing Faery.

Sidney could relate. To her, losing the Mortal Realm would be equally as horrifying as Disenchantment. She just didn't fit into Faery. Okay, so she belonged in Faery, but she had always felt like she stood on the outside. Unnoticed and insignificant.

It had been years since she'd left her parents' home to serve in the MR, but some emotions ran deep and were hard to shake. She wondered now if her parents ever found a few moments to think of their middle daughter off serving the MR as a tooth collector. Likely not. She was on her own, and she liked it that way. Mostly.

A giggle over in the nonfiction stacks prompted her to *shush* the two girls who had discovered the anatomy section. They were the only patrons this afternoon. Most days were slow like this.

Most mothers didn't allow their children to come to the library unescorted.

"What is with all the uptight mothers in this town?" she muttered. "First they eradicate the Easter Bunny and the groundhog, and now . . . me?" Sidney's lower lip wobbled. "Who's next? Santa Claus?"

Catching her head in her palms, she closed her eyes. "It's like being overlooked. Again."

Why did she so desperately need to feel, well, needed?

Seeking distraction from her thoughts, Sidney sorted through the card catalog. The flipping of the crisp new cards gave her simple joy. Just last year she'd helped create all new records for the catalog because the old ones were wearing thin. The library hadn't the funds to computerize, nor did they have the desire to. Sidney appreciated that.

She bent to pull out a bottom drawer. Most of the day she had to herself, unless a field trip brought in a classroom. That was the best time to survey for her night job. If there was a loose tooth in the bunch, she'd notice it and could determine the exact hour of detachment within a few seconds.

Oftentimes she beat the ScryeTracker™, knowing which kids she'd have to collect from that night. Another small thrill that delighted Sidney.

Oh, yeah, she stood on the literal pulse of the community. Not.

It was a job that needed to be done. And she did it well.

Closing the drawer, she rubbed her fingers together. Dust? Lisa never did do what she was supposed to. Sidney sneezed and her eyes teared.

"Ahem."

As she sprang upright, Sidney's shoulder hit the open card drawer and she let out a yelp. Instant awareness of her loud outburst made her blush. She scanned the room, and her eyes fell upon the sexy sandman, standing before the desk. Smiling at her.

"You?"

"Me," he replied easily. "You didn't hurt yourself, did you? Are you crying, Sidney?"

"Me? No, no, it's the dust. Allergies, don't you know. Pollen does a real number on me, too." She sniffed.

"Here."

Dart pressed a soft handkerchief into her palm and Sidney sniffled into it. Thoughtful of him. She managed a brave smile and finally glanced at him.

Toadstools and moonbeams, could a man get more attractive?

Dart's pale green sweater matched the new leaf buds on the nearby forsythia bush. He didn't glow, because he wore glamour. Didn't matter, he still shone. His golden hair, tousled and sun-bleached, swept across broad shoulders, framing a square, strong jaw. Wide hands with long fingers splayed across the counter.

Sidney noticed hands. Men had either the rough, gruff,

gnarly hands she wouldn't go near with a hot mitt and tongs, or the long, narrow wraith hands that made her cringe before they got close enough to shake. A few had masterful hands. Just the right shape, large and manly, with perfect fingers, graceful in movement, and warm at first touch.

A woman might find herself wondering what it felt like to have one of those hands caress her cheek. Just a stroke. Slowly, barely there.

"Sidney?"

"Huh?" Realizing she held the white hankie clenched against her cheek, Sidney tossed it at Dart. "Er, right. Thanks. Better now. Much better. You must be getting ready to go out on rounds?"

"Yeah, I start early. There are a few little ones across town who need my help. Usually kids sleep like logs. It's the adults and their crazy schedules—what with all the stress and tension—that really keep me busy. But Lacey Johnson's mom has been letting her eat Fruity Bonkers for supper because she's been feeling guilty for working two jobs to pay the bills. Talk about a sugar rush. Lacey needs my help if she's going to get any sleep tonight. What about you? Tooth business booming?"

Sidney glanced aside to staunch another threatening teardrop. "I don't have any pickups tonight. I got a letter from a kid the other night," she said. "Says his mom told him the Tooth Fairy doesn't exist."

"No way."

"Yes, way." Sidney caught a sniffling sigh at the back of her throat. "Rumors like that, it doesn't take long for them to become real. Once kids lose their Belief, well . . ."

"Don't even speak it. I understand completely."

A warm hand twined within her fingers. Sidney thought surely she'd die right there. Die the good death of enchantment so bold. The feel of him, so much bigger than she, and a confident rock to her lacking convictions, well, it felt great. Better than an entire field of strawberries.

"Without belief, I cease to exist," she whispered. It was getting harder to keep a tremble from her voice, but Sidney tightened her jaw and held her head up. She squeezed Dart's hand. "Which would mean I'd be packed off to Faery and reassigned. I'd despise a demotion to flower faery."

"I'd miss you."

"You don't even know me, Sandman."

"I want to know you better."

He lifted her hand and placed a kiss to the back of it. It was a tender morsel. Sidney's jaw loosened, and the tears threatened to pull a Niagara on her. Moments like this she felt so helpless, and utterly . . .

"What are you doing here? In a library?"

"I want a book?"

"Aha." He wanted a book like she needed to join a convent.

What had she been doing? Utterly losing it to the dysfunctional Casanova? What kind of power did he hold over her? *Don't look in those gorgeous eyes*, she coached. *Be stern.*

"What sort of book?"

Pressing his elbows onto the desk, he leaned in and flashed the charming grin that, despite her best efforts at a stern front, sent a wicked flush up the back of Sidney's neck. "What sort do you have?"

"Sort? Who comes to a library without any idea what book they need?"

"All right." He straightened. "You got me. I don't need a book. I came to see you, Sidney. But don't worry, it's not a date. Just a 'Hey, how are you' kind of thing."

Uh-huh. What did he think, to make her another notch on his bedpost? She was so not willing to play that game.

"I'm working." She tugged a sheet listing new releases out from the drawer and grabbed a pencil. There was nothing to write or do with the paper, but it looked good. "If you don't want a book, then I can't help you, Mr. Sand."

"I can play your game, Sidney."

Don't look in his eyes. Those deep, wide, charm-soaked orbs. "I don't play games."

"I'll take that book then. Give me something on . . . romance."

The lead in the pencil snapped against the paper. Sidney huffed out a breath. "You don't read romance."

"I'm just starting. Give me the latest. A bestseller."

"Very well." She rapped the pencil eraser on the desk. "Where's your library card?"

"I need a card?" He slapped at his shirt pockets, then gave a surrendering shrug. "Okay, let's skip the bull. I *do* want a date, Sidney. I just don't understand why it's so hard to get one with you."

"Because I'm discerning? Because maybe I value the fact I've served as Reverie's tooth faery for three decades and don't want to mess that up?"

"Whew, three decades? You really are one of those uptight follow-the-rules kind of gals."

"Uptight?" Did the man not have a compliment to hand? He'd done nothing but put her down since their first crash.

"That came out wrong. I don't think you're uptight; I think you're gorgeous, Sidney. I haven't been able to stop thinking of you since we crashed."

"How many times you use that line on the flower faeries?"

"Once in a— Hey, now that's not fair."

"Isn't it?" Sidney turned and plucked a book from the cart behind her and set it on the desk before Dart. "Take this one. Let me know what you think of it, will you?"

Dart tapped the hardcover titled *Romance for Dummies*.

"All right then," he said slyly. "I can take a hint. You want romance? I can do that. Talk to you later, Miss Tooth."

Chapter

7

" 'Talk to you later, Miss Tooth,' " Sidney mocked as she popped a box of frozen eggs in the microwave. She wasn't big on cooking. If it came in a box, she was so there.

"What kind of stud does he think he is? We're not all fast and easy, Sand. Some of us are discerning and won't jump into bed with just any man, I'll have you know."

Uh-huh. Right. And she was so behind that statement. Mostly.

While the eggs sat in the microwave, Sidney strode into the bedroom to find some clothes. Her unrumpled, *untwisted* sheets blared at her.

"I'm just not that into him," she muttered. "I bet the sandman has never known what it's like to not feel needed. Everyone wants that guy."

Once she convinced herself Dart Sand was uninteresting and not at all sexy, she could move ahead and resume her life.

"My dull, uninteresting, follow-the-rules life."

Sighing, Sidney pillaged her closet. Polyester flew overhead; cotton bounced off walls; rayon and corduroy got chucked over a shoulder.

She stood at the edge of the double-doored closet,

ankle-deep in scattered shirts and pants and dresses. And go-go boots. And fluorescent crocheted shawls.

"Why I ever believed Day-Glo was fashionable after the eighties is beyond me," she said with a bare-toed kick to the crinkly, sharp stuff.

The doorbell rang. Sidney gripped a slip of polka-dotted green cotton to her bare chest. "Who could that be?"

Panic scurried up her arms and prickled her neck. She never got visitors. Who had time to socialize?

She shot a look at the mirror. In an unglamourized state, her hair, drying every which way after a shower, hung in heavy ringlets down to her elbows. The pale moss color had always bothered her. Why not blond, like a summer wheat field?

She slapped on a glamour. The mossy hair was replaced by frizzy mortal brown, her wings cloaked, which always gave a brief pinch between her shoulder blades.

The doorbell rang again.

Pulling a cotton sundress over her head, Sidney headed toward the front door. Barefoot, shoving up the left strap that refused to stay on her shoulder and wondering when she'd ever gotten this slim-fitted dress, she tugged open the door to a bouquet of huge mauve peonies.

Rearing back at sight of the frilly petals, Sidney stifled a sneeze. "I hate flowers."

Dart's brilliant gold eyes appeared above the bouquet. "Seriously?"

"They make me—*achoo*!"

Dart tossed the flowers over his shoulder to land on the front stoop. "Then it's a good thing I brought this."

There on his palm sat a small white plastic box, emblazoned with red lettering.

Overwhelmed by his thoughtfulness, Sidney grabbed the gift. "Cinnamon." She turned and strode across the living room. He'd bought the Target brand of floss she loved. And waxed even!

"Can I come in? Sidney?"

Oops. Handsome stud standing in the doorway. Get your priorities in order, Sidney.

"Yes, come in. You must be hungry after a long night of work. I've eggs cooking. Er, did I invite you over without realizing I did so?"

"Nope."

Right. The man was pursuing her—for that notch.

Sidney placed the floss dispenser on the counter and gave it a possessive pat. Any points lost with the flower fiasco were made up and doubled with this attentive gesture. And her favorite flavor. What a guy.

Catching her chin in hand, Sidney preened over the gift. Out the corner of her eye, she noticed a six-foot-plus sandman brandishing a silly grin. He stood in the center of her living room. Staring at her.

"Er . . ."

She tugged at the skirt of her dress. No, wasn't stuck in her underwear. (Because she hadn't time to put any on—brazen faery.) Was it her hair? She smoothed back the unruly tresses, struggling a bit when the stuff stuck in her eyelashes.

"Is something wrong, Dart? I don't hate flowers; I mean, you didn't have to toss them. It's just, they remind me of those silly flower twits and tend to make me sneeze."

"Sorry about the twits—er, I mean, well, they don't matter. The way you look now, Sidney . . . so happy. Your smile is like the sunrise. What makes your smile curve up on the right side a little higher than the other?"

"Er . . . I like floss?"

Dart crossed the room and took her in his arms. He performed an amazing feat, sweeping her backward and bowing over her, without making her feel like a marionette.

And he kissed her. Sidney had to clutch at his neck and slide her fingers through his soft, silky hair to hold the lip-lock.

Was it something she'd said? What *had* she said? Whatever it was, could she get that in writing?

Pressing against his rock-hard chest, Sidney managed to get a breath in edgewise. "What are you doing?" she gasped.

"I'm kissing you. Please tell me you've kissed before."

"Of course I have. Get over yourself, Sand. You think you're such a stud?"

"I've been told once or twice."

I know better, she thought. *Premature dusting, eh?* But she wasn't infuriated enough to say something so horrible.

"Just . . . let the dog off the leash, will you? I don't fall for flirty winks and sweet talk like those silly flower giglets."

Dart hung his head and nodded. "You wouldn't. You're not like them."

Sidney bristled. So she didn't know how to dress, or to style her hair. Didn't give him a right to make comments like that. "You're such a . . . a player!"

No, Sidney, calling him names is no way to get a repeat performance.

"You don't want me to kiss you?"

"Of course I do. I just—ichor-dripping sprites, maybe in your world everyone who breathes your air falls under the spell of your charm, but in my world—"

Another kiss stopped her tirade. It was short. Simple. Two mouths briefly colliding.

"You *are* attracted," Dart said.

Gold eyes traced back and forth between Sidney's eyes.

Had she ever felt the touch of a moonbeam? It was cool yet electric. Beguiling.

"How could I not want to kiss you, Sidney? You smell gorgeous—like cinnamon floss and strawberries—and look tasty."

"I do? Huh." She spread her palms across the skirt of her dress. "Thought you didn't like polka dots?"

"They are a bit much. But you—everything about you."

Strong hands bracketed her shoulders. The scent of him, earthy and warm, filled Sidney's senses. "This is nice, just the two of us. Why do you wear a glamour when you're at home alone?"

Because it was too easy *not* being herself.

"Why are *you* wearing glamour?" she countered.

"Had to get here somehow."

"You didn't fly?" Most faeries traveled in small form and could cross an entire town in but minutes.

"I took the bike."

"Bike?"

"Street chopper. Seven hundred pounds of titanium, leather, and roar. There isn't a sweeter ride in Faery."

"I see. I bet the flutter-twits love it, too," she muttered. "No iron?"

"Had it specially made. Not an ounce of iron on the entire thing. I get vaccinated against iron sickness once a year."

Her eyes fell to the muscular biceps he rubbed where she knew they gave the vaccine. "They hurt."

"Yeah." A bend of his elbow pulsed up the muscle. "You want me to drop the glamour, I will—"

"No!"

Warmth flushed Sidney's neck and cheeks. And it was moving lower. That loose, melty feeling she got when in the sandman's presence was doing its job, relaxing her muscles and making her insides all squishy.

Good thing she was wearing glamour or her wings would be violet.

And if the sandman dropped his, well, she wasn't sure how she'd react to his moonbeam glow. A simple kiss would not serve. She'd have to shove him on the couch and have at him. Bet he'd like that. She, running her hands all over those tight, tanned muscles. Licking the hard ridges on his abdomen that rolled, lower and lower, until she'd have to go so low—

Dashing out her tongue, she tasted the remnants of Dart's kiss. Twice now he'd planted a nice one on her. And twice she'd decided to like the faery despite all the warnings that screamed he was a player.

The image of her tongue dancing across his hard body had not gone away.

"Sorry about calling you a player. Kiss me again, Sandman."

They landed in each other's embrace like two honeybees colliding mid-air.

Sidney slid her hand down his granite abs. Real, all of him. Not a daydream or fantasy. And he was kissing her. *Mercy, mushrooms, and midnight moonbeams! Rules? Who cared about the rules?* She wanted this fling.

And she would have it.

Dart muttered something against her mouth, but the sensual husky tones got lost in their kiss. He pushed Sidney's hand away. She drew him closer.

Too late. A cloud of glimmering dust filled the air. And Sidney went down, snoring.

Chapter

8

Sidney woke, sprawled in the center of the kitchen floor. Beneath the counter, a stray baby carrot brandished a coating of dust thicker than a rabbit pelt. That was the problem with living in the MR; brownies developed a superior attitude and wouldn't work for faeries here. Like they were so hoity-toity working for the feeble mortals.

Feeling like she'd been hit by one of those huge mortal semitrucks, she gripped the edge of the counter and pulled herself up to stand.

"Wha—? What in toadstools happened?" Rubbing her eyes, she felt grit roll away and down her cheek.

"So he really *is* trigger-happy with the dust. What do you know? The dude gets aroused and—poof! Dust city. Can't be good for a man's sex life. Or the faery he's having sex with."

Sidney yawned and straightened. "Though the nap was good. That dude must be an insomniac's dream."

A note scrawled in rushed script lay on the counter. Sidney read: *Sorry. I have a problem.*

"Well, duh."

Didn't mean to put you to sleep. Hope you can forgive

*me. Too embarrassed to stick around. Won't bother you
again.*

What was with all the notes lately? They all harbored
doom!

"Too embarrassed? Poor guy. How does someone like
that have a relationship? Hmm, should keep him from being retrieved for rule breaking. Suppose he dates those
silly flower faeries 'cause they just giggle and probably
don't mind being dusted to sleep in the middle of a good
make-out session."

Didn't they desire more? The big wazoo? Payoff for all
the foreplay and crazy acrobatic maneuverings? Obviously, such reward wasn't possible at Dart's speed.

Yet he was a charmer.

Remembering the way he'd looked at her made Sidney
smile. Wrapped in Dart's arms, she'd felt melty and a little naked, but a good naked. It had been a long time since
any man had given her the glad eye.

And she wanted it again.

An extra helping of dust for Mrs. Henderson this evening.
Dart hovered over her pillow, dusting her. Half a foot
away sprawled the snoring body of a sleeping gorilla. Mr.
Henderson was big, hairy, and loud. How anyone could
sleep through that racket was a wonder. Which was why
Dart paid special attention to the pretty mortal woman
tossing about on her pink satin pillow.

As his dust settled and began to take effect—Dart had
some very potent fellows—Mrs. Henderson relaxed. Her
mouth curved into a smile and her hands slid up to her
breasts. And then she cooed.

Dart smirked.

They dreamed about him, the mortal women. Nothing
wrong with that. Why shouldn't they have sexy dreams

about the man who could take away their troubles and gift them with peaceful sleep?

Fluttering up and away from the king-size bed, Dart wandered aimlessly as his thoughts found him rehashing this morning's disaster at Sidney's house.

He'd dusted her. And she'd dropped like a log.

Now there was one female who likely never dreamed a sexy thought about him.

The master of the sleep dust had a little problem. Only it wasn't so little. Dart dusted women prematurely all the time.

Prematurely? Stones, he shouldn't even be dusting a potential lover. The last thing he needed was for a half-dressed, almost-ready-to-climax female to drop into a snore.

It was killer to his sex life.

Which was why he dated the twitter-fly flower faeries. Overwhelmed by the sandman's charm, the giglets went along for anything—just to be in Dart Sand's bed. So what if coitus interruptus was the name of the game? They just giggled, kissed him on the forehead, and then fluttered away.

And never came back.

He'd heard the scandalous whispers. Made him want to crawl into the shadows. He couldn't prevent the dusting. He didn't know why it happened.

Dart swerved to avoid a floor lamp boasting gaudy red beads about the hem of the shade.

They didn't come back because they were dissatisfied. Like he wasn't?

The last time he'd had great sex had been—had he *ever* had great sex?

And what was with his inability to control his dust? He could dole it out to mortals whenever needed. It wasn't as though he flew through the air leaving a trail like some of the sprites did.

Yet when he became aroused? Wham! Poof! Snores.

It wasn't right. A man wasn't, well, *a man* unless he could please a woman. But Dart had no idea how to change it.

After he'd left Sidney's house, Dart had flown through the park and stopped to chat with Steve the Faery. Dart had asked Steve's advice about pursuing Sidney.

"Are you sure about this? You gotta really want her," Steve the Faery had said. "'Cause that tooth faery is no day in the park."

Dart had nodded and answered, "Yes."

He really had a thing for Sidney Tooth, feisty faery extraordinaire.

"Sidney won't have the patience for me," he muttered now. "She's been around. I'm just a player to her. I'm surprised she even let me in the front door."

Certainly she would not invite him back after he'd dusted her. Again. He shouldn't have left her lying on the kitchen floor, but he'd panicked.

"Maybe therapy?" Dodging the dangling fringes beneath a drapery valance, Dart searched for the open window where he'd entered the Henderson house. "Do I have some deep-seated childhood angst that makes me want to blow my dust before I can get it up?"

That was just wrong.

Now he was starting to think like those mortals on that TV show he watched religiously. The one with the bald doctor who spoke in anecdotes. Okay, not *religiously*. If anyone asked, it was only occasionally, but thanks to TiVo, he never missed an episode.

"I've never felt this way about a woman before."

This time he wanted it to be right. To not scare her off.

To be able to satisfy her. And to have her look upon him, not necessarily with lust but with respect.

"Tall order."

You gotta really want her. 'Cause that tooth faery is no day in the park.

So she had a freaky sense of fashion. And her hair could certainly use some taming. And she did like obscene gestures. And for some reason she preferred mortal glamour to her real appearance. But that was outside stuff.

Those grass green eyes. They looked *into* him. Melted him. And yes, challenged him. Which was a cool thing. Dart had never met a woman like Sidney, one who was willing to challenge his shortcomings.

"She's one smart lady. And that figure." He traced the air, drawing her shape as he flew along. "Va-va-voo—*ouf*!"

Forehead slapping against the window, the rest of Dart's body followed. Flattened against the clear glass, his body sagged and he slid down the window like a horsefly splattered on a windshield.

Chapter

9

Sidney edged by Cooper Henderson, who stood in the medical section, wielding a book on snoring. She smiled at him, but he tucked the book under an arm and headed to a reading nook.

She'd scanned the children's mythology section—all books on tooth faeries were gone.

"Non-believers," she muttered grumpily.

The adult mythology section was bare of tooth faery literature as well. She pondered looking up the sandman when a red-spined book caught her eye. She pulled it out.

"*Sex for Dummies*. How did this get filed in Mythology?"

Kids. They never ceased to surprise her with their curious minds. It gave Sidney a chuckle.

"Didn't think the Reverie library allowed books like this. Must have gotten past the *mothers*."

She paged through, and though there were no pictures, the subject headings were blush-worthy. "Teaching an Old Dog New Tricks." "Using Feathers to Sweep Him off His Feet." "Self-Cultivation 101."

"Self-cultivation? Oh, toadstools. I'm so tired of doing it all myself."

Sidney replaced the book and pressed her forehead to the row of book spines before her. "I thought being independent was what I wanted. And it feels great. But . . ."

Lately, alone didn't feel so great. Alone was this big gaping hole in her chest. Alone got her a mortgage but no love. Alone meant self-cultivation.

"I've put him off and pushed him away. He's probably already on to the next flutter-twit. I had my chance, and I spoiled it."

A sigh echoed in the quiet library.

Tugging out the book again, Sidney paged through and stopped at the chapter called "Dress Sexy to Catch His Eye."

Sidney sat through the entire night mindlessly watching a rerun of the *Matrix* trilogy. She loved the kick-ass moves and tried to incorporate them into her own job whenever a vicious cat decided to take her on.

"My job," she muttered, and followed with sigh number thirty in an evening of sighs.

She scratched her belly and tugged the white terry bathrobe. Fluffy green turtle slippers eyed her with plastic googly eyes.

No faery would be caught dead wearing turtle slippers.

Dart was right. "I wear mortal glamour like a security blanket."

Another sigh.

Glancing to the ScryeTracker™ on the arm of the sofa, she eyed the blank screen. No new pickups reported. It was as if the children of Reverie had all started brushing and going to regular checkups, and those darned teeth actually enjoyed chewing Cheez Doodles and sipping corrosive soda.

Sidney knew better. Selfish non-believers, lurking in

the dark with lipstick sneers, were tossing any and all fallen teeth.

How could a group of over-combed, high-fashion, Aqua Net–shellacked moms wield such power? Actually, it was just the one mother, and the rest all followed like mindless sheep.

"I'm a classic," Sidney murmured. "They can't get rid of me."

She hated this feeling of lacking control. But how to change things if she didn't know where the teeth were?

Sniffling, Sidney settled deeper into the array of velvet pillows on the couch. She'd returned home after reading the chapter on dressing sensually, showered, and spent more than a few hours in front of the mirror, plucking, tweezing, and grooming.

The picture of the woman on the cover of the book, wearing a pretty, curve-hugging dress that flounced out around the knees, had been easy enough to glamourize.

For all the good it would do. Sidney had gotten all dressed up with no place to go.

"It was just a practice run," she reasoned.

Keanu Reeves took to the air in his long black priest's coat, with the villain in pursuit. They soared upward, defying gravity and the logistics of flight.

"That's not how you fly. Amateurs." Sidney clicked to another station, then, knowing she wanted to watch the movie, clicked back to it.

Lately she was so . . . uptight. Easily angered. On edge.

Had to be the job security. That would make anyone irritable. But she didn't like feeling this way. A girl couldn't sustain uptight for long before she became . . .

"An angry uptight mother who lives to take fun away from her children."

Was that it? All those mothers. They were uptight. Angry

"Unsatisfied," Sidney decided with a nod of her head. "In need of sex? Like me?"

Huh. It made curious sense.

But knowing the underlying reason for the mothers' bad moods didn't change things. Sidney was still out a night job. And her sheets were still far too smooth and in need of twisting.

She clicked off the television just as the doorbell rang.

Sidney sat bolt upright. Who could that be? She glanced out the window. The sun had peeked over the horizon as she'd sat muddling in a media stupor.

A whole night had passed without a single tooth retrieval.

Feeling imminent tears sting her eyes, but knowing that whoever stood outside wasn't going to leave, because now the bell rang steadily, she stomped over and opened the door.

The guy who had left a note stating he wouldn't bother her again had returned. With lilies.

Sidney cocked an elbow high on the door frame. "Dart."

"Sidney."

Did a faery have a right to be so handsome? Sidney felt sure there must be a rule about it somewhere. How was she supposed to follow the no-fraternization rule if the sandman was sexy and pumped, and . . . were his wings the slightest shade of violet?

She looked down and to the side, surprising herself with her embarrassment. Dissatisfied, eh? Just like the mortal mothers who had become her bane. She really was more mortal than faery!

"What's wrong?" he asked.

"Er, lose the flowers, will you?"

"Right." A toss relegated the silly bouquet over his shoulder. "I brought you something else." Lifting his hand, he displayed a gift.

Sidney snatched the travel-size plastic bottle of crimson mouthwash.

"I'll have you know that's not an easy flavor to find. All the stores offer is the minty fresh green stuff with fluoride."

"Yuck."

"But I know you're a cinnamon kind of gal. Fiery and gotta lot of bite."

The sandman really did know how to treat a girl.

And Sidney reacted. She grabbed Dart by the head and pulled him in for a kiss. No tentative I'll-take-your-measure-and-decide-if-I-like-you kind of kiss. This one meant business. This one was all about showing him exactly what his moonbeam glow gave her a hankering for.

While not breaking their lip-lock, she stepped back, luring Dart over the threshold. It didn't take long for him to bracket her hips and lift her up. She wrapped her legs about his waist. The turtle slippers clicked appreciatively behind his back. He walked across the floor while the kiss journeyed to new depths. Stars, she liked tongue dancing with this guy. And he tasted like cinnamon floss. Bonus!

He set her on the kitchen table and Sidney wrapped her legs about his hips to keep him close. A kiss to the corner of her eye felt like a pixie landing on her skin.

"Why'd you come over?" she managed between kisses. "I thought you weren't . . ."

"Going to come back?" he answered. "Embarrassed?"

"Uh-huh." She tugged at his shirt, wanting to feel hard muscle.

"I am still. But there are more important things than my pride. I mean—" He broke the kiss but maintained a forehead-to-forehead closeness. "I've been thinking about you and your situation all night. You can't let those ridiculous mothers do this to you. The kids can't stop believing in the Tooth Fairy."

The top button popped off Dart's shirt. She hadn't intended to do that, but since it had already happened—Sidney quickly unbuttoned the rest. Talk was cheap. She wanted the sandman. Now.

"Sidney, your job?"

"Uh-huh."

He clasped a wide, strong hand over hers as it landed on the waist of his jeans. Spoilsport!

"Right, my job." Reluctantly she shook off the ardor that threatened to swallow her better senses. The guy wanted to talk. He had said he wasn't going to return, so the fact he *had* returned should caution her to go slower. Not scare him away.

She could do that.

"I've never been faced with this kind of situation in all my decades in the MR," she said. "I don't have a clue in a mountain of toadstools. Except maybe . . ."

"I have a clue."

"Really? So you've been thinking of me?"

He pulled back his hair to reveal a good-sized egg at his temple. "I still have a bruise from flying into a window at the Hendersons' because my mind was on one sweet tooth faery instead of dusting."

Sidney stroked the tender skin. "Poor guy."

He took her fingers and kissed them with deliberate slowness. Dashing out his tongue, he tickled the curve of skin between two of her fingers. Did he want to talk or make out? Mixed signals, anyone?

"Ah . . . Dart?"

"Right. You make it hard to concentrate, but I will, because this is important."

Toadstools.

"So this is what I've come up with. We need to go to the head mom's house. Take a look around. We might find clues."

"Clues to what?"

"To what her deal is," he said. "To understand why she feels it's okay to strip her offspring of childhood beliefs. If this gets out of hand, one day it's Reverie, but soon it's the world."

The immensity of what could happen stymied Sidney. The world could change because of one mother's misdirected morals. No more tooth faeries meant loss of Belief and confused, disenchanted young children worldwide. How to alter a non-believer's perceptions?

Look at her! The faery who didn't believe all that much in herself lately thought she had a clue?

"I have a sort of theory on the subject, too," Sidney offered.

"Which is?"

Stars, stones, and toadstool circles, the man's eyes had depth. A faery could hop right in and splash about in those gold pools. No life preserver necessary. Send her in for a good long soak.

Sidney's jaw dropped. The motion snapped her out of her drooling appreciation of the finer things in life. "Er."

"See something you like?" he dared coyly.

"More than floss and mouthwash," she murmured, her body relaxing and her lips moving dangerously closer to his.

Dart's eyebrow lifted.

"But this theory I have." Anything to keep her from an all-out attack on the sandman's oh-so-kissable lips. "The mortal mothers? They're not satisfied with their lives. They . . . need things." *Like sex. Oh, baby, let me swim in those eyes.* "And, and they're angry they don't have what they want."

"You think?"

She nodded. "I know."

"Sex?"

"Right now?"

"Sidney." He leaned in and tweaked her nose with a fingertip. "We're talking about the mothers. You think they're dissatisfied and taking that anger out on you because—"

"Because the entire town of Reverie needs to get laid. And you—"

He nuzzled a kiss to the underside of her jaw.

"—are responsible."

"Me? Whoa now, Miss Tooth, I think you lost me somewhere between angry villagers and soft tender kisses. Me? How am I to blame for the mothers' trying to take your job away?"

"Well." It had just come to her. But it made a lot of sense. And Sidney had never been one to sugarcoat things. (Especially since sugarcoating always did a number on tooth enamel. Four out of five dentists agreed.) "You are the best sandman around, aren't you? The fastest? Most thorough?"

"Yeeesss," he answered cautiously.

"So, you've been *too* good. You're putting the entire city to sleep when, well . . . maybe those women need a sleepless night to get them back on track, so to speak."

"No snoring, more sex?"

"I think so."

"Huh." He propped a hand at his waist. "Makes sense. You, Sidney Tooth, are one smart faery."

"I try." She fluttered her lashes, but one of them stuck. Too much mascara. But she made a save by flipping her hair over that eye. Awkward sexy at its finest. *Oh, you go, Sidney.*

Not.

Dart swept aside her hair and traced under her eye, which effectively released her from lash-mesh. "If I didn't know better, I'd say you're all made up to go out on a date. Is this eye shadow? Who you planning to seduce, Sidney?"

"Only you."

"But you didn't know I'd come."

"I had hopes."

Did that sound desperate? Sidney didn't care. He'd come back. She wasn't about to let him get off with a note from his mommy this time.

She gripped the sandman by his waistband and pulled him in for another kiss. "I want you, Sandman."

"Whoa. You are the fastest faery in the Mortal Realm, Sidney. Take it easy. I thought you were concerned about the mortal women of Reverie?"

"They can suck toadstools, er—I mean—oh, Dart. I came to the conclusion about the mothers because I'm in the same boat. I want. I . . . need . . ."

He leaned in and kissed her. Warm, soft, promising. Moonbeams clashing with sunshine. "We've got time."

"We do? Because judging from your propensity to . . . erm . . . well, you know, I'd think the quicker the better."

Dart turned and sat on the table next to her, arms crossed over his chest. Oops, she'd said something wrong. Again. And yet he wasn't fleeing. Yet.

"I like you, Sidney."

Yes! "I like you, too, Dart."

"I mean, I *really* like you. Not like, you know . . . those others."

"Flower faeries?"

"Yeah. Not like those giggly twitter-flies."

"So why do you date them?"

"Don't make me explain, please?"

"Of course I won't." But it killed her not to know.

It was probably as she suspected. The flutter-twits were all so dull in the noggin they only saw Dart's attractive outer side and didn't care that he couldn't finish the deal.

Must be a status symbol of sorts, to have been with the sandman.

She could get beyond the premature dusting bit. Well, *eventually* she could get beyond it. If she could stay awake long enough to do so.

Sex for the heck of it was fine. But a man's insides were important, too. And Dart had great insides. He cared about her. Look at the thoughtful gifts he'd brought. And he'd expressed concern over her job disaster.

"There's something different about you, Sidney. Something calm and yet erratic. Wise and foolish. Gorgeous and goofy. You're a mass of contradictions."

"You got a problem with that?"

"Not at all! You fascinate me. A guy could spend forever with a gal like you and never grow bored."

He'd said *forever.* Did he realize that women picked out the most benign words from a man's conversation and could elevate them to high-alert, be-still-my-heart status?

"I miss my family," he said. "But I like the MR."

"Faery ain't got nothing over the Mortal Realm. You said earlier that you live here? Sort of?"

"I don't go back and forth to Faery daily, but I don't have a permanent residence here."

"So how do you—?"

"I rent. But it's not working for me anymore, this gigolo lifestyle. I need family here. My own family."

And he called *her* fast?

"I need to take things slow, though. With relationships, in general. I've an issue to work out. It's just me; you gotta trust that."

Strangely relieved, Sidney pulled the skirt of her dress over her knees and tugged her robe shut. Whew, she was disheveled. And it felt freeing and wild, yet a little inappropriate after the sandman's confession.

She wanted family, but not right this second. She hadn't

even taken the man for a swing yet. One must never seal the deal until after the merchandise has been thoroughly tested.

"You want to go reconnaissance that mom's house today?" he asked. "Most mothers are gone to the beauty salon during the day, and the kids are in school. This afternoon would be a perfect time."

"I suppose." She'd rather have sex with a handsome sandman. "Yes, that sounds good. Work."

And no play. When had she tossed her uptight and follows-the-rules crown?

"If you promise to take it easy on the dust tonight when you're doing rounds in any house with a kid who may have a loose tooth."

"Deal." Dart headed to the door so quickly, Sidney had to turn to check if a band of marrow-sucking spriggans were on his heels. "Meet me in the park in a few hours. See ya, Sidney."

She waved him off. The mouthwash glinted near her elbow. She picked it up and swished the red liquid back and forth. The motion stirred bubbles to the neck of the plastic bottle.

"That man really knows how to romance a gal." Sigh number thirty-two landed in the atmosphere. "But how to save him from himself?"

Chapter

10

Mid-afternoon sifted cool needle-shaped shadows from pine trees across the green stucco façade of the Hanson residence. Dust motes crept through the air but didn't dare to land on the polished mahogany dining table. Couches and chairs sat militant and white, a furniture-store display. No evidence of Jimmy's toys or that a child even lived in this home.

Sidney thought surely there must be a robo-maid stashed in the closet to chase off the minutest speck of dust. Must have some fierce brownies working this house.

"This is what you call anal," Dart said. "I think you're right, Sidney. There's been no extra-curricular sheet Olympics going on in this house."

Sidney agreed.

Both were small, easier to reconnaissance that way. Dart hovered in the kitchen, inspecting the glass cabinet fronts that revealed goblets arranged from tall to short and by pattern. "I hate wine goblets."

"Wait until you see the kid's room," Sidney said. "I'm surprised the twerp isn't sent to military school for the infractions against dirt, grime, and general disorder in that room. Let's head this way. What's wrong with wine goblets?"

"I had a bad experience a few years ago," Dart said as he followed. "Some psycho insomniac wouldn't fall asleep even when I brought out the superpowered dust. She wore me out. As I was catching my breath on the bedside table—*clank!*—she trapped me inside a goblet. Wine dripped down my wings and got them all sticky. It was a nightmare."

"You were *Seen* by a mortal adult?"

"Yeah. The SSF wasn't too pleased about that. Did they care I cut my wing trying to escape? Oh, no, you're getting written up, Sand. One more slip-up and it's retrieval time."

Sidney shuddered to even consider being retrieved back to Faery. "So what are we looking for?"

"Not sure." Dart flew down the hallway. "Did you say they have a cat?"

"Yep. Big white fluff-monster. You've never seen it on your rounds?"

"I work so fast, I rarely take in the surroundings." He paused in the doorway to the master bedroom, hovering in a macho pose, shoulders thrust back and chin lifted. Yeah, the guy was a super-fast stud faery.

Fast wasn't always good. *Or satisfying,* Sidney thought. She preferred things slow and easy. But not too easy. Slow and gradually working up to faster. And harder. And—

"I got a whole town to do in one night, Sidney. I can't be leisurely."

"Sure, but you're skipping some houses tonight, and don't forget it."

She fluttered in a meandering path down the hallway. Keeping thoughts of sex from her mind wasn't going to be easy with Dart flexing his muscles. And then there was that cute tight butt below his wings.

And what about those wings? Faery wings came in all

shapes, sizes, and colors. But the bigger the male's wings, the bigger the, er . . . well, she had heard.

Dart's wings stretched above his head, past his shoulders, and well below his ankles. Huge wings.

Huge.

Something grabbed her by the arm. Sidney flittered around and crashed into Dart's chest. Her wings fluttered double time, but he wouldn't let her go.

"Cheer up, Sidney," he said.

"I am cheerful. Mostly." She was freakin' horny, is what she was.

"I'm going to help you. This is not the end of the Reverie tooth faery, I won't let it be."

Wings deflated and Sidney sighed. "If you say so."

He leaned in to kiss her. It was a soft morsel, a soul-touching, heart-slaying taste of bliss. Sidney's wings lifted.

Dart peered over her shoulder. A grin tickled his face.

Oh, stones, were her wings shading violet?

"I think we should get to work before I find something much better to occupy myself with," he said. A quick kiss to her forehead and he fluttered off. "I'll check the master bedroom!"

"I can think of better things to occupy myself, too, Studman."

Sidney preened a hand back over the tip of her upper left wing. It was pale violet—a transformation from her usual dull rainbow of pink, aquamarine, and gold—but if he'd kissed her any longer, her wings would have colored as deep as Oberon's royal cape.

She fluttered without direction down the hallway. It had been a while since she'd had someone who made her wings color and her toes tingle. Too bad any attempts at foreplay resulted in her snoring.

"There's got to be a way to slow the dude down. Hold

off that dust. Does he dust every time he gets excited? Whoa."

Sidney caught her body against a billow of thick fabric. She'd fluttered right into the velvet drapery at the end of the hallway.

She cast a glance over her shoulder. No sandman in sight. "Most embarrassing."

"Meow." Below, a fat fluff-ball's enunciation sounded very much like kitty laughter.

"Oh, yeah?"

Sidney swooped down for the target. Skimming the head of the beast, she left a trail of dust in her wake. She hadn't the ability to put anything to sleep, but she did pack a powerful discombobulation dust.

The cat wobbled. As it stepped down the hallway, each paw hung and swayed. It almost toppled but then miraculously landed its footing. Sidney would have laughed, if she weren't so glum.

"I got it!"

Dart shot out into the hallway and gestured for her to follow. Sidney joined him inside the master bedroom. "What'd you find, Studman—er, I mean Sandman?"

Watch it, Sidney.

He led her to an open drawer. They fluttered into the dark depths, half-filled with lacy underwear.

"Is this some kind of twisted hint to see my undies?" Sidney wondered as she landed a silky blue pair. "I'll have you know I don't do undies."

Not lately, at least. Hee!

Dart had been about to speak, but he suddenly gave her a double take. "You don't?"

If it hadn't been dark as a king-size pillow crushed against a Temper-Pedic mattress, Sidney might swear she saw his wings shade purple. Stars, but she *could* see in the dark, and they were purple.

"Not a stitch."

The sandman's swallow was audible. *Heh.* It was good to do that to him. A girl had to keep a man guessing.

"So what do you have?" she asked.

"This." Dart kicked back the top of a small Altoids tin. Inside, a clatter of teeth rocked across the bottom.

Digging her hands into the collection—an entire set of baby teeth, Sidney surmised—she drew up a smooth and nicely weighted tooth. Sniffing it, she then tapped the enamel. "An eight-year canine. Now it's twenty to thirty years old, I'd say. Female." Nano-divots pocked the surface. To the untrained eye, unnoticeable. "Excessive use of fluoride. Minimal flossing. Yep, this belongs to the mom."

"How do you know that?"

"It's my job, Sand. I do it well."

She may not be as fast as a sandman, but woe to the faery who tried to match her in tooth knowledge. She'd give a mortal forensic team a run for their DNA labs.

"I wonder what the deal is?" she said. "All these teeth. A complete set. It's as if the tooth faery never visited her."

"Maybe she didn't."

"That's impossible."

"Nothing is im—"

A grip of Sidney's hand cut off Dart's words. She clenched his shirt before his neck. If his wings had been shading purple before, now his face surpassed that color.

"Listen, Sandman. I've been Reverie's tooth faery for thirty mortal years. Do you understand what that means? Upright. Rule-abiding. Respected. I've never missed a tooth."

"Never?" he squeaked.

She released her clutch and the sandman gasped in a wheezing breath. Dramatic, but warranted.

"Never," she spat.

"Huh." He toed a pre-molar inside the tin. "Doesn't explain all this."

"No, it doesn't."

Sidney flew out from the drawer and sat on the edge of it. Below, the cat hissed and whipped its tail menacingly. She delivered it a nasty mortal gesture and muttered, "Underskinker." The mood to kick feline butt didn't even tweak at her.

All those teeth. Unclaimed.

Had she—? "Impossible." Maybe?

"This troubles me," she said when Dart joined her. "But if the woman never received a visit from the tooth faery, that certainly explains her venom toward me now."

"That would do it. Is it possible she was off your radar thirty years ago?"

"No, headquarters has an advanced tracking system. The ScryeTracker™ is infallible. I can't believe this. Is it possible? I . . . missed a child?"

What she required right now was what she got. Dart's silence. She didn't want to hear any *Well, maybe you were wrong*s. What she *needed* was what Dart did next. He hugged her.

And Sidney released her worries and melted into the warmth of his presence. It was as though he were holding an umbrella over her head, sheltering her from cold rain. Sometimes just being in the company of another put things right. At least in her heart.

"We'll solve this," he said after a while. "For the kids."

His concern for the children impressed her. Put a warm glow right there in her bosom.

"You plan to have kids someday, Dart?"

He answered easily, "Twenty or so."

An average brood for a faery family. Though Sidney would certainly consider the advantages of nanny pixies should she ever push out a brood so large. Perhaps ten would be reasonable. No chance of any children getting forgotten or unfed then.

She sighed. "I hope you get your wish. You'd make a great father."

"You think? Thanks. You'd be a great mother."

"Right." The man was in the market for a family. The idea wasn't half so frightening to her now as it had been when he'd first revealed his insistent need for family.

He'd softened her, and she liked the feeling.

"So how'd you manage to stick around this town for so long?" he asked. "I thought all Night Workers were reassigned yearly."

"I follow the rules. Keep a clean record and don't rock any boats. You can put in for renewal at the end of a service year if you want to, and I do. I like this town. It's a great place to live."

"Huh. I usually use up my three strikes before the year is up. But I've seen a lot of the world that way."

"You like to travel?"

"Getting tired of it lately. Like I said, family . . ."

"Yeah," Sidney agreed on a sigh.

"You're an amazing woman, Sidney. Far too upstanding for the likes of me."

"Don't say that. I'm just a woman who needs . . ." *love*.

A small part of her resisted that confession. It wasn't right. It could never be right. He was the means to her decline, the utter destruction of all she had worked for.

So why didn't her achievements mean as much now that she was sitting next to Dart?

"You need what?" he prompted.

"Nothing. I'm satisfied, like you. You seem perfectly at ease with the life you've made for yourself."

"There are things about me that need to, well . . . slow down first. I'm all about instant gratification. Totally opposite you. I don't think I'd have the patience to stay in the MR without, well, you know."

"Having sex as often as you like?"

He smirked. "I'm not that much of a stud. But I do have needs."

"I have those same needs. I've overlooked them lately. But I'm afraid, Dart. I don't want to screw up this great situation I have here in the MR."

"You need to learn to fly under the Realm's radar."

"Yeah? Like you do so well, Mr. One Strike and I'm Out?"

"True. But I can help with your other needs. The personal ones."

Like sex. Neither spoke it, but Sidney sensed both thought of it. Talk about white elephants. This one glowed.

"Let's rock"—Dart nodded toward the bed—"before puss pounces."

Sidney hadn't noticed the cat had jumped to the bed. It flicked its tail and prepared for a leap. They both took to flight as the feline sprang. A tormented meow accompanied the cat's graceless fall from the edge of the drawer. Claws tore through wood as the beast clattered to the floor.

Sidney followed Dart down the hall, her hand in the sandman's. They stopped to hover before a collection of photographs hanging on the wall.

"I think I know how you can keep your job. It'll be a backup plan should my not dusting have little effect tonight." Dart reached for Sidney and pushed back her hair over a shoulder. Such a gentle act. She bowed her head. "Are you willing to try?"

"I'll try anything once."

"Oh, yeah? Now you're starting to sound like me."

He leaned in and cupped the back of her head. Sidney knew what was coming, and she closed her eyes.

A mid-air kiss was delightful. Wings fluttering and heart thumping, the intensity increased with their motion and the adrenaline pumping through her wings. He traced her lips with his tongue.

The touch scurried all through her body. Her nipples perked. Had she been wearing underwear, it might have grown moist. She became even softer than when he'd just been holding her.

The low moan that hummed from Dart's throat told her he enjoyed the kiss as much as she. Would he dust her?

Sidney couldn't risk falling into a dead snore. Not with a cat prowling nearby.

When she opened her eyes, she focused on the picture over Dart's shoulder. A mortal girl with blond pigtails, probably ten years old, leaned against the trunk of a blue Chevy truck.

"License plates in Florida!" Sidney shouted.

"Wha—?" Dart was still surfacing from the kiss.

"That's it!" She shot down the hallway toward the open window. "She grew up in Florida. It wasn't my territory. Some other idiot tooth faery forgot her. It wasn't me!"

Chapter

11

"I'll take this one." Vanessa Henderson set the book *Analyzing Your Dreams* on the counter, her library card gleaming on top.

Sidney slashed the card, then tried a bit of conversation: "Dreaming about flying?"

"I wish." Vanessa blushed.

Whoa. What had she said?

Vanessa looked left and right. There was no one in the library, but she practiced caution with a low whisper. "I've been dreaming about a sexy man."

"Nothing wrong with that, is there?"

"No, but he's only four inches tall. What do you think that means?"

Pushing the book across the counter, Sidney merely shrugged and kept back the laughter until Vanessa exited.

"No way," Sidney sputtered on giggles when the library was clear. "I wonder if Dart knows she's dreaming of him? He's such a stud, even the mortal women dream about him."

My stud, she thought. Which reminded her, if she wanted to keep said stud, she had some research to do.

Slipping into the office, she then tapped into the Faery

database through her ScryeTracker™. Her contact took the necessary info: child's name, date, location.

"Sandra Hanson. Female," the systems operator repeated. "Age: thirty-six mortal years. Current city of residence: Reverie, Minnesota. Er, right. That was a casualty from the er . . . *incident.*"

"Incident?" Sidney stared into the handheld like it was going to combust.

"Can't give you details. You're not authorized. Let's just say that's why Night Workers are not allowed to fraternize. Things go wrong. Teeth get forgotten. Flowers die. Birthday parties are minus faery godmothers. Anything else you need, Tooth?"

"Erm, no?"

"Before you go . . . there's a notation on your record here. Having a little trouble in Reverie, are you?"

"What makes you say that?" They knew. Of course, she'd known they would know.

"You haven't picked up a TLFR in days."

Because none had been reported. Duh.

"Well, that's not unusual," Sidney quickly replied. "It's a small town. Teeth go in cycles. Some days, kids drop them like marbles. Other days, there's nary a toothbrush taken out at bedtime. No problems here—"

"Hold on, Tooth. Sidney Tooth. Reverie registered tooth faery number one-seven-eight," the operator said, now all business. "Prepare for retrieval. You've got twenty-four mortal hours."

"But—"

"Signing out."

Sidney dropped the ScryeTracker™ onto the desk with a clatter. Retrieval in twenty-four hours? Her stomach flip-flopped like a claustrophobic koi in a kiddie pool.

"Retrieval?" She plopped onto the creaking office couch, arms spread.

Was all hope lost?

"I hope your plan works, Dart. Or I'm one recalled faery."

Dart's plan to *not* dust the mortal mothers could go off without a hitch. Unless the mothers avoided sex for reasons beyond Sidney's understanding. It was entirely possible they had good sex lives but were just naturally uptight.

"He knows what he's doing. He seems to be up on skulking about and flying under the radar. He's like a mortal James Bond. Mostly. Okay, not so much. More like a surfer Casanova. All gold eyes and charming smiles. And those huge wings," she said appreciatively.

Her thoughts easily drifted from dire to desire. "No fraternization, eh?"

Though, apparently, a lot of hanky-panky was overlooked, so long as the faeries didn't do *relationships* in the MR. Which explained why Dart hadn't been written up on his numerous—make that hundreds—of infractions.

Hundreds? It was an uneducated guess. For all she knew, it could be—no, not thousands. Never.

"Don't think about it, Sidney. He's in your hands now."

And with imminent retrieval looming over her shoulders, why—Sidney snapped upright. Fists formed. She didn't give a fruiting toadstool about the rules. Fraternization? Bring it!

But she couldn't jump into the pool without a solid plan. So far, her adventures with the faery sex god of Reverie had proven entertaining but far from satisfying.

What was so special about Dart that she was willing to work with his problem? She wasn't so desperate she couldn't consider the next guy who fluttered by. Okay, so they didn't flutter by her. Ever.

"He's different. He . . . likes me for who I am, polka

dots and all. So what about who *he* is? Why the uncontrollable dusting? Is it because he gets excited too quickly? How to slow the dude down? Or maybe I need to speed up, beat him to the punch? Hmm . . ."

That did make sense. There hadn't been a chapter about it in the sex manual, but she was smart; she could figure this out.

She deserved a wild affair with a sexy sandman. And she now had a deadline. Twenty-four mortal hours before all chance to have sex with the sexiest night-duster she had ever known was ripped from her needy grasp.

It was time to go for it.

How to win the heart of a woman who had seen it all, and had little patience for a faery with a dusting affliction?

Keeping his promise to Sidney, to avoid the houses of any mother with a child who had a loose tooth, Dart muddled on the park bench. He wore glamour, and a mortal man walking by on the sidewalk nodded in acknowledgment. Not far from where Dart sat, flower faeries tended their blossoms. Little glowing faery lights blinked suggestively violet.

They wanted him.

He wanted them.

No, he didn't.

Really?

"Yes, really."

Closing his eyes and leaning back against the bench, Dart put a vision of Sidney into his thoughts. Saucy, eccentric, and so attractive. He couldn't pinpoint what it was about her, but he knew whenever she was around, he felt great. Better than with the twitter-flies.

She appealed to parts of him that he'd been unaware he possessed until now. Parts that made him want to protect her from harm, sadness, or disappointment. And another part of him simply wanted to see her look at him with respect.

"Because she's a real woman."

No silliness, no giggling attempts to bed him for the mere sake of bedding him. Sidney did have a kooky side, and he liked her laughter. And how many women were so easily impressed by floss?

Close by, the air vibrated. Dart opened one eye. As he'd thought, a flower faery buzzed near his head.

He reached up and flicked the faery away with a snap of his forefinger. As she bounced and bobbled through the air, her protests stirred up an entire brigade of twitterflies. But they weren't angry, no. One of their ranks had been refused? The sandman was free game.

A swarm of violet-winged faeries aimed for him, and began to tangle in his hair and sit upon his shoulder. Their seductive whispers initially enticed, but then memory of Sidney's bluebell laughter resounded in his brain.

"Enough!"

He dusted the entire swarm.

Faery lights hung in the air, momentarily suspended, then dropped. Tiny sleeping bodies littered the ground at his feet.

"That's right." Dart carefully stepped over the fallout. "This sandman is no longer interested."

Time to bring out the big guns.

Sidney slammed the clothing on hangers down the metal bar. The depths of her closet were revealed. It was dark. It gave off a dull sequin glint. She hadn't been back there in years, perhaps decades.

"I remember that one dress. . . ."

Squeezing in through the crush of clothing and the wall, Sidney inserted herself into the musty darkness.

Polka dots dusted her knees and creaky vinyl knee-high boots crunched beneath her bare feet.

Working completely by feel, she scavenged the dismal depths of her pitiful life. The last time she'd worn that pillbox hat—she didn't even want to know.

The vinyl rain slicker with the Day-Glo smiley faces? "What in a hobbit's footbrush had I been thinking?"

Sequins brushed her cheek. The balloon-like sleeves of a velvet number muffled her breathing and she had to shove forcefully to push a spot clear to stand in.

And then she felt it. The soft glide of jersey. It was thin and red. She'd glamourized it to fit her years back after overdosing on episodes of *Sex and the City*.

"Time to let this faery out to play."

Chapter

12

A huge bouquet of white daisies with yellow centers greeted her. Sidney looked over the officious bunch of weeds, offered in clutched fingers. Dirt-crusted roots grew from the bottom of the bouquet. She smirked.

"I'll have you know Mrs. Larson next door doesn't take kindly to thieves."

Dart dropped his hand, swinging the flowers at his side. He tried a weak smile. "What about you? I thought these might have less pollen than the lilies."

"Achoo!" She turned and walked through the living room.

Dart tossed the flowers over his shoulder. They landed on the stoop next to the other heaps of wilted, rejected offerings.

"Give it up on the flowers, will you?" Sidney rubbed her itchy nose.

"All right, the flowers are history. Good thing I brought this for you, too."

Something wondrous sat upon the sandman's hand. Sidney didn't have to look close; she knew exactly what it was.

A Turbo 6000 SuperSwift Toothbrush/Tongue Cleaner/Palette Pleaser®.

Sidney grasped the holy grail.

The handle was carved from Brazilian rain forest trees that had fallen naturally, not been cut by deforestation crews. The bristles were not plastic but rather a natural substance that gave plaque a kick in the patootie. And it had an engine—yes, an engine—that vibrated the entire head across the surface of the tooth 6,000 revolutions per second. Yeah, that was per *second*, baby.

"I think I'm . . . in . . ." *Love?*

No, too soon for that confession. But the sandman had just handed her a key to her heart. He *understood* her.

Sidney dove in for a kiss. Which was forceful. It toppled Dart from his feet. They landed on the couch, their lips still locked.

No man treated her so special and then slipped away like a shadow at high noon. The body crushed against hers, so solid and fierce, fit to her like butter to bread. The cinnamon taste of his mouth worked like an aphrodisiac. And the toothbrush wielded in her hand became her sword of triumph.

The sandman wasn't getting out of her house unmolested this afternoon. That's just the way it had to be.

"You're wearing something new," he managed between kisses and gropes. "Red?"

"You like it?" Sidney gripped the front of his shirt and tore it open. Buttons popped. One plastic disk pinged Dart's nose, landing on his forehead. She snapped the rogue button away. "I thought I'd try something closer to current fashion, give or take a mortal decade. A little less outrageous, a lot more—"

"Sexy and delicious. You are a wanton, Sidney."

"Got a problem with that?"

The sandman squinted as he gave it a brief think. "Not at all."

Shrugging his fingers back through his tousled hair, he looked her over. Sidney sensed a bit of shock, maybe . . . reluctance?

"Oh, no, it's going to happen this time." She moved closer, but he stopped her renewed attack with an abrupt palm.

"It is, Sidney. But give me time to catch my breath. And look at you. Let *me* look at you. Woman, you are more beautiful than a meadow glittering with glow bugs on a dreamy summer night."

The way he breathed the words tickled fiery tingles along Sidney's spine and over her scalp. And the way his eyes slowly traveled her body, starting there, at her breasts, caressed by the red jersey, and moving along her waist and lower, heated her all over. But she didn't need stoking—she was already there.

Sidney leaned back against the couch arm, propping her elbows. She stretched out her legs, bending one, and when she did so, the jersey slid up to her thigh. *There, look at me,* the pose said.

It made her feel wondrous to have the sandman ogle her. But it wasn't a blatant, *hey, baby,* kind of stare. No, this one touched her. There. And there, on her hard, tight nipples. And oh, there, where she squeezed her legs tight to trap the sensation of wanting to fly.

There would be no flying today. Grounded and naked was how Sidney intended this afternoon to proceed.

"It's not too much?" she asked, tugging at the slim line of the skirt.

"It's all I need." Dart leaned over her and kissed the top of her breast. "If I weren't wearing a glamour, my wings would give me away. Why *are* we wearing glamour? We're alone, Sidney. There are no mortals to see us."

"Point taken." An uncomfortable cringe attacked her sudden slip into wanton sex goddess. "Er, you first."

"Gladly."

With a magnificent toss of his head and a shimmy of his shoulders, Dart shook off his glamour. Wings unfurled and curled slightly forward. Moonglow radiated from his skin. And his eyes beguiled with golden enchantments.

Sidney sighed.

"Now you," he encouraged. "There's no reason to be shy. You can be yourself with me, Sidney. Don't you trust me?"

"Of course." So why was she suddenly skittish? She'd started this foreplay, and she wanted to ride it to the glorious finale. "I just . . . It's been so long. I've become used to wearing glamour. To being . . . mortal."

"You've become so attached to the MR, you're not sure where you belong anymore."

He had that one almost right. "I belong here, serving as the town's tooth faery. But as for what I do when I'm not working the night job . . ."

Dart took her hand and placed it over his heart. "You belong here, Sidney. You are a faery, not a mortal. Be one. For me?"

The stud was right on the toadstool.

Sidney nodded. "I've spent so much time in the MR. I'm this close to being completely mortal. I don't want to become Sidney the Faery, and end up sitting on a park bench gnawing Krispy Kremes. I want to be me. Sidney Tooth."

"Do you trust me, Sidney?"

"Of course I do."

"Then show me," he said.

Right. She was Sidney Tooth. Reverie registered tooth faery number 178. She was smart. Strong. Caring. Not so bad on the eyes, either. She knew exactly what she wanted in life. A good secure job, a home to raise a family, and some twisty sheets.

So why not be herself?

Sidney pushed away from Dart and stood. Hands to hips, she drew in a breath—and held it.

Could she do this? Taking this step meant abandoning her uptight, rigid alliance to the rules, and very possibly her position here in the MR.

Deep in Dart's eyes, the twinkle of trust and admiration flashed at her.

One self, coming right up!

Sidney shook back her head and released the glamour. Her frizzy mortal hair grew lush, wavy, and moss-colored as it spilled to her elbows. As her wings spread and unfurled, the red jersey slid from her shoulders to hug the tops of her arms and nestle upon her breasts.

Dust glittered about her.

The release of glamour felt as if she'd shucked off chains. The air felt lighter. Her breaths came more quickly, seasoned with joy. Sidney let out a sigh and went with the freeing feeling.

When she opened her eyes, Dart's wings shimmered and waved gently—they were violet.

"I've got to have you now." He wrapped his arms about her waist. "Sidney, I adore you. Not just because you're beautiful, but also because you're unique. You're tough. You're feisty. You're hot. You are like no other faery in this realm."

"Mighty kind of you to say, Sandman. I want you, too, no matter the consequences. It's time this faery started living. But we're going my speed tonight." She stood on tiptoes to inspect his gaze. His eyes glittered with want. An aura of moonbeams spat from him like tiny sun storms. "And . . . I'm going first."

"Huh?"

"That's right." She sashayed past him, destination: the bedroom. "Me first, then you."

"I don't understand?" He followed her like a good little sandman.

"You will, Studman, you will."

It was all in the perspective. The sandman obviously functioned via visual images and arousal, as did all males of any species. So Sidney turned off the lights and pulled the shades. They could still see in the darkness, but the shadows softened the curves and emphasized the sultry mood. It slowed the pace, which was what she initially wanted.

She made sure to undress Dart before she completely stripped. His wings curled forward and stroked her cheeks, a warm summer breeze to her cool autumn flesh. The sensation shivered through her body and rocketed out her toes.

She touched him all over, running her fingertips lightly, teasingly, over the abs that felt like polished stone, beneath his pecs, and down the inside of his strong arms. And that wings-to-private-parts ratio of comparison? So right on the mark.

Huge.

Breathing rapidly, the sandman raced toward incoherency. "Sidney, I can't . . ."

. . . hold off much longer. Close to dusting, Sidney sensed, so she switched to rocket speed.

She shoved Dart hard. He landed on the bed. The rough move gave him pause, knocking him out of ultra-lust mode and into startled wonder.

Just what she needed. A pause to his overwhelming and hummingbird-fast libido.

Lifting her skirt to her thighs, Sidney crawled onto

Dart. He didn't protest her forwardness and, in fact, moaned appreciatively as she fit herself onto his huge, hard length and went for the ride.

The trip was short, but she wasn't complaining. Climax rocketed her toward a slippery edge she had no desire to grasp. Soaring over that edge, she dug her fingers into Dart's sun-burnished hair, and called out as orgasm streaked through her body.

She'd done it.

And as her wave began to drift away, Dart mounted the top of his. The edge tempted him closer, and he surfed it. He called out, "Tooth faeries rock!" and climaxed.

Dust glittered about their embrace.

Sidney dropped into a snore.

"I get it now," Dart said. Sidney yawned after being shaken awake. "You first, then me. It worked!"

"And it was good," she agreed sleepily.

"Really? Even though you had to hurry?"

"Better than elderberry wine and chocolate-dipped strawberries. I figure with a little practice we could get slower and slower. I may even be able to stay up past the morning news."

"You're the best, Sidney. No other faery would have been so selfless."

"Selfless? I took my pleasure first, in case you hadn't noticed."

"But you did it so we could both come."

"Yes. You just need to learn patience, Dart."

"I've always been impatient. If I want something, I get it. I don't wait around. Guess that comes through in my sex life as well. Here I thought it was some childhood thing that I needed therapy for. You're perfect, Sidney."

"I wouldn't go quite so far. But I have been known to have my moments. Ready for another go?"

"Only if you're ready for another nap."

Hours later, Sidney counted five orgasms and four cat-naps. Not a bad tally for an afternoon well spent.

As Dart exited the shower, scrubbing his hair with a towel, he sang a pop tune all the mortal kids were currently raving about. He shook his entire six-foot-plus body, wings flinging droplets about the room and across the sheets.

"You are worse than a dog."

"But you like me anyway?"

An irresistible smile curled her mouth, and her whole body tingled with the delicious lingering vibrations of after-sex. "I think I just may."

"You don't commit easily, do you?"

"I can't help but wonder how the rules are going to interfere with our liaisons. Dart, I don't break the rules; I follow them. I don't want this to end, but you know . . ."

"No fraternization between Night Workers. It's easy to get around those rules. I do it all the time."

"Yeah, but I have a feeling all those *fraternizations* have been overlooked for the very fact they all lasted less than ten minutes. Am I right?"

He sighed.

"Come here, you big hunk of sex god."

Dart crawled onto the bed and snuggled next to her. The wet from the shower shimmered like jewels on his moonglow flesh.

"I'm saying a relationship might be harder to hide from the guild. We've got to be careful. I don't want to get sent back to Faery now that I've found someone I want to spend all my off-hours with." *Yawn.* "You know?"

"I won't tell a soul."

"They have ways of tracking us."

"I know. I've always wanted to be off the radar, you know? Suits my free and easy lifestyle."

"If you were off the radar you wouldn't be able to work as a sandman."

"Yeah, but I don't define my life by my job, Sidney. I could do anything if I put my mind to it."

"In this realm? How would you live? You don't have a mortal job."

"I've got my ways. Let's not worry about it just yet. First, I want to save your job, because it is so important to you."

"Thanks for understanding."

"It's what I like about you, Sidney. You have a purpose, and you don't sway from that. It's all about the kids."

"It is. And their Belief only grows thinner the closer this tooth faery gets to retrieval."

"We ready to enact the backup plan?"

Sidney yawned, tracing the edges of sleep. "Right behind you, Studman."

Chapter

13

"You tired?"

Sidney stifled a yawn behind her palm. "What makes you think that?"

The sandman's dust packed a heck of a wallop. This relationship would take some work, but she was determined. Certainly, she couldn't argue with being well rested.

"Sidney?"

A nudge stirred her from insistent slumber. "I'm good, I'm good."

"We should leave now. There's not much time."

"I know. The plan. To save . . ."—*yawn*—"the . . ."

"The tooth faery!" He tickled her.

Sidney shrieked out laughter and rolled from the bed to land on the heaped bedspread on the floor. "All right! I'm awake! Let's do this!"

Ten minutes later, they were dressed, and ready for action. Tight, dark blue jeans emphasized Dart's huge attributes. And Sidney intended to make sure no flutter-twits ever got their hands on *that* again.

Herself, she'd searched her closet for an understated outfit (no small task). Finally, Dart paged through a magazine and showed her a picture of a fashion model. Perfect.

Sidney glamourized the look. Simple black leggings and a fitted black T-shirt. Stealth and blending with the surroundings were necessary for reconnaissance work.

When Dart got an eyeful of her figure, hugged in all the right places by the clingy black fabric, he tugged her into his embrace. A kiss beneath her chin stirred up silly shivery bumps along Sidney's arms, and she giggled.

"I love your laughter, Sidney. It's like rain on bluebells. Let me see if a touch here, under your breast where I know you're ticklish, will make you laugh again."

"Chill, big boy. I'm not sure I can stay awake as it is."

"Right. We have a mission. But first." He grabbed her hand and led her outside to the front stoop, cluttered with wilted flowers. "I want to be with you, Sidney."

"I know that. I do, too."

"I mean forever. And I'm willing to do whatever it takes to make it happen."

She smiled, but it was forced. Whatever it would take was asking too much of him. Forever wasn't possible so long as they both belonged to the Night Worker's Guild. "Let's just get through tonight, all right?"

"All right, lover."

Sidney hid another yawn behind her hand before she turned to kiss her lover. "Let's stop and get some Red Bull at the gas station first. Fruiting stones, what's that?"

Dart mounted the huge street chopper parked in front of her house. "Hop on, baby. Now I'm going to take you for a real ride."

"I thought . . ." That they'd get small and fly.

The deafening rumble of the engine startled Sidney so she almost fell from the stoop. "That's not what I'd call stealth!" she shouted over the roar.

The sight of the powerful faery sandman seated upon a huge titanium monster did things to her resolve.

Resolve? Turkish toadstools, it did things to her libido.

Did they have time for a quickie? On the bike?

"Stones. Let's do this before my tawdry sex goddess crown sparkles so brightly I attract all the resident faeries."

They arrived at the Hanson house and fluttered outside the mother's bedroom door. Sidney pulled a white dust mask out of her pocket and pulled it on, placing it over her nose and mouth.

"What?" She caught Dart's confused expression. "It's a safety measure. You know, in case you decide to get crazy with the dust."

"I understand. You might catch some residual dust. No problem, sweetie. I still love you."

Sidney paused, halfway into the room. She spun about, wings fluttering madly. "You what?"

"Love you." He flew by her, brushing her forehead with a barely tangible kiss. "Cat's here," he said.

Sidney joined his side. *Love, eh? Ah. Well. Great. Nice.* "I guess I um, er . . ."

"You what?" He focused on the cat across the room, sleeping on top of the open dresser drawer where the baby teeth were stashed. "Get all horny with a medical mask over your face? Can't wait to jump me?"

"Are you going to dust the woman, or what?"

"Not until you finish your sentence, Sidney. What is it you guess about me?"

"I don't guess anything. I love you, all right?" She punched him on the arm. "Now get to work. Dust the woman while I distract the cat."

Rubbing his arm, Dart flew over the bed. "Gotta love a woman who likes it rough."

The two of them had known that Dart couldn't *not* dust this mortal woman, as he had the others. She was divorced, so it wasn't as though a sound sleep was making her dissatisfied and grumpy.

With a grand motion of his hands, Dart dusted Sandra Hanson, who was already sleeping. No chance would be taken tonight.

Sidney flew toward the cat, pushing up her sleeves as she did. "Here, kitty, kitty," she called. "You want a piece of me?"

The cat sat upright, sniffing the air. Its whiskers flickered. It looked directly at Sidney and narrowed its wicked gaze.

"I know, I'm so sexy you want me, don't ya?" Sidney teased. She turned and tugged down the back of her pants, mooning the feline.

It was probably the tongue-sticking-out part that really pissed off the cat. The feline leapt, slashing the air with razor claws, but missed Sidney and landed on the floor with a frustrated meow.

"Huh?" Anorexia Divorsosa stirred on the bed.

"More dust!" Sidney cried, and then bulleted toward her furry opponent.

"Got it!" Dart, in position over the dresser drawer, redirected aim and flew back over the pillow.

Sandra Hanson woke and saw the faery glowing like a shard of moonlight. "What the—?"

A shower of dust spumed her face. Her head dropped onto the pillow, blond curls splaying over her gaping mouth.

Sidney flew back and forth at the end of the bed, luring the faery-ichor-hungry feline in her wake. "Hurry, Dart! Get the teeth!"

"Working on it!" He soared down to the box and lifted the lid.

Meanwhile, Sidney lost sight of the cat. She hovered next to the dresser, catching her breath. "How you doing, Dart?"

"It's heavy!"

"Just get them out, and I'll take care of the transport. Yeiih!"

She hadn't seen the feline sneaking under the king-size bed. Sidney's reaction time was limited. Two furry paws pinned her to the thick Berber carpet.

Dart dragged the tin of teeth out from the underwear drawer and dropped it to the dresser top with a clatter. He swung a look to the bed. Still snoring.

"Should have changed size for this," he muttered, pushing the tin toward the edge of the dresser. "I don't know how she does it. Course, she only has the one tooth to retrieve. Wonder where she carries the money? Must be a tooth faery trade secret."

Like his dust. Only that was a secret he was trying to tame. And Sidney had helped him. He'd actually had sex with a woman, and brought her to orgasm *before* dusting her to a snore. Who would have thought?

He really was the studman she claimed him to be.

"Nice, Dart. You *are* the faery."

But he still had a lot of work to do. Fast was fun, but he wanted to linger with Sidney, draw out her pleasure, and make her so giddy that she dusted him. He'd meant it when he'd said he wanted to spend forever with her. But that wasn't going to happen without sacrifice and hard work.

Sidney was right; he needed to learn patience, to delay gratification. It would be tough, but the learning part— which involved Sidney, naked—would be worth the challenge.

He sat on the corner of the mint tin and leaned backward onto his palms. "Stars, but I love the woman. Any chick who can tame my dust problem, *and* kick a cat's—"

It suddenly struck Dart—he didn't hear anything. Not

the sound of mortal snoring, or the sound of a faery's wings frantically fluttering as she led the furry white predator on a goose chase.

Diving to the edge of the dresser, Dart peered toward the floor. The cat had his woman pinned, and as far as he could see, Sidney wasn't moving.

"That—that . . . underskinker!"

He dove.

"What the hell is going on?"

Dart put on the brakes mid-air. The mortal sat upright on the bed. He'd already overdosed her. "How much dust does one mortal need to stay asleep?"

Hanging there, Dart looked down. The cat flicked its tail madly. The love of his life lay pinned beneath vicious clawed paws.

To his left, Sandra Hanson crawled across the thick down bedspread. Being seen by a mortal would surely see him instantly retrieved back to Faery.

But nothing was going to hurt his woman.

"I'm coming, Sidney!"

Dart rocketed downward. He landed on a mass of fur and whiskers. Impossible to get a grip on the silky thick stuff. Sprawling out his limbs, he managed to grope and secure whiskers with both hands. Demonic green cat eyes held his stare.

Faeries made tasty kitty treats. Dart had lost a good friend last year after a run-in with a Persian prizewinner. Nasty ball of fluff. He still couldn't banish the image of his friend's wings sticking out from the cat's mouth.

The beast shook its head, Dart plastered across its face.

"I don't think so!" Dart yelled. "No cat is taking this faery down."

He couldn't get a look at the ground. "Sidney?"

"I am not awake," boomed out from the edge of the

bed. "I have to be dreaming. Pussums, what is that awful thing on your face?"

"One very brave sandman," Sidney said as she fluttered by Dart.

"You're alive!" he yelled, and then the cat flung him across the room. The wall caught his flailing faery limbs with a smack and a crack of wing.

"Big nasty bugs!" the mortal woman cried.

Dart shook his head to jar the reverberations of the landing. Just in time, he opened his eyes to see a paw swipe toward his face. Claws glinted with deadly threat. He dodged but took a cut to his shoulder. He shook off the pain and flew beneath the cat's belly. Long cat fur tickled his shoulders.

Dart chuckled, and dusted the cat. The feline dropped.

"Why didn't you think of that in the first place?" Sidney called from her position on the dresser. She wielded a crisp dollar bill, folding it to shove into the Altoids tin.

"My dust has never worked on animals before," Dart said. "You must have worn the critter out for me."

Then he soared up to float before the mortal's face. Blond curls *poinged* here and there. Pink tape stuck across each eyebrow peeled back like cringing caterpillars.

"You're so stubborn even the sandman's dust won't put you out." He then made a rude gesture he'd seen Sidney perform earlier.

The mortal woman's eyes rolled backward; she wobbled, and passed out.

"An offensive gesture," Sidney said, joining Dart's side. "That'll do it every time for the leader of the Hyper-Anal No-Fun Brigade."

"You okay?" He turned and gripped her by the shoulders, inspecting her from crown to toe. "You don't look the worse for wear, but you could have broken bones, inner trauma."

"I'm fine." She tugged down the dust mask. "A little stunned a cat finally got the better of me. If you hadn't jumped on it when you did, I might be kitty nibble right now. You saved my life, Dart."

Dart hugged her. "Promise me you'll never do a dangerous thing like that again?"

"Now that would be a tough promise to keep. What say we go haggle over the possibilities of it between the sheets?"

"You got the teeth?"

"All collected and sent to central receiving," she confirmed, fluttering out of the bedroom.

Dart followed her down the hallway and into the living room. "Should take you off the retrieval list, eh?"

"Let's hope so. Oh, Dart, there's ichor on your shoulder."

He puffed up his chest and Sidney pressed her hand over the wound. He was warm and had been working hard. She loved the smell of him, all ichor and virility and residual dust. Her hero.

"A claw slashed at me hyper-speed," he said. "Nothing to worry about. War wound—wait one spriggan second."

"What?" She searched her lover's eyes but couldn't figure what he was thinking about.

Dart groaned, gripped his chest, and dropped, landing on the plush cushion of the couch.

"Dart!"

"Maybe it's bigger than a wound," he muttered, moaning and coiling in on himself. "Aggh! I think . . . I've been killed."

"What?" He was joking, surely. The ichor had already stopped dripping—

"Call it in to headquarters," he gasped, reaching for her hand and dramatically clutching at his chest. "I'm down. I'm hit. Dart Sand is no more."

"Dart, I don't understand. What are you . . ." And then a mini LED lit above Sidney's head. "Right. The sandman is dead. I'll contact them immediately."

She whipped out the ScryeTracker™ and dialed in to headquarters.

"We've just received an entire set of Sandra Hanson's teeth," the operator confirmed as a greeting. "Good going, number one-seven-eight. Your retrieval has been marked in abeyance."

"Great. But I'm calling to report a fallen sandman."

"Which one is that? Let's see, Dart Sand is the Reverie sandman. What's up, Tooth?"

"He's dead," she said, perfectly calm but with a wink to Dart. "Cat got him."

"Eww. That's never pretty. I'll send in cleanup immediately."

"Unnecessary," she hastened. "There's . . . nothing left to clean up. He was swallowed whole."

The operator made a gagging noise. "Very well. Thanks for reporting the casualty, Tooth. We'll get a new sandman on the job immediately. Signing out."

Sidney tucked away the ScryeTracker™ and bent over Dart, who now lay casually across the couch, smiling.

"You're good at the sneak, you know that, Sidney?"

"I've never lied to headquarters before."

"But don't you see? We did it. I don't exist in the MR now. We can be together without worry of breaking any rules."

"Clever. But you gave up your job. For me?"

"I couldn't imagine a day without you in my arms. I need you, Sidney."

"You do?"

"Come here and kiss me, darling."

Dart's kiss was better than anything Faery had to offer. Toadstools, his kiss could make everything *in* Faery more palatable. Because when she was in his arms, the rest of the world didn't matter. She loved this sandman, and he'd sacrificed for her.

"I need you, too, Dart. Let's make this work. What's this?" She shrugged her fingers through her lover's hair and pulled out a long white cat whisker. "You know these things are good luck?"

Dart took the whisker and tucked it into Sidney's hair. It stuck out like a flecheless feather, but it looked regal nonetheless. He drew back and asked, "So what do you say to some permanent fraternization?"

Epilogue

Reverie Elementary School was in the midst of Dental Hygiene Week. Sandra Hanson had volunteered to take the second-grade class on a field trip to the dentist. As the last kid scrambled to find a seat on the bus, Sandra clapped once for attention. All eyes turned to her.

She shoved up the bridge of her black-rimmed glasses. "Remember, kids, brush two times a day. Floss, and keep your teeth sparkling for when the Tooth Fairy comes."

Eager nods and wide smiles revealed gaps where teeth had fallen out. Each sparkling gem had been placed under a pillow in hopes of the Tooth Fairy's visit.

"And don't forget," Sandra continued, "next week is Easter. Is everyone ready for the Easter Bunny?"

All through Reverie, mothers were relaxing and loosening their stringent rules. Kids laughed more. The Horticulture Club had even decided to donate the east garden, which never did flourish—cactuses, don't you know—to be a sandbox for the children.

It was as though the entire city had sighed—thanks to a few sleepless nights and some raging good sheet twisting.

* * *

Sidney switched off the ScryeTracker™. Her retrieval had been canceled. Since she and Dart had picked up Sandra Hanson's baby teeth, Sidney had been registering anywhere from six to a dozen TLFRs a night.

Life was back to normal. And yet, not.

To the Realm, Dart was dead. Which meant he could no longer work as a sandman. Unless he took on a new identity. Which he was keen to do. But not right away. He was simply enjoying being with Sidney during the few hours she had between night and day shifts.

Setting aside the ScryeTracker™ on the dresser beside a half-eaten bowl of strawberries, she then turned into the warmth of Dart's naked body. He slept peacefully on the new sheets she'd bought him for his birthday. Organic black cotton with white polka dots.

Hey, who said she had to go cold turkey? Certainly not her lover.

He'd already asked to move in with her and for her to quit the library. Seems he knew how to play the stock market, which was why he'd never needed a day job. She'd consider the offer. To have her days free to spend with Dart would be delicious.

But complete withdrawal from not breaking the rules would take time. She wanted to toe the line. If anyone ever found out about Dart, they'd both be on a fast retrieve back to Faery.

At least they'd be together.

This morning their foreplay had lasted a little longer than the previous morning. Dart had been able to hold off his dust, and he hadn't even minded when Sidney had grabbed the face mask from under the pillow seconds before he dusted. She was so proud of him.

"Dust me, lover," she whispered as her climax faded and the sparkle of his dust settled over her. "One more time."

A Little Bit Faery

BY LEANDRA LOGAN

Thanks to Monique Patterson and MaryJanice Davidson for taking on this project with enthusiasm. It's been such fun!

Thanks to my dear friends, Susan Johnson, Lois Greiman, and Michele Hauf, who supported my battle with breast cancer this year. I'm overwhelmed by your many kindnesses and feeling much better.

Finally, a double thanks to Nancy Yost who covered me on both fronts. Much appreciated.

Chapter

1

Isle of Man

It seemed Tia Mayberry had had one too many nectar fizzes. Again.

Or so observed the weary doortroll on duty at her lavish co-op, Treetop Towers, shortly after extracting her finger from the night buzzer.

"I'm perkily fine," she slurred, her buzzer finger landing on his chest. "You're bad, Woodburn. Leaving your pest, er, post."

"Pest" seemed more appropriate as Tia tumbled over the threshold into the bony troll's arms. Luna faeries were generally taller than most species of the Enchanted Realm, and this particular Fey was tallest of all. Not to mention more cushy at the curves. It always took some effort to right her on her high cork heels. "Tonight is different, Tia," Woodburn cautioned, giving her a shake.

"I'll say! I had to buzz and buzz. Who knows how much attention that fetched!"

Unfortunately, plenty. Rather than steer her toward the service elevator for her usual discreet ride upstairs, Woodburn drew her a glass of water at the front desk. "I've been down the hall at an emergency meeting of the co-op board," he explained. "Giving testimony about weekend shenanigans that have become intolerable. That threaten the sterling reputation of this singles co-op."

"Must be a real loser to slow that petty trio of Luna party bitches on a Saturday night," she mused. "Who is this miscreant? Uh, let me guess. The witch who brews yucky green smoke stew?"

"No."

"The pied pipers who lure pesky squirrels into the heating ducts?"

"No."

"Oh, I know. The goblins who—"

"The miscreant, Tia, is you."

"Me?" Tia squealed as Woodburn whisked her toward the meeting room. "Not *me*."

"I am truly sorry," he intoned, pushing her through the door.

Tia stumbled inside the bright room to find some milling tenants, who quickly parted ranks to reveal the Co-op Cuties. Glenda, Shante, and Keelee, stunning Luna specimens with wavy lavender hair, baby doll features, and huge lustrous wings sprouting from rail backs. They closed in on her now, their undulating bodies making their party dresses of purple, gold, and red shimmer.

Growing up with these Cuties had been tough due to Tia's many un-Luna-like characteristics. Though generally now more resilient to their gibes, she couldn't resist smoothing her straight waist-length platinum hair, tugging at the crocheted daisy minidress that clung to her ample curves.

"Where have you been?" Glenda taunted. "Out on the town or visiting Mamma?"

Agog with nectar fizz, Tia wondered which sounded worse: spending Saturday night with a parent or striking out on the dating scene long before midnight. Actually, both sort of sucked. "Does it really matter?" she spouted.

"Certainly it matters," Keelee insisted. "You carry the reputation of Treetop Towers every place you go."

"It's come to our attention that Treetops has taken quite a beating from you lately," Shante accused. "Reduced to the most common dives, slurping nectars squeezed from substandard plants. Rejected by everyone from hunched-back elves to sons of witches. Is it any wonder we hope you were at Mother's for a change?"

"So I've hit a rough social patch. It's wrong of you three to single me out this way."

"It isn't just us." Glenda smugly unfurled a sheet of paper in her hand.

Tia seized a horrified breath. "Is that . . ."

"A petition for expulsion," Glenda verified. "You know full well tenants pay good money for Treetop bragging rights, to be a part of our cutting-edge professionals network. It's come to our attention that you are single-handedly making us a laughingstock."

"I have a lease, authorized by the manager, Minkie himself."

"Pushed through with pressure from your mother. We know all the pathetic details. In any case, a lease can be broken with enough tenant signatures."

"It takes two-thirds in favor."

Glenda smiled at her list. "We've got that and then some."

Tia's heart fluttered in sheer panic. "All of you should understand my search for someone special."

"Search?" Glenda hooted. "It's become a desperate hunt!"

"'Hi, I'm Tia,'" Keelee mimicked. "'I live at lush Tree-tops Towers. Come back for a mergy merge merger?'"

"I don't sound like that!"

"When that ploy fails," Shante asserted sternly, "there's your early return to stagger drunkenly about the lobby."

"I try hard to sneak in," Tia admitted at some cost to her pride. "Woodburn takes me to the service elevator."

" 'Carries you' is more like it. And the agony doesn't end there. You pule into the night."

"That's humming, taught in yoga class here. I opt to sing away the pain."

"Excruciating pain, it seems." Glenda read on. " 'Described by tenants as tuneless. A keening wail. Ankle caught in bear trap. Cobra venom seizure.' " She paused. "Odd, as we Luna faeries are renowned for our lyrical voices, our siren ability to lure seafaring ships into the rocks. A difference," she thought to add, "as inexplicable as your tolerance for iron. Which segues us into another complaint about your menial job as a metalworker."

"Custom jeweler! And puling is in the ears of the beholder." Scalded, Tia snatched the paper away.

Glenda shrugged. "Help yourself. It's only a copy. Destroying it will not preserve your home here."

"Plainly, I don't belong here, after all. I will be out by midweek." On that, Tia whirled on her high cork shoes.

"Uh, Mayberry," Keelee intervened.

Tia did a slow swivel, gripping the paper tube in a tight, nervous fist.

"You're out tonight. Tomorrow is May first and we have a tenant waiting."

"Even more pressing, we have a social life waiting." Glenda glanced at her watch. "By the time we return, we trust you'll be long gone."

Head spinning in alcohol and anguish, Tia struggled for some comeback. "What about my damage deposit?"

"Waiting for you at the front desk. That's one thing we can say in your favor: you played it ultra-safe with the furnishings. No drunken lord or marauder ever broke as much as a teacup playing house with you."

"Not my fault!" Tia wailed. "I would've welcomed a drunken lord—most any marauder."

"Woodburn will help you pack," Shante offered. "And tip him well. He's the only one who offered."

It was nearing 3:00 A.M. when Tia arrived at her mother's cottage by the sea and slid a key in the lock. A spill of moonlight through the windows gave the modest furnishings of the living room a soothing glow.

As Tia hauled in her last suitcase she heard a clop of slipper on the staircase, caught the shadow of a winged figure bearing a lantern and hefty stick.

Whisking the door closed, Tia swiftly called out, "Only me, Mamma!"

"Tia, dear?" Maeve Mayberry galloped on, her long nightgown billowing.

"Don't be alarmed."

Maeve's alarm only deepened as she gazed upon the all too familiar cluster of worn leather suitcases.

Tia cringed. "Care to welcome home your long-lost daughter? Mamma? Mamma," she said more forcefully, "put down the stick."

Jerking to attention, Maeve slowly lowered the length of wood.

"Somebody might get clobbered," Tia chided.

Maeve's eyes narrowed slightly. "Yes."

Tia gently took the stick and the lantern from her mother's fisted grip and set them on a table. "I suppose you want an explanation."

"Don't see a way around it."

"Well, that co-op is full of snobs!"

"All your friends, Tia," Maeve said quietly.

"I grew up with them, yes. Or should I say I grew up alongside them?"

"Oh, child." Maeve sighed. "I thought with a little effort, you could manage to blend in, finally win them over."

"I tried. For eight long months, I tried."

"Exactly how bad are the damages?"

"They threw me out!"

"Oh, no." Maeve frowned. "That will take some fixing."

"Mamma! When will you accept that you can't mend my life like a holey sock! When will you allow me to simply be me?"

"Admit it, Tia. You've never been sure who you want to be. One minute you wanted to tame and tint your platinum hair Luna lavender; the next you were flaunting it like a wild unicorn's mane. You insisted on vibration lessons to lift and quicken your voice; then you were auditioning for the school choir with your low, flat thrum. You wanted lenses to green up your stark blue eyes; then you were accentuating them in blue powder. There was even that push to pull your square white teeth in favor of a false bridge of tiny cream pearls."

"Of course I was conflicted growing up. There isn't another creature on the Isle of Man who shares my characteristics."

"God blessed you in a very special way—"

"Oh, knock it off! I haven't bought that line in ages."

Maeve grimaced. "Just how did the board plead their case against you?"

Tia reached into her handbag for the crumpled petition. Maeve took it to the lantern. "Damn Minkie! In my day, a goblin was as good as his word."

"Wasn't his fault. The Co-op Cuties got enough signatures to override him."

"He should've intervened before it got this far. When I think of how I cooked for him . . ."

"All those lovely stews."

"Actually, the desserts were the most challenging."

"I don't remember any desserts."

Maeve cleared her throat and concentrated on the paper. "I thought that place would be the answer to my prayers."

"Surely you mean 'our prayers,' Mamma."

Maeve flashed a startled look. "Of course, dear. Mingling with that upscale crowd—flaunting that trendy address—seemed a surefire plan to put you on the fast track. In range of a handsome, successful lord smart enough to appreciate your qualities as I do. After all, one was all we really needed. . . ."

"While having the Treetops address got me into some cozy positions, something always went wrong. What, exactly, I have no idea. Do you?"

Maeve gave her fingers a nervous flutter. "Do I what, dear?"

"Have any idea why I am the last virgin standing of my generation!"

"Surely not the last."

"Even the crooked horned unicorns are—locking horns."

"I so hoped there was one male on the Isle destined to love you."

"That is one tale this faery isn't so sure of anymore."

"You mustn't give up until you've turned over every rock. Not literally, of course. Unless it becomes absolutely necessary," she added lamely.

Tia wrinkled her nose. "There must be a flaw in my strategy, Mamma. One I can't finger. Perhaps if you finally have the Talk with me, we can sort it out."

"Surely you jest."

"What, exactly, have you always found so difficult about the ages-old tradition? You tell me about mergence and I get all squirmy and shocked."

"You are twenty-eight—way too old."

"Even if it is a little past due and I'm no longer likely to get squirmy and shocked, I need help. Specifically tips for success."

"I am no expert," Maeve blustered. "I was dazzled once, by your father."

"A visiting Scandinavian lord on holiday," Tia dutifully recited, "struck down by a wicked Cailleach attempting to rob his fishing party."

Maeve hung her salt-and-lavender head. "Such a shame he never even knew you were on the way."

"About the Talk."

"A useless waste of energy, dear."

Tia bit her lip. "I suppose there's one consolation. I'll always have a home with you."

Maeve's silver brows jumped. "I thought you'd fight for your place at the Treetops. I mean, there is the principle to consider."

"I don't know. A new tenant is already set to move into my apartment."

"When?" Maeve demanded sharply.

"Tomorrow." Tia stifled a yawn behind her hand. "All I want to do now is curl up in my old comfy feather bed, in the home where I spent my happiest hours." She looked around the old fieldstone walls with a bittersweet smile.

"Uh, that won't be possible, Tia."

"What?"

"I've sort of turned your bedroom into a sewing room."

"Mamma!"

"I've always had that much confidence in your charms."

Tia scowled. "You mostly always wanted a sewing room."

"Can you blame me for indulging? I've been helping you pay for that crackerbox palace for eight months."

"Guess there's nothing for it, then. I'll have to sleep in your bed."

"Suppose we can try it. Unless you'd like to take the chaise," Maeve lilted, gesturing to a lumpy slope-backed sofa near the fireplace.

"You had it restuffed then?"

"Well, no."

An hour later, snuggled under a soft comforter in Maeve's cramped feather bed, Tia felt a sharp jab in the ribs. She sat up with a shriek. "Mamma! Are you having some kind of fit?"

"In a manner of speaking." Maeve turned up her bedside lantern.

Tia leaned into the light with a wizened look. "Did you eat pecans before bed again? You know they give you a fit of indigestion—"

"Tia, I nudged you on purpose. You have a very disturbing snore, dear."

"Ridiculous. I wasn't even asleep."

"You make a very loud sound all the same. Barely tolerable even when we had a stone wall and cork earplugs between us."

"You always said your collection of cork was for plugging mouse holes!"

"Some of them are— Never mind. What is the source of that sound?"

Tia sighed deeply. "Humming. The latest meditative trend among Treetop tenants. Everyone is doing it, Mamma."

"Really, when it was on the list of tenant complaints?"

"I suppose I may sound a little different from the others. But you've always fought prejudice in my name, encouraged me to follow my heart."

"Maybe we should have the Talk after all."

"You mean it?"

"Yes. I believe if I am to ever sleep again, we'll have to finally face the music, among other things."

Back downstairs in the kitchen nook, gossamer wings twitching, Tia shared a cup of tea with her mother at the old pine table.

"Now, Tia, tell me exactly what happens when you . . . mingle."

"Things start out fine. Males attracted to my exotic looks often are eager to get to know me. Many of them speak directly to my larger breasts, but I know my eyes can be kind of piercing at first sight."

"And then?"

"Things start to heat up with flirting, dancing, kissing."

"And—and—"

"Abruptly, the spell is broken. There's always a prior engagement remembered, or a headache, or a sickly parent in need of aid. The Isle of late seems teeming with throbbing noggins and ailing relatives."

"Do you, by chance, try to carry a tune?"

"Sometimes. But that doesn't seem the deal breaker. I've even tried to ask a male in mid-retreat with no success. No offense to the Luna species, but as I was fated to carry Father's genes, I wish his bravery and cleverness had been a bigger part of the mix. I'm out of nerve and strategies."

"As it stands, dear, I think you carry more than enough of your father."

Tia reared in astonishment. Maeve rarely spoke of Gustave and always glowingly. "What do you mean?"

"Gustave isn't quite who I made him out to be."

"You mean he wasn't a visiting faery lord?"

Maeve attempted a lilt. "The visiting part is true."

Dread began to well in Tia's stomach. "What are you saying?"

"Gustave wasn't a faery. Not even a Gustave!"

Tia was not a full-blooded faery? This meant not only that she didn't know who her father was, but that she didn't know *what* he was. "You wouldn't be this distressed over an elf or leprechaun," she speculated.

"And you wouldn't be a dazzling eleven hands tall!"

"Is Papa of the marine culture? A kraken?"

Maeve jerked her head.

"But he is an amphibian."

"Oh, yes. The bits of him you carry will never dissolve in salt water."

"A warlock, by chance?"

"Think lower. A lower species," she articulated.

"Just tell me, *please*."

Maeve sucked in a breath. "I'm afraid your father is human."

Tia's cry of denial was sharp and instant.

Maeve reached across the table and squeezed her hand. "It explains so much, doesn't it? Your ability to work with iron while the rest of us are repelled. Your general physical handicaps . . ."

"How did this happen? How could you let it?"

"It wasn't a well-thought-out decision, I admit. Your father was part of an American fishing party sailing the Irish Sea. They were drawn to the Isle by the sound of our musicians playing the 'Londonderry Air.' The large group debarked and followed the music to our glen. They joined our circular dance—"

"That old come-on."

"The music and movement of the reel are mesmerizing to humans! Especially visiting ones without the good sense or willpower to resist."

"They could not have joined in unless the clan allowed them to *see*."

"My crowd used to do such things for selfish amusement," Maeve confessed ashamedly. "Of all creatures, humans are so easy to manipulate, entrance."

"It's so unlike you to take advantage of a lesser creature."

"Normally, such a lark only involved harmless fun. But things got out of hand that night. We all drank too much."

"Well, you never could hold your nectar, could you?"

"It wasn't the tame honeysuckle you enjoy, but a human beverage from the ship—rum—blended with my family's strong elderberry wine. It surely packed a punch. Everyone at the party grabbed a partner. Unicorns mated with zebras. Manks with Siamese. Which explains some of the misshapen, misplaced horns and tails of your generation. Anyway, we made crazy love in the moonlit forest, in the dirt on a tangle of tree roots. Rough and earthy and uninhibited."

Tia watched her mother's eyes deepen to a wondrous emerald. Maeve an edgy lover? Giving herself to a limited human? Had the Isle of Man gone mad? "Maybe your head was so muddled, you remember the story wrong."

"Not on your life," Maeve purred. "The merger was incredible." Closing her eyes, she gave a snaky quiver beneath her prim cotton nightgown.

"So this mortal had his way with you and went on his way."

"Like most humans in his position, he likely woke up in the forest at dawn with a headache and, at most, a sketchy memory he mistook for a dream. He did have good intentions through the night, however. Even confided his address."

"Which you never followed up on."

"I was young and didn't want to risk the humiliation of his benightedness. At the time a cover-up seemed best for us. I naively figured you'd blend in."

"How strange, with all that revelry, I seem to be the only resulting human half-breed."

"Naturally, it was my hope to find you some company. Prejudice being so strong, however, I was leery of asking friends what effect the humans had on them. Especially wise, as everyone went on to pretend the event never happened. But believe that Blot and I always kept a lookout for any potential offspring."

"Blot knows?" Tia pictured the effusive leprechaun and cringed. "All these years, he's listened to my blither about Father without a complaint."

"He was essential from the start, hiding me until your birth, helping me concoct a Scandinavian faery lord to account for your fair hair and blue eyes."

"Funny Blot never tried to look up my father. As a pot of gold regulator for the Rainbow Council, he spends endless days in the Mortal Realm."

"I couldn't trust him with John's identity—John Winter is his full name. Blot felt my honor had been compromised, wanted satisfaction."

"So in essence, you're saying my human condition somehow repels males."

"Put bluntly, you smell. Only during moments of arousal," Maeve insisted above Tia's shriek. "As Luna faeries have for centuries found mating with humans repulsive, I believe the faeries have an innate reaction to their scent. They get a whiff of something off and you're done."

Tia clutched her chest. "I am doomed to virgindom because I stink?"

"Not necessarily. There is a big Mortal Realm out there full of men who must find a woman's earthy scent appealing."

"You're suggesting I switch realms! Live among the primitives?"

"You are undeniable proof there is more to humanity than our realm allows. Rise above Enchanted ignorance; give mortals a chance. If nothing else, you're bound to get to know yourself better."

"Even perhaps get to know Father," Tia realized.

Maeve tensed. "Odds are he won't remember, Tia."

"My facial features are similar to yours at that age, though. I might jog something inexplicable inside him, make him believe an old dream."

"You would be obligated to approach with caution. It's the only fair way."

Tia rose the following morning to find Blot seated at her mother's kitchen table. The squat leprechaun, dressed in his favorite green velvet suit jacket, hat, and britches, did not at all look his usual jolly self.

Maeve, swathed in her woven vine robe, hovered with a pan of her special butter brittle. "I've given Blot the particulars. He'll drop you off."

"To think your father has been under my nose all these years," Blot grumbled. "I headquarter in Central Park, you know."

"He'll also get you the best exchange rate on your money," Maeve added.

"All under extreme protest. You have a fine life right here, Tia."

Tia nipped some brittle from the pan. "From the Fey who spends most of *his* time in the Mortal Realm!"

"For every rainbow path on my gold route I cross ten thousand mired in moral bankruptcy. It's no place—" Blot paused to survey Tia's best pink iridescent minidress with flared skirt. "You're even dressed for him, aren't you?"

"Blot," Maeve chided, "nothing can threaten your place with us."

"Of course not." Tia kissed his green cheek. "Now, can we hurry along?"

Blot rose and followed Tia to the living room, where her unpacked suitcases sat. He begrudgingly grasped the largest two.

Maeve hugged Tia. "Be well. Keep in touch."

"Thank you for finally telling me."

Maeve turned then to Blot. "Haven't you forgotten something?"

Blot dropped the cases to sweep Maeve into his arms for a kiss.

Maeve giggled. "I mean John's address."

Chapter

2

Isle of Manhattan

Alec Simon was seeing things.

A regular occurrence after a night of clubbing, especially under the influence of Libation Station's specialty rum drink, Stalking Zombie.

Normally, it turned out to be nothing more than a fat pigeon on his fire escape. But this was a bird of an altogether different feather. Flowing platinum hair, hourglass body in shiny pink party dress. Heavenly. Especially the gossamer wings keeping her in a holding pattern two stories in the air.

"Something the matter, baby? Thought I heard you groan."

Alec self-consciously twisted on the sofa to eye the redhead standing near his galley kitchen. "Guess the leg is twinging a bit."

"It shouldn't be. You lost the cast last week."

Alec shrugged. He'd been blaming everything lately on the broken leg, the last of his injuries to heal. And it was proving a hard habit to break. Like his recent affection for tequila. "How's the nightcap coming?"

"After serving you all night at the Libation, I'm pretty sure you've had enough. How about some juice?"

"Forget it, Mindy."

"The name is Lindsay."

"C'mere then," he asked impulsively. "Quick."

Lindsay sashayed over, her tight black uniform swishing against her nylon hose. She dropped on the sofa beside him and leaned in. "What's up?"

"Not that." Alec pried her hand off his crotch. "I want your opinion on something. At the window."

She squinted at the dark glass glazed by streetlight. "Like what?"

"Something wild," he confided excitedly.

"Like what?"

"Well," he admitted more slowly, "a flying girl."

Lindsay bounced huffily on the cushions. "Sounds like you've had *way* too many. But never mind, I'll do the heavy lifting." Moving her hands to his shirt, she began to unbutton it.

He stopped her lunge for his belt buckle. "Check outside for me, will ya?"

"Okay." She stomped across the room to the windows.

"Open it wide. Have a good look."

"Gotcha." She turned back coyly, then raised the sash and dipped out. Tipping her bottom high enough to show some thong 'n' cheek, she made a show of looking out over West 60th Street.

"See anything special?"

She wiggled her bottom. "Do you?"

"How can I? You're blocking the view!"

Lindsay wiggled back inside. "If you don't want me, just say so."

"It's not like that."

"Sure it is." She stalked to the sofa with a tug to her

uniform. "You've been screwing anything that moves over at the Libation for weeks."

"It's not you, honestly."

"Oh, so you've suddenly had your fill of hero sex? I'm supposed to buy that? I knew the boobs turned out too small. Or is the nose still too big?"

"It's all nice," he assured. "They're really calling it hero sex?"

"As if you didn't know, you fickle shit. At first the girls just wanted a shot at the brave fireman from the newspaper. Then word got around about how good you are."

"I am?"

She tossed her arms in the air. "How should I know!"

His brows jumped in interest, then crashed down again. "Sorry."

"Time to say good night, Alec."

Alec patted the sofa, filling his eyes with puppy dog appeal. "We could just sit here awhile, see what develops."

"On hallucination watch? How stupid do you think I am?"

"I don't know—"

"You jerk!"

"C'mon, Mindy, be a sport. I have to know if I'm losing my mind."

"I vote yes!"

"I've got details. Pink dress, shiny white hair, shimmery pearl wings."

"Sounds like a faery."

He snapped his fingers. "Right!"

She snapped a tight smile. "Right. You're on your own."

He twisted round to track her moves as she grabbed her purse and jacket from a chair. "Would it be so wrong to see a faery?"

"You're on medical leave! Physical and *emotional* stress. Do you really think it smart?"

"Hey, my problem is totally physical. Feel free to pass that around the club."

"Fine."

"And on the subject, can you bring my cane before you go?"

She glared at the hinged black stick leaning against the entry closet door. "Funny thing about that crutch."

"Cane."

"You don't need it the way you used to."

"Of course I do!"

"You forget all about it at the Libation once you're smashed. That makes the cane a crutch, Alec Simon. That makes your head more messed up than your leg." On that she slammed the door.

Alec twisted to look out the window again—to find the faery was back! Peering curiously at him—as if eavesdropping. "Hey, you!" He pulled himself up and stumbled to the window. No sign of her. *Dammit!*

Naturally, she couldn't possibly exist. He was bored, that's all. Trying to escape the clutches of Lindsay. But Lindsay was right about one thing: he couldn't afford to see a faery, on top of his other troubles. Even if she was the most captivating creature ever!

Early afternoon the following day, Tia stood on the sidewalk outside the brownstone building on West 60th Street belonging to John Winter. Her first bit of luck stared back at her in the form of a For Rent sign out front. What better place to study mortal behavior than right under her father's roof?

Last night's eavesdropping had left her shaken. After Alec Simon's apartment had gone dark, she'd curled up on his length of fire escape to ponder developments. Apparently, faery spotting was not a common practice, not necessarily a good thing when it happened.

Could humans possibly deprecate faeries much in the way faeries deprecated them? Raised with faery pride, dissimilarities notwithstanding, she hadn't counted on a reverse prejudice here. Now it seemed wisest to tuck in her wings for the time being until she got a better reading on the realm.

Where to start had been the first nagging question.

By dawn there was only one thing for it. Shop till she dropped at Manhattan's famed stores. Judging by the joyful human females poring over the latest mortal fashions, she'd found a salve common to both cultures! Hopefully, the first of many.

Entering the brownstone's lobby, she found the inner door locked. Full names were proudly listed at her Enchanted Realm co-op, but this one merely had apartment numbers—six in all, beside call buttons. Apartment 2B, however, was listed as Manager. She pressed that button.

"What?" a male growled through the intercom.

"John Winter?"

"No."

"Hello, hello?"

"What?"

"Doesn't John Winter own this building?"

"You taking a survey?"

"I'm not a measurer of property, no," she replied with some bewilderment.

"Not a geographical surveyor— Oh, never mind. John hasn't lived here in years. Anything else?"

"Yes!" she said quickly. "I'd like to see your vacancy."

The front door buzzed. Juggling her bags, she made a mad grab for it.

Skipping up the stairs, she found 2B at the top to the

right. She raised her fist to the door, only to have it swung open in her face.

There stood the man she'd eavesdropped on some twelve hours ago, Alec Simon, dripping wet and nearly naked. His moist black brows crunched warily but not altogether unpleasantly. "Do we know each other?"

How tempting to pour out her heart. He had liked her at first sight after all. But in the end he had rejected the possibility of her existence. As uncharacteristic as it was, she decided to err on the side of caution.

"You look so familiar," he pressed.

"Impossible. I'm new in town."

"Still . . ."

"What a nice towel," she noted sincerely as her eyes slid to the white swath at his hips. "Looks remarkably soft and fluffy."

Amusement touched his mouth as he tightened the length of terry. "So you want to see the place."

"Please."

"Come in a minute." Still holding his towel, he managed to pull in a few of her bags labeled Bergdorf, Saks, and Bloomingdale's, then shut the door behind her with his bare foot. "I'll get dressed."

"Suit yourself."

He grinned and marched off.

"Nice furniture," she called after him.

"All the units come furnished," he called back.

"Including towels?"

He appeared moments later in blue jeans, T-shirt, and tattered moccasins, his damp jet hair combed neatly. "Well, no."

"Maybe I can borrow one of yours."

He snagged a ring of keys off a hook above his stove. "We'll see."

Alec easily grabbed up all her shopping bags this time

and led the way down the hall. Pausing at the door marked 2D, he inserted the key, then ushered her inside. Tia looked around the bright, cheery space identical to his.

"Interested?"

"It's smaller than my old place."

"Everyone new to Manhattan says that. You are new?"

She nodded. "I do like it. How much is the charter?"

"Rent?" He told her.

"Do you accept cash?"

He looked surprised. "Sure. I'll give you a receipt, of course."

Dipping into her tote bag, she produced a roll of bills. Noting his surprise, she assured him it was genuine United States currency.

"Yeah, I can see that. Just so you know, flashing anything valuable around the city can be dangerous. Might want to keep a grip on that handbag."

"And you a grip on your towel."

He sort of coughed and chuckled all at once.

She counted money into his palm and he promised a receipt. "I'm Alec Simon, by the way."

"Tia Mayberry."

"Where you come from, Tia?"

"I come from . . . Scandinavia."

"Really. I've always considered that an interesting place."

"Me, too. Until lately," she muttered. But it was impossible to sulk while gazing into those intriguing eyes of Alec's. Troll brown in color. Always dull and lifeless in the Enchanted Realm. Yet here on him . . .

Alec broke the spell by waving fingers in her face. "You still with me?"

"Sorry to go adrift. It's just . . . your eyes don't look like mud at all."

"Why, thank you."

"They're rich and warm and golden, like my mother's butter brittle."

"So, do you need help recovering your luggage?"

"No, thank you."

"Are you sure? Is it stashed far?"

As far as the nearest fire escape. "I have a plan," she assured him.

"Great." He extended her the key ring, then held on to her hand. "You've got two apartment door keys on there—these two. This larger one is for the main door. And this smaller one is for the mailbox in the lobby."

"You lock up letters?"

"Certainly. There's a lot of crime in Manhattan."

"Being nosy is a crime here?"

"Damned if it shouldn't be. No, thieves are interested in valuable stuff like checks and credit card applications. Isn't that a problem back home?"

"Not much paper product crime. Life in general is fairly quiet."

"Hey, are you sure you want to relocate here in pandemonium central?"

"No choice but to start over once you've hit rock bottom," she murmured. "No sense in doing things the same old way, either. One day soon, Alec, I hope to be accepted for exactly who I am."

"There's no better city for letting it all hang out," Alec declared.

"So how does a girl get started?"

He hesitated briefly. "A girl could have dinner with me."

"Oh?"

"Don't you want to?"

"You just seemed so out of sorts—on the phone, I mean," she thought to add. Seemed unlikely he'd appreciate last night's second-story eavesdropping.

"Well, that's because I've hit rock bottom, too, I suppose."

He shyly raked his thick black hair. "So what do you say? Care to rub some of that enthusiasm off on me?"

"Rubbing's good."

"Seven o'clock it is."

As he turned to leave, she laid a hand on his bare, damp arm and squeezed it with a gentle purpose. The tingle of strength and energy made her belly tighten.

"Yeah?" he prompted softly.

She blinked back to reality. "About that towel."

He set his hand atop hers and squeezed her back. "Coming up."

Alec returned to his apartment after delivering an armload of towels and some basic snacks, happier than he'd been in a long while. Tia was sweet, not bothering to hide her interest in him, not quick to set any terms on their date. Apparently, they raised 'em right in Scandinavia.

How strange, when he was finally driven to the edge of sanity with a faery sighting, he meet a very real and appealing substitute.

He'd been too plastered to retain many details of his hallucination, but he wanted to think she was no more stunning than the girl next door.

All he knew for sure was that he had turned a corner when he turned down Mindy's surface advances. He could and would get a grip back on reality. Once again take control of his doubts and fears.

Moving to the galley kitchen, he rifled through his fridge for half a submarine sandwich and some potato salad. Ferrying the food to his coffee table along with a Coke, he parked in the middle of the sofa and used the remote to switch on the television. He flipped through the channels to land on ESPN and leaned forward to reach for his sandwich.

It was then that a blur on the fire escape caught his eye.

A tip of gossamer wing?

He launched off the cushions and charged the window. Raising the sash, he peered out. Nothing. Aside from a fat pigeon perched on the black iron railing.

Closing the window, he took a long steadying breath. He'd seen the wing of the pigeon. It was lots smaller and duller in color. Just the same. He was buying that. He could live with that.

Alec chose a friendly neighborhood restaurant for dinner. He explained this to Tia as they exited the building that evening.

She paused before him on the sidewalk. "Am I dressed right?"

"You're asking the guy?"

"I don't have other friends yet. So you'll have to fill in every which way."

"Well, okay!" He snapped his fingers. "First off, lose the sweater." Tia obediently peeled off her cardigan, tossed it to him. "Now, give us a twirl."

Arms posed, she rotated in the tight blue sleeveless minidress that accentuated her tight, lush curves. "It's from the new spring line," she confided.

"How I love the springtime," he raved. "And the dress."

"How are the shoes?" She tipped up a tan skimmer with bow.

"They look comfy, which is good, because we have a three-block walk."

Alec readjusted the pastel sweater on her shoulders and they began to move down 60th Street with a stream of pedestrians.

"I'm used to walking almost everywhere," she confided. "Are you fond of nature, Alec?"

"Guess so. I do like Central Park."

"I can't wait to see that."

"We'll go soon."

The moment Alec ushered Tia through the front door of Forliti's Eatery, the plump and motherly owner was at his side and on his case.

"Who is this beautiful woman, Alec?" she demanded, taking Tia's sweater to a small cloak area behind the register.

"Tia Mayberry, this is Marie Forliti. Friend, snoop, and the best Italian cook this side of the Atlantic."

"Wonderful to meet you, Marie."

"You've done wonders to Alec's disposition, Tia. He's actually smiling again and navigating without that stick!" Her beaming face shadowed a little as Alec took off his leather jacket and revealed the folded cane tucked inside it. She frowned but took both to the cloak area.

"Tia just moved to the brownstone. Thought as building manager, I'd help her get her bearings."

Marie patted Tia's shoulder. "Well done, young lady. Alec hasn't had dinner conversation with anyone but Charlie Gibson in quite some time."

"Who is that, Marie?"

"The newscaster," she replied with some surprise.

"Tia is also new to the country," Alec explained.

"Should've known by the accent. When I first came here forty years ago, people thought I sounded different."

Alec smirked. Judging by her speech, Marie hit town four minutes ago.

Marie led them to a booth in the rear, underneath some fisherman net made of string, dotted with plastic fish. Tia took a keen interest in it as she slipped along the red-and-white-striped bench. What tore her away was the sight of Alec sliding into a seat across from her.

"Aren't you going to sit with me?" she asked.

Alec was nonplused. "Was planning—"

"An easy getaway?" Tia winced. "Do you already have a headache?"

"Not at all."

"A sick relative?"

Alec balked. "Not within miles."

She patted the seat beside her with a smile. "Then sit over here."

Heart zinging with pleasure, he unfolded his large frame from the booth and took his place beside her. Just like high school. Marie was gonna love this.

Sure enough, she had a twinkle in her eye when she bustled over. "How thoughtful of you two, not tying up two menus at once."

"Anything to conserve menus during the rush," Alec grumbled with humor.

"Shall we save on dishes and utensils as well?"

"No, Marie, bring two of everything."

"What is your specialty?" Tia asked, scanning the menu uncertainly.

"Toasted cheese ravioli," Marie promptly replied.

"Sounds delicious."

"Make it two," Alec said, handing back the menu. "With a bottle of the house red."

"One glass or—"

"Just do it, Marie."

Chuckling, the owner sidled off.

"She likes you, Alec," Tia observed warmly.

"I'm handy with carpentry and plumbing; my mother is long gone. I'm just the sort of project Marie likes."

"What happened to your mother?"

Alec shifted on the bench to find her stunning blue eyes full of sincere curiosity. "Both my parents died in a fire when I was nine years old. For whatever reason, I alone managed to escape—with some help."

"Is that why you became a fireman?" she asked tentatively.

"Actually, yes," he admitted quietly.

"Fairly traumatic, huh?"

"Tia, how do you know about my job?"

Startled, she fiddled with her cloth napkin. "Someone told me."

"Thought I was your only friend."

"Some tenant. In the hallway. Didn't catch his name. A tall one."

"Probably old man Hansen in 1C. He likes to talk. As much as you do."

"Ask me something personal in return if you want."

"Okay. What led you to John Winter's brownstone?"

"So he does still own it?"

"Yes. And your answer to *my* question is . . ."

"A short woman in Macy's told me about it." She fumbled with her napkin. "Lucky break, I suppose, her knowing John Winter."

"Everyone in the city knows him. He's a rich, powerful businessman who owns a half-dozen companies and a full dozen skyscrapers."

"Really," she marveled.

"What is strange is anyone believing he would be living in the brownstone. He's often mentioned in the newspapers, the subject of magazine articles. It's common knowledge that he has a thirty-acre estate in Bernardsville, New Jersey, a penthouse on Central Park West, and a winter place in Montecito, California—just to name the high spots."

"I probably just assumed he lived there. So how do you know him, Alec?" she asked eagerly.

"I went to college with his son, Ken—in fact, we were roommates all four years. John thought I was a good aggressive influence on Ken, who's the shy and earnest type."

"So John has a son," she said softly. "How old is he?"

"Twenty-eight—like me."

"Really." Forehead puckered slightly.

"Does that matter?"

"I'm twenty-eight, too." For the first time all day, her smile seemed forced. "Any other children?"

"Not that I know of."

"What is Ken like today?"

"He's living in Cincinnati with his wife. They teach at a junior college."

"You must miss him."

"I wish Ken lived closer, of course. But we're still great friends. As are John and I. Living in the same city as John, managing his building, I see more of him than ever—and his wife, Helen."

"The family must mean a lot to you."

"Very much."

"I'd like to meet them sometime."

"Noticed."

The wine arrived, brought by the young man destined to be their server. Alec poured them each a glassful.

Tia tasted it approvingly. "Every bit as good as my mother's elderberry."

"She makes her own wine?"

"She's well known for it. Mamma supported the two of us for many years with her recipe. That and her embroidery."

"What about your father, Tia?"

She gulped more wine. "He vanished. Before I was born."

"That's lousy."

Her brilliant blue eyes flared. "I'm not sure he could help it."

"But he must've made the choice not to support you."

"He and Mamma shared only one night. He likely never knew . . ."

"About you," Alec finished self-consciously. "Sorry."

"It's fine."

"I suppose you're used to the situation by now."

"Does anyone ever fully recover?"

"I'd like to think starting a family of my own will help," Alec confided.

"A nice complement one day to your career, I imagine." He hesitated. "Yeah. Sure."

"I want it all myself, too," she confided, "family and career."

Eager to shift off the subject of his work, he asked about hers.

"I craft jewelry." She touched the choker at her neck. "This is mine."

"Beautiful." He couldn't resist fingering the necklace, mostly to caress her creamy throat. Still, the silver squares imbedded with deep purple amethysts were worth close inspection. "You make a good living back home?"

"Good enough. I was in demand, you see, due to a common metal allergy."

"Really. I had no idea such a thing was ever common-place."

"I choose to think of my immunity as a small slice of serendipity."

He lifted his stemmed glass and clinked it to hers. "Good for you."

"Good for us, smiling up from rock bottom." She sipped with a coyness that made him rock solid inside his briefs.

The ravioli was, as always, heavenly. Pillows of firm pasta filled with a secret creamy cheese blend topped with a crispy Parmesan layer.

"Naturally, I'm hoping to find the same kind of work here," she confided, mowing her last ravioli pillow through the last dribble of red sauce before popping it into her mouth. "Though I imagine the competition will be keen, without the same immunity boost."

"Maybe I can help. Steer you in the right direction."

"That would be great," she enthused.

Her unguarded warmth was melting him to a defenseless puddle. But he was comfortable with it. There was an exciting sincerity humming between them. Nothing like his artificial Libation Station conquests of late. "Just off the top of my head, I'm thinking maybe some place in Soho or Greenwich Village might be interested. Trendy galleries and shops there sometimes take stuff on consignment. Or a bigger jeweler might be interested in putting you on staff. Are you good at fixing things?"

"Oh, I can work magic with any metal."

She stared dreamily into his eyes then, making him so glad they didn't remind her of mud.

When Marie reappeared tableside, Tia thrust her empty plate at her. "May I have a refill please?"

"Why, certainly." Marie took the plate and the empty bread basket. "You must be very hungry!"

"I'm hungry for several days after I fly—on a plane, of course."

"We all get hungry when we travel," Marie agreed with a wink. "Seconds on the way. My treat."

It was shortly after ten when Alec and Tia finally landed back on the street.

"Want to go home?" Alec asked.

"No." She drew her shimmery brows together in challenge. "Do you?"

"Not at all."

"Still no headache or anything?"

This had to be a running joke with her, the idea that he was apt to cut and run. As she looked totally serious, he pulled his arm around her shoulders. "There's a funky little jazz club I've been dying to try."

"Somewhere new and exciting?"

With her along? "It's bound to be."

"Lead on!"

It wasn't until they were in the cab and rolling that Alec realized he didn't have his cane. Or more to the point, Marie hadn't returned it with his jacket.

Settled back on the seat beside him, Tia read him indulgently. "You don't really need it, do you?"

"Maybe not."

"You can tell me all about it, Alec. You can trust me to understand."

Alec gazed away, out the window at the dark city streaking by. She would try to understand, he was certain. But there was no guarantee. In any case, this was a night for magic and smiles. "Another time, okay?"

"You can always find me right down the hall."

The nightclub, in a basement in the garment district, was called The Panic. Due to the name, Tia expected glaring pandemonium inside, but instead she was treated to a dim, low-key atmosphere.

"Like it?" Alec murmured in her ear as a young woman in black led them to one of the small round tables.

Tia half-turned as she moved. "It reminds me of a sea cave. Seductively hollow with an earthy thrum."

He held out a wooden chair for her. "No doubt about it, Tia, you have life stories of your own to share."

A male server, also in black, appeared for their drink order. Alec requested a ginger ale. "The wine was enough for me," he told Tia over a flickering candle. "I don't want any blurred spots later. But have what you like."

"We have many house cocktails," the server chimed in.

Tia's toes tingled under Alec's dark arresting eyes. She'd been up to trying some exotic mortal cocktail, then recalled the nectar fizz highs on her pathetic quest for romance. The buzz, while pleasant, had gotten her nowhere. "Make that two gingers," she finally said, hoping it was something half-tasty.

A stage stood twenty feet in front of them, boasting a

trio of musicians playing jazz. Tia loved the mortal rhythms and began to sway in time to them. The tune was easy enough to pick up on, but she kept mum, bearing in mind that her hum had been compared to a cobra venom seizure.

Alec rose to remove his jacket and hang it on the chair. "Let's dance."

"Are you sure?"

"My leg is fine."

"I know. . . ."

"So what's the problem?"

"I'm just growing so attracted to you, Alec."

"No harm in that. Is there?"

Guess it depended upon how good his sniffer was.

As Tia stood, Alec was swift to peel off her sweater. Grasping her bare arms, he pushed her forward. "That cardy's been in my way all night."

The band was playing a slow, languid number with a squealing sax. Alec held her close and guided her in slow circles, deftly shifting between several other couples. Melding into his strength, she matched his steps and his heartbeat, let the music wind through her.

It was the most erotic moment of her life.

Certainly she'd be stinking to high heaven any minute. *Just how would this one get away?* she wondered. He claimed to feel fine and had no relatives to fall back on. Perhaps in his case, it would be a house afire.

Wired with tension, she put herself on high alert. Moments turned into longer moments. Still, he said nothing. Even as she picked up her own musty scent, he said nothing. Could he be suffering from acute nasal blockage?

There was no clean break between a smatter of songs, so Alec never stopped steering her around. Tia snuggled closer, fully aware of the turgid flesh now pressing urgently against her belly.

It was time for the ultimate test. To hum that tune. Close to Alec's ear. Ever so softly, of course, so as not to cause an angry stampede in the cramped space.

To Tia's utter amazement, no one gave her so-called puling a second glance. As for Alec, he merely kissed her temple and called her his songbird!

Suffused with relief and pleasure, she swiped away a trace of tears.

Perhaps there was a place for her in this world after all.

Chapter

3

Alec and Tia barely made it inside her new apartment before they were locking lips and tugging at each other's clothing. They tussled on to the bedroom, Alec bare-chested, Tia bare everything.

Tia was bursting with excitement. It was really going to happen this time.

In a slow, fluid motion, she dropped to her knees to unbuckle his belt, urge down his zipper. She pulled away his pants and placed a hand over his bulging boxers. With fascination, she began to massage the outline of his shaft.

"Slow down, honey," he rasped. "Like to have my shoes off first."

Her huge eyes lifted to his. "Am I doing it wrong?"

With a wizened scowl, Alec yanked her to her feet. "Don't say it. This isn't your first time."

"Will that pose a problem?"

"Not exactly. It's more a matter of choice—for you."

"Then there is no problem." Clutching his face, she pressed her mouth against his.

Alec broke free. Eventually. "This is a big deal. You gotta be sure."

"I'm far from innocent, Alec. Have, for instance, skinny-dipped with males back home for years and years."

"What group was this? The deaf and mute society for the blind?"

More like the strapping male faery society by the bay. Certainly a better subject for a rainy day, with little emphasis on the "strapping" part due to Alec's new possessive gleam.

"I just don't understand how you made it this long," he persisted as she oozed into him like an itchy kitten. "Especially rubbing up against a man like that!"

"Must say, there's a lot more talk than I expected."

"You think?" Taking the challenge, he ground his mouth against hers, kicking off the last of his clothes.

Years of pent-up frustration had Tia kissing Alec back with gusto. Toe-to-toe, mouth-to-mouth, she reveled in every untested masculine edge. The pebbly surface of his tongue inside her mouth, the scratchy chest hairs scoring her breasts, the roughened fingertips skimming her curves. All moving against the grain, causing a heady friction.

Counter this with the smooth sensation of his penis undulating against her tender belly as if pressing for entry.

Weak at the knees, Tia was certain she'd soon melt away.

Deciding to save herself, Tia wound her arms around his neck and gracefully leapt up to ride his waist.

Locked between her thighs, Alec sucked a breath. Then began to knead the curved flesh of her bottom. Tia shuddered as his fingers pressed deep into the firm butt muscle with a massaging motion, grinding his cock into her sensitive pubis. Then with a flying leap worthy of a winged lord, Alec propelled them onto the bed.

Tia landed flat on her back with a broad smile, which faded as Alec retreated from the mattress. She swiftly raised herself up on elbows, eyes slitted. "Oh, no, you don't."

Alec whirled in the middle of the room. "What?"

"No headaches tonight."

He chuckled and reached for his pants. "I'm just digging a condom out of my wallet."

"Oh." She sank back on the pillows with a sigh.

Alec climbed back on the bed fully sheathed. Then after a moment's hesitation, he lowered over her. She swiftly wound her legs around his middle and clamped hard with earnest eyes.

"Don't hold back on me."

Ever so gently he dipped his hips and teased her opening with his cock. "Okay?"

She slanted him a smile. "Carry on."

He pushed inside her then, plainly struggling to take his time. She gasped in delight as his erection grew inside her, invading her tight untried tunnel.

Testing her muscles, she gave him a small, tentative squeeze, spurring him to move inside her. Deeper, then out again. Once, twice, in and out. With intense concentration he picked up a gliding rhythm that Tia sought to match, lifting her hips against his with a skin smack. The core of her being twisted and tightened until she could take no more.

She gave in to a sweet dizzy release, distantly aware of Alec jerking inside her. Sinking on top of her, he was careful not to crush her. His heart beat fiercely against hers for some moments before he rolled away.

They lay silently in the darkness, working to breathe again. "You waited for me, didn't you, Alec?"

He rolled up to stroke her moist forehead. "To make it special. After all, everyone remembers their first time."

She cuddled closer. "I imagine they do."

Alec was busy cooking in Tia's galley kitchen the next morning when she shuffled in with mussed hair and heavy bedroom eyes.

"You're dressed."

"And you not so much." Setting down his spatula, he slid his hands underneath the shawl collar of her robe and kissed her deeply. She was beautifully naked beneath the terry wrapping, which, he happened to note, still held a price tag from Saks.

She welcomed the kiss but smacked his shoulder afterward. "I thought I'd wake up in your arms."

"Tia, it's mid-morning."

"You slept this late just yesterday. I woke you, remember?"

"A lot has changed since yesterday. I'm feeling more like myself. And the real me gets up early to make the day matter."

"The clothes are different," she noted. "You even went home!"

Her abandonment issues were overwhelming—far worse than his. All because of her father's absence? Sensing this might not be a good time to dig deeper, he playfully tapped her nose. "I went out to buy breakfast fixings. You can't expect to live on air."

Leaning into him, she traced her tongue along his mouth. "That is not what I hoped to live on today."

"Hmm, your first time must have gone well."

"Don't make me squirm over telling you."

"I know you didn't have to." Riffling his fingers through her luxuriant platinum hair, he kissed her cheekbone. "But I hope we'll always tell each other things."

"Hmm, yes."

His hand slid deeper to cup her full, warm breast.

"Something's burning, Alec."

"Oh, yeah. . . ." Suddenly he realized she was talking about his omelets! With a yelp he whirled to take the pan off the burner and shut off the heat.

"I can save them," she assured, busily taking over.

Gripping the spatula, she gave the browned half-moon shapes a flip and slid them onto the two ceramic plates set on the counter.

He took a plate, his free hand closing on the one holding the spatula. "You, Tia Mayberry, can save anything."

Alec knew part of reclaiming his old active life was returning to the gym three times a week. Technically, his place of fitness was a health club on 86th Street with a panoramic view of Central Park West. A high-roller hangout where the elite struck deals over cutting-edge energy drinks. Where he was merely a long-term guest. Courtesy of the respected mentor he called Trey.

Better known at large as John Winter III.

Alec was lying on a weight bench, hoisting a barbell, when he spied the mogul himself standing behind a spotter.

"Alec! They called the house to say you were here."

John wanted to see him that badly. It was enough to give his conscience a good hard prick. He set the barbell back on its rack, sat up on the bench, and shook John's hand. "Sorry I haven't been in touch."

"No matter, we're together now." John beamed and patted his back. "We could take in a spinning class if you like."

Alec didn't like. But like the rest of Manhattan, he had trouble resisting the persuasive John Winter.

Half the stationary bikes were occupied at that hour of the afternoon. A girl named Becka sat on the top bike at the head of the class. Armed with peppy music and drill sergeant instructions, she always rode them mercilessly.

Alec spared a sidelong glance at John, pedaling madly on a bike beside him dressed in tank and shorts similar to his own. Few people saw the dignified industrialist in such skimpy clothes, his corded suntanned skin awash in sweat.

Even fewer were on terms intimate enough to address him as Trey. That honor was restricted to friends and family members. Alec was openly delighted to be accepted in not one but both camps.

Alec knew John would never speak during the workout. The music was too loud, the exertion too strenuous. It would also be an insult to Becka as she coaxed the cyclists on their feverish ride.

Though happily married for close to thirty years, John always charmed the ladies. Always.

A brief shower and a change to street clothes had him and Alec settled in the health club dining room.

"I feel I should be treating you to something better to celebrate your recovery, Alec," John said.

Alec glanced fondly across the table at the silver-haired gent, touching his salon-clipped moustache as he perused the menu through reading glasses. "It's the company that counts."

John smiled. "Right. Can't beat this place for a confidential chat."

Alec tensed slightly, wondering what he had in mind.

"Helen's been asking after you. A lot."

"Sorry. I've been hiding from everyone."

John regarded Alec wryly over his lenses. "Helen is my only concern, as she warms my bed."

"You can assure her I'm better."

"I'd rather you show her."

"Of course."

Soon they turned their attention to their waiter. Settling their order, Trey peeled off his glasses. Grooves of distress marred his face. "It still tears us up that you were hurt on my property. You of all people, Alec. Why, you weren't even supposed to be on duty."

"All part of the firefighter game. The crew was short, so I got the call." Alec gulped from his water glass, still finding this subject difficult to tackle. Thank God he hadn't tried to explain it all to Tia yet. She admired his strength, and how he longed to keep it that way.

Tia. He'd glanced down into Central Park frequently as they hauled ass on those bikes. She was down there some-place waiting for him.

Take as long as you like, she'd said. There was nothing she enjoyed more than romping through the trees.

She'd actually said *romp.* A sample of genuine play-fulness that he was finding so infectious. He hadn't bought a girl a Frisbee since junior high. But he'd done it today. Tia had been thrilled with the yellow plastic disk. They would toss it around the park the moment he got back.

Separated by thirty stories, he couldn't totally block out those skinny-dipping guys she'd ogled on nature *romps* back home. Why none of them had ever seduced her he couldn't fathom. Why she struggled so between self-confidence and terror he couldn't fathom, either.

She was stunning enough to give a man a headache. Like looking into the sun too long.

Surely no one at the park would pose him any real com-petition.

But should he have bought her the Frisbee before they parted? Or waited until after? Tia, warm and shiny as the sun, frolicking on her own with a Frisbee.

Possessively, he wondered who was tossing it now.

"Alec!"

"Sorry." Alec struggled to reconnect. "We both have to get over what happened, accept that too many were at the wrong place at the wrong time."

"Naturally, I have less sympathy for the hooligans and tramps who caused the trouble."

"College kids and homeless people."

"Trespassing on my property. In the dead of night. Playing with fire."

"Well, the homeless were obviously trying to escape the cold snap. As for the students, they were green freshmen from NYU involved in some sort of hazing stunt. Several of them dropped by my room at the hospital to express remorse—you saw them."

"You shouldn't let them off the hook so easily," John muttered.

"Ask anyone at the station and you'll find we all carry the same mission: to save lives without passing judgment."

"I felt both sides were more than anxious to blame the other. That didn't seem very noble."

"There was a lot of confusion at the site, of course. Everyone fearful of being held responsible."

John abruptly leaned into the table, his tone urgent. "So when will responsibility be determined?"

"You probably know more at this point than I do."

He settled back with a low snort. "They aren't sharing a thing with me. No matter how many strings I've tried to pull."

"Sorry, Trey. But it is common procedure in a case like this."

"Stonewalling my inquiries, as if *I'm* a suspect."

"I don't believe it. You were, after all, with me much of the night!"

"It's your chief, Kevin Mitchell, at fault, I figure. He'd held a grudge since I bought his Tribeca apartment building and flipped it to condos."

"His family lived there for three generations at a manageable price," Alec reasoned. "Now he's holed up someplace in Queens, miles from the station."

"It was strictly business. It's what I do."

"As these investigations are department business. They're always fair."

"Plainly it was a stupid accident! I can't figure what's taking so long."

"I suppose the nonprofit you were donating the building to is the most impatient."

John's expression softened. "The women's shelter, Arms of Tomorrow. Helen's become their champion, you know, tirelessly rounding up supplies, medical and spiritual counsel. Under the circumstances, I felt it only right to arrange another site for them in Chelsea. It's not as large or convenient as the Fifty-sixth Street building, but at least it's not barbecued."

"You moved on that fast."

"That part was easy compared to appeasing the authorities. It's so awkward with my annual banquet for outstanding heroism slated for Saturday. Here I am, set to distribute plaques of bravery to, among others, your crew—for my very own fire. With the investigation at a frustrating standstill."

"You don't know it's at a standstill," Alec insisted. "I'm sure—"

"You keep using the word 'sure.' Which is a damn sight different from being positive. You're usually so on top of things at the station."

"Truth is, I haven't been to the station lately."

"I know you're not back on the roster yet."

"Trey, I haven't been back there at all."

"Why the hell not!"

Alec bowed his head. "I've been struggling with doubts about the job."

"I don't believe it. You've wanted to fight fires since you were a kid! Are damned good at it!"

"A firefighter with doubts is no damn good," Alec uttered.

"You haven't outright quit, have you?"

"No. I've been stalling around instead, using that cane as a prop for my lingering *emotional* disability."

"Can't believe you didn't confide in me sooner."

"Only recently admitted it to myself. Very recently."

"That's something anyway." Despite this concession, John's mouth settled into a disgruntled line. "Seems I finally understand why you won't commit to the awards banquet."

"I'm a work in progress, Trey. Just like the investigation."

"Oh, I don't mean to sound so contentious."

"You have a right to defend your reputation. It's deserved."

"Just like you have a right to expect my support. Nothing has changed since that first day Kenny brought you home from college on holiday break. I instantly spotted in you a kindred spirit, with drive, ambition, resilience. You were the second son I always wanted and just what Kenny needed, somebody to lure him into sports, show him how to throw a punch—how to date indiscriminately, for Pete's sake! Not that he's exactly followed through on any of it."

"Those skills are most useful at age twenty anyway."

"It's been tough to see him crawl back into his shell, though, married to a bookworm, teaching kiddie arithmetic in the outback."

"He teaches trigonometry at a junior college! And Cincinnati is a metropolis, with museums and galleries, even electricity and running water."

John brushed off Alec's attempt at levity. "I'll tell you what I told him on the phone just last week. You want an executive post in my organization, it's yours. As soon as tomorrow. You can sit at a computer all day devising strategies or crunching numbers. Whichever your pleasure."

Alec groaned. "I can imagine Ken's answer. You can imagine mine."

John smirked. "So who isn't sure he doesn't want to play fireman?"

"Point taken. I will drop into the station."

"When?"

"Soon."

"Like tomorrow? Tuesday nights are potluck."

Alec's mouth curled. "You remembered."

"You miss enough of my events to make it matter."

"I was planning to corner Chief Mitchell at a quieter—"

"And make it all look staged?"

"My comeback? Honestly, I don't expect a standing ovation."

"No, Alec. *Your* questions about *my* fire."

"Mitchell won't tell me if they're holding back any crucial findings."

"At least find out if there are any crucial findings. Find out if they're earning the taxpayers' money."

Alec smiled faintly. This appeared to be a thinly disguised campaign to get him back on the job. After all, the Winter enterprise owned dozens of properties to take up his time. And by all appearances the fire was an accident perpetrated by trespassers. Perhaps most important, John was always good under pressure, sure of his well-groomed reputation. "I promise to do what I can," Alec said fondly.

"Great. Let's celebrate with some dessert."

"The dessert here is way too nutritious. But let's have coffee. I want to tell you all about your new tenant."

Tia fell in love at first sight with Central Park, a wondrous haven of green with traces of home.

She and Alec had parted ways on the West Side near the Reservoir at 86th Street, on the promise they'd meet up in two and a half hours' time and she wouldn't wander off too far on her own. She had stood in place while he'd crossed the street, waved when he waved. She even waited several minutes after he entered a skyscraper, just in case he felt the urge to wave again.

After that, however, she stepped behind a bush to let it all hang out. Which to a Luna Fey meant spreading her wings in all their gossamer glory.

Bowing her head in concentration, she urged her wings to sprout from the ridges of her shoulder blades, while at the same time shifting into a dress of rose petals in place of her street clothes. Making certain she was still undetected, she took a deep breath and willed her heart rate up far beyond human endurance. She stretched and flexed. Then with a brisk flapping motion, she lifted herself several inches off the ground and into another dimension boasting far less gravity. While not totally invisible to the naked human eye, she was moving at a much quicker vibration. At best, someone with extremely keen senses might catch a glimpse of wing or shadow.

She continued to hover in place, waiting for the rush that signaled a full recharge of her Enchanted energies. Then in a shimmery streak of gossamer and platinum, she tore off in a horizontal glide.

Tia soared low over the park, marveling that the city jungle of concrete and steel could boast water, trees, and grasslands in splendorous relief.

Swooping over a lake boasting paddleboats, she sank low enough to ruffle the hair of some children, rescue a fallen robins' nest, even slow a runaway stroller on a footpath. It occurred to her that she could always find quick rejuvenation here from the stresses of mortal life. A single hour attuned with nature would always rejuvenate. If she did indeed decide to stay on.

It was in the quickened zone accessible to all Enchanted creatures that she eventually spotted Blot sitting in a tree quite near her spot of liftoff. The roundish leprechaun was dressed in his favored green velvet outfit, sitting atop a towering forty-foot oak, basking in a dapple of sunlight. With equal measures of affection and frustration, she swooped up to surprise him. With great success, as he promptly teetered off his lounging branch, yelping all the way down.

As expected, he landed squarely on the soles of his green boots, with, at most, a bruise to his dignity. After all, no species indigenous to the Isle of Man had better buoyancy than the leprechaun, not to mention the unparalleled ability to relocate in a blink with or without passengers, turn invisible, and, of course, tote huge amounts of gold.

He wasn't on the ground seconds before rolling over to the mortal dimension, in the guise of a Caucasian midget, his green skin paling to paste, his velvet suit melding to street clothes. Tia was quick to land as well. Cooling down with deep breaths, she inverted her wings and shifted her rose petal dress back to her original tight-fitting jeans and a striped blouse.

Hands on hips, she confronted him in dismay. "Are you spying on me?"

Hopping up on a nearby park bench, he smugly thrust a fat finger in her face. "It is you who's come to my turf!"

She grew sheepish. "Guess I have. Though perfectly by chance."

"In any event, I'm glad you're here. I have been worried."

"You shouldn't—"

"Mostly for your mother's sake!"

"She didn't seem worried. This was her idea."

Blot paced the length of the bench. "Parents often lament their own ideas. Maeve is roiling in confusion and guilt. Should she have worked harder to find you a male who could stand your . . . features? Worked harder to hide those features in the first place? Or should she have told you the truth sooner? Chased after your father like a devoted sea-spotted terrier earlier on than that!" He spat out the last in utter distaste.

"Conflicts we know you don't share."

"We are what we are," Blot maintained. "Enchanted beings. Should be more than enough."

"Still, you spend most of your time here."

"For my work. Can't regulate pots of gold from my seaside cottage. So what are you doing in the park, Tia, if not to track me down?"

"I'm here with a friend. Who should be back any minute now." She dashed over to the bushes, only to return with the Frisbee in her hands.

Blot was hot on her heels. "Where did you get that thing?"

"It's a gift."

"I've seen them around the park. Humans delight in throwing them."

"I'm out to try their favorite things. Choose my new favorites."

"You already sound pretty chummy about being one of 'em."

"I'm off to a good start. Managed to lease space in my father's building."

Stoically he folded his arms across his small barrel chest. "How handy."

"Aren't you even going to ask if I met my father?"

"Did you?"

"No."

His droopy face lifted slightly.

"I will meet him eventually. My new friend, Alec, is a friend of his."

"That was quick."

"Men here find me much more appealing, even aromatic," she confided.

"So you're bound to let your human side simply take over?"

"Not necessarily. In an ideal situation, I'd be accepted as half 'n' half."

"What mortals call a dairy product. Please go home, Tia, before you lose your Enchanted edge, before the real heartache sets in. Surely you understand that the realm you consort with will be your dominant one."

"Can embracing the human be worse than the heartache of my last few years on the Isle? Shunned by old classmates who thought I'd outgrow my abnormalities, rejected by males with marginal wit and intelligence—singing voices worse than my own? Which, by the way, isn't a problem here. My singing is considered good," she confided excitedly.

"How startling." Blot cleared his throat. "I mean, how sterling."

"It seems smartest to let nature take its course, pull my strengths to light. Soon enough I'll know who I am and where I belong." Tia beamed affectionately. "C'mon, let's throw the Frisbee together, like the natives do." She trotted back to put some distance between them and artfully fired off the plastic toy.

Blot humphed as the whirling disk sliced him squarely in the paunch.

Alec's anxiety melted at the sight of Tia launching their Frisbee into an aging midget's midsection. She hadn't landed some Adonis after all. Probably had, in fact, chosen one of the safest playmates in the park.

"There she is up ahead," Alec confided to John. "Tia!" Alec called out.

She turned, froze, and gave a jerky wave.

"Honey, I want you to meet John Winter. The owner of our building."

"Oh." Her tone and eyes went softer than Alec had seen out of bed.

"Tia's been dying to meet you, John."

"Has she? How nice."

Alec would have liked to see more than John's genial public relations smile, after the glowing description he'd given Tia. But the Winter family was reserved by nature, and always slow to trust in the way many rich people are— due to the large number of opportunists floating around.

"Love the . . . building," Tia chirped in a gap of silence.

"Alec tells me you're visiting far from home," John said pleasantly. "Under the circumstances, I'd never insist you sign a long-term lease."

"Why, thank you."

Alec thought Tia was staring at John rather intensely, as if trying to squeeze something more from the moment. It happened with acquaintances, familiar with the mogul's celebrity. Though come to think of it, Tia hadn't known who he was.

"Alec, John, this is . . ." Tia wavered over the little old man beside her.

"Mr. Blot," he intoned. "Just showing this young lady how to toss one of these things."

John's deeply tanned face crinkled in amusement. "We saw you in action."

As the smaller man's expression darkened, Tia took back the Frisbee and touched his arm. "It was so nice meeting you, Mr. Blot."

He bared pointy yellowed teeth. "Yes. How kind of you, Miss Mayberry, to insist we meet again soon."

Tia cocked a platinum brow. "Guess I'm a real nice gal."

"Rest assured, I have your number. Alec. Trey." With a curt nod, Mr. Blot was off.

"I must be getting along, too," John intoned. "Good day, Tia. Enjoy the firehouse chili, Alec."

Chapter

4

"You told that little guy your last name. Where you live." Alec shut the magazine he was reading and gazed at Tia, nestled beside him on his sofa. "I still can't believe it."

Tia, intently watching a man named Jay Leno on the television, wrinkled her nose at the interruption. "I knew you'd come back round to it eventually."

"There's just something about the guy. Not sure what."

She made a funny sound, though she remained glued to the screen.

"Equally not sure what kind of magic he worked on you."

"No spell of any kind. Honestly."

"Good to hear," Alec returned with more humor. "Though he looked magical. Give him a little green suit and he could have leapt off a box of Lucky Charms."

"What are Lucky Charms?"

"A children's breakfast cereal with a leprechaun spokesperson."

"Sounds like a healthy role model. A strike against Enchanted discrimination."

Alec fingered her luxuriant white-blond hair. "Oh, Tia, I love you."

This tore her interest away from the program, sent her bouncing right into his lap! "You do, Alec? Really?"

He flinched. "I love so many things about you, I— What the hell, I do believe I'm falling for you." Grasping her chin, he locked in on her ever-hypnotic peepers. "In fact, I know it."

"You aren't fighting it, are you?" she demanded abruptly.

"No, no. It just seems so impossible, meeting you at such a low point, zipping up to such a high one so quick."

"But isn't that what happens with the right blend of chemistry?"

"Yes, honey. It'll just take some time to make sure it's real for us. We don't want to rush ahead and hurt one another."

"A part of me would like to lose myself in you forever," she admitted in raw candor. "No more questions asked. But as you know, pesky questions have a way of creeping in."

"Now she has questions!" he lamented. "No questions for Mr. Lucky Charms."

She sighed indulgently. "I'm sure he's harmless, Alec."

"He struck me as the kind who could become a real pest."

"I won't let that happen."

"Okay. Enough said."

"So, Alec, do you think John Winter liked me?"

"What's not to like?"

"That's sweet. But do you?"

"You really are anxious to make new friends today."

She busily rearranged some of the dark hair that had tumbled into his vision. "I just think John would be worth the effort, being so special to you and all."

"He is. You'll charm him in no time, probably even be invited to call him Trey, an honor reserved for his closet posse."

"Trey," she repeated. "Guess I did hear that mentioned. Does it have meaning?"

"He's the third John in his family—Trey."

"Sounds like a lovely arrangement." A smile flooding her face, she wrapped her arms around Alec and snuggled in close. He felt a stirring of desire. They hadn't done it on the sofa yet.

"What did he mean, about the firehouse chili?"

"Huh?"

"John," she pressed. "When he said good-bye."

Alec rubbed the back of his neck to find it stiff. "He wants me to work my way back into the station."

"Have you been kicked out?"

He laughed, albeit edgily. "Nothing like that."

She stroked his cheek. "Please tell me about it. Prove that you want to move beyond the chemistry."

"Okay." He shifted on the sofa but held her fast in his arms. "Since my injury on the job, I've sort of avoided visiting the fire station. At first it was because I was pretty badly hurt, having fallen through a floor. It was all I could do to get to my doctors and therapists. Then, more recently, I discovered my breaks and sprains were healed. People started noticing, too."

"Like Marie."

"Yes. What no one understands is what caused my fall in the first place. What keeps holding me back emotionally even now."

"The original fire from your boyhood?"

"Yes," he said with surprise. "How'd you . . ."

"Merely a guess. We're all defined by childhood scars."

"My dad's burning cigarette started the blaze in the living room. It soon spread upstairs to where my mother and I slept. I remember waking to the stench of smoke, opening my door to confront a wall of flames. Then remember slamming it shut again, running round my room in helpless circles. If I try I can still taste the smoke, feel the cape of my superhero pajamas billowing off my shoulders."

"Superhero?"

"Fictional character with magic powers."

"Ah."

"At any rate, I was in dire need of a real hero just then and he came on a whine of siren. Drawn to the window, I pushed it open. A giant fire truck stopped out front. Out popped a crew of firefighters, among them Gus Martin. Through the melee he was soon scrambling up a ladder to my window. A regular guy underneath some impressive gear, I came to find out. But on the job, fueled by a desire to rescue others, he became superhuman.

"All went well at first. He managed to get me over the sill and onto the ladder. Neither of us was prepared for what happened next, though, my terror over the second-story height. Several rungs down I jolted in his grip. We both lost our balance and fell. Both broke some bones," he admitted morosely. "Gus held no grudge, though. We mended together in the hospital. He was there when I got the bad news about my folks. He was around as I lived on with my crabby grandmother. Through Gus I learned the true meaning of heroism: ordinary guys who take on the extraordinary. I realized I wanted to follow in his footsteps. Save some lives myself. I was doing a pretty good job of it, too. Until that last blaze."

"Go on," she urged gently.

"Quite unexpectedly, I seized in panic. I'd gotten everyone on the second floor out the window and on the ladder—as is procedure. Then as it was my turn to bail, the floor beneath me began to give way with a resounding crack, opened wide to shooting flames. At that moment, my unconscious opened wide, jogged loose the buried memory of that childhood fire. I hesitated only briefly, to anticipate the horror of taking another long fall. Unfortunately, it was enough time for the floor to give way under my feet. It was so out of character for me, I still have trouble accepting it," he finished bitterly.

"Did something set this fire apart from others? Some added pressure?"

"Probably. I went in knowing the building belonged to John—"

"Our John?"

"Yes." He smiled faintly at her wide eyes. "The minute I heard there was a small crowd trapped inside, I worried the Winters were among them. I'd dined with John and Helen earlier, and while there'd been no mention of a stop there, the building was earmarked for a charity of Helen's. It was feasible they'd brought people around for a visit. As they are the closet thing I have to parents now, the department shrink relates my fear for their safety to my old fears for my parents.

"The scene was chaotic from the get-go. A mix of trespassers who knew they shouldn't be there and were not eager to hand out names. For me, it was an emotional course for disaster. Not that that is any excuse."

"Oh, Alec, the last thing Gus would want you to do is toss off your career over one hesitation."

"I know. He'd insist everything happens for a reason, to teach us a lesson, help us grow into better people. There's nothing wrong with being a fragile human being. The trick is to play on strengths and work on weaknesses."

Tia nodded, as if especially partial to this last nugget of wisdom.

"But what if the weakness is permanent? What if I'm now a true agoraphobic?"

"Give yourself a break, Alec. You were under extreme personal pressure. If it ever happens again, I'm sure you'll bank your emotions properly."

"I'd like to believe I can. But it isn't enough. I have to

be back a hundred percent. As it is, I'm having trouble even imagining it. Can't even get comfortable on my own fire escape."

"You did find the nerve to give up your cane."

"I was so busy trying to impress you at Forliti's, I simply forgot it. Damned if I could think of a way to take the stick up again without looking totally idiotic!"

"You don't want it anymore. You know that."

"I do know," he relented. "But it was my last claim to physical injury. My co-workers are bound to start asking tougher questions now about my return. This is all your fault, Tia, tweaking my machismo, forcing me to chase you with two good legs."

"Let me back you with a little boost." She squeezed his arm. "Take me to the chili party."

The offer was unexpected and, he realized, comforting. "You are always hungry!" he complained with feigned gruffness.

"Always." To prove it she sank her teeth into his earlobe.

It was nearing 6:00 P.M. when Alec stood with a fussing Tia outside the Midtown Precinct on 51st Street and 3rd Avenue.

"You look great."

"Not too casual, Alec?"

"Blue jeans and T-shirts are the norm. Trust me, you're perfect." Alec ushered her inside.

"Alec! Welcome back!" Joyce Fortney, stationed at the front desk, wasted no time rushing up to give him a hug.

Alec introduced Tia as his date and neighbor. He was grateful for the chance to first use the label on the sweet older woman in order to gauge the ever insecure Tia's reaction. Luckily, Tia appeared quite satisfied with the non-committal tag, shaking Joyce's hand.

Without question, his rowdy co-workers would tease him mercilessly if and when they discovered how fast and crazy he'd fallen for this rather unique blonde. With the weight of his job in the balance, he wasn't up to it tonight.

Alec led on to a homey room in the rear, bright and cozy with tables, comfy furniture, and appliances. The space rumbled with activity as men and women, some in uniform, mingled, with bursts of shouts and laughter. Much of this activity stalled as Alec stepped in. The pause was very brief, however, followed by a chorus blasting his name.

He could feel Tia meld against him as the crowd stampeded them.

"The hero returns!"

"Slacker!"

"What took you so long?"

The well-wishers circled and budged, all the while eyeing Tia with the unabashed interest common in families, even blended ones of choice.

Alec finally held up both hands. "Good to be home." Applause filled the room. When it died down, Alec spoke up again. "Just to bring you up to date, this woman is Tia Mayberry. Yes, we're on a date. Yes, she lives in my brownstone. No, not in my apartment," he added, causing a few chuckles. "Go easy on her. She's new in town. Oh, I assured her you've had all your shots."

He instantly regretted the last crack. Sure enough, Tia's high lyrical voice caressed his ear. "Are they vaccinated against anything dangerous?"

"Later," he murmured, kissing her cheek. He turned sharply then as a hand touched his shoulder. "Oh, hey. Tia, this is Chief Kevin Mitchell."

She surveyed the tall, big-boned man with thinning brown hair. "Lord of the station. How nice."

Mitchell looked momentarily startled, but his smile

never wavered. "Heard through the grapevine, Alec, that you'd given up your cane. Figuring you'd be showing up any day, we rinsed out your coffee mug."

Right on cue, Amelia Ross, the redheaded beauty of the station, sidled up with said mug in hand. "Cheers, Alec!"

Alec accepted the steamy ceramic cup and sipped. "I've missed this tar." He explained to Tia that this was a way of welcoming a crew member back.

"Won't be long now," Tia chirped confidently.

"He's in the minute he passes the official evaluation," Chief Mitchell put in easily, apparently considering it a mere formality. "Well, enjoy the chili. I can't stay myself." With a nod he turned on his heel.

"Say, ah, Chief."

Mitchell spun back. "What is it, Alec?"

"Is there any progress on *the* investigation?"

The chief scowled. "You asking for yourself or the building's owner?"

"We both have an interest," Alec admitted.

"We're down to tying up loose ends. That's all I can say."

"Can you blame Trey for wanting his property released, for worrying about the investigation?" Alec normally made it a point to never call John Trey except to his face, as it seemed like a celebrity name–dropping ploy out in public. But here it just popped out in the heat of the moment.

No doubt Alec's divided loyalties added to the chief's consternation. "Winter shouldn't have any worries unless he was involved in setting the blaze."

"John Winter would never do that!" Tia's disruptive cry drew stark attention from both males. "I mean, Alec, you're such a good judge of character."

Alec cringed. "The chief is a very good judge of people, too."

The chief's face darkened. "If you tell him anything,

tell him his fancy banquet honoring you guys isn't going to sway our findings."

"That banquet honors a lot of people every year. You go every year. He isn't trying to pull anything."

"You do deserve the award," Mitchell conceded. "But I just announced that I won't be attending. The press will be snapping photos. I need to appear impartial to the public until this arson mess is officially cleared up."

"When is this banquet?" Tia asked.

"Saturday night," Mitchell replied. "Make sure Alec gets there, Tia. Dancing and a nice dinner will do him good."

"Oh, I will."

The chief glanced at his watch. "I have a meeting at my son's new school soon, in *Queens*. So you'll have to excuse me."

"What has he against Queens, Alec?" Tia asked as Mitchell lumbered off.

"Oh, the chief got stung when John flipped his apartment building to condos. When he couldn't afford to buy his place, he moved out there."

"Can he investigate the fire in an impartial way?"

Alec's defenses rose slightly. "Of course. He treats all the rich power brokers around town with nearly the same disdain. We share a tight bond around here, Tia," he went on under her skeptical look. "Work together, play together. Everyone tries to get along."

"Why didn't you tell me about the banquet?"

"Because I'm not going," he said quietly. "Don't feel I deserve it."

"You saved everyone!"

Everyone but me. "Don't press it here."

Moments later, Abe Spence, resident cook, gave a holler from a doorway. "Soup's on! Get your lazy asses back here, pronto."

Alec wound his arm around a startled Tia. "He's rude but a great cook."

"Then he's forgiven already."

The next few hours passed leisurely. Alec and Tia were allowed to move about without more fanfare, but the crowd was surreptitiously tracking Tia as she packed food away like a hungry trucker and tossed around her glorious waist-length mane of platinum hair. As he watched her mingle with a number of other females for the first time, new things registered in Alec's mind. How her small feet barely touched the floor as she moved. How her lush hips swayed hypnotically. How her voice rose over others' no matter how she worked to modulate it.

Captivating mysteries he wanted to explore layer by layer.

Eventually, the party began to break up.

"Hey!" Dick Kroft, the night shift supervisor, called over the din. "Don't forget to empty your lockers for the refurbishing tonight. There are still some empty cardboard boxes available in the locker room for the slackers."

This was news to Alec, so he grabbed a box. He led Tia through the cavernous storage area housing the fire and rescue vehicles. Like all visitors to the station, she seemed intent on lingering to inspect the large shiny trucks, but there wasn't time tonight. With a tug he urged her along to the locker room.

A crowd tagged along, but most of them only shuffled around the gray steel lockers with their arms folded. For no definable reason, the tiny hairs on the back of Alec's neck prickled as he fiddled with the combination dial on his own door.

Lifting the catch, he opened the door with a creak, then stepped back in with a grunt of surprise.

The interior was loaded with faery paraphernalia! Photos, cartoons, and crude sketches on station paper pasted to every surface. Dolls of paper and plastic hanging by strings from coat hooks.

All this was accompanied by a chorus of "When You Wish upon a Star."

Kroft stepped up behind him. "That waitress from Libation Station sure was steamed when you dumped her—over a hallucination!" He guffawed, causing a chain reaction of belly laughs.

"You didn't really see anything that night?" Joyce asked in worry.

Alec forced a chuckle. "I'd hardly get my job back if I did, now would I?"

"So you haven't seen her since?" Abe demanded.

"That was a treat for the totally sloshed," Alec said uneasily.

Another round of laughter followed. Alec had all but forgotten Tia until she pushed him aside for a closer look at the locker.

"Shame, shame on all of you!" she cried, bringing the room to a quick silence. "This is nothing to be laughed at. Alec is always sincere—"

"Hush." Alec took hold of her arm.

"But this isn't funny! Faeries—"

"Tia. Please." He squeezed her arm a little tighter. In a louder, jovial voice he said they were taking off.

Alec hustled Tia to the street and kept on walking. Stopping at a bus bench two blocks down, he parked her on it. "What is your problem tonight?"

"Where to begin!" she wailed. "First you are criticized for backing John Winter. Then you are mocked for believing in faeries."

"You are overreacting to everything. John's innocence will come out in due course. As for the locker, the guys just like to clown around. It's what we do to one another. Though I do wish they hadn't found out about my little hallucination, when I'm struggling so hard not to appear nuts. When I've already put it behind me," he added half to himself.

"So you really think denying faeries will help you win back your job."

"Win back my sanity!"

She promptly burst into tears. "Oh, Alec, I feel so foolish."

"Everyone will understand you were just nervous, anxious to fit in."

"More than you know, Alec," she babbled almost eerily.

"Not my fault. I've been waiting patiently for you to explain yourself, Tia. I've told you so much, even admitted to loving you."

"And I've loved you, Alec. Why, with every passing hour I've worried more about . . . this." Popping up from the bench, she stepped into the shadows. Standing very still with arms at her sides, she bowed her head. With a soft, high hum she began to vibrate.

The process was so fast, Alec barely had time to register the transmutation. Where his new girlfriend once stood on the sidewalk in blue jeans, shirt, and Keds, now hovered a creature in an iridescent pink dress and golden slippers, sprouting a pair of shimmery white wings. Strange and foreign, but to Alec Simon in particular, instantly recognizable, right down to the slippers.

"You. You." All he could manage was to point and gape.

"I am the apparition you've apparently been working so hard to forget."

It was Alec's turn to sit on the bus bench. "How could you not tell me!"

"After your conversation with Mindy, I was afraid to."

That's right. She would've gotten an earful and eyeful there. No wonder she always seemed one step ahead of him. Bending over, he buried his face in his hands. "I thought I was getting back on track. I thought I had a fresh start, with a cool new girlfriend."

"We are fresh. I am cool."

His head snapped up again. "You aren't even human!"

"There you are wrong. I wallow in your disgusting condition by a full half."

"Excuse me?"

"My father is human," she snapped impatiently. "I came here from the Enchanted Realm to explore what I hoped would be my better half. You were quickly convincing me the Mortal Realm is an upgrade. But after tonight I can see both realms suffer from equal stupidity and prejudice." Her shoulders sagged slightly even as she fluttered in place.

He was dumbfounded. "I can't be responsible for a whole nation's bias."

She hovered closer, her lush lower lip extended. "At the moment, your opinion is all that matters."

"This is crazy. Beyond words—"

Then suddenly words no longer mattered when, on a whiplash flap, Tia up and vanished into the night.

Alec headed home, stopping outside the brownstone to gaze up at Tia's apartment, looking empty and dark. If she was there at all, she was hiding.

Alec kept his place pretty dark as well once he was inside. Kicking off his shoes, he settled into his living-room recliner in front of the glow of a muted television. The History Channel was rehashing the Battle of the Bulge. While he usually enjoyed old war stories, he found himself more focused on the window facing 60th Street. Primed for a flash of gossamer on his fire escape.

Did he really want her to show up?

Had he hurt her deeply?

So many anxieties Ping-Ponged round his head, along with the intermittent ring of dual telephones.

John was trying hard to reach him on both his cell and his landline, surely anxious for news on his chat with the chief. Normally, John had him on the first ring. But right now, his convoluted feelings for Tia outranked everything else. That realization rose out of nowhere as his hand froze in mid-air over the cordless resting nearby on his end table.

While John was as close to family as Alec came these days, his gut was telling him that Tia could potentially move in even closer. That she deserved this stretch of reflective stewing.

So what did the two of them really have?

Chemistry. To look at her was to desire her. A reaction she openly shared.

Loyalty. She swiftly took an active interest in his challenges, coaxing him to face his professional demons, supporting John in his plight at the fire department.

All she'd really done wrong was not return his confidences as quickly as she should. Which on one hand caused her to spout off embarrassingly in front of his colleagues. Which made him less receptive when she did finally spill.

But again, understandable after eavesdropping on his scene with Lindsay. To arrive here for a fresh start, only to discover more prejudice in her path, must have been tough.

On the surface of things, it appeared tonight's breakdown was mostly his fault. But surely fixable, if he wanted it badly enough.

All through the years, what he wanted most was to re-create the stable home life he had shared with his folks.

Settle into a haven of ordinariness where he could escape the stress of his job.

With Tia, there were bound to be kinks in this mortal domestic setup.

In her defense, however, she was already trying to figure out what he needed and trying damn hard to deliver.

All this, of course, was merely speculation limited to his own scope. He couldn't sort any further without her input. A part of him felt she should apologize first for draining his secrets while hoarding her own. Due to her insecurities, however, she'd never initiate amends. No matter how long he stared out the window. It would be up to Alec to step up. He hoped it wasn't too late.

Alec awoke the following morning to a pounding on his door. It was at that moment he realized he'd fallen asleep in his recliner. He scrambled to pop the lock and remove the security chain without bothering to check the peephole.

"Alec. Finally."

"Trey. Come in." Alec stepped aside to allow John Winter passage.

"Why haven't you been picking up?"

Alec self-consciously raked back his hair. "Fell asleep in my chair."

"You make it to the station?"

"Yeah."

John dropped into the room's best chair, a hand-crafted leather one he'd gifted Alec with last Christmas. Alec suspected John had bought it mostly for himself.

"Spoke to the chief," Alec admitted, moving into the kitchen for a drink of water. "He isn't handing out favors. Any findings are still on the down low."

"No wonder you avoided my calls, trying to spare me the news."

Alec shrugged from the kitchen. Worked for him.

"Thanks, anyway, for trying."

Alec reappeared in the living room, rubbing his fresh, itchy whiskers. "The process is fair. I'd stake my life on it."

"Kevin Mitchell is making an ass of both of us. Keeping the probe alive in the newspapers, now publicly refusing to attend my awards banquet."

"Sorry about that."

"I need you there more than ever!"

Still unsure if he'd attend, Alec shrugged.

John lifted a stoic chin. "I don't know why I bother with these ceremonies."

"Because you care."

John brightened a little. His cell phone beeped then with an incoming text message. He glanced at it and rose. "I have to go." Alec followed him back to the door, where he paused, shifting his long body elegantly against the door frame in a way Alec had never before considered. "If you hear of any breakthroughs, even rumors, let me know."

"Of course."

"And don't rule out Saturday."

"I won't." Alec studied his mentor closely then, the intriguing blue eyes shifting from flint to gleam in a heartbeat. He'd seen it all a thousand times before as John got his way. Yet it gave Alec a distinct tug of déjà vu.

"Something the matter?"

Alec jerked back to attention. "Nope."

"Stay in touch." With a pat on Alec's shoulder, he shot off down the hall.

Alec sort of half-closed the door on John. As Alec waited

for John's steps to clear the staircase, he thought back to the last time he'd seen that look of sated smugness.

He'd been on top of it, in his own bed, buried in reams of platinum hair.

How could he have missed the obvious set so clearly before him!

Chapter

5

Barefoot, dressed in last night's clothes, Alec marched down the hall and pounded on the door marked 2D. "Open up! I know you're in there."

"You can't know for sure."

"Well, I sure do now. Open up, Tia."

The lock rattled and the door opened the length of the security chain.

"John Winter is your father!" Alec quickly accused.

The door smacked shut, only to fly open wide on its hinges. Tia popped out in the hall to look around. Alec used the opportunity to herd them both inside.

"I finally put it together, the string of clues. The way you asked for him first thing. The way you defended him—though I thought you were merely supporting me. But what really just cinched it was John himself in one of his pouts. Lounged at my door like his jockeys were pulled up too snug, then suddenly loosened. Sort of a catch and release. You look like that sometimes, too. Around the eyes. You share those startling baby blues. . . ."

She opened her mouth and closed it. Folded her arms and kept them folded. "We are not speaking."

"There it is! The Winter glimmer!"

She simmered with energy now, Alec noted. She never could keep quiet long, and under the circumstances—

"Did he recognize me, Alec?" she asked in a burst.

"Well, no. Don't think so. C'mon, tell me how this is even possible."

"The usual way." She made a crude motion with her fingers, jabbing one through a hole.

He couldn't help but laugh.

"This is not amusing."

"Tia, Tia, I find you totally amazing."

"Suit yourself," she said loftily.

"Listen, I'm sorry I reacted badly last night."

"You don't care to believe in Enchantments, that is your privilege."

"I must have always believed a little bit. I did acknowledge you at first sight. If I'd been alone, who knows what might have happened."

"What got you running back today, though, was my connection to your precious John, the idea that his blood runs through my veins."

"It did get me over here faster. I was already eating humble pie, though, wondering how I could ever get you to open your door to me, when John arrived to give the game away."

She sized him up. "This humble pie does wonders for you."

He shook his head. "To think that Winter blood flows through you."

"Yes. Though mine is rich violet in color, singular to the Luna species."

"So you're *Luna,* huh?"

"Yes."

"That common in Scandinavia?"

"No."

"Am I going to have to pry every detail out of you?" he demanded.

"Not sure I want to stick my throat out."

"Neck."

She whirled round just in time to catch him biting back a grin. "Next it could be a foot. Sticking a foot—"

"Tia! That's no way to talk to your fresh-start buddy."

Her stony face began to crumble. "You hurt me deeply last night, Alec. You would have thought I grew horns instead of wings."

"I had every right to freak over your strange origin. I also felt betrayed. You could have told me the truth sooner and didn't. As it is, you went on to have that mini-breakdown at my place of work, where my fitness is already in question."

"I never meant to harm you. I was only reacting to insults that seemed directed at me. Don't forget, my fitness is also in question—caused me to leave home!"

"The crew is harmless. Responded in a way humans raised on tales will."

"So no one in your realm freely accepts the Enchanted."

"Oh, I think if you advertised around town, you'd find pockets of believers."

"But it isn't mainstream anywhere."

"Like anyone who is *different,* I think you'll suffer through a period of adjustment. It seems in your best interest to lead with your human qualities."

"I'm not sure that is best for me."

"Just one of the many things we'll have to work out. What I need first is a better idea of exactly who you are." He moved to her sofa, identical to his own minus some beer stains, and patted the cushion beside him. She didn't join him, however. Instead she chose to pace.

"All right, Alec. Here goes."

* * *

Alec's head was spinning thirty minutes later. A small girl grappling with her half-breed existence in a world of Enchanted creatures. An existence due to a young robust John sailing the Irish Sea off the Isle of Man. Lured forth by a siren's song? High on rum and elderberry wine! Making love in the forest!

"Mortals rarely remember the experience," Tia ultimately explained. "At the most it seems like a dream."

"Still, you've been hoping John would remember."

"Of course! While my eyes, hair, melodious voice, even teeth, are unquestionably human, I do share Mamma's facial features. There's a chance, albeit slim, that I could jog loose a memory he's always mistaken for a dream."

"Just the same, I think he would have said something by now, don't you?"

"He's seen so little of me, really. Given time . . ."

"John has long been grounded in practicalities. Wealth and power fuel his dreams."

Tia hung her head. "I don't want to disrupt his life in any way."

"Your news has the potential to do just that. If a whiff of his *adventure* got through to the media, they'd attack like hungry sharks, until John's dignified public image was picked clean. Even worse, in my opinion, would be the suspicion that he cheated on his wife. You and Ken are both twenty-eight."

"I am almost twenty-nine. And faery gestation is faster. His tryst with Mamma could be months off," she reasoned hopefully.

"Only John would know the timetable, and only then if he remembers."

"You are so quick to his defense at every turn, Alec."

"It's what I do. What we do for each other. Family strategy."

"Exactly what I want for myself! Can't you see that?"

It all was, in fact, sinking in with clarity. Particularly his unwitting new role as middleman.

"Come on, Alec. Do you think you can see to my best interests along with John's or not?"

His heart twisted under her achy yet defiant gaze. He launched from his chair to embrace her. "I will do everything in my power to get you into John's life, of course. If you follow my strategy." Her chin wobbled slightly, but it was hardly the nod he was looking for. "C'mon, Tia. I have every right to guard my relationship with the man. If you cross some line, it will be the end for both of us. Once John stops trusting someone, he's out for good." Reading her pained surprise, he added, "John isn't a saint by any stretch. Never one to yield."

"Not even for a long-lost daughter?"

He smiled faintly. "He did always fancy one. Use your patience and charm wisely, you might at least become the lovely mortal girl he stole away from somebody else."

Plainly, this idea fell below her expectations.

"Tia, that might be the limit with John—forever."

"But you'll be willing to accept my Fey traits . . . won't you?"

"A work in progress," he confessed mightily.

"I suppose I should appreciate your honesty," she begrudged.

Pinching her chin, he pressed his mouth to her forehead. "I came back. You let me in. Give us a chance."

Tia was thrilled when Alec allowed her to choose the itinerary for their day. Missing the natural glories of the Isle of Man, she chose to spend the day in Central Park. Roaming bridges, glades, meadows, bridle and lake paths that she'd swiftly explored on wing had her relating animated memories of her home.

"Sounds beautiful," Alec remarked as they paused by a duck pond.

"Oh, indescribably so. Hope you'll want to visit one day."

"That's possible?"

"I can arrange transport one way or another. The rest would be up to you, your decision to believe what you see."

John must have believed, Alec realized. *People sure ran deep and mysterious.* "Do you expect to return often?" he thought to ask.

"I don't know. I'll need some arrangement with Mamma."

Alec pushed aside a hank of silver-blond hair to plant a kiss on her cheek. "I'll do everything I can to make that happen, Tia."

Tia drew a small tight smile. He probably would. Still there were so many unexpected terms. Could she conceal her faery origin if necessary to fit into normal human society? Could she stand to be around John, playing the friend, while bursting to reveal their kinship?

Alec expected these things right now. Insisted it was for the common good. She felt she had no choice but to trust him until, if, and when she knew better.

On the last leg of their outing, the couple wandered outside to the neighborhood market. Alec stood by with a plastic basket while Tia inspected produce with a squeeze and a sniff.

"Rest assured, I know my onions," she whispered when the market's owner, old Mr. Bellamy, glared at them for the umpteenth time. "Other vegs as well."

"Still, pick up the pace," Alec urged. "I'm getting hungry."

"Such things are never rushed in the Enchanted Realm." She wrinkled her nose over a misshapen potato.

"Those spuds all look the same."

"Yet they are not. Vegetables, and fruit for that matter, are as varied as humans and faeries."

Bellamy loved that one, Alec noted with a grimace. He wondered if he could ever get used to public amusement over Tia's sincere observations. Felt like hell no!

"Have you considered planting your own garden, Alec?"

Alec liked that idea. Bellamy, not so much. "I think a garden would be nice. Someday, when I have that dream house—with a yard."

"Maybe some space in Central Park could be adopted."

Alec handed their basket to Bellamy.

It was sometime after dinner in Alec's apartment that he and Tia decided to tune out the History Channel in favor of the bedroom. It was sheer relief to abandon the cares of the fully clothed, as well as worries over species, and issues of paternity, to focus on the timeless act of intimacy.

Later, lying in the darkness beside a gently snoring Tia, Alec had no clue of the time. His boxers were presently covering up his clock radio on the nightstand. There seemed nothing wrong with allowing the traffic sounds outside his brownstone to lull him to sleep.

A perfect plan, if the cordless phone, standing to attention underneath Tia's scrap-of-lace excuse for panties, hadn't started to ring. Flicking off the panties, he grabbed the handset. So intent on sniffing the panties, he hadn't bothered to check the caller ID. "Hello." He cleared his throat. "Simon here."

"Busy, Alec?"

He flung the panties to the foot of the mattress. "No, sir. What's up?"

* * *

Tia awoke to a dark room and empty bed. Alec's boxers no longer concealed the clock. The green numbers glowed 3:38.

Pulling on Alec's gray T-shirt, she padded out to the living room, where a single lamp glowed. She was certain he'd be watching the TV box humans so admired, but the screen was blank. The tickle of spring breezes soon drew her to the window—and Alec, perched on the fire escape.

She eased onto the sill. "Can't sleep?"

"The chief called. He'd like me to take my fitness test day after tomorrow."

"That's wonderful!"

"Ya think so?"

"It's the only way forward. You didn't turn him down, did you?"

"No, told him to pencil me in."

"That's a step."

"Considering he writes everything in ink, I'd say the date is set."

"So you're angry that you didn't have a choice?" she tentatively asked.

"I'm angry because I know I won't pass! Then the truth will be out. My last shred of hope for a quiet recovery over."

"All is not lost. You made it out here."

"Barely. Looking down still makes me sick to my stomach. I would never conceal this weakness from the department—probably couldn't anyway."

"I can help you, Alec, if you let me."

"What can you do that my physical therapist and shrink could not?"

Shifting on the sill, Tia flapped her arms.

"Don't say it."

"But you'll love flying!"

"Most men only have to *jump* through hoops to get the girl."

"It would take your complete trust," she acknowledged. "But it may be the only quick fix dramatic enough to work."

He surveyed her dubiously. "You have experience carrying passengers?"

"More than one on occasion. After extensive training."

"You get high marks?"

"My wingspan is shallow, likely due to my human genes. But I passed."

"I suppose we could take a shot at it. If you remember I'm no Peter Pan."

She laughed melodiously. "Oh, Alec, there can be only one Peter Pan."

"Silly me."

"I would like to add one condition," she said rather defiantly.

He slanted her a weary, wary look. "What?"

"Your promise that we'll attend the banquet Saturday."

"Gee, I'm already under enough pressure."

"You'll feel like celebrating if you pass your fitness test."

"That's a huge *if*."

"Your chief invited me, so in a way I don't even need your okay."

"You'd go without me?" he squawked.

"I know I won't have to, Alec. You'll pass and want to celebrate."

"How 'bout we leave it as a maybe?"

The next night, Alec brought Tia to the fire site on 56th Street. Together they stood on the sidewalk in front of a broken-down two-story building tucked between a high-rise and a trendy boutique, presently a dark hollow shell, void of life. The property was surrounded by orange fencing, as well as No Trespassing signs, bearing multiple threats of punishment by law.

Alec forced a grin. "What a week. Scored a new girlfriend who can make me insane and cure my insanity all at the same time."

"A true example of irony."

"Your average American couple, really."

"You say the nicest things," Tia said wispily.

Alec gazed up with a deep, tense breath. "Guess it's time."

"We could have taken flight anywhere, Alec. Even from your fire escape. Are you sure you want to be here?"

"Yeah. If I'm going to face my demons, this is the only place to do it. Plus I'll finally get a look at the scene without technically trespassing. We won't be touching a thing, not even the floor." Digging into his pocket, he extracted a small LED flashlight. Clicking it on, he confided that he had brought two.

"I won't need one. I have excellent night vision. If you tell me what you're looking for, I can be of great help."

"Any signs of arson. Deep charring on walls and flooring. The smell of accelerant. Multiple fire patterns." He extended his arms, sending his beam of light skyward. "They grow up and out in a V pattern. These are all the things we hope *not* to see."

"For John's sake."

"To some extent. Off-the-record. Officially, this isn't even happening," he related edgily. "The best I can ever do is tell John I got a reliable tip."

"Which means I won't get a mention," she complained.

"Tia, please, while the night is still dark."

"Yes, we do need the cover of darkness. Flying this slow, even the Earth's lowest creatures can spot me."

"Knock humans all you want. You're still one of us."

"I will attribute your weak humor to nerves." She sighed with strained patience. "First lesson is a caution. Flying is like mergence, Alec. Once you do it, you'll want more. And more."

He clipped his flashlight to the string of his black hooded sweatshirt. "Don't distract me now, honey."

"I am only saying it will take enormous energy to carry you. I won't be pressured in the future by your every whim."

"Huh. It does sound like sex. Married-couple sex."

"Now you're distracting *me,* Alec. I can't think about a wedding *and* teach you the ropes."

"Stick to the ropes. What do we do first?"

In response, Tia went into transmutation mode, bowing her head and rolling her shoulders slightly. Wings sprouted, her jeans and top melded into a backless rose petal dress.

Alec inhaled sharply, certain he'd never get over the wonder of it all.

"Touch one, Alec," Tia urged, stroking the tip of a gossamer limb against his cheek. "Soft enough to caress. Resilient enough to polish silver."

The graze of the iridescent material against his skin sent an electric current down his spine. He struggled to focus on something mundane. "You use your wings in your work?"

"That's right. A zip over gossamer webbing gives each metal piece I create a lasting sheen."

He blinked, urging back his bearings. "Okay. Lasting sheen. Now what?"

Tia removed a silken braid that had appeared at her waist during transmutation. Stepping up behind him, she drew the rope around his middle several times, cinching them snugly together.

"You meant 'ropes' literally?"

"This braid can hold a ton."

"Oh? Your people ever do a human stress test with this thing?"

"It's not the rope about to snap here, Alec," she fumed. "My whole life is at stake!"

"Which is why I am being so darling right now. No! Don't twist round. Just checking my knots."

"What's your knot of choice?"

"Trust, Alec."

"Okay, okay."

Suddenly Alec felt a whipping of air behind him. Wind pressure increased until he thought his hair would blow off the top of his head.

They were rising! Inches off the concrete! Dangling in place, picking up wing velocity, he realized he hadn't discussed with her how they'd enter the building. He barely had time to process the thought, however, as they lifted, angled, and swooped up through a broken-out window on the second floor!

Hovering vertically in the dark interior of the second level, he fumbled for the flashlight dangling from his flashlight string. The small LED beam was strong, a welcome complement to the paler moonlight streaming through the holes his crew had chopped in the roof to vent the flames.

Getting his bearings, he spotted the jagged hole of his fall only feet away. His body jerked against Tia's as he relived the helpless falling sensation. The all-encompassing dizziness, his heart being sucked up his throat.

"All right?" Tia murmured in his ear.

He inhaled deeply to steady his nerves. The nasal shot of kerosene and charred wood mostly made him want to gag.

Fire sites always stunk, of destruction, waste, and loss—all too often human.

It was common to deal with such things. He'd been good at it for so long.

And he could be good at it again. If only he could wrestle past his old demons once and for all. Seemed a matter of keeping his cool keeping the faith.

"What next?" Tia prodded.

"Circle slowly near the walls!" he shouted over the swish of her wings.

"Take it easy," she soothed. "I have excellent hearing."

"Huh?"

"Nothing!" she shouted back.

Alec gritted his teeth as Tia slowly began to rise and slant. Then let out a yelp as they did a jarring 360 spin! It was like somersaulting on the loopy-loop ride at the carnival—without a seat belt, or even a seat!

"Sorry, Alec," she said, righting them once again in a vertical hold.

"You said you were trained for this!"

"I am certified. Regulation textbook training."

"What about your experience carrying passengers!"

"A gaggle of kittens over a raging sea."

"Tiny kitties?"

"There was also a troll rescue. All of them squirmy."

"On second thought—"

"No second thoughts! I am perfectly capable. It's only a matter of balancing your weight. I'm getting it." Using her arms as added support around his middle, she leveled off and began to flutter toward the nearest wall.

Alec lost himself in the evidence as they floated in a horizontal hold along the perimeter, darting his flashlight at the charred walls and flooring. Plainly, this was no accident caused by drinking college kids or homeless people trying to cook. Rather, it was outright arson. There was no mistaking the stink of kerosene—an arsonist's best friend—or the core burns it caused in the wood.

Though hardly the work of a pro. Accelerant was slopped everywhere, making it a wonder anyone got out safely.

Not for the first time, Alec wondered if some unlikely character had pulled this off. Such as a disgruntled neighbor on this street, bitter because Helen's charity would have lured lower-income traffic to the upscale area of shops and offices. Maybe a few of them were in cahoots. Then again, John was on many a shit list for any number of dealings. Even Alec's own fire chief resented him. The investigation had to be tough going.

In any case, this was news better kept to himself.

Completing a full pass over the second level, Tia swept them to the center of the floor. Suspiciously near the hole.

Alec forwent preliminaries. "I'm ready. Watch out for jagged wood."

Raising them directly over the gap, Tia plunged them through feet first. Alec felt his heart slide up his throat, only to come back down as they landed inches from the charred ground floor. He could see the disturbance where they'd likely hauled him out. Not that he remembered much after hitting the ground.

"All right, Alec?"

"Yeah. *Yeah.*"

Tia fluttered along the lower perimeter, which showed similar signs of arson.

"Good enough!" Alec shouted in her ear.

Upon hearing this, Tia took Alec's breath away by swooping back through the hole in the floor. While Alec leaned slightly toward the window where they'd entered, Tia kept going straight up, right through a hole in the roof!

Flapping wildly in the crisp spring night on sheer gossamer wings, Alec never felt more exhilarated—or scared out of his wits. But all was good. He'd done it! Faced his greatest fear and conquered it.

All that was left was a gentle landing. The sooner, the better.

"Congratulations, Alec!"

"If this didn't cure me, nothing can. Now let's head for safer ground."

"This doesn't have to be the end."

Exactly what he was thinking. *"Please land."*

"Let's take a quick tour of the city first, see the Statue of Liberty. C'mon, don't be a goblin."

Her tone clearly intimated some deficiency on his part. Not fair to a man who had skied the Alps, river rafted in the Boundary Waters, hiked the jungles of Costa Rica. But all she knew at the moment was her man had some exasperating limits. His macho pride had him giving in.

There was no denying the ride was spectacular. No doubt what news crews and tourists saw from helicopters. Alec and Tia headed south along the East River, over the medical center, the East Village, zooming out over the water—where it was especially damp and chilly—to Lady Liberty in all her glory. Tia was enraptured enough to circle once, twice, a total of three times, until he was nearly shivering out of his skin.

If he could have reached her bottom, he would have paddled it. All he could manage, however, was an urging nudge of elbow.

Getting the message, she soared back, north along the Hudson over the West Village, the twinkling lights of the Theater District.

As they came up fast on their 60th Street brownstone, Alec began to wonder how on earth they were going to land. As Tia dipped and slowed and scanned, he sensed she was wondering the same thing.

He couldn't help but be reminded that he weighed a damn sight more than some kittens.

They ended up dropping into Central Park, skidding in a pond near the Hallett Nature Sanctuary.

They slogged to the water's edge like a couple of drowned rats. The only thing with any spring left between them was a pair of gossamer wings. Pulling off his hooded sweatshirt, Alec wrung it out. "We'll have to walk home from here. I didn't bring my wallet." Then he thought to pat his front jeans pocket. "My key ring is gone!"

"Is it so important?"

"It's the one with all the building keys on it." He slapped the sweatshirt down on the lawn. "Dammit!"

"Don't give up yet."

"For all we know, Lady Liberty is chewing on them."

"I doubt it."

"Why?"

"Remember that three sixty we did in the building?"

"Oh, right. That could've jogged 'em loose, along with my kidneys."

"You go on home, Alec. I'll fly back for a look."

"I'd better come along."

"No. You're angry, annoying, tired. And heavy. Very heavy."

He preened. "You say the sweetest things."

She preened back. "I can zip back, make use of my night vision, and land on my feet near the brownstone again in no time. In fact, I wager I'll beat you back there, ready to let you in for a nice, hot shower."

He aimed a finger at her. "You're on."

Sure enough, when a sodden Alec trudged up to their building gripping his soaked hoodie, he found Tia perched on the top step, dressed in her original dry jeans and shirt. He decided to forgive her smugness, however, when she held the ring high above her head and jingled the keys in glee.

"You found them! Thank . . ." He paused as she popped

up and held them out of reach. "What are you up to now?"

"A negotiation break. I swept you off your feet. Now it's your turn to sweep me—onto the dance floor."

"Oh, Tia—"

"I know you want to pass the fitness test first. After tonight, that certainly will happen."

"There is no guarantee."

"If and when it does . . ."

"Look, there's more to the story now that we've seen the arson signs. John will soon be notified officially. That banquet could be extremely awkward."

"Not before Saturday night, surely! He doesn't have to know we checked on the building."

"Just the same, he's sure to ask me if I heard anything. I've never lied to him yet. I can't imagine starting now, at a public event in my honor."

"You can stall. Evade the issue." She wound her arms around his soggy body and kissed him thoroughly. "Please, do it for me."

He smiled down at her, touching her loose silvered hair. "There'll be other nights, other dances."

Her baby blues gleamed. "Really? When?"

"The Winters love their fancy dress parties."

"How often do *you* attend, Alec?"

"Whenever I can't worm out of it."

"I thought so! You own a couple sad-looking suits and a total of five crumpled ties."

He tapped her nose. "You've been snooping."

"Don't change the subject. Don't be so difficult!"

He surveyed those blue eyes again, noting a deeper tension he'd missed. "What am I missing here?"

"A dazzling party hosted by my father," she coaxed. "The chance to waltz in his arms as well as yours."

"So he's your real target."

She blushed. "Not exactly. Not totally. Surely you can understand how irresistible this opportunity seems. To dress my best, put on a radiant face similar to my mother so long ago. It could be enough to jar his memory, validate an old dream."

"Ah. Guess I do understand. Say I go along with this scheme."

"Yes, Alec?"

"Will you accept the verdict either way? If John has no clue to who you are, will you settle into the idea of friendship?"

She bit her lip. "Suppose I'll have to, won't I?"

Alec was seated on the stoop of the brownstone later Friday afternoon when Tia alighted from a cab. "Where ya been?" he called out merrily.

"Buying the perfect dress for tomorrow night," she blithely announced with the sweep of a Nordstrom garment bag.

"Pretty sure of yourself, aren't you?"

She leaned over the stoop to kiss him. "Pretty sure of you."

"As it happens, you have a right to be. I passed inspection! Back to work on Monday." Popping off the steps, he grasped her waist and lifted her in the air for a twirl on the sidewalk. Caught off guard, she squealed. He kept turning with a laugh. "This is how humans fly when they're happy!"

"Would you like to go for another real ride, Alec?"

He swiftly set her down. "Not really. Let's go upstairs."

Back in her apartment, Tia airily whisked the garment bag right by him. "This is going to be a surprise. So don't follow me to the bedroom."

"Guess I'm more interested in the kitchen anyway. Anything to eat?"

"Help yourself!" Tia laid the bag on the bed and went to check her hair and makeup in the dresser mirror.

"Found your tools of the trade!" Alec called out.

"Oh, yeah."

"You working on something?"

Tia gazed down at two pieces on her dresser, a narrow silver one buffed to perfection and a charred nugget of as-yet undetermined metal. "Something pretty for the gala. A surprise."

Tia returned to the kitchen fully expecting Alec to be examining the black felt roll holding her glittery craftsman tools. Rather, he was peering at two far more mundane red ceramic mugs bearing traces of tea.

"So which tenant have you been ear-bending?" he teased.

"Would you like some tea, Alec?"

He sank into a chair. "Not in this lifetime."

"Let's go out, to Forliti's."

"You're evading the question," he realized with surprise.

"I think I'll have some tea."

He snagged her arm. "Tia, we made a deal to be direct with each other—answer questions as asked."

"Okay, it was the little man you met in the park."

"Mr. Blot? Didn't waste much time." His dark brows narrowed. "I knew it was wrong to give him your number."

"His name is simply Blot and he didn't really need my number. He already sort of had it."

Alec squeezed her arm. "What are you saying?"

"He is a dear friend from the Enchanted Realm. Specifically, a leprechaun."

He released her with a flick. "We actually discussed him. You should've told me then!"

"Your instant dislike for him has made it awkward. As

has Blot's disapproval of my mortal quest here. He's not exactly in favor of me spreading my wings beyond the Enchanted Realm."

"He's important in your life," Alec realized.

"Very." Tia went on to explain Blot's role as family friend, his illustrious job regulating the pots of gold at rainbows' end. "He should be retiring soon. I'd like nothing better than to see him seriously romance Mamma. All he'd likely have to do is stick around the Realm for a change and turn up the steam."

"Still not sure what rubbed me the wrong way about him," Alec conceded.

"Maybe nothing."

"No matter. For you, I'll give the imp a chance."

"Don't ever insult him with a prissy name like that, Alec. Blot has magical powers you don't want to mess with."

"Such as?"

"He can relocate anywhere in a blink—taking anyone he wishes along. Temporarily freeze creatures like statues. Cloak himself in invisibility. Carry several times his body weight."

"Huh. Maybe I'll tap him next time I need a lift."

"My suit is lost! The cleaners lost my suit." Late Saturday afternoon Alec barged into Tia's bedroom, where she was scooting around wrapped head to knee in terry.

"The drab brown one?" she asked hopefully.

"The very sharp navy one."

Tia pulled open her lingerie drawer with a shrug. "If they were going to lose one, it is too bad —"

"They lost the only one I was having cleaned of course! That's what I get for taking it to the overnight place." He paced between the bed and the dresser, distracted by her holding up two pairs of lace panties.

"Pink or beige?"

"You want my opinion on what to wear *under* the dress I can't see yet?"

"Eventually, the dress will be coming off. So . . ."

He narrowed in on the quandary. "Let's do pink."

"So you like pink."

"I dunno. They're . . . lacier."

All of a sudden the air between them seemed heavier. Tia could feel herself melting into his desire. "Alec! You need to go buy a new suit."

He snapped back to attention. "No time to have it altered."

"They can tack it up. Humans must have an idea."

"Yes! You're right. I'm going to head for Madison Avenue, bring my shoes, shirt, and stuff along." He tugged her close for a kiss. "I'll hurry."

"No reason we can't meet up at Winter Towers."

"Oh, no. I want to be the first to see you in that new dress. Wait for me in the vestibule. I'll swing back for you."

Tia tried not to glance too compulsively at her watch as she waited for Alec in the brownstone's lobby that evening. It was drizzling outside, which had already sent her back upstairs once for an airy gold chiffon scarf to keep the moisture from her lacquered chignon. Preserving the specific style was a priority, as it was her mother's favorite. How, Tia was certain, Maeve would have worn it seducing seafaring males.

It might not be sensitive to reveal herself to John outright, but there seemed nothing wrong in giving nature a nudge in the right direction.

Finally! A streak of yellow at the dark curb and a honk of horn. By the time she had the heavy glass door open, Alec was alighting on the steps, looking handsome in a new suit, as slick and black as his hair and shoes.

"Hold it!" Alec pushed her back inside to view her in the golden light of the cramped lobby. He ran a tender eye over her clingy peach shade gown, stalling on the exposed cleavage adorned with a topaz necklace. He attempted to remove the scarf from her head, but she pulled back with a smile. "Don't you dare muss me."

He affected exasperation. "How this reminds me of senior prom."

"What's that?"

"I'll tell you tonight in bed, while I'm working on those pink panties."

"More and more I think we'll have our busiest night in bed yet."

Easing Tia into the cab ahead of him, Alec instructed the cabby to Winter Towers on FDR Drive.

Tia watched out the window as they approached from 47th Street. The glittering glass and steel skyscraper dominated the strip of buildings overlooking the East River.

John Winter, vital king of New York City! An amazing contrast to the vague father image she had long carried of a perished faery lord.

Traffic was snailing along the drive as doormen at the brightly lit entrance assisted guests out of vehicles. Finally, it was Alec and Tia's turn to alight.

Alec whisked her inside the building, where they melded with a throng of formally attired people moving toward the elevators. Tia felt a rush of excitement in the crush as Alec introduced her to friends, all the while keeping a possessive hand at her waist.

Plainly, he was tremendously proud of her.

She was proud of him as well for so many reasons. Not only did he conquer his fears, but he'd also come to accept who she was at rapid speed.

The ballroom on the fifty-first floor proved to be a wonderland of gold foil walls trimmed in white with massive crystal chandeliers hanging from a high gilded ceiling.

Tia did a starry-eyed pirouette to take in the ambiance. That was when the chiffon scarf fell off her head, landing on her shoulders.

Alec's smile faded as he inspected her hair, a lustrous platinum sweep high above her neck. "What the . . ."

"Don't touch it!" Her fingers flew protectively to the narrow silver leaf-encrusted arrow. "It holds everything together."

"That's what scares me. Where did it come from, Tia?"

"It's of human origin. . . ."

"Obviously. It's a man's tie clip."

"Oh. That's rather disappointing."

"Did you keep it secret because it's from the fire scene?"

How frustratingly clever he was. "I kept it secret mostly to dazzle you, along with the dress."

"It isn't from the fire then?" he asked in a near plea.

"Sorry, but I couldn't resist it," she confessed in a gush. "Lying in plain sight beside your keys. Plain to me, anyway, with my sharpened night vision."

"I trusted you to return there alone."

"It was charred beyond human restoration. Strained even my skills. C'mon, Alec," she reasoned under his growing thunder. "Your chief lord said they were tying up loose ends; surely the item was dismissed."

"Overlooked, not dismissed. Big difference there when it comes to evidence."

"You think it's important then?"

"You'd be amazed by what our lab of human *minions* could have done with it."

"I am sorry. Don't let it spoil the whole party."

"The party is over as of now."

"You can't mean it!" She grasped his lapels, but he already seemed half-gone as his head spun over hers.

"I can't explain right now, am not even sure you deserve an explanation."

"Give me thirty minutes, Alec," she begged softly. "I don't have to dance with John; just let me greet him, looking as I do. Then I will return the clip to the exact place I found it."

"That's no good."

"Why!"

"You've tampered with it, Tia. No one will believe it survived the fire."

"All right, all right." She puffed nervously, rubbing her hands. "All is not lost. There was another piece."

"Another one!"

"Yes, a smaller nugget with a post. I left it behind because I couldn't think what to do with it."

"Thank God for that much."

"For all you know, I may have cracked the case wide open," she nervily reckoned.

"Not your case to crack. How the hell I wish you'd just butted out."

She retreated a notch. "Please take my word—"

"Your word?" Alec's features twisted in fury. "What good is that!"

"What a horrible thing to say, Alec Simon."

"I feel horrible. Sick."

"Fine. You're not my date anymore. Get unburdened."

"I think you mean lost. Get lost."

"Oh, just do it." Tears streaming down her cheeks, Tia scooted for the safest haven known to females the realm over: the ladies' room.

Alec paced out front of the ladies' room, knowing he already should be on the phone to Chief Mitchell, busily avoiding this affair. Even if it was the last thing he wanted to do. No, the last thing he wanted to do was leave Tia to her own foolish devices. She needed to leave. Now. He huffed over it some minutes before asking a blue-haired matron entering no-man zone to check up on a comrade in peach.

"A spat?" she clucked.

"Yeah. Sort of."

"You don't look sorry enough yet."

"Please, check up on her."

The matron returned moments later to report no one was in the restroom. It probably would land him briefly in purgatory one day, but Alec barged inside for a look. Sure enough, Tia was gone, save for her chiffon scarf, which he found underneath a slotted vent.

It occurred to him then that he knew more about Blot's powers than hers. Stood to reason, however, that she was too proud to be stuffed into a cab and had opted for a squirmy trek through the building's air duct system. Served her right! At least a part of him thought so, the part that was horrible. As sick as he felt, the night was only going to get sicker. Pocketing the scarf, he left.

After all they'd been through, Alec didn't think to look up once.

With both exasperation and relief, Tia swooped down from the ceiling of the restroom. Willing her wings back between her shoulder blades, she moved to ease open the door and slip in behind a group of women. Snagging a glass of champagne from a passing waiter, she took a self-pitying slurp and looked around. The ballroom was jammed with milling guests. If Alec was still among them, he'd moved on. So must she.

For a start, she would leave when she damn well pleased. After she had a word with John Winter.

Tia began to mingle in the hope of spotting John, passing the time with firefighters she'd met at the station. Servers with trays of champagne cocktails kept going by and she kept accepting them. They dulled the pain as adequately as nectar fizzes did back home.

Also like home, she seemed to have blown yet another romantic prospect. Her mother would not be pleased. Especially as there was less excuse. It wasn't Tia's scent or her singing this time. It was stubbornness grounded in humanity.

"Too many of those can spoil your appetite."

The smooth male voice caused Tia to spin on her white strappy Jimmy Choos, slosh champagne on an elegant jacket sleeve. John Winter's sleeve. He was positively resplendent from head to toe, his short gleaming hair the same unique shade as hers, his trim figure doing justice to his perfectly cut tuxedo.

A breathless Tia presented him a dazzling smile. While he . . . stared intently at her hair.

"We met in the park," she began wispily.

"Never mind all that, Tia. I know exactly who you are."

"How . . ."

"A little leprechaun told me, that same day in the park."

"How strange he didn't let me know."

"He left it to me because I asked him to, assured him it was the right thing."

Tia loosened up. "So, you remember your tryst with Mamma?"

"Fondly. Though once I returned home, I did choose to move on. Hope you can understand."

The secret child in her put up a feeble protest. If only he'd returned once! But he had no way of knowing all he'd abandoned. And the journey back would have been a long uncertain one. "No hard feelings," she whispered.

"Blot tells me Maeve is doing well."

"Oh, she is. So, you have no doubts about my relation to you?" she pressed.

"None. Your Winter features are prominent."

"I'm not here to make trouble for you," she assured. "Alec has explained how sensitive your reputation is. He's been emphatic about protecting it."

John scanned the room, nodding to passersby. "Where is he, anyway?"

"He's off cooling down," she improvised. *The cruel,*

insensitive goblin. "We had a little difference of opinion over the way I've handled this clip in my hair."

"You're using it to grab my attention," he stated practically.

"Well, yes. With my hair done this way, I—"

"Don't bother to explain. It was pretty nervy, but I myself have been guilty of grandstanding on occasion. Alec tends to be more cautious."

"Still, he'd do most anything to please you, sir."

"Am I wrong to assume you share those sentiments?"

"I'd like nothing better than to be your daughter, your friend—anything!" Her joy and relief nearly bubbled over. "Though I have come to understand the prejudice humans carry for anyone Enchanted. Realize it won't be easy for us."

"Sometimes human stupidity makes good business."

"How?"

"When you leave yourself open to the impossible, you sometimes get a jump on everyone else."

"How?"

"For the time being, let's just say, I have no quarrel with the Enchanted."

She could only smile in bewilderment.

"Don't worry about Alec," John went on. "He can be relied upon. We'll be one big happy family; I'm sure of it."

"Where to begin?"

"Start by calling me Trey."

The mention of family, access to the revered nickname, all without a hitch. She could barely breathe. "What about your wife?" she thought to ask. "Alec says she's wonderful, but I am bound to be a shock."

He pulled a small tight smile. "She's totally manageable."

"I can barely find the words to express . . ." Turned out she didn't need them, as he was no longer listening, but rather, making a phone call. To bring a company car around to a rear entrance, as it turned out.

John disconnected and settled back on Tia. "There are no limits for you in my operation. If you can follow directions."

"Operation" seemed a little cold in describing familial ties. But Tia did at times struggle with human terminology and John was, after all, very businesslike indeed. "Thank you, Trey. I'm grateful for this chance."

"So it's safe to assume you'll run a quick errand with me."

"Now? Leave your own party?"

"No one will miss us if we hurry."

She hesitated a merc half beat. "If you like."

"Good. We'll take my private elevator down to the car. Don't say another word, not even to my driver."

Alec bumped into Helen a short time later in the ballroom. The unassuming redhead always looked a little out of her league at these functions, in a way that even a designer gown like tonight's aqua stunner couldn't cure.

"Alec! So glad you're feeling better."

"Have you seen Trey?" he asked with strained cheer.

"Sure. Just caught him slipping out an exit with a woman in a peach gown."

"You know her?"

"Why, no."

"Can you describe her at all?" he pressed more sharply.

"Young, blond. Frankly, dear, I've learned to look the other way."

Her words, spoken at this time and place of enlightenment, rocked him significantly. Alec was forced to humbly acknowledge that he, too, sometimes looked the other way rather than allow John's image to distort. What mattered most right now was that the blonde in Trey's grip had to be Tia. A vulnerable daughter in waiting who might not know better than to look the other way.

"Thanks, Helen. For everything." On impulse, Alec hugged her gently, knowing full well it might be their last.

Tia didn't know what to expect once John's Town Car came to a stop on a dark street corner someplace in the city. John gave the driver instructions to vamoose, then alighted on the sidewalk to aid Tia, rather constricted in her gown.

Turned out they were standing before the fire-gutted building on 56th Street. Grasping a lantern, John held out his arm. "Shall we?"

Tia gazed at the orange fencing and warning signs still in place, then at the Town Car's red taillights already winking in the distance. Unease crept up her spine and, presumably, into her expression.

"Surely you can't be surprised, Tia. After all, you brandished the clip."

"You know it's from the fire?"

"Of course, child. It's mine."

Her jaw dropped.

"You really didn't know?"

Tia shook her head. "I spotted it retrieving Alec's key ring—after a little aerial inspection we made. Thought it would look good in my hair. Thought this particular style would remind you of Mamma."

His expression shifted oddly in the shadows. "Certainly it made all the difference. Lovely."

"So, what are we doing here?"

"I want to utilize your charming powers for a small search."

"Alec is already so angry over my meddling here."

"As I said, he errs on the side of caution. And would prefer to protect me inside the confines of the law. But in this case, the law must be bent. Allow me to explain," he said as her chin wobbled. "I lost the tie clip and a cuff link here a week before the fire, helping shift some furniture around for my wife. If Chief Mitchell were to uncover either piece of silver, I'm afraid he'd try to use it as evidence against me. You see?"

Tia nodded with more confidence. "The chief doesn't like you much."

"I hoped the pieces were lost for good. That is, until I spotted the clip in your hair."

"Both pieces were concealed in rubble and hopelessly charred. I only happened upon them due to my keen Fey night sight."

"Both? Did you by chance already come across the cuff link as well?"

"Yes."

"What did you do with it?" he demanded.

"Left it in the rubble. Unlike the clip, I judged it beyond repair."

His excitement was palpable. "I would be grateful if you'd retrieve it for me. Immediately."

Tia paused only briefly. "Would you like a lift through a window, like I gave Alec?"

He gave a brusque laugh. "At my age, I'd rather enter by a side door." Switching on the lantern, John eased them inside.

Tia's edginess grew as they delved into the black, dank space. Gagging slightly, she decided it looked a whole lot worse, even creepy, from the bottom up.

John set the lantern on the floor and waved. "Go about . . . your thing."

"Give me a moment. I have trouble transmuting when I'm nervous."

"There's nothing to fret," he said impatiently.

Tia took a deep breath and bowed her head. Before she

could sink into a trance, however, an all too familiar third voice echoed harshly through the room.

"Tia! What are you doing here?"

She snapped up her head. "I was invited. And you?"

"Please, stop and listen."

"You wouldn't listen to me at the party. While Father was more than happy to listen."

"I'll bet."

"Alec," John snapped, "if you're going to upset her, I'd rather you leave."

"That would make it easier, you lousy crook!"

"Oh, so it's that way now," John mourned, affecting hurt.

"Yeah, it is."

"You're jealous of Tia."

"No!" Outraged, Alec held out his hand. "Tia, I know it's a lot to ask—"

"You are not the boss of me! Get that through your noggin."

"No, you don't need any boss—"

"What she does need is a father," John intoned, smiling her way.

"This is a very sad day, John," Alec muttered.

"Yes, you dropping the ball here when I need you most."

Tia inhaled as the men began to stalk round one another. "What is the matter with you two? I am capable of saving the day. I'll fetch the cuff link and this whole arson matter will be settled to Trey's satisfaction."

"Yeah, with your wings and sight, you're the perfect partner in crime on this caper."

"That's just cruel, Alec. What's happened to you? Has Chief Mitchell offered you a bonus for dragooning Trey?"

"Likely a promotion," John suggested mournfully.

"Don't be such a little fool!" Alec boomed.

Tia gasped. "You're the fool, Alec. Mean and thought-less."

"You've probably got a point," he relented. "I've been blinded far too long by the lush Winter reality. I may not deserve you, but John deserves you even less. Don't start down my slippery path, give him his way."

"You seem out of your mind," John lamented.

Alec's retort lodged in his throat as a corner of the room lit up in eerie green. As Blot took shape in lepre-chaun regalia, Alec's distrust promptly resurfaced.

"Tia, m'dear, I heard your cries. Are you all right?"

"How could you hear her cries?" Alec demanded.

"I have kept a wavelength open out of deep concern," Blot replied, tugging at his green velvet jacket.

Tia seized the opportunity to outline the circumstance and seek his opinion.

Blot beamed gently. "It seems you're on the brink of a bright new start in life. Go for it."

"Hang on, Lucky Charms," Alec cut in. "Suddenly you approve of Tia's involvement with humans?"

Blot sniffed. "A wise creature knows when he's licked."

"Thing is, I sniffed something off about you that first day in the park."

"But you don't know what," Tia taunted. "Blot has been nothing but a wonderful protector of my mother and me." Bowing her head, Tia began the transmutation to faery.

Soon all would be lost—the arson evidence, Tia's chance to detour John. Unless Alec could think of something. Then, recalling the stubborn tick in his brain about the leprechaun, it came to him. "I've got it, Tia! Blot and John only pretended to be strangers in the park. They al-ready knew each other. Must have, because in the end, Blot addressed John as Trey."

"Everyone knows his nickname," Blot sniffed. "I merely took the liberty."

"That is reasonable, Alec."

"It's not reasonable that John allowed it. He should've been pissed as hell."

John smiled. "I'm softening in my old age. Now, Tia, if you will."

"What if they're lying, Tia? You gotta wonder why."

"I don't know what to wonder anymore!"

"Believe in us," Alec pleaded. "Trust me when I tell you the clip and the cuff link cast huge doubt on John's innocence."

Tia regarded Alec in pity. "You misunderstand. Trey lost the pieces days before the fire."

Alec grimaced. "I personally saw the silver on him an hour before the blaze. I told you we had dinner that night."

"Nonsense!" John raved.

"Tia," Alec said in a steelier tone, "I trusted you at seven hundred feet. You have to know I only want what's best for you."

She met his eyes then with an agonizing groan.

"I'm sorry, honey, but he likely thought you wore the clip in some kind of power play. That's why I tried to shoo you out of the ballroom."

At this point, John Winter impatiently snapped his fingers. "Blot. Plan B."

Blot disappeared. Only to reappear moments later, to Alec's amazement, with a burden twice his size. A plump, squirming female with gray hair sprinkled in lavender, dressed in a robe that appeared to be made of vines. With a wicked grin the leprechaun curled his thick velvet-sleeved arm to his captive's neck, tight enough to make her sputter.

"Enough," John ordered. "The point is made."

"What point?" Wrenching free of her unsuspecting captor, she whirled to face him. "Blot? Have you gone mad?"

"Oh, Mamma," Tia lamented.

"Tia?" Maeve whirled to the spill of lantern light.

"Maeve." John balked, stepping closer. "You're old and wrinkled!"

Maeve sniffed haughtily. "The bloom is off you as well, John Winter. What is the meaning of this, anyway? Tia, are you all right?"

"Save yourself, Mamma. Fly home."

"Without explanation? Not on your life."

"Ah, but it's all on *your* life, Maeve," John crowed, his face distorted. "That's the crux of Plan B." He snapped his fingers again, provoking Blot to produce an iron chain, which he wrapped loosely around Maeve's fleshy waist.

Maeve gasped in outrage. "You dare threaten me with iron?"

"How it will singe faery skin." John winced wickedly. "Ouch."

Maeve attempted a wiggle. "Blot, you are in the deepest peril."

"I do regret this unpleasantry," John continued icily, "but our little girl is behaving badly. When I urgently need her help."

"Tia," Maeve lamented, "how on earth could you stir up this much commotion already!"

"I am a loser here, too. Misunderstood by everyone. Even the horrible John Winter mistook my sincere outreach for a cat-and-mouse scheme."

"Well, excuse me, young lady, for thinking you're every bit as conniving as your old friend Blot!" John thundered.

"What is your connection to Blot?" Maeve demanded. "Answer me, John. I won't allow Tia to do your bidding until you do—threat of iron notwithstanding."

"Blot and I have a long history. He paid me a visit shortly after our *merger*. Your own fault for keeping my address in plain sight."

"Rolled up in a hollow twig in the back of my cupboard," Maeve drolled. "But then, Blot is as snoopy as a spinster."

"Blot was most determined to sink his claws into me. I was already fairly successful, you see, infatuated with Helen and her family's social connections. He tricked me into admitting that I remembered our union, then blinked me back for a look at your brat with glaringly human features. The last thing I wanted was for him to deliberately pique your interest in this realm. So I began to pay him money to keep his fat mouth shut. Soon I paid him to get proactive, to play the attentive friend/suitor in order to distract you, squash any future ambitions in my direction. Eventually, he began to do all sorts of jobs for me here, putting my interests far ahead of his gold route. His cunning and magic make him a most valuable nemesis in mortal business affairs."

"He earned his money," Maeve grumbled. "Always pretending to be jealous of you, John, forever encouraging Tia and myself to settle."

"Oh, he was deathly jealous of me from the start. That's what made his betrayal to you possible in the first place."

"So it was more than a little envy, was it, Blot?"

"Yes," he breathed over her shoulder. "If only you'd ever gazed upon me with any true desire. We would have roasted John on a spit. As it was, Winter's offer was more fulfilling than yours."

Maeve gave a harsh laugh. "No wonder Tia is a loser in love, with my poor example."

"Tia is not a loser at anything!" Alec thundered.

"Who is this young man?" Maeve asked with new sweetness.

"Shut up, all of you!" John roared. "Tia, go scoop up that cuff link. If you don't, I'll have Blot brand your mother like the old cow she is."

Alec's heart wrenched as Tia poised in uncertainty. "C'mon, John, this was always a job for Lucky Charms."

"The little tub has developed cataracts," John spat.

Alec couldn't help but blurt out laughter. "This whole thing seems like a clumsy circus with you as dastardly leader. I mean, what were you doing even lighting your own fire?"

Alec hoped to keep him talking and the pompous mogul couldn't resist defending his circumstance. "My hired hand was picked up on an outstanding warrant—got the call during our alibi dinner. The supplies were already here, so I decided to use them. It was imperative to get it done, you see, with those low-rent moochers set to take over my prime real estate. Helen had no right to promise them the place on her own, even if her parents owned it originally. Things got worse when I got here to find those kids and homeless people milling round. Handy fall guys, but they did make me nervous. I lost my footing upstairs in the dark and tore my shirt. Off popped my clip and cuff link. I could only hope they'd escape human detection—which they did. You can only imagine my shock tonight, first to spot Tia flaunting the clip like a seasoned conniver, then to discover she was only trying to dazzle me with a stupid faery hairdo!"

Alec stepped up on John, only to halt as he whisked a revolver into view. "Another step, Alec, and I tell Blot to freeze you solid. Damn uncomfortable for a good hour. If it's any consolation, I never wanted you hurt by any of this. But even my real son never gets in the way like you have here. Now, Tia, do as I ask or Mamma gets a lifetime allowance of iron in one dose."

With a deep sigh, Tia zipped up through the hole in the floor. She returned moments later holding a small black chunk between two fingers. Steadying the gun, John extended his free hand.

Tia recoiled. "Release Mamma first."

John nodded at Blot, who tightened the chain against Maeve's robe while hissing in her ear, "Tell her to turn it over."

With a cry of rage keen enough to hurt Alec's eardrums, Maeve whirled on Blot. Belly to belly, she kneed him in the groin with a mighty jerk. Howling, he dropped the chain. "Turn this over, you sack of shit!" she bellowed, twisting his nose between two crooked fingers. Writhing in pain, Blot sank to his knees. "You see, John," Maeve said conversationally, maintaining the pressure, "the snoot is a leprechaun's only true weakness."

John reared. "Now you tell me."

"Hear me well, Blot," she vented. "I'm going to tell your mother."

The leprechaun trembled. "Please, no."

"She's truly insufferable, waltzing around, bragging about her son the pot of gold regulator. Which leads me to believe that even the Rainbow Council still considers you above reproach, regulating to the best of your ability. A hint of scandal and they'll yank your prized route away. Then, they'll start reviewing your numbers, checking coin inventory in those pots—bound to come up short. Oh, yes, I can see the inevitable comeuppance to you and yours is worrisome. Years of degrading labor in the teeth-grinding mines!" She released his nose with a crank sharp enough to make Alec's eyes water.

"You've got me," Blot whined. "What's your terms?"

"Find a new home, Blot. Away from both the Isles of Man and Manhattan. And don't think we won't be watching."

Blot popped off in a flash of green.

The gun-wielding John, meanwhile, used the distraction to grab Tia, causing her to scream and slap his face.

"You little bitch," he seethed, raising the butt of the gun over her head.

Maeve swooped to Alec. "Stop him, sir!"

Alec was already on it. Lunging forward, he grabbed for the gun. Forced to let go of either the weapon or the faery, John shoved Tia to the sooty floor.

"Just leave, boy," John growled, struggling against him. "Not . . . too . . . late."

Suddenly the gun went off between their hands. Alec recovered quickly, using the kick of the shot to slide a right hook into John's jaw. The older man dizzily tumbled to the floor.

Alec regarded the women, now hugging one another. "Okay?"

"The shot went up," Maeve reported, hugging her daughter fiercely.

Sirens now wailed in the distance. "Probably for us," Alec predicted. "I did call for backup."

"As if you needed any," Maeve cooed.

"Mamma, I think it best we fly away home," Tia whispered self-consciously.

"What? With this fine young man all over you like a harbor mist?"

"I have messed things up even with this human. Pushed him off when he deserved my faith. Fell for John Winter's tricks."

"Tia," Alec interceded, grasping her close. "I am in no position to judge good judgment! Especially in relation to John. C'mon, we clicked in the first place because we both needed a fresh start. It's still true, simply minus a couple of father wannabes who don't deserve us anyway. We have each other, and your mother. Nice start on family if you ask me."

"Oh, Alec," Tia choked, "how can you desire this sooty mess?"

His eyes crinkled. "I happen to know you clean up nicely."

"What's our next move here, Alec?" Maeve demanded as the sirens neared.

"Tia's got to ditch that cuff link."

"Where?" Tia asked.

Alec glanced down at the unconscious mogul. "Put it in John's suit jacket pocket. He did want it, after all." The sirens whooped to a stop now. "I already reported that I was following John here on a tip. I'll say I found him rummaging around. He confessed to setting the fire, tried to involve me in a search for evidence. He pulled a gun; we fought."

"What about us?"

Alec grinned. "You have wings, Mamma. Use 'em."

"Surely John will protest your version."

"Admit to being trumped by his faery daughter and lover? Not a chance. He'll sic his lawyers on the case and hope to hell you ladies don't talk."

No sooner were Tia and Maeve soaring off than Chief Mitchell appeared in the doorway with a posse. "Sorry it took me so long, Alec." He hoisted a groggy John to his feet. "If it isn't Mr. Winter. Sorry I missed the showdown, but it's always down to that damn commute."

Epilogue

Four months later

"Back here, Alec! My mamma is being unreasonable again."

"I am his mamma, too," Maeve sang out cheerily. "With a marriage certificate on aged cedar parchment as proof."

Alec entered his roomy new kitchen to find Tia and Maeve seated at his new maple table. "What's the issue today?"

"Mamma insists on exposing her wings where any neighbor might walk by and see them."

Alec hedged round those wings, on display in a drape back top, to drop a kiss on Maeve's head. "As long as the blinds are drawn, what does it matter?"

"A man should be leery of his mother-in-law," Tia protested. "Complain of her in whispers at night after mergence. It is tradition in realms world over. But you two . . . thick as thieves."

Alec returned the older woman's serene smile. "We give her familial security and this is how she thanks us."

"You do all you can, Alec, even returning with us to

the Enchanted Realm for our wedding ceremony. You do still retain those memories?" Maeve queried.

"Every spin of reel, every mind-bending cocktail. Every vow."

"For the first time ever," Tia asserted above their exchange, "I feel I belong someplace. Our behaving human makes that possible."

"I am not human!" Maeve chortled.

"Still, you promised to blend in for the sake of neighborhood harmony."

"The principality of Queens is sure to surprise us one day. I suspect there are shape-shifters housed right down the street. A former toad at the grocer if I ever saw one. Not to mention a wandering tomcat with some very intelligent eyes."

"Even so, let's hold off and let them reveal first."

"On the subject of marriage and neighbors," Alec intervened excitedly, "I've been considering a mortal wedding ceremony in the backyard—to make it legal here as well. I have a weekend off at the end of the month. There's not much time, but we can keep it simple."

"The missus next door is on pins for this news," Maeve half-complained. "She budges in on every small thing."

"Elizabeth *and* Kevin Mitchell have been nothing but wonderful since Alec lost his Winter-owned apartment," Tia countered. "Steering us to this house, instigating a block party to introduce us."

"Chief Mitchell is grateful that I rolled over on John. Just the same, I only followed my conscience." Alec sighed. "Turns out I knew him no better than you did, Mamma."

Maeve sniffed. "I choose to pretend I never knew him. Though I imagine in the event that he is locked up, he will while away the hours remembering the splendor of *me*."

No doubt! If not for that single night of splendid mergence, John Winter III would probably have gone on unfettered with his lies, schemes, and betrayals.

Levering to her feet, Maeve announced that she'd pop next door with the good news.

"Uh, Mamma?"

"Yes, darling son?"

He pointed to her wings. "For now, leave any true confessions to the cat."

"Oh, yes." Flexing her shoulders, she drew her gossamer blades flat against her back and threw a sweater over her shoulders. "Ta-ta, children. A human salutation I picked up at the block party."

"What's 'ta-ta' mean?" Tia asked as the screen door bounced after Maeve.

"It means . . ."—Alec playfully drew her into the living room, where he tugged her atop him on the sofa—"one suffocating snoop is off to visit another." With a rich laugh he cradled her close for a long smooch.

Tia came up for air with a grin. "You are so good with her, Alec. I cannot remember the last time she giggled."

"The pressure is off her now. Blot's no longer feeding her anxiety and she's let go of her deepest secret."

"I imagine she has a few secrets left," Tia wagered.

"We all have some, I suppose. Or maybe they're simply discomforts we avoid talking about."

"There's something I'd still like to know about you, Alec."

His forehead bunched. "Like what?"

"Does our happy ending compare with the one of your dreams?"

"It's different," he admitted. "For starters, I never expected to settle down with a girl who skinny-dipped off the Isle of Man."

"Seriously, you expected to always be part of the Winters' wealth and excitement."

"It's proven easy to give up what never existed. John was only out for himself all along. What you and I have is a real, equal partnership. Ironically, I feel amazingly grounded. Married to a girl who can fly, yet grounded," he emphasized.

"I get it, Alec. Very amusing. In return I have a secret for you."

"Uh-oh."

"It's a sweet one." Straddling his thighs, she cupped his face. "I am with child."

Alec's jaw dropped. "Are you sure?"

"Mamma guarantees it."

Alec sank back in the cushions. "Mamma knows first?"

"Only because *you* missed the spots on the bottom of my feet."

"That's no symptom of human pregnancy. Looks like heat rash."

"What of my filmy fingernails?"

"No good, either. Thought it was pearly nail polish. Now if you had a tummy ache or a craving for pickles or some light-headedness—"

"I do have those things as well!"

"Now those signs I would have recognized."

Tia nestled in the hollow of his shoulder. "You know what this means?"

"It means I'm going to finally be the dad I've always wanted."

"What else?"

"I'm gonna make damn sure that wedding comes off in the backyard!"

"Oh, Alec, it means that despite its predominant human genes, the baby will still be a little bit faery."

Alec stroked her cheek. "And that makes you happy, Tia?"

"Oh, yes."

"Then I'm happy, too."